THE BERWICK CHRONICLES

VICTOR SIMPSON

FriesenPress

Suite 300 - 990 Fort St
Victoria, BC, Canada, V8V 3K2
www.friesenpress.com

ISBN
978-1-4602-7080-6 (Hardcover)
978-1-4602-7081-3 (Paperback)
978-1-4602-7082-0 (eBook)

1. Fiction, Science Fiction, Adventure

Distributed to the trade by The Ingram Book Company

CHAPTER ONE

PROFESSOR STAFFORD COLLAPSED, CRASHING HEADFIRST ONTO THE control panel. I caught a glimpse of the accelerator lever pushing forward under his weight. In horror I heard rather than saw the computer whirl into action. I saw Neil's younger brother Nelson trying to pull the Professor from the machine. He was one of us five researchers and the lucky one. The rest of us froze on the platform as the world started to stretch around us. The elongation of the room stretched us and our lab into impossible shapes and suddenly our world disappeared. We scientists, Beth, Neil, Sarah and I, stared into total darkness as we found ourselves floating in the air without the platform or any point of reference other than one another.

It felt as if we drifted in this void for an eternity. I peered at my illuminated wristwatch; to my surprise, the hands were *spinning* backwards at an incredible speed. Sarah, the smartest and youngest, grasped my arm and held me closer as she had done the night before. She thrust her wrist in front of my face showing me her digital chronometer; the brightly lit numbers also sped backwards. In her clipped New York accent, she whispered in my ear, "Jonathan. It's all wrong. We should be going forward not backwards in time." Her athletic body firm and strong tensed next to mine as she added, "What did that old fool Stafford do to us?"

My eyes adjusted to the dark, and I glanced over to my right. Beth, our couch potato, stood outlined against the nothingness. Her facial features reflected a silhouette of awe and joy.

Neil, the fourth member of our team, was a statue frozen in terror, grasping Beth's hand as if it were his lifeline from this horror. I thought Neil was afraid, but Sarah, Beth and I were ecstatic. We had become involved in time travel research in hopes that one day we would have it.

1

If I could redo the accident would I still have stood on the contraption, and time traveled with my friends? I don't know. How much have I changed? How many have died? How many more will die? All these deaths happened as a result of Stafford's mild heart attack, and my foolishness.

As fast as we entered the void, we returned to the real world. The smell hit me first, pungent and earthy. I now lay on the floor of a stable, or to be precise in the tack room. The four of us lay where we were before the blackout. Except now the building no longer functioned as a research facility. The millions of dollars of scientific equipment no longer lined the walls. Straw was everywhere. We were in a horse stable.

I couldn't articulate a word; only uncoordinated syllables escaped my vocal cords. Sarah regained her equilibrium first and asked, "When are we? This looks like the 19th century. This building hasn't been a stable for over a hundred years or more." Then her violet-blue Liz Taylor eyes sparkled as she said, "We did it."

Beth struggled to her feet and ventured to the door. She peeked out. "Quiet, there are some grooms out there. We don't want them to know we're here. Well, not yet anyway. We need to know what's going on out there. There's never been a report of time travelers in history. We don't want to be the first."

I timidly cleared my voice to speak when Neil expressed my thoughts in a shaky almost nervous stutter. "The accelerator screwed up. We've traveled back in time more than a few years. How do you explain a century or more Jonathan? How do you explain it?" His last few words sounded almost hysterical.

Beth put her arm around him. "It's all right Neil. We'll work it out." I could tell he didn't believe her but said nothing.

We glanced at each other shaking our heads. Sarah pointed at me and whispered, "You're the theorist, and you designed this experiment. Explain it to us."

I looked at them with a blank expression on my face. "I can't explain it. It's all wrong. No, not wrong, impossible. We can't be here."

Neil grabbed my arm, with both terror and anger in his voice, "It may be impossible, but we are here, wake up and smell the coffee."

I didn't like violence, and I felt threatened by Neil. I turned red and knew I should do something but instead just shrugged my shoulders and said, "Sorry" in the soft pathetic voice I used when I felt intimidated.

"Quiet you two. We have to get out of here and find a way home." Beth squeezed her eyes closed to keep from crying. Her false bravado had cracked. She started to shake. Neil's anger had calmed down; he took her hand and gently wrapped his arm around her as he stroked her hair. They had been lovers since Neil joined the team five months earlier.

Sarah sneered at Beth and Neil. "Beth, the only way home is to live another hundred or so years. We're trapped in the past. Sure, if we had all that crap we left back in the lab we might after ten or twenty years devise a way to travel forward in time. Well, if we're lucky," she wriggled her nose at us. "But we don't have that. We only have the clothes on our backs."

Beth asked through her tears, "What can we do?"

How were we to return to our time? How were we going to survive? We'd lived in an academic environment all our lives. We didn't know how to survive outside our own world.

"Adapt. Look, listen and learn," was Sarah's simple reply. "But first, we have to get out of here."

Blinking the tears away, Beth still looked panicked but peeked out the door again. "Okay, the grooms have left the barn."

She gingerly opened the door and crept out of the tack room. We followed, just like in a prison break movie. We skulked our way out into the courtyard. The buildings looked like the Oxford we left, but just a bit different. There was a block of classrooms across the courtyard from the stables and we watched students heading off to their various classes.

We dressed as did our generation at university of our time. It was difficult to say from what era the students we saw belonged. They wore a mishmash of clothing. Some wore scholarly garb; black robes with funny hats and others wore bucolic dress. However, many others wore a gaudy assortment of robes in various colors from red, green, orange and even white. We assumed it was a special day at Oxford calling for outlandish dress.

After seeing the students and the familiar campus, Beth regained some of her bravery. "Follow me. If this place has the same layout, I know a place we can go. Come on."

We hurried out into the mid afternoon sunshine like all the students. The weather gave me the impression that whatever year we arrived it still was May. We tried to be inconspicuous as we entered the fray of students. Our modern dress should have told everyone we didn't belong in that time. However, the preoccupied students gave us the once-over stare, but none ventured to ask any questions as they rushed off to their classes. We marched across the square and entered the classroom building kitty corner from the stable.

Once inside the building, we mingled with the students. Beth pushed her way to the front, and we followed her up a flight of stairs. We went down a hall where she stopped in front of an impressive mahogany door larger than any other we had seen in the building. Beth yanked at the door turning the knob with all her strength, yet it didn't move. She rummaged around in her knapsack and extracted an old skeleton key, and inserted it into the lock. To our surprise, the door swung open. She rushed us into the room. The room had large windows, and bright light streamed across the floor and onto the office furniture. I observed all the trappings of an ecclesiastical monk. Luckily, no one was sitting behind the desk. Beth ran over to the wall behind the desk. Solid blocks of stone formed the partition. She gently pushed on a stone, a second later pushed on another rock and a secret door opened. We scurried in.

I almost yelled. This was too much, a secret room at Oxford. This wasn't Windsor Castle or some phony scary movie set but a real college. I felt overwhelmed.

Beth read my mind and answered my silent question. "I had this office for three years when I did my PhD here. I found this place during my first year. They constructed this room when they erected the building, but I checked the plans, and it never was recorded. From what I could discover, the purpose of the room was to hide priests during Henry the VIII's time. Now we have a safe place."

A high window allowed light into the room. The dust almost a centimeter thick gave credence to Beth's next statement, "The room may be sparse, but no one has been in here for years. We should be safe." The twenty by twenty-foot room had two chairs and a cot. Six tapers stood in a candleholder, and a yellow piece of parchment lay on a small desk, but no writing appeared on it.

I shivered all over. This hiding didn't suit the way I thought time travel could be. I wanted to meet the people from the past. I pulled at Beth's sleeve, "Why don't we just ask someone about this place?"

Beth shook her head. "Jonathan, are you stupid? We don't know anything about this time or these people. Who knows what they might do?"

I frowned and looked at my friends. "Which one of you is a history buff? No one answered, "If this is no earlier than 17th century we should make out OK. That is if my memory is correct."

Sarah piped up. "No, I agree with Beth. Until we know what's happening, we'll stay hidden." She thought a second then added, "We need to inventory our resources. To see what we have, so we can survive in this time."

"Right, everyone turn out your pockets and see what we have," suggested Neil.

We examined the contents of our pockets. We had our cell phones. We had money. We had pens and paper. Beth had her knapsack with a can of hair spray, a couple of Mars bars, a bottle of water and her laptop. Our knowledge of history and science should enable us to survive in this time. If only we could put a date to our present time.

I picked up Beth's knapsack. "Beth, is this new? What is it made of, it's a very strange material."

She grabbed the bag from me and started stuffing her belongs back into it. "I told you this morning my mom gave it to me when I visited her last weekend. Her father gave her about five meters of this material. He told her that it fell off a back of a lorry during the war. It's supposed to be fabric from the blimps they flew over London during the Blitz."

As we talked, we heard the door to the office open and someone came in. Dead silence fell over our hideaway. Beth whispered, "This room is nearly soundproof but whoever designed it constructed it so we can hear what's happening in the other room. Put your ear to the wall and listen."

Our ears glued themselves to the cold stone blocks and listened to the person in the office. We heard a deep voice singing a medieval chant. It didn't sound Latin or English, but a bastardization of each. At first, I could barely make out the words but with perseverance I understood what the male voice said. He ordered lunch; a salad, chicken noodle soup and a roast beef sandwich.

We looked at one another and scratched our heads. "Was he talking into a telephone?" I asked.

Sarah shook her head, "I didn't see one in the room as we passed through it. Anyway, it didn't sound like how you speak into a telephone."

Someone knocked at the office door as we discussed the merits of the telephone or possibly a cell phone. I heard another male voice as someone entered the room delivering the ordered meal. The servant had no time to prepare the meal, maybe twenty or thirty seconds had elapsed before he entered the office with the food. I wondered how that could be possible. Moments later, I could hear the occupant of the room leisurely consume his lunch. Eventually, he left merrily singing a dirge of some sort.

I shook my head and whispered to the others, 'This guy is either a happy undertaker or very disturbed"

We waited a few minutes and entered the office. This time we searched it. The room contained books, papers, cabinets and shelves with jars of herbs and other dried plant material, but no phone or any mechanical devices, not even a clock.

Beth and Neil sat at the desk trying to decipher documents stacked in a basket. I studied a wall hanging, and Sarah took a book off a bookshelf and started reading. We examined everything in the room trying to discover facts about our new world. I jumped three feet when the door sprung open and a surprised servant stood mouth agape, eyes wide with astonishment and then horror as he stared at the four of us.

CHAPTER TWO

I SURPRISED MYSELF AND AT THE SAME TIME HORRIFIED MYSELF. I grabbed the intruder by the folds of his robe and dragged him into the room. My heart sounded like a jackhammer in my chest. I had never used physical force against anyone before in my life. I played sports but nothing with violence, no hockey or football or even basketball.

Still out of breath I whispered, "Close the door, Sarah." She closed the door before any eyes strolling down the hall could see my act of aggression.

I wrestled the stranger into an overstuffed chair that faced the large oak desk in the room.

Our captive stood about five-foot-six, no match for my six-foot-two frame, yet I could feel large muscles under his black robes. His red hair was tied into a long ponytail. He looked to be in his forties.

After my first attempt to question him, Beth took over and ordered him to speak. "Who're you and what's your job around here?"

In a strong highland accent, he said, "Canna hardly understand ya lassie. You're not from around here, are ye?" Then he added, "The question is who are ye and what are you dooin here?"

Sarah asked the next question, "What year is it?"

"Lassie, from your tongue you aren't from anywhere I know, and I've been throughout the land." Sarah's New York surliness showed as she sneered at him.

Then her expression changed and a grin crossed her face, as she said, "Sir, you're good at misdirecting our questions, but now it's time to answer them."

He laughed. "I'll be answering yours, if you be answering mine. I'm Angus Paterson, and I'm a captive slave of the Order of the Red Master. Young woman with the harsh tongue, it is as we reckon it twenty years past the second millennium."

We looked at him as if he had donkey ears and tulips sprouting from his head. "What are you saying? You're a captive slave of the Red Master, and the year is 2020? That's impossible, that's the year we left," gasped Sarah.

"You're crazy man!" was Neil's eloquent reply. Neil still looked sick and ready to vomit at any moment. Time travel didn't suit him.

Angus studied all of our reactions, nodding his head up and down and said, "Aye sir, you four are wanderers. It is true ye aren't from aroun' here or even from Great Britain as some call it. Nay, ye are a strange breed from your clothes and talk and your lack of knowledge. Wha' are ye and where are ye from?"

Before we could answer, we heard a noise in the hall. Angus became frightened. He picked up the plates on the desk. Beth went over to the concealed door and opened it; we pushed Angus into the hidden room with us. Beth shut the door as the office door opened.

Angus turned to us. "Wha' are ye people? Whit are ye doin' here?" He whispered so whoever entered the other room wouldn't hear him.

Sarah looked into his eyes. "You tell us first, and we'll tell you what you want to know. Tell us about this place and your world. As you have surmised, we are strangers in your land, and we know nothing about what is going on here. Please tell us and we'll tell you everything we can about us."

He looked at her long and hard. It was obvious he was assessing her, and in turns us. Finally, his face broke out into a smile. "Ye are all so young and serious. I'm close to twice your age and have seen all of this world and what it has tae offer, but the likes o' ye I've never seen. I trust in your ignorance and your will to know."

He looked at us standing there, "Ye foor look like I'm speaking in a strange toongue. I know the Master's English's well as my native dialectic." He smiled again, "I was a prisoner at this school for many years and know how to talk that dry tongue the educated speak. From now on I'll put on my best English." Humor was evident in his voice.

"There are six realms to this land of Great Britain. My realm, the Highlands is in the North, what the others call Scotland. The other five are Northumbria to the south of my land, Mercia in the center, Wales to the west, Ireland the land across the western sea and Wessex, where we are. This is Oxford, the center of learning for all the realms. In the war of '09 a Brigade of Wessex's Winchester Lancers under the command of the Red Master captured me as I commanded my army in the invasion of York. The room we just left is the Lord of the Wessex's or as the world knows him, the Red Master. His office when he visits Oxford is where you surprised me." Angus stopped talking, and looked perplexed, "It's strange he doesn't know you hid in his office and are now only a few feet from him. He knows everything. He can read minds. He has powers beyond anyone I've ever met. I've tried to escape six times, each time he knew and tortured me with mind control. He's the most powerful Wizard in our lands. I've heard he talks with the Ancient Ones."

Beth looked at him with a glint of humor in her eyes, "Your army, what did you mean by that?"

Angus had the same glint in his eye, "Well lassie, you caught that did yea? The Thane of the Highlands they called me. It's a family responsibility, my father and his father and as far back as the Masters have recorded history a Paterson has sat on the throne of the land. The MacDonald's and the Wallace's and even the Stuarts have ruled their fiefdoms, but for a millennium my ancestors ruled and suppressed rebellion in Scotland. That's why the bloody Red Master keeps me here so one of his puppets can rule in my place. My son is still too young to rule. The Red Master has appointed a Fraser to rule my land. I'm afraid before my boy reaches the age of twenty-one the Red Master will assassinate him. If my son Ian leaves no heir, the realm will fall into the Red Master's hands." Angus fell silent, brooding over what he just had told us. No one spoke. We also brooded over his fate and ours. Finally, he looked up at us, "Who might you young lads and lassies be?"

"We are travelers from far away, but from this exact place. I'm Jonathan Jackson. This is Sarah Cunningham. That's Neil Bjornsen next to you, and Beth Clarke is standing on the other side of you. We are all scientists working on a project at this University, but not this University. It's hard to explain. Anyway, we worked on a machine that would allow us to travel forward in time. It wasn't ready for humans to travel in it, but an accident happened, which brought us here. We thought we had traveled back to the late 1880's or 1890's, but this is nothing like that time in our history. Where are we? We don't know unless—" I was recalculating everything in my head, putting the pieces back into a logical order and consequently reshuffling them. "Christ, we didn't time travel. We traveled dimensionally. We're not in our world. This world is like ours yet not quite right. It's just... different."

My colleagues all groaned. Beth asked, "Can we get back?"

I asked Angus, "Do you have any scientists or equipment for electrical power?"

He looked at me if I were talking Greek, "The Masters banned science in all the realms a millennium ago. The use of science destroyed the lands over the sea to the East. Legend tells us that happened more than a thousand years ago; according to the tea caravans, the land is a vast sterile desert that takes months to circumnavigate by camel. The Wizards tell us no one who goes into the barren land ever comes back."

He paused to think and finally he said with awe, "The Prophecy." He stopped talking and for a longtime he seemed to drift away. He refocused and looked at us in a new way. "In Berwick in Northumbria the Orange Wizard's land, it was prophesied travelers from another dimension would come to our world, which would change our lives forever. The Archbishop of Canterbury has preached there are many worlds that use the same space and time to live out their lives. The Prophecy tells about worlds like ours and others much different and that on occasion these worlds collide. When that happens, calamities befall both worlds. The Orange Master knows more about this Prophecy than anyone. I asked him about such crossings to the otherworld, he spoke of the calamities that could destroy both worlds. He told me that is why the council of Grand Wizards banned science those many centuries ago." In further explanation he said, "A scientist in Ireland crossed over the line to another world. That world turned to powder and the winds of time blew it into the unknown. The Irishman returned barely alive. His last words "Our world will suffer ..." He died and his body turned to dust before the Orange Master. The lands far to the west disappeared; the black seas filled the void that was the land of promise. The Orange Master told me the scribes of the White Wizard Blalock wrote in the Berwick Chronicles all the scientists' notes of how to cross to the other worlds."

Neil asked the question on our lips, "Angus, can you guide us to where the Berwick Chronicles are located?"

Angus looked sad, "I'm bound here by a spell. I can't walk off the grounds. If I do I fall into an unconscious state. Only the Red Master can bring me back to life. Even if I escaped out of Wessex, it is a dangerous journey through hostile territory. The shire at Berwick is far away. We would need an army to fight our way to the Berwick castle. That's where they guard the Chronicles. Brownies guard the road to Berwick, they are fierce and deadly. The Brownie army

is the most vicious of the Fairy tribes. Even the Leprechauns are no match for them. I saw them take on the White Wizard's army when he attacked Northumbria, he had gnomes but the Brownies killed them all. They ate them after the battle, it was horrible. It sickened my troops to see it; we always kept our distance from the carrion that they are."

"When you fall unconscious, is it long-term or does the Red Master bring you back right away?"

"Well, it's usually a few hours before he brings me back."

"Have you ever seen him bring back anyone else from unconsciousness who has tried to escape?" asked Beth.

Angus thought a minute, "Yes, once another slave ran away. He gave her a drink of— some green liquid. Yes of course, he kept it in the study. Right you are." His voice took on a jovial note. "It happened during my first month in Oxford. The Red Master ordered me to polish his boots. They brought in this young woman who appeared dead. I overheard the guard inform the Master she had tried to escape. The Master laughed and went to a locked cabinet and pulled out a bottle of green liquid. He glanced at me and ordered me out of his study, but I saw him put the bottle to her mouth. Five or six hours later I saw her in the kitchen peeling potatoes, as if nothing had happened."

Wide-eyed I listened to his story then Sarah broke the spell. "Can you find some clothes for us so we don't look so conspicuous? We need to leave this place. Do you have any money we can have?"

A wry look came across Angus's face, "Nay, I'm a slave; they don't let me have such glittery things as gold and silver. Aye, I can get us some traveling clothes, but alas, as I said I'm just a poor slave. If you feel you have a little larceny in you, I can show you the treasury; we can take a few bags of sovereigns with us."

Plans took form; we decided to leave after midnight when the town would be asleep. Angus explained the Red Master didn't live at Oxford but in his Castle at Windsor; he traveled every month to Oxford for special meetings of the Supreme Red Council at the University and would stay for another two days. The Red Master permanently assigned Angus to the University to be his personal servant.

"Now my lads and lassies, you've gotta be clear, if the Red Master catches us it will be torture for me, but for the likes of you it will be much worse."

Sarah looked at the floor and finally into Angus' eyes, "The plan is good. We must attempt to return to our world." Her piercing violet eyes searched his soul and she continued, "We are trusting you. We may be peace loving academics, but if you turn on us we have nowhere to hide and like cornered animals we'll fight tenaciously to survive." I looked at my friends and couldn't envision them fighting their way through the lunch lines at McDonald's.

After Angus left our hideout, we waited with anticipation as he purloined clothing for us. He arrived back just before six with clothes and food. He also brought a book of the history of the lands and maps of each realm.

Beth, a native of England, looked amazed. "I'm gobsmacked, the map of my village is identical with what I remember. I lived there all my life and it has never changed. Yet in this upside down world it's identical." Then she read some of the history, "Holy crap, the history is all ass backwards. It talks about the early invasions but there is no War of the Roses or even Henry VIII or Elizabeth. It's all magic stuff from the arrival of the Vikings."

We looked at the maps, read short parts of the history, and shook our heads. Beth was right. It was insane.

Angus looked on us with amazement. "Your world sounds boring beyond compare to mine, no wars, no magic, no intrigue. Oh well, let's get out of this place. I back to my kingdom and you to your world of science and placid living."

"I have planned this escape for almost seven years. It will take all of us to get to the gold in the treasury. You will also have to help me in the Red Master's suite. We need to take a few of his precious trinkets with us and that bottle of green liquid. We'll make a stop at the armory as well. In this land, one does not go by land or sea without personal protection or a body-guard, not man, not wizard, or beast. You'll learn why when we pass through Nottingham or even Warwick."

At midnight, he had us dressed in the native garb, full of native food and ready to steal what we needed to escape this land. I had butterflies fluttering in my stomach. I'd never stolen anything in my life. Well, I didn't count the Three Musketeers bar the Safeway employee caught me with. I didn't know you had to pay for them. As an adult it didn't fit into my moral attitude or my lifestyle.

Angus led us off to the armory. We were scientists and none of us had military training in weaponry or self-defense. This was going to be our induction into violence and crime.

Neil looked excited and in a stage whisper said to me, "I never thought I'd be stealing gold. I've always dreamed of being a pirate, but I never thought I'd be in a land where it could come true."

Angus brought us down to the dungeons in the building. The roughly hewn stone walls dripped with moisture. There was a set of iron bars in front of us and a hulking large soldier dressed in chainmail with a halberd in his hand. His dark foreboding eyes pierced into my soul. He stood tall and his well-trimmed black beard made it impossible to gauge his age. He was mean looking and did not look friendly at all when he saw Angus.

"It's past curfew, what the hell are you servants doing here? If you don't return to your quarters I'll call the sergeant of the guard and you'll all be in irons before the crow sounds."

Angus moved a few feet closer and reached into his pocket for a box. The guard looked confused, "Move along." He lowered his weapon and now the spear end was pointing at us. Angus tossed the guard the brightly decorated gold box. He grabbed for it and a cloud of blue mist wafted out of the box and encircled the soldier's head. The guard instantly dropped to his knees coughing, and in the next instant passed out.

"What the—" was all Neil could say.

Angus answered the unasked question. "When I'm not busy, I look in on the wizard classes. I've watched this one about ten times over the last few years. The wizard teaching the class calls that potion, 'Blue mist at night, soldier is out like a light.' Works every time, I practiced on the scullery maids."

He searched the guard, finding only a concealed dagger and the key to the barred off area leading to the armory. He turned to Neil. "You're about the same size as the guard. Remove his clothes and put them on, you are to take his place until we return. Remember, no one goes in no matter what. You have orders from the Red Master himself, you're from— let's see—, yes, you're from London, you just arrived this morning."

Neil looked at the guard and then down at himself, "Angus, this guy's huge, I'll swim in his uniform, let Jonathan."

Angus looked stern, "No, I need him with me, just tighten the belt and you'll look fine." Then he smiled, "I have faith in you laddie, you can do it. Just look mean."

Once Neil was standing guard, we continued. There was another guard down the corridor. This one was guarding a large wooden door studded with iron spikes. If possible, this guard was meaner and nastier looking than the first. He commanded that we halt a good twenty feet away from him as he pulled out his sword. Earlier Angus chose Sarah as the temptress to his plan and provided her with a sultry dress the local young women had a liking to wear. She enhanced this by applying makeup and pulling at the clothes in strategic places. She walked just a little closer to the guard ostensibly to show him orders from the commandant. As she showed the paper to the guard, Angus started muttering. The chant sounded the same as we heard from the Red Master.

The guard looked confused and laid down his sword and started to remove his armor. Within seconds, he was no longer a disciplined soldier, but a boy being shy and awkward around an attractive young woman. As we came past the guard, Angus bumped into him and grabbed him behind the neck, pinched a nerve and dropped him unconscious to the ground. We looked to Angus.

"It was simple. Sarah pleasantly distracted him and I therefore could manipulate his undisciplined mind. I told him remove your armor and, get rid of the sword. Think good thoughts about the young woman. You're just fourteen and she is your first girlfriend. With all that on his mind, I could then walk up to him and render him unconscious. It's a trick I learned from the wizards. The wizards misdirect weak minds like this all the time. Get his keys and weapons."

When the weapons and the keys belonged to us Angus opened the door and we marched into the inner sanctum of the armory. "Right it be. You my recruits need weapons to suit your body." He looked at Sarah and said, "A delicate flower like you should only carry a dagger. You will always be a temptress."

"You sexist pig," she scoffed

With dexterity he had never seen in his world she had him on the ground with her foot on his neck. "I'm not just a pretty flower. In my world, a girl has to take care of herself. I took classes in martial arts. In high school I was the state's archery champion and in my under graduate years I was on UCLA's fencing team when we won the NCAA title. I'll choose my weapons and never again think of me as a temptress. I'll fight if we have to and tempt who I want." She batted her Liz Taylor eyes at him as she pulled Angus from the stone floor.

I had never seen this side of Sarah. I knew she enjoyed outdoors and ran with me for exercise, but martial arts and fencing didn't seem like her. I thought I knew her yet she never told me about her extracurricular activities. What else didn't I know about her?

Like me Angus looked dazed, and finally chuckled, "There's plenty this Highland oaf needs to learn about my new friends. Lassie, if we have to fight I want you on my right, I saw that look in your eye. You have killer eyes." Then he winked at her.

The armory had swords, pikes, bows and arrows and every other weapon in abundance. Searching the armory thoroughly we chose the weapons we would need. We left loaded down.

Angus put me in shoulder to knee light chain mail armor with a helmet and added a sword, a dagger, and a bow and arrows for good measure. I could hardly walk, especially now that I wore the red pants and shirt of the Red Master's army. I also wore the blue cape and jacket of an officer. He decked each of us out in similar fashion. With his new respect for the women folk of our time, he also dressed Beth and Sarah as officers. The femininity of both of them was hidden beneath the uniform and armor of the Red Master.

Angus said, "We have six hours before changing of the guards and their check of the armory." Unfortunately, that night they changed the guards every four hours. An officer and four guards met us as we climbed the stairs to the main floor.

"Angus, do you have any more of that Harry Potter magic in your cloak? Those four don't look too happy." I looked like a warrior in my blue tunic and red pants, but I felt like a circus clown. I couldn't wield a sword or shoot an arrow if my life depended on it yet at any moment it probably did.

One of the soldiers marched down the hall right to us. Angus whispered behind us, "I know the sergeant who is trooping his men to their posts in the armory. If he sees me, we'll be done for."

Neil stood as tall as he could in his oversized uniform, and marched in his best military imitation. "You men, stop. My officers are here inspecting your command. The men in the armory are good for another hour. I need you to prepare transport for us; we leave for London on the hour."

The sergeant stared at Neil, "You're not from Oxford are you?"

Neil took on a haughty attitude, "Of course I'm not you idiot. If I were, you would know who I am. I'm from London."

The sergeant was no fool. "I didn't hear about this. Show me your authorization."

I pushed forward, "Sergeant, you don't know because it's a secret inspection. You have done well. Send two of your men back to fetch your captain. We need to evaluate his soldiers' performance." As the words escaped my mouth I could hear the unbelievable lies catch in my throat. Lying and stealing didn't suit me. I could feel myself blush.

The sergeant looked confused. "Yes sir. Jones and Roberts go and see if Lieutenant Thomas is available to chat with these officers from London."

I reckoned with two of his men gone, we had a better chance of fighting. Visions of swords clashing and men dying filled my head. My stomach tried to crawl up my throat, and my bowels pushed their way out of my rectum. As soon as the two disappeared out of earshot, I returned to reality and felt the sword my hand now grasped. I shook so hard the pummel wouldn't stay in my hand; my first medieval sword fight awaited me.

Beth dressed approached two of the soldiers and to my astonishment showed them the can of hairspray from her knapsack. She sprayed some of the mist, and they became intrigued with the aerosol and the smell of the droplets. She sprayed more this time into their faces and ignited it with her lighter. The act of violence shocked me as much as it did the three soldiers. Before I realized what had happened, Sarah had taken the sergeant to the ground, and karate chopped his windpipe. Angus and Neil subdued the other two with singed hair.

"You are a surprising band of travelers," Angus said hurrying us along. "Take them back to the armory and we'll tie them up. Let's be quick about it. We don't have much time." "Acquiring our traveling money in a land of slaves is not an easy task, but you have Angus to show you the way." He exploded with a hearty laugh. "How many gold coins will your pockets hold? I bet more than you think."

CHAPTER THREE

OUR NEXT STOP WAS TO THE TREASURY IN ANOTHER BASEMENT ROOM with walls a foot thick on all sides and ten guards at the twelve-inch solid iron door. Not even the Red Master had authority to enter without permission of the Council of Seven and co-signed by the head Coin Counter or the Count as Angus told us the academics called him.

"Angus, we're not bank robbers and as thieves we are a poor substitute for the Great Train Robbers. How are we going to do this?" Beth whined.

Angus no longer had a smile on his face. He looked the image of the warrior king his ancestors bred him to be, yet a moment later a childish grin started at the upper corners of his lips and spread across his face. "Follow me and I'll tell you."

We crept down one of the halls on the teaching floor. We stopped in a room with a big padlock on the door. Angus slipped a long piece of metal out of his pocket and jabbed it into the keyhole of the lock, after a few seconds of twisting the metal the lock snapped open. "They use cheap locks in this place. One of my father's court jesters taught me that trick. After I told my father, he had a locksmith replace all the locks with some from a village in Northumbria called Yale."

The room looked like a science lab but none I'd ever seen before. Lazy students had strewn the wooden lab desks with odd objects that resembled ancient apothecary tools like pestles and mortars as well as instruments that looked foreign to me. Strange charts covered the walls showing versions of the periodic table with elements that I couldn't identify. However, to any university student the layout was similar to science labs in which they had studied. Once in the classroom, Angus took us to the back of the room to another locked door. He performed the same prestidigitation with the small steel rod, and we slinked into a room full of bottles; each held about a gallon of a clear liquid.

"Be extremely careful with this magic fluid, it destroys whatever it touches. This is the advanced alchemy class. Every Wizard student must make two pure gallons of this stuff before they go on to their next level of alchemy."

Neil gingerly picked up one of the gallon bottles when the door from the classroom swung open. He stumbled, and the bottle started to slip through his fingers. Angus yelled a highland scream that had to wake up his dead ancestors. Neil caught the glass bottle inches from crashing to the floor. The door caught him on the side of the head as it finished its swing and to everyone's surprise, a woman entered the storage room. She looked even more frightened than us. "My stars Angus, what are you about? Who are these pretend soldiers you have with you and what are they doing with the corrosive potion bottles?"

Angus was speechless for a few seconds. "I'm escaping tonight and these four are dimension travelers, like in the Berwick Chronicles. Don't try to stop us." His hand went to his sword, and a growl escaped from his throat. "We have passed the point of caring. We'll do anything to escape the Red Master. We have no choice but to continue."

I watched her with eyes that I drank in her every movement. She was exotic; no, more than exotic, she was original and erotic. From that first moment she opened the door. I wanted her, not just once physically, but I wanted her for all times and as an equal, as a soul mate, as a lover and as my partner for life. Sarah, my companion and lover, was just a dim memory; this woman was real and overpowering. I heard her in my mind speaking to me. I could smell her sweet and stimulating breath even though she stood ten feet away from me.

It was like time had stopped and only the two of us occupied the room. Her voice told me she wanted to come with me wherever I traveled. She whispered in my mind as lovers do. After that I heard her voice, "Angus, you know I'm a prisoner here like you. Furthermore, like you, I'm of royal blood. My father will give you whatever you want, if you help me escape." She could see him waver, "If you take me, I will be your most valuable weapon, remember I'm a Welsh Black Witch."

Her stare was fierce, "I will go with you. I won't indulge in further discussion." Finally, she looked directly at me. "There is one in your group that draws me to him. One that I sense is going to destroy our world as we see it today and bring us into a world unimaginable to us. I will follow you to help him fulfill his destiny and mine. I will be his Seer. I will be his magician and his teacher. Jonathan, I will lead you from the dark into the light. My black arts will take you farther than the stars."

Everyone looked at me, no one with more penetrating eyes than Sarah. "What shit is this Jon? How did she know your name? What's going on?"

Sarah said angrily, "What the hell is happening? Jonathan? Speak to me, you look like you're a thousand miles away."

Angus broke into Sarah's anger, "Robina, I think he's spoken for. Yeah, canna take him as your own. He's not one of us, he's an outsider."

Robina's eyes transmuted from soft blue to flaming red, "He's mine, heart, body and soul. I don't give a gold coin for his past or to whom he's betrothed, it's our future I can see, and I'm entwined with him forever." She looked at Sarah. "I see your future too. You are wise and you are dangerous. If we are to be enemies, I'd have picked none less worthy than you. As allies, we can make the Prophecy come true. The Berwick Chronicles predict the two witches and the man with the heart of a lion are destined to go where no wizard has gone before. If you believe that, we are to be together as well. Let me have him, you shall have a Master of this world for your own and the four of us will change the universe."

Angus put his arms around Sarah. "Oh my God, I'm such an idiot. I should have seen it. It's your eyes, the most violet of eyes. The Chronicles foretell you and your Lord, with the Black Witch and the Emperor, will rule this world and many others. It's the Prophecy." Suddenly he stopped dead; his face took on the look of terror. "The rest of the Prophecy is not good. Not good at all."

Beth shook her head, "This is straight from Macbeth. Get real people, we're scientists. The sexy Professor has the hots for Jonathan and Sarah's jealous. I would be too if she made moves on Neil. So she makes up this big story to weird us out. It's crap."

I stood there in the middle of this debate watching the ball going back and forth over the net. I could still feel the lust for this Robina creature, thinking this is my life they are talking about. Robina continued to talk to me in my mind, enticing me with her words. The others had no idea what she told me and how she affected me. They blathered back and forth but I listened only to Robina. Then I heard Angus break into the maelstrom.

"Like I said before, you're not from around here. There is a Prophecy and some witches and wizards can read the future. In our world anyway, so take heed." He took a deep breath. "If the Prophecy comes true all our lives are in danger, not only from the Red Master but also from more than I can say. The Black Witch is right, we must act as allies. If we fight among ourselves we will all die."

Sarah looked confused, "I don't like what everyone is saying. If this world works on different principles than ours, we have to learn them." She glared at Robina with lightning in her eyes. "I'll fight you for Jon, take that as a given. I'm not sure I want him forever, but he's all I've got here and he's a good friend. However, if what you say is true, we need you to teach us how to survive in this world of yours and how to use magic." Finally in a voice that sounded like thinking aloud, she said softly, "Can I trust you? Can I trust a Black Witch? Can I trust a woman who is stealing my lover? Can I trust anybody in this strange land?"

Robina spoke, "I like you Sarah, I could put a spell on you and you would forget Jonathan. I could give you a love potion and you would fall in love with someone else or I could just kill you. All are possible without leaving this room. Remember that, but also remember I'm your friend. We'll have to learn to trust each other. The Prophecy described us as sisters or so close to sisters we are siblings of heart and soul."

Angus broke the magic of the moment, "We have to go; the soldiers will soon be looking for us. Robina, we are going to expropriate the gold the Red Master took from us and our families. The Red Master's treasury will pay us back before we leave. Are you with us?"

She laughed, "I've been with you as soon as I saw my Jonathan."

I couldn't stay quiet any longer, "Now we're six, let's get the money and leave this place." As I walked out of the room, I took Robina's hand in mine.

Angus said, "Not so quick, we need the bottles."

I looked at all the glass bottles and determined that each was full of hydrochloric acid. Angus was taking one from the rack. It alarmed me; if the bottle dropped, he would suffer serious injuries, permanent scars or even worse. It would create a big hole in the floor and probably splash on all of us. Before I could voice my concerns, Beth responded to his actions. "Be careful, it's called hydrochloric acid, it's deadly. What you say about it is truer than you know."

Robina nodded, "Angus is the only one that I allow to move the bottles when the class has prepared them."

He smiled at Robina, "A smart lass, very smart lass, we need a cart to carry the bottles. Robina, is the one in your office big enough to carry thirty bottles?"

She laughed, "Yes my magic cart can do that." Less than a minute later we were loading the bottles into a cart like contraption that moved on its own. We started on our way to the treasure.

The six of us hurried down the hall with the cart following us. Angus led us on a march through the building, upstairs and downstairs, until on the main floor we came to a nondescript room. "Ah, here we are. This is the slaves' waiting room. When our master is busy, we either come here or go to our allotted workplace. If he requires us to stay close to him we come here and relax with the other servants. Then our master summons us by sending a servant here and we go do his bidding. The other remarkable quality that's noteworthy about this room is that it's right over the treasure-house of the Red Master's Order. Well, not the complete treasure-house, but the most sacred part. See that circle on the floor? It's a bit faded now. I put it there seven years ago when I first realized what sat directly below this room. I painted the circle and drilled a ring into the floor. Finally I set up a block and tackle." He pointed to the ceiling and the wall next to the door. "I worked at it for two years to develop the plan and another five years to prepare the room. Tonight we'll see if it works."

Robina looked around the room and gave a squeal of excitement, "You old rascal, you've painted the floor with a red circle. Is that where we are going to use that class project of mine?"

He pointed to a tall stepladder in one corner and a rope attached to the wall. "We'll need them both to go down the hole and back up again." He hooked the rope from the block and tackle through the eyebolt in the floor. "Now I'll uncork one of the bottles and start the proceedings."

He was true to his word; he opened a bottle of the deadly liquid and started to pour it around the faded red circle. The acid bubbled and crack-led as it hit the floor and ate through the stone. The first bottle ate away a ring in the floor three inches deep and two inches wide over the outline of the circle. The floor now showed another layer of unknown depth made of copper. The second bottle ate through that, bubbling off a foul odor. We watched as Angus repeated the process many times until he stopped and asked for our help.

"Lads and lassies, I need you to hold on to the other end of the rope that's through the block and tackle. When I break through I don't want this whole floor to fall into the vault below."

During all this Robina stood by the door with a smirk on her face as she watched Angus work up a sweat. Her attitude seemed strange to me, but I was in a strange land. Robina was the most exotic and strangest of all the inhabitants I'd met. I loved her.

After another fifteen bottles of hydrochloric acid, the floor was floating in the air. All of us pulled on the rope until the remaining ring of the floor was ten feet off the ground. Angus tied off the rope to a shackle on the wall. The rest of us watched as Neil and Angus lowered the big ladder into the hole.

I had never been a criminal let alone a bank robber before, yet the excitement of the breaking through the floor caused my heart to jump in my chest like a kangaroo. I felt giddy. Robina handed me a candle and told me it would never burn out and purred, "Magic, you know, has its practical uses."

I took the everlasting candle from her and looked into the vault. The light sparkled, reflecting off the wealth contained in the room. I saw boxes of coins full to the brim. There were gold pieces, some as big as sand dollars, filled chests big enough to bury a horse. In one box lay a life-sized golden stallion. In many boxes I could see silver bars and coins which showed no tarnish. They glistened so brightly in the artificial light. Directly below me I smelled the exotic aroma of incense such as the Kings of the East brought to baby Jesus on that first Christmas long ago. Barrels of rubies, emeralds and diamonds caught my eye. Just seeing such wealth thrilled me, and the thought of taking it overwhelmed me. I didn't feel like a crook, yet I knew I couldn't justify my actions. I didn't care as I saw other precious stones that I could not name sparkle in my eyes. Just one or two in my pocket would be enough for me. Then I thought a few more to fill a knapsack on my back. I could not resist.

"Jonathan, you're blocking the way, get down the ladder." Angus pushed me down. Once all six of us stood among the treasure trove, I noticed several other containers full of jewelry and silver and gold utensils. On the far wall opposite the door stood several crated paintings, all of them of exquisite quality reminiscent of the 16th and 17th centuries of my world. They reminded me of many of the pictures I saw at the National Gallery. There must have been other treasures, but we didn't have time to explore. Angus bid us to take all the coins and gems we could carry and leave everything else.

Robina laughed at seeing the treasure. "I'll take five times what he stole from me; no ten times. The Red Master is a brute and deserves the wages of his sins. The Order when it hears of what we have taken will deal with him. What magic have you arranged to carry this out of the coin room and eventually out of Oxford?"

Angus showered us with gunnysacks reinforced with pillow cases, "Fill them up, I've hundreds of them. I've had them hidden up here for years."

Robina shook her head and smiled, "Angus, I forgot you're a practical man, hard work and cunning are your skills. I would have used magic to pull off this caper. I won't interfere, you have this well in hand. Your use of the acid was clever, but I would have used a spell."

Angus laughed, "And the Red Master would have you in his prison waiting for the executioner. This is a dead zone. No magic works in or around the vault. You can't use magic in this room. If you did an alarm would sound and the guards would surround us in a minute. Come on, let's get the treasure loaded up and get on the road."

I stuffed the bags I took with hundreds of gold coins; all the coins with strange faces on them, with dates and names written in a strange form of Anglicized Latin. My arms ached from lifting the bags of coins. Robina never left my side but had her hands in the barrels of jewels and her bags bulged with beautiful stones but none as gorgeous as she.

"That's enough for now. Start handing them up to me." Angus had climbed back up the ladder and knelt on the floor above. We formed a line and passed each bag up the ladder to Angus. Then we filled more bags to their brims and passed them up to the room above.

Robina passed me a ring she had found in one of the other strong boxes in the room. "Jonathan, put this enchanted ring on and don't take it off. The ring binds us as one."

"Robina, I don't know."

She snuggled up close to me and kissed me with passion. I tried to protest but her lips tasted like honey and fresh strawberries. As I became aroused, she whispered into my ear, "That ring belonged to the Black Master, my great-grandfather. Lord Geoffrey of the Red Order tricked him and used special magic to remove the ring and afterwards sliced my ancestor's head off. It is powerful, never take it off, it will protect you." She winked at me and continued "As long as I'm by your side it will protect me as well"

Sarah pushed Robina away from me, "You're a bitch. What are you trying to do, fuck him right here with all the gold and diamonds surrounding you? Is that how you get your kicks? Get back to work. We have another fifty bags to haul up the ladder."

Robina kissed me again and nonchalantly picked up a dagger from an open chest. Cradling it as if the weapon needed tender loving care like a newborn child, she handed it to Sarah. In a sweet loving voice she said, "In time we'll be the best of friends. Until then carry this dagger, it will protect you always when you're in danger." The dagger had a black handle and a vicious looking black blade: an assassin's knife. "If you choose to use it on me so be it, but I'd rather you use it on our enemies. Once we leave this vault, we'll have every member of the Red Order after us until we're dead or escape this world."

We left the coin room and removed the ladder. Angus lowered the floor section back in place. He looked serious, "Now we had to transport the booty out of the building and into the stables." Angus laughs, "Now for my magic trick. Neil and Beth, come with me." The three left us in the slaves' room and about five minutes later returned. "Strip," Angus ordered, "you are now going to be slaves. Put on these rags but bring your uniforms too. We'll pretend we're taking the laundry to the washing area; we're going to the stables."

Neil and Beth pushed in six large wicker baskets on wheels. "It's going to be tight but divide the bags into six piles and load the baskets. Each of you will push one out to the stables. We'll load them on the two wagons I stole. That's our transport to freedom and back to the Highlands."

Robina gave Angus a sad look, "Keep your memories of the Highlands Angus. It'll be a long time before any of us sees Urquhart Castle or Isle of Skye. I fear we have many misfortunes and tests to try us before any of us reach home."

Angus shook his head, "Robina, you're a professor of potions, not foretelling. You're full of it; let's get the wagons loaded. We have still to get the green potion from the Red Master's room."

The rest of us looked at Robina with fear in our eyes for we believed her. We whispered among ourselves.

Neil pushed his basket, "This mobile basket weighs a ton. How are we to push it to the stable?"

Huffing and puffing Beth piped up, "It's impossible. I don't know how we can push them. None of us are that strong."

Robina overheard us and winked, "The wizard in charge of the laundry enchanted the baskets, once we leave the room you'll only be pushing about fifty pounds of gold, the rest is traveling by basket motion. That's how this world moves, magic instead of machines."

We passed two security patrols with our work of drudgery; they didn't even poke the baskets but only ogled Robina and Sarah as they hurried by.

We returned to the scene of our entry into this crazy world as we stepped into the stable, which fifteen hours before had been our lab. I almost cried with feelings of homesickness. I so wished it could have been a dream, and I would wake in my bed in Wheatley, just east of Oxford.

We stowed the treasure in the wagons and covered them with straw and heavy canvas tarps. "Neil, you and Beth stay here and guard the wagons. Put your uniforms back on and stand guard like soldiers. If anyone asks, you're waiting for four members of the Red sub-council that are going to London for secret talks on machine destruction in Wales," ordered Angus in his Scottish Lord's voice.

Beth and Neil looked at each other. Finally Neil spoke, "What crap is that?"

"Don't worry, any guard that hears you say that will walk away, they don't want any problems with any council members, sub–council or not."

Angus and Robina stayed in their slave garb. Sarah and I returned to our red pants and blue tunics of the Red Master's officer's dress in compliance with Angus' orders. We marched in front of the two slaves who moped along behind us. Up to the third floor we marched, heading for the private sleeping chambers of the Red Master. In this most protected of rooms in Oxford, the Red Master kept the potion Angus desperately needed to make his escape. The elixir sat sealed in the Master's most guarded locked cabinet. I shook all over. I knew this was where our plan was likely to fail. I imagined myself on the scaffold with a man dressed in black holding an axe in his huge arms ready to chop my head clean off. I turned green.

"Stop you four." a gruff voice from behind us commanded. All four of us stopped and turned. Two vicious soldiers dressed like Sarah and I advanced down the hall towards us. One had his hand on his sword the other carried a large mace. Robina moved forward into me and melded her body against mine. I could feel she sought my protection.

The bigger of the two said to the other soldier, "They're the four we're looking for."

CHAPTER FOUR

THERE WE STOOD, SARAH AND I MASQUERADING AS RED ARMY OFFI-
cers and Robina and Angus dressed as the Red Master's menial slaves.
The fiercest looking men in any world approached us with their weapons
pointed menacingly towards us. They looked like the wickedest troll or orc
that fiction could produce. The surprise on our faces turned to panic.

Before they could advance a step further towards us, Angus started
talking, "Hello, fine sirs. You know me; I'm Angus the Scot, your master's
most trusted servant. I bring these soldiers and my assistant to his quarters
to carry off some of his personal possessions to take to Windsor Castle in
London." Angus looked at them and back at us, scratching his head. Looking
at the guards again he said, "Looking at you stout fellows, I think I should
take you and not these weaklings. Put your weapons down and let this
scruffy bunch guard the hall. You can carry the boxes for me."

The biggest and probably the senior guard said with contempt, "You
scurvy blighter, do not think you can give us orders. We are to stay here until
relieved. Take your riffraff and get your boxes and be quick about it."

We breathed a sigh of relief as we marched past the guards and down the
hall. Again, Angus used his piece of metal to gain entry into the Red Master's
chambers. A guard slept in a chair outside the door to the Red Master's inner
chamber. I stopped in my tracks and made small movements to flee. I could
not contain myself and in a high-pitch whisper said, "Angus, what`s going
on here? Isn't the guard posted here to protect the Red Master?" With my
heart beating what felt like five hundred times a minute, I continued, "Is the
Master guarded by magic or are we caught in a trap?"

Angus gave me a serious look then smiled. "No Jonathan, The Red Master
is so conceited he would never use magic to guard his own door. This is his

most trusted guard. He has killed hundreds while guarding his master. He would never sleep at that door even if he had not slept in a month. I gave him a draft of sleeping potion before I left the Master this evening. He will sleep for another ten hours."

The experience so far had shattered my nerves. I felt the bile in my throat and my innards twisted like a snake had curled up inside me. I wanted to run. Run as fast as my sprinter's legs would carry me. The guards gave me the fright of my life, didn't they see I was an officer and shouldn't be fetching and carrying for a slave? Now I was only ten feet away from the most powerful man in this world, and I was stealing from him. It felt like I had slunk into the Oval Office as the President slept at his desk and stood by his side taking his trophies off his desk. This had to be a dream.

"Jonathan, don't fret. I put a spell on the guards outside, nothing harmful, the weak like them are easy to misdirect." Robina interlocked her hand in mine, "See, aren't you glad I'm with you. Now let's see what this Wizard is reading."

Robina started taking down books from the shelves of the Red Master's home away from home mini-library. The room was a comfortable size, larger than a Don's room, decorated in Elizabethan England décor; strong oak beams and smoky white stucco covered the ceiling and walls. A fireplace big enough to roast a boar stood against the wall next to the door to the Master's bedroom. The simply-furnished room consisted of a few oak chairs, a table for eating and another for paperwork or making potions. Two walls gave a scholarly atmosphere with hundreds of leather-covered tomes. The lead windows on the wall opposite the entry door looked over the courtyard.

I watched Angus search the cupboards in the bottom parts of the bookcases. He searched frantically for the green liquid. I started to amble over to the cupboard to help him search when Robina whispered to me with excitement in her voice.

"Oh my god, Jonathan, look, it's the original *Saunders on Wizardry and other Crafts*. I've read about this book of books but to think I've found one. The Ancient Council of Wizards only allowed twelve tomes copied to be by their scribes." She opened it up and I saw beautiful hand printed text with pictures and diagrams illustrated in color as if done by Da Vinci or even Rembrandt. "This book is worth a hundred times more than the gold and diamonds we have in the wagons. The magic in this book makes whoever reads it one of the rulers of the world. Hold on to it for me Johnny." She put her arm around my waist and drew me closer to her. "You don't mind me calling you Johnny do you, lover?" Her breath overpowered me with its sweetness and its feeling of hot desire.

"No, Robina, I'll protect the book with my life." With passion I had never felt before she kissed me. I couldn't breathe or even think. I wanted her now. I was in mortal danger and it didn't matter, I wanted her.

Sarah broke the moment. "You two make me sick. Let's get what we need and leave this devil's den before he wakes up and eats us for breakfast."

"Quiet, my sister or you'll wake the devil yourself." Robina started taking other books from the shelf. She had found one of the Red Master's robes and used it to make a large bag to carry the books.

Sarah walked over to the table covered in papers, and by candlelight she sat down to read the Red Master's private correspondence. I thought of Sarah's and my life before the accident in the lab. I wasn't a thief nor was she. We saw ourselves as moral and honest members of society. Yet take us out of that society and we find ourselves robbing banks, breaking into private residences and reading private documents, probably confidential state documents. I shook my head and realized how thin our morals and honesty became when your world crumbles around you. I could justify every action I had done in the last twelve hours. Yet in the world that I now found myself, I was a criminal. A fugitive of the worst kind, and I knew it would never be any better.

I watched Angus scoop up a hand mirror with an ivory and gold handle, a wooden box the size of a case of beer and a glass bottle full of green liquid.

"Jonathan, come here and find something to carry these treasures in, but be careful of the liquid, that's what's going to save your good pal Angus and your new love Robina from an endless sleep."

I found a large leather bag by the other piece of furniture in the room, a grand oak desk stained with ink and dark with age. Angus sat on the floor prying open the center drawer. He searched it and pulled out a stack of papers written on large parchment in gold and black lettering, some with large wax seals in green, red, black and white.

"Let's go, we've found what we came for, it's time to leave this place forever."

Sarah found a rapier of such beauty it was a work of art. A ruby sat at the end of the pommel and the blade was as thin as a rat's tail, but shone like the

North Star on a clear frosty night. I saw the rapture on her face; it was more sublime and loving than when we made love.

Robina saw it as well. "Sarah, you've found your own true love. Its name is the Reaper. It has made many a widow throughout our lands. The Red Master earned his post by the expert use of that small weapon. With your dagger and the Reaper, you will be a woman of legend in this world."

Sarah swished the weapon and the blade sang a song of death through the air. A grin came to her face. "I like it, I like it a lot. I did some fencing in my undergraduate years." She winked at me. "This blade is an exquisite weapon."

As Sarah fondled the sword, Angus said, "We have to go. The college will swarm with troops in a few minutes. We've got everything we can carry."

Robina stood firm. "No, Sarah has the Reaper, Jonathan must have the Buffoon. His personal guard always carries it."

"No, Robina, there is no time and it's just a myth, the sword is not foolproof."

She gave him a withering look. "That's why it's called the Buffoon, it is foolproof. The White Wizard of five hundred years ago created it so even if a fool guarded him the sword would kill his assassins. It is ideal for Jonathan." She skipped over to the sleeping guard and cut his belt holding the sword from his waist and gave me the weapon to replace the one I carried.

"Now," she said, "no matter what, that blade will protect you from harm and defend you against the best of the best. It doesn't matter how inept you are with a sword, you will win the fight. It is old magic, no potion or spell can defeat that magic. Many have tried and none have succeeded. Only cunning can vanquish the holder of the blade. This weapon will never fail you."

The four of us took on a military bearing and marched from the room. The guard sitting in his chair barring the door to the inner chamber of the Red Master still slept blissfully. On the way down to the main floor Robina stopped. "I have to go to my room and grab a few of my precious belongings before we leave. Jonathan and I will meet you in the stables in five minutes."

"The hell you will. We must leave now or we'll never leave this town alive."

Robina's eyes flashed red. "I have to collect up my valuables. They mean the difference between life-or-death for us. Wait." I felt a tremor in the air and the smell of ozone burning filled my nostrils. I could see the smoke form in the air around us.

Angus was trembling. "You have two minutes. We'll wait in the Red Master's office. Hurry."

I entered Robina's bedroom/sitting room. The interior had the commanding authority of its occupant. If I had to describe the room, I would say the decorator lived-in the 1960's Haight Ashbury district of San Francisco. The word psychedelic came to mind. I could feel myself becoming aroused. The burning incense infused the room with a stimulating aroma. I needed her right now and I could feel she wanted me as well. In a hoarse voice I said, "We only have a few minutes. We don't have enough time."

In a husky voice she replied, "I'll stop time, we must."

I had my tunic off and she her peasant blouse. As I smothered her in kisses, I directed her towards the bed when the door flew open. "What the hell are you doing?" It was Sarah standing in the doorway with both hands on her hips and a look of utter disgust on her face.

Robina looked up and in an insolent tone said, "What does it look like. I'm to bear twins for the Lord of this world, a boy and a girl. It is time."

Sarah had the rapier in her hand. "Not now and not with him, grab your treasures. The college is swarming with soldiers all looking for us. Shit, Jonathan, put your pants on, you look ridiculous."

Robina and I rearranged our clothing and she stuffed the precious items she needed in her pillow case. I sulked in the middle of the room trying to avoid Sarah's enraged eyes and trying not to stare at Robina. I felt cheated yet amused in the same moment. My eyes strayed to Robina, and when our eyes locked I knew that destiny meant us to be together.

We reached the main floor without difficulty. Six soldiers blocked our way at the main exit from the Red Master's building. The soldiers all tall and forbidding gave me a frozen lump in the pit of my stomach. We had to pass them to link up with Angus.

"Halt, you three are under arrest. Throw down your weapons."

The soldier yelling at us stood over six feet six inches tall, his muscles looked more chiseled and larger than Arnold Schwarzenegger's. He drew his sword and the others followed suit. I felt my bowels turn to water and tried hard not to make a mess in my red pants.

Sarah took command. "Robina, take the saber from my right side. Jonathan, take out your sword. I'll use the rapier. We'll put our backs together and form a triangle with our swords facing out. If we have to fight we'll give them a few stingers before we die."

I couldn't believe what I was hearing. "Sarah, we're scientists, not 16th century musketeers. We can't fight real soldiers." My knees were wobbling as the soldiers approached.

Robina's hand found mine and she whispered, "You can do it, remember the ring. Think about us, not about the world you left behind. Just think of what you need to do, the sword will answer your commands."

Next she turned to Sarah's ear. "My sister, you're a warrior, that sword will not fail you. There are only six of them, do it now."

Like a jack-in-the-box, Sarah sprang from our defensive position and attacked the huge leader of the group. I followed her lead and stormed the two giants in front of me. My peripheral vision saw Robina slashing her sword at two others. Sarah's magic Reaper could do no wrong and in her trained hands it looked so simple for her to dance around her opponents letting her sword do its worst.

A wave of red infected me. Like tinted glasses everything turned a crimson hue, my emotions changed from black fear to killing red and I attacked with fury. I had never used a real sword in my life. As a child, I had wooden sticks and played Robin Hood or some such game but in reality you didn't count to ten and start again. As clumsily as I fought, I did damage to my two opponents.

On my left, Sarah's footwork mystified her adversary. His bulk made him ungainly and she sashayed around him making his every thrust pull him off balance. I saw the coup de grace. Her rapier cut into his tunic just below the heart and sliced upwards spraying blood over her head. The expression on her face was pure joy.

To my right, Robina struggled with difficulty against the two soldiers she fought. She had her back to a wall. They jabbed at her. Her body made spasmodic movements to avoid her attackers' thrusts. Each thrust of the enemy barely missed her. She threw a handful of dust from her leather pouch at her attackers. Whatever potion Robina tossed at them induced them to cough. The soldiers dropped their weapons and collapsed on the hard stone floor.

I continued fighting, my opponents were now bleeding from gashes and deep cuts. The two soldiers wouldn't surrender to my awkward swordplay. They charged me. When I put my sword up in front of my body to my surprise I parried their attack. I stumbled backwards falling to the floor. My sword stood straight up like a lone stalk of corn after the harvest. One of the soldiers in his zeal to finish me fell on it. The other could not stop and ran his friend through. Then he couldn't get his sword disengaged from his comrade's back. In terror he ran, leaving me lying on my back with his dead comrade skewed upon my sword.

I involuntarily vomited on the cold stone floor and squeezed my ass tight as I feared I might release my bowels in a messy explosion.

I looked around and discovered Robina laughing at my plight. Sarah was still in the passion of battle, she had just beheaded her foe, an ugly barbarian creature. Most likely, he was the pride of the Red Master's Army. Blood sprayed over Sarah's face again mixing with her first kills. Her eyes glistened and the savagery on her spattered face froze my soul. She loved the kill. I approached her slowly not wanting to be her next victim.

"Sarah, it's over. They are all dead or gone." She looked at me with eyes that didn't register who I was. She raised her sword and I pulled away.

Robina yelled, "Sarah, Sarah. It's your sister, it's done."

Sarah's eyes refocused on my face and she ran to me. I clasped her to my chest trying to smother her desire to kill. The smell of blood mixed with her perspiration overwhelmed me. "It's okay, Sarah, we've won. We survived without injury, let's get Angus and escape this madhouse."

"Jonathan. I loved it. I killed two human beings and I loved it. My soul cries out for more. I feel so alive in the heat of battle. With that sword in my hand I feel invincible."

Robina pushed me away from Sarah and hugged her. "Little sister, it's all right. Your nature is that of a warrior. That sword brings it out in you. In this world, you can do the impossible and follow those inner drives that your world wouldn't allow you to do. You're free to express your true nature. You're a fighter. Praise your talents and understand yourself. I'm a witch and Jonathan is a King. Each of us has a role to play in the Prophecy. I knew mine since birth. You have found yours, and one day Jonathan will realize his."

I thought, a king, what bunk. I promptly vomited again. I wounded a soldier and killed another. I'm not a warrior. I'm not a killer. I'm a theoretical physicist. I stopped from vomiting a third time as Robina wrapped her arm around me and guided me to Angus in the Red Master's office.

The bodies of the soldiers still littered the entryway door as we sprinted to the stables. We had escaped the building, but how far could we go with the University on alert knowing of our dash for freedom? We explained our last half hour's exploits to Beth and Neil as we loaded our new loot into the wagons. With the two buckboards, two teams of four horses and six riding horses hitched up behind, we snuck out of the stable and hightailed it to the main gate out of Oxford.

I sat snuggled next to Robina in the wagon. Sarah sat erect beside my new lover, still looking disgusted with me. I held the reins in my hands as Robina explained to me how to guide my team of horses out of the town. I could drive a car, but a horse was another matter. I wanted them to go left, they would stop. Go right, they would try to turn around. Every second we delayed I knew the Red Master would catch us, and still my horses would not obey.

"Don't be so controlling let the horses make some of the decisions. They've pulled wagons for years. They can anticipate your route. When they don't do what you want be firm, but be decisive, don't pull one way then the other. They will stop when you tell them, and go when you say the right words. Calm down."

It was easy for her to say, but my stomach tied itself in knots. The damn horses weren't like my Mini Cooper. Even with the horses not obeying my commands, the gate to the open road raced towards me. If we made it past the Red Master's guards we had a chance. That didn't seem possible. Once through the gate, neither Angus nor Robina would be able to help us. They would suffer from the Red Master's spell. We just hoped the green liquid would bring them back to life once we could dribble it down their throats.

The dawn was still two hours away. At that hour of the night, no one ventured on the road out of town. Only the street lamps guided us to the city gate. As we drew nearer to the road to freedom, a man-at-arms stood in front of the closed gate with crossbow in hand. Angus yelled for us to stop. I could hear fear in his voice. Robina told us that each of the towers on either side of the gate housed a company of soldiers.

"Robina, there's no way we can get through the gate unless it's open, and from what you tell me there's no way anyone will open the gate for us." If as a robber I might lose my hand, as a murderer of the guard I would lose my life. I fell into despair. In five seconds I let my mind turn to mush. My thoughts didn't flashback to show me my life, but flashed forward and showed me what I would miss if I died in front of the closed gate. In those few seconds I decided I had to win whatever life and death battle destiny had planned for me.

Robina's hand squeezed mine. "Your destiny is a King's Crown; there is always hope, desperate as it may be, we will find a way."

CHAPTER FIVE

ROBINA SEARCHED THROUGH THE PERSONAL POSSESSIONS SHE HAD retrieved from her room. "Ah, it's here. Jonathan, stop the wagon thirty feet from the gate. Then run up to the gate and put this beside it and light the string leading from the ball. Hurry back here or death will take you in little pieces."

I smiled at her, "An explosive, you've made black powder in your lab."

"You know of such alchemy? We don't reveal such knowledge to the ordinary people; it's against the Wizard's code of conduct. How do you know? Of course, your world has science."

"Yes, we have what you call black powder, we call it TNT."

After that she yanked two more long tubes from her bag and she told me, "These are smoke makers. When I say run, go and set the explosive, I'll ignite the smoke and I hope the Red Master's soldiers won't kill you before you gain the protection of the gate. Once you reach the gate set off the charges."

I looked at the hulking man-at-arms in his full armor and crossbow standing in front of the gate. I had taken part in killing a man a few minutes earlier, and then both Robina and the she-warrior Sarah stood beside me. This time I had no such comrades-in-arms. I stood alone on the battlefield.

The goliath of a warrior, swaggered in front of me taking aim at my heart with his crossbow and in a deep whisky tainted voice screamed, "I said halt. Or you in the officer's uniform will have my arrow through your heart."

Robina shook her head and laughed. "What a fool. Sarah, take the dagger I gave you and throw it at him."

"Christ, Robina, even if I could hit him he's covered in armor. It would be like hitting him with a stick."

"Do as I order, all our lives depend on it. Now throw the dagger."

The man-at-arms guarding the gate had his crossbow aimed at me. From his body language I could tell it was time. To my left I watched the dagger fly through the air. I observed the blade then the pommel go end over end through the air. The guard had his visor down on his headgear with only the slit open so he could see. The shiny steel armor covered his whole body. The little dagger had no chance in hell to do any damage.

The wagon still rolled slowly towards the gate. "Now run." Robina touched me on the shoulder as she yelled. I scrutinized the guard. I saw the soldiers in the towers; I knew death waited. I allowed fate to decide my life or death. I ran as fast as my sprinter's legs would carry me towards the gate. The two smoke bombs exploded in front of me. The man-at-arms yelled. At first, I thought he screamed at me to stop, however, a second later peering through the billowing smoke I watched him fall to his knees.

From behind me I heard Robina yell, "Johnny, retrieve Sarah's dagger." She yelled at Sarah next, "Mark another kill on your belt, sister. You just helped open the door to our freedom."

I heard strange zinging sounds as I darted through the smoke to the gate. An arrow landed in the ground at my feet. Then another arrow crashed to the earth on my left. Twenty more arrows followed falling all around me. The zings sounded almost like the whelping of a helicopter. I reached the man-at-arms now lying on his back. Blood sprayed out of the opening in his visor. The dagger had pierced his left eye to the hilt. All eight inches of the blade had penetrated his brain. It took me a few seconds to pluck the blade out of his eye socket. As I withdrew the blade arrows struck the dead warrior. To my surprise, a few penetrated his armor.

I tucked the dagger in my belt and sprinted to the gate to light the fuse. I retrace my steps back to the wagon. I prayed I wouldn't end up in little pieces like the gate. I spun around to return to Robina when I heard a cry coming from the wagons. I immediately imagined an arrow protruding from my new lover's eye like the Bayeux Tapestry showing King Harold's demise at the hands of William the Conquer. The cry continued, and I realized the screams came from a man's voice shouting in pain. I exhaled a sigh of relief and scampered back to the wagon.

The explosion rocked the ground and showered our two carts with debris and body parts. I couldn't hear, but I could see Robina yelling in my face.

From the way her lips moved I could tell she ordered me to drive the wagon as fast as I could out of the town through the gaping hole in the wall.

Fire, broken rock and split wood lay everywhere. The horses bucked and refused to move. They didn't seem thrilled with making their way through the breach in the wall. However, Robina, whip in hand, had the poor beasts galloping through the gate. As we passed under the destroyed passageway, I watched Robina wilt and collapse, succumbing to the Red Master's curse. I could hardly find a pulse. She breathed so shallowly it took me a few seconds to realize she hadn't died. In a tender motion Sarah took Robina in her arms and held her close, just as I imagined a sister would. I drove the horses through the rest of the destruction and they raced down the road heading north. I continued craning my neck to see if an army of cavalry chased after us. I kept the horses galloping for as long as I could and after twenty minutes they told me I had to stop. Not being a teamster or a horse person I had to obey even though I feared the Red Master would capture us within seconds.

I ran back to Angus' wagon to grab the green liquid to revive our emancipated slaves of the Red Master. To my horror, I discovered an arrow in Angus's left leg. "What the hell happened?" I screamed at Neil

"Calm down, Jonathan. He'll be all right. Before he passed out, he explained to us that we must wait until he's conscious before taking out the arrow. If we did it while he's still under the spell, he may never regain consciousness. As we passed through the gate he said Robina would know the magic to save his life."

Beth broke in, "We'll wake Robina first and she'll instruct us how to deal with the arrow in Angus." Beth started to cry, "He's a brave warrior, I owe him my life. When the arrows started to rain down on us he covered my body with his. The archer aimed for me, not him, but it struck him. He saved my life." She put a hand on his head. "I feel all the gold in that wagon is not enough to pay back what I owe him." Then she caressed his brow.

I took the green liquid and rushed back to Robina, who lay in the back of the wagon. I forced a few drops of the liquid into her mouth and as that slid down her throat I gave her a half mouthful. Angus wasn't sure how much to give so once that gurgled down I gave her another half mouthful. Then we waited.

Five minutes passed and nothing happened. I fidgeted. I knew we had to vamoose, yet I didn't want to continue with Robina still unconscious. After ten minutes, I decided we must give her more liquid, but Sarah cautioned, "No, that's enough if we give her more we might not have enough for Angus. Let's move on, I'll watch over her." Beth and Neil nodded in an agreement.

I didn't want to go, but then again I didn't want to stay in the middle of the road with an army chasing us. I knew theoretical physics, and how to solve such problems but I didn't have a clue how to solve real life tactical war problems. "Let's get moving." I croaked, "The bad guys will be after us. Sarah, remember when we went driving out this way two weeks ago in our world? We found that little valley you fell in love with. How much farther up the road is it?"

She looked at me as if I had spoken Klingon and had two heads. Then a smile came to her face. "Yes—why yes, back in our world it's about two miles up this road and to your left. If this world is similar to ours, it will be a good place to hide. Remember that overgrown path we found? Maybe it's here as well."

We reined in our horses and scooted up the road for another fifteen minutes stopping every few hundred feet looking for the side road we took two weeks earlier.

Sarah walked in front of the wagons searching the side of the road for our path. She jumped up and down and pointed to a break in the foliage. "Over here, Jonathan."

The dawn was just breaking as we started down what we thought would be a good hideout to rest and revive our friends. Neil jumped down from his wagon. "We have to obliterate our tracks or the Red Master's Army will follow us right down this trail." He broke off some bushes and took Beth with him. We waited as they erased our wagon tracks for about a quarter mile down the road.

We moved slowly down the rutted wagon trail. After about five minutes we stopped. We heard a thunderous sound from the road. Sarah whispered. "It's the Red Master. Sounds like a hundred or more riders, followed by wagons, and hear that, there must be soldiers running behind. Let's move on quickly. They may double back once they realize they've lost our tracks."

Neil shook his head, "No, they're going too fast to track us. They're heading north, probably all the way to Scotland to capture the escaped king. We are the unknown. He thinks we're Angus's supporters or members from his army come from the north to free him. Scotland is where he's taking his army."

The rough path disappeared in places in the long grass. We pushed on for an hour letting the horses, graze every half mile of so. Finally we found the site Sarah and I loved so much on our picnic two weeks ago. I stopped the wagon and surveyed our hiding place. The path to the valley lay just behind a copse of willow trees next to a winding stream. Robina's condition concerned me. She had not regained consciousness and almost three hours had passed since we escaped through the Oxford gate.

"Robina, Robina, wake up." I held her in my arms kissing her lips and rubbing her hands and forehead. She looked like a beautiful stone sculpture, cold and immovable. I became frantic, holding her tight to transfer my warmth into her. I kissed her cheeks, my tears falling onto her forehead as I stroked her hair. I did everything I could to stimulate her.

My whole soul ached. I didn't know what I would do if she died. I had only known her for eight hours, yet for me she represented everything I wanted; no, needed in my life. As my life was ending with Robina's condition, Beth's cell phone began to ring.

"Oh my god," She screamed. We rushed to her as she dug in her bag to find it. "Hello, who's this?"

"Holy Christ Professor," Beth answered, "Where are you? No professor, the machine didn't transport us back in time but to another dimension. It's terrible here, it's like hell right now; an evil sorcerer is chasing us. Yes professor, it is the same year and date as when we left. We are in that wooded area that you told Sarah about a few weeks ago. Can you help us?"

The Professor said something then the line went dead. For over an hour we tried to awake our comatose friends. We sat in the wagons giving each small quantities of the green liquid. We became frantic nothing was working. Then we notice movement in the woods.

Out of nowhere, a band of brigands swarmed out of the trees. I wrestled my sword from

my belt and scurried back to the wagon where Robina still lay motionless. Neil raised his crossbow to fire. As I looked at the bandits forty feet away one fell face first with an arrow between his eyes, a few seconds later another fell with an arrow in his chest. I heard Sarah's blade sing beside me. Both of us stood on the wagon awaiting the fifteen men. Many of them wore white tunics but five or six wore white with a black skull and crossbones emblazoned across the front of their tunics. The pirates charged our wagons in a headlong dash with every one of them screaming some foul epithet of how they would drink our blood. Our horses spooked and started to move erratically.

The brigands now had less than fifteen feet to cover before they confronted us. I watched a third and a fourth fall to Neil's mastery of the bow. A black pirate threw his spear. The thud of it hitting human flesh attacked my ears. It had connected with one of my companions. I knew it wasn't Robina as I stood over her like a guardian angel. Sarah was standing like a rock next to me but that is all I could see with the battle in front of me.

"Don't worry, Jonathan, we can deal with them. If we can't, well it'll all be over in a few minutes." I didn't have Sarah's fatalism. If we didn't kill them, I could see us being sport for them for some time in the future. Inch by inch killing or raping us until we no longer amused them or gave them enjoyment.

The first six charged the wagon; I swung my saber Buffoon at the first one but missed, inadvertently cutting the nose and ear of the attacker next to him. Sarah's rapier sliced the throat out of the one I missed. An axe toting thug whose arms were as big as tree trunks swung at my feet. I jumped up like a Cossack dancer and in my graceless return to the wagon-deck nearly severed his head. They now surrounded our wagon. Sarah and I attacked and parried. Still un-bloodied, but each attack forced us closer together. My nerves on first seeing the devils surface from the woods reacted like Mexican jumping beans, but once I swung and cut off the first attacker's nose and ear, I felt only elation.

Beth screamed from the other wagon as four of the pirates swarmed her. A pirate had crept up behind her and grabbed hold of her by the ponytail that she wore when she traveled. Without even aiming, Sarah removed the dagger from her belt and threw it at the man groping Beth. The blade struck the brigand in the back and he dropped Beth. He crashed into two of his fellow attackers. The last of the four attackers stood licking his lips. He stared at Beth in her ripped tunic and exposed breast. The man lowered his sword and reached out for Beth's ample chest. For his lechery he lost his hand, and finally he lost his heart to Beth as she plucked it out of his body on the point of her sword.

Two of the pirates in trying to climb on to the wagon pulled the tarp off revealing the bags of gold. Their attack stopped as two of the bags spilled on the ground with coins rolling willy-nilly around the wagon. Three pirates dove to the ground trying to pick up the elusive coins. In the confusion, Sarah cut down two more of the thieves. She knocked me to the ground as she ran her rapier through my opponent. On the way down my sword sliced through two of the coin collectors. I landed on the back of a third and put the pommel of his sword through his forehead.

Of the original fifteen or so pirates five remained intact; the others lay dead or senseless on the ground. The survivors had seen the gold. I could tell their minds whirled debating whether to charge the wagons and have one last go at killing us. Either fight for the gold or run, they had to decide and quickly.

Sarah yelled to me from her perch on the top of the wagon, "We can't let them go, they'll bring back more of their sort to steal our gold. We have to cut them down before they decide what to do. Let's go." She leaped down from the wagon extracted her dagger from the back of the dead man. We charged across the field yelling as our opponents did only a few minutes before. To our surprise, the five started running back into the woods.

Sarah loped like an antelope through the brush. Her grace and her speed through the woods caught two of the more rotund pirates. One turned to fight. She cut him down without any effort or remorse. Sarah didn't even miss a stride. The second pirate didn't know what hit him. Her rapier pierced his heart from behind. I sprinted through the forest like a deer. I ran marathons in cities. That was on a more uniform surface. Yet I still had the moves and the speed. My quarries ran more ineptly like pigs. One fell in front of me and I stumbled over him, my sword catching him in the belly ripping his innards and spilling them across the green grass. The second turned to face me. As I charged him; he parried, but unfortunately he fell backwards over a log. He smashed his head on an ugly jagged rock, that battle was over before it began.

The final brigand was swift of foot and we chased him into the valley that Sarah and I fell in love with two weeks prior. He scurried into a small cottage. I jogged behind with ragged breath and feet feeling leaden. I thought how picturesque the scene looked, smoke curling from the chimney of the stone and wooden building next to the various greens of the forest. I laid my eyes on the corral in the back of the cottage. It contained high spirited horses and even a contented milk cow munching on hay. I knew if I looked closer, I'd see chickens and geese. But I had other life-and-death problems to keep me occupied. The lone outlaw invaded the cottage. Before we could gain entry, he sprung out. He held a man between him and us, a hostage.

I stopped dead. It was Neil's brother, Nelson and he wasn't wearing sixteenth or even seventeenth century clothing. He was dressed as we left him in the Professor's lab, in jeans and safari shirt. The pirate had a knife to Nelson's throat and had his hands and feet tied with rope. He could hobble but not walk.

"Now my hardies, we have an Oxford standoff here, don't we? I propose a trade, this fine soul for your gold. Say the word and I'll unhitch my horse and all the gold I can carry and you have your friend. Or he dies and I take your gold anyway." He pointed his knife at the twenty-first century man.

I stopped dead, with mouth open and sword still in my hand but drooping to the ground. The pirate could see my astonishment. "You know this bugger, do you mate? He's a strange one, he is. But he has red blood like the rest of us." The knife in his hand gently sliced the throat of the denim-clad captive. A thin line of blood bubbled from the wound and trickled down the tanned throat of the prisoner. Nelson grimaced but didn't utter a word or even cry out.

I had seen my share of movies where the psychopathic killer has the hostage by the neck. The experienced hostage negotiator either talks the killer down or a sharpshooter ends the standoff. I didn't know the first rule about negotiating standoffs, and didn't have a shooter in the wings. However, I had to do something, "Where did you find this strange looking creature?"

The brigand laughed, "You're not from around here either, you speak like this blackheart." The knife cut another thin line across the throat this time just a little higher. "You're his friend, he's looking for two men and two women just like you. He talked a lot when we first met him, but once we tied him up he's been real quiet." The pirate wiped the blood from his knife on his jerkin and yelled, "Get out of my way, find me two horses burdened with gold and saddle up my black stallion. You stole that gold, or are you just stupid, traveling without an escort with such treasure?"

Sarah now stood beside me. "You don't want that gold mister 'cause if anyone found you with it the Red Master would eat your balls for breakfast. I hear he loves sweetmeats."

The bandit's face turned white. Then he laughed and spat on the ground, "You're a Goddamn liar, if that's the Red Master's gold he'd be here by now, skinning you alive."

As he was trying to assess if Sarah was telling the truth about the gold, Beth ran up. "Come quick, something's wrong with Neil. The spear went right through him and I can't stop the bleeding. He just went into convulsions." Beth hadn't repaired her tunic, and Neil's blood covered her bare chest. The pirate leered at her and I could see him lick his lips.

Sarah's face turned to utter revulsion as she looked at him. In one swift move, she threw her dagger the fifteen feet. It curved as it flew through the air missing the captive. Then the blade entered the pirate's mouth. I watched as the hilt stuck between his teeth. Blood bubbled out of the brigand's face. He fought death to speak. His eyes dilated. He fell to the ground onto his own knife. Nelson collapsed beside him and I ran to free him from his bonds.

"Oh my god, I thought I was dead, I've been with them for 20 minutes. They're the crudest, cruelest bastards I've ever met. My brother-in-law was a Hell's Angel out of Oakland but compared with these assholes he was a choirboy."

I put up my hand, "How did you get here Nelson?"

Before he could answer, Beth was yelling at me, "Help me. We have to save Neil. And we still have your love bunny and Angus to try to bring back from the dead. Come on, we can talk to Nelson later."

CHAPTER SIX

SARAH SPRINTED TO THE WAGON AND ARRIVED FIRST. I FOLLOWED only seconds behind. Neil lay in the wagon with his hands neatly crossed over his chest and Angus in the same prone position beside him. They both looked like corpses; motionless, and with their eyes closed. Angus had an arrow in his leg, and Neil a spear through his chest. Beth could hardly breathe as Sarah knelt beside Neil. She shook him and cried, "Neil, Neil, it's me, talk to me Neil, Neil."

Our newly released captive ran after us to the wagons. On spying the two wounded men he yelled in pain, "No, no he can't be dead." He fell to the floor of the wagon wrapping his arms around Neil. Beth pulled him off and started fussing with Neil.

I grabbed the newcomer. "Nelson, how did you get here?"

His didn't answer me and said, "My brother's hurt. Let me go!"

Cradling his brother's head he related, "When your team disappeared yesterday, The Professor and I follow your tracking devices on your phones. It took a lot of work, but we did it. By morning we found you, and The Professor sent me to bring you back."

Before he could say any more Neil coughed, and blood spewed through his teeth. Neil gurgled rather than spoke, "What's happening?"

His brother grabbed his hand. "It's me Neil. It's Nelson. I've come to take you home."

Neil's eyes opened, and a smile came to his bloody lips. "Nelson, I know you're a death dream but speak to me little brother." Neil coughed, and more blood frothed from his mouth.

"I've come to take you home. Everyone is waiting. We've refined the equipment. We can go back to our world, I can take us there."

Neil's eyes rolled back in his head, and he slumped down. Nelson cradled him closer to his chest. "Neil, Neil, you're safe now, Neil."

His body gave a violent shake, and his eyes opened once more. "Thank you, Nelson." Then Neil quietly died.

Beth started to weep. Nudging Nelson away from Neil's body she wrapped her arms around her dead lover. Sarah led Nelson away and I just stood there and silently cried. Beth yanked the bloody spear from Neil's body and taking the spear in two hands rammed it into the heart of each of the dead or wounded pirates. Her violence made me think of the love I had for Robina. I immediately ran to her.

My heart beat faster; I didn't want to lose her. I watched Beth's pain, I couldn't bear that. Like Angus, Robina lay like a corpse in the bed of the wagon. I took her frigid hand in mine and rubbed the delicate fingers. I held her close to my chest. Tears dropped from my puffy eyes leaving watermarks on her dress. A single tear dropped on her face and gently trickled down her cheek and slipped into her open mouth. I heard a light cough as the moisture rolled down her throat. I released Robina when her whole body gave a shiver. Then like a snake shedding its skin, she shook herself awake.

I gasped with surprise as she awoke and spoke as if she had never been asleep, "Oh, my love, I was dead and now I'm reborn. You shed the tears of life. You made me alive again."

She grabbed me and pulled me down in the wagon with her. I couldn't resist. How could I? The Prophecy said I was the father of her children. The battle had made me realize life and death sat on the opposite side of the same coin, one side you win, the other you lose. Life meant passion and commitment; the other side looked like oblivion. My passion for life exploded, and I needed her more than I needed air to breathe. She quenched my passion and we lay in the wagon looking up at the lazy clouds in the sky, and I recognized in those clouds my commitment to her and to the Prophecy.

She yawned and asked, "What happened to you and the others when I traveled to Hades and spoke to the dead?"

I gave her the short version of our battle with the brigands.

She jumped up from the bed of the wagon and pulled me to my feet. "We have to see this Outlander and then tend to Angus. The guards always use poison arrows. It's lucky that curse sent Angus to hell. The poison may dilute over time. I'll examine him and decide if we should bring him back to life or leave him in hell for another hour or so."

I followed her over to Angus' wagon. Beth sat calmly beside Neil holding his hand and whispering in his ear. Her rage had subsided and grieving took over her emotions. Beth ignored us as Robina pried Angus's eyelid open and pressed her left eye next to his, leaving less than a centimeter between each eye.

"Ah, just as I thought, I'll make a poultice. We'll need Beth to watch him until I come back." Robina gently shook her. "Dear, I need you to look after the living. Watch Angus. If he moves fetch me. He is in an extremely danger-ous place right now."

She looked around and asked, "Where are Nelson and Sarah?"

Beth pointed to the cottage, "He returned there to find his equipment. They took it from him."

Robina nodded, grabbed my hand, and we hurried into the woods. "Show me where this cottage is, we must find Sarah and your Outlander." As I rushed her through the forest, she stopped every so often to pick flowers and small bits of greenery.

She handed me a daisy and said, "We each pick one petal at a time and say, he loves me for one petal, and he loves me not for the next one you pull off. Now it's your turn, pick one, and say she loves me. I'll pick one and say he loves me."

We played the game until we both ended with the love me petal. "See, I told you our destiny has made us lovers."

We came to the cabin and stopped to catch our breath before entering. The long dead builders of the cabin had constructed it from roughhewed logs with mud and straw pushed between the chinks. It had stood in this secluded spot for more years than anyone could say. On walking into the cabin we spied Sarah and Nelson sitting together at a large kitchen table involved in an intense conversation. I noticed the homemade furniture, a bearskin rug and a large fireplace which dominated the main room. Embers of a recent fire still glowed in the grate.

Sarah looked over at Robina and sneered. "I can smell it on your clothes. Bitch." Then she looked away.

Robina, who didn't seem fazed by the attitude of Sarah, asked in a soft almost melodic voice, "Tell us who this man is and why he is here and of course where he came from." Robina's eyes turned from a flaming red when we made love to a soft pale blue when she spoke to Sarah.

Sarah took a deep breath and the anger in her voice melted away. "This is Neil's younger brother. When Professor Stafford phoned Beth they knew where we were and the day and time the communications started and ended. They had worked through the night on the machine that brought us and rewired the equipment to send Nelson here once they found us. He's one of our team from the lab."

I stopped her. "Why haven't we sent any calls or received them from our world?"

Sarah just shrugged. Nelson said, "It's the sunspots. If they are active, I've theorized they displace the electromagnetic field that allows radio waves to cross from one dimension to other and even images. You know ghosts walking through walls and flying saucers all that stuff is one dimension interrupting another."

Robina broke into the conversation. "I'm going to make tea and see if there are any biscuits." Then she looked directly into Nelson's eyes. "You need to have some hot tea, it will calm you after seeing your brother die."

Nelson shook his head. "I'll never be the same; he died in such a horrible way" He took a deep breath. "The last few hours have drained my emotions. I feel nothing. I thought I was dead a hundred times with those bandits. I just feel so numb."

Robina stoked the fire in the fireplace and hung a kettle from a hook over the rekindled flames. I watched the steam curl out of the kettle in ghostly wisps. "I found some biscuits and cups for tea." I had watched her and knew she materialized the goodies out of thin air. It was magic.

She cleared the table of the debris left by the pirates. "Ah here's the tea." She poured two cups, one for Sarah and one for Nelson. "You two eat and drink up, Johnny and I must wake Angus. I'll take a cup out for Beth; she's in a bad way."

Robina clasped me by the hand and started to drag me away. I resisted and said, "Lover, I want to hear more from Nelson, like how he got here and the design of his machine."

She gave me a kiss. "Later, Johnny, we have work to do, remember our good friend Angus?"

"Damn," I realized I'd forgotten about him, the poison arrow, and his deathly appearance. "Sorry, you're right. We have to go." I turned to Nelson and said, "We'll be back shortly to hear more about your experiences. We have to tend to one of our wounded."

As we returned to the wagons, I spied Beth. She looked so forlorn with Neil's body on one side and the corpse like Angus on the other. I turned to Robina, "I'll get the green liquid, and we'll start reviving him."

"Not on your life. That green liquid is not what he thinks it is. It's a hypnotic drug. The wizards use it to sedate and control. That's why it took me so long to recover and why only your love revived me. First, we have to repair his wound then bring him back. I'll need that spell book we expropriated from the Red Master. Pick me twenty of those blue flowers by your feet." Once I handed them to her she started to mash them into a paste.

After ten minutes of incantations and preparing a blue paste from the flowers I picked for her she nodded to me. "It's time."

To my horror, she instructed me to cut the arrow shaft from Angus' leg and then dig the barbed head out. I'm not a surgeon, and I felt relieved that Angus still slept when I rummaged in his thigh to remove the arrow. The hole I made was large and messy but Robina stuffed it with the blue paste.

"You're not a Nun of Mercy, but you're good."

I took one of the white tunics from a dead pirate and wiped my bloody hands. "What's a Nun of Mercy?"

"There is an order of nuns who have mystical healing powers. It's better than magic if your wounds are serious or life threatening. They take donations for healing, pennies if you're poor and gold sovereigns if you're noblemen. There's a convent of them in Stratford-Upon-Avon."

Then she glanced down at Angus. Robina gave a big sigh and started to revive the undead Scot.

She again chanted passages from the large book. Finally, she turned to Beth, "Dear; I need your help. It's essential you sip the cold tea I have prepared then force the other half of the cup down Angus' throat. It may be hard but you must do it. Then I'll provide you with a chant, and for ten minutes you must repeat it over and over again. When he awakes, all will come clear and your sorrow will disappear. It's crucial I go back to the cottage and talk to Sarah." Robina turned to me. "Johnny, we must go back now." She turned to Beth, "Please Beth, do what I asked."

On our return to the cabin, Robina stopped at the body of the leader of the brigands. "This is not good. This isn't an outlaw, it's the White Master's son. See the white tunic and the black skull and cross bones on it? That's the coat of arms of the White Master." She thought for a few seconds, appraising the dead. "This is not good. It appears as if they came to Oxford to assassinate the Red Master. Hand me your sword." She cut two fingers off the corpse. "This ring," she pulled it off one of the bloody fingers, "has the seal of the White Master's family and the crown tells me it's the first son." She threw that finger away and squeezed another ring off the second finger. She looked at the finger more closely. The finger had a cracked nail, blackened with dirt and calluses where it held a sword. She threw that finger to the ground as well. "This ring is magic and exceedingly important. See the stone, it is a communication stone. If you rub it, the Doppelganger of this ring reacts. The two wearers of the rings can see each other in the crystal and can talk to one another over long distances. I know the White Master wears the other. She tore a piece of the dead man's shirt and wrapped the ring in it. "This ring is dangerous; we must bury it deep into the earth far away from the dead.

She stuffed the ring in the pocket of her dress and looked down at the dead. "We can't leave them here. Someone will find them. We must bury the White Master's assassins and leave this place at once. The White Master may already know you killed his son, and who you are. Worse, he may know who all of us are."

"This is impossible. We defeated them with only one casualty. They should have massacred us. How could we be a team of assassins? It doesn't make sense."

"Maybe in your world you deplored violence and acted in a pacifist manner, but in this world you are warriors, very efficient warriors at that. I stood with Sarah in battle and recognized the ferocity in her eyes. She's a warrior who would at no time give up and at no time lose. I glimpsed in you the drive to find a way to survive through your intelligence, and with Buffoon by your side, you'll never face defeat. You fight like a lion. Beth will show her worth in time."

We sauntered back to the cabin in silence holding hands and thinking of what our future would bring. When I opened the door to the cabin, we found Nelson and Sarah both laughing, and completely enchanted with each other. Sarah spoke first, "Jonathan. Nelson had dinner with my mother yesterday.

He took her to that little place in Abingdon where Neil got so drunk we had to use a wheelbarrow to get him to the car."

I noticed her eyes sparkled and she looked younger. Robina put her arm around me and slipped me a peck on the cheek. To my astonishment, Sarah laughed. She seemed happy with Nelson.

Robina said, "Nelson, tell us what happened."

"Once we found you, we packed everything up and went to the location in our world. Then we duplicated the experiment and I arrived here just outside the cabin. Next thing I knew the outlaws confronted me. They called me a wizard and after that said something about the Red Master. They beat me and brought me inside. Then they stripped me of my locator and communicator. Without them, there is no way back. Sarah and I searched inside and outside the cabin but didn't find them. The leader pocketed them. It's crucial we must find them."

I jumped out of my skin, "You have a way back?"

He nodded. "It's all theoretical, but yes, I'm positive the Professor's hypothesis will work. If we recover the locator and the communicator, all of us can return to Oxford. We'll just have to wait until the next solar storms erupt, that's when I can communicate to the lab. Once they receive our signal from the locator, they'll flash us back to our own dimension."

Sarah and I gave a sigh of relief mixed with a glimmer of hope. But not Robina, who said, "That's not the way back. The Prophecy tells us that it is the Berwick Chronicles that gives us the way. Not your science, not your gadgets, it'll be magic that will solve our dilemmas."

Nelson stood and pulled Sarah up with him. "We have to find the leader. He has my belongings."

I said, "Let's go. I know where he is." We started to leave, but Robina stood by the fire.

"You are on a fool's task. The White Prince would have destroyed any such gadgets. I'm going to stay here, warm my hands in front of the fire, and smell this wood burning. The sweet scent of an oak fire relaxes me and I'll think of the journey ahead of us. Remember we must leave this place within the hour. We now have two grand houses after us, the Red and the White. Fly and find your toys. Move the wagons closer to the cabin when you return."

I loved Robina but couldn't understand her attitude towards technology, or for that matter, this world's attitude towards it. We found the dead White

Prince. I hadn't noticed the first time I came across him the sack on his back. Inside I found Nelson's instruments. They must have broken when the prince fell over a rock out cropping. The transmitter had shorted out, and the smell of ozone wafted from the open sack. We wept. Sarah and I craved so badly to leave this world. The smell of ozone told us we had only one choice, and that was Berwick and the Chronicles.

Nelson spoke first, "There's no way I can reproduce the equipment." Then he bowed his head.

I tried to put on an optimistic face when I said, "Nelson, we have the greatest minds in theoretical physics and the most talented conceptual engineer. We can do it. Sarah is more than brilliant and can help and Beth is the best with hardware, creating it and modifying it. You have the knowledge; we just need to find a place to build it."

Sarah shook her head in disbelief, "Jonathan. We are in a world where wood and iron rule, not the technology we require. We can't do it."

I gave a toothy grin. "Yes, we can. It may take years. We just have to start at the beginning. Remember on Star Trek when Spock made that computer when they were on earth in the 1930s? We can do that."

Sarah looked at me and rolled her eyes, "Jonathan. I don't know what I saw in you. That was television, not real life, get real. It's impossible."

It hurt, but I knew I was correct, if we put our minds to it, we could recreate Nelson's machine. We had the right minds, the only variable, time, stood in our way to complete our task and return to our world. Just the lack of time and no safe place to work could foil our return. Then I remembered Angus. "Let's see what's happened to Angus."

We arrived back at the wagons. Angus stood beside his wagon on a stave he must have cut down in the forest. Beth sat in the wagon. The two didn't notice us at first. Angus was joking with Beth and related a story that made her laugh. She put her hand on his sleeve, and he looked as happy as I'd ever seen him. Beth saw us first and waved us over.

"Robina is fabulous; she revived Angus within minutes of the two of you leaving. It must have been the tea. I enjoyed it myself even though it had cooled." She looked at Nelson, "We took Neil off the wagon and placed him over by the trees and covered him with a tarp. Angus suggested we could bury him here."

Angus yawned and said, "we'd better bury the bodies, an' soon. We dinna' want anyone finding them. These arneae a vagabond gang roaming the forest. They're a White Council's raiding party and frae' what I've seen, probably an assassin squad. You three did well. And you, Nelson, I hear ye popped in from the same world ma new friends came frae'." The Thane of Scotland became serious and put on a somber face, "I'm sorry this bunch o' hooligans murdered yoor brother. I hear ye did hae a chance to speak ta him afore he died. I know how yu feel, I remember the day ma brother died in ma arms on a battlefield in the highlands. It's no' a good omen."

I noticed Sarah fidget and then take a deep breath. "I smell something strange. I can almost taste it."

I took a deep breath and sniffed the air. I smelled something also. "Sarah. I think it's the dust, see it coming from the east. In the dust, I smell horses and sweat."

Angus sniffed as well, "Ye newcomers are good. Ye're natural-born trackers. That's the army returning. They're marching back ta Oxford. I would have never noticed it. I can smell the sweet flower in Beth's hair, but no' the stink of an army on the march. My years at Oxford hae taken ma away from the battlefield for too long. To think ye defended the wagons and killed every single one o' the White Master's assassins. Ye hae earned commissions in ma army that is for sure."

"Once they march by, we can leave this place and find a safe place to hide until the hunt for us cools down," suggested Nelson.

I nodded my head agreeing when Angus spoke again. "Na, we canna rest. We'll be on the run until we reach ma homeland. The word will go oot we've taken something of value from the Red Master. Every low life in the land will be after us. Every Wizard and his apprentice as well. Oor worst enemy though is the Red Master, we've made him look a fool an he canna abide by that. No, he has to kill us himsel' and regain his possessions and his pride. The army is coming back but the Red Master is no' stupid. He will hae left sentries up an' down the road looking for the booty an' for us."

Robina walked into the clearing and spoke, "I've heard what Angus has said. He's right. We have more enemies than friends in this world. I would guess even my father, the Black Lord, is looking for us. Angus' land is our only refuge. We must bury the dead and leave."

"Angus. Why are you speaking in a Scottish brogue? I asked.

He winked and said, "Na young man. I'm a Scot, and I went to Oxford so a can talk the talk, I dinna go there of ma own free will. When I'm outside of Oxford, I'm a Scot not an Englishman. I'll speak ma mother tongue."

Angus then surveyed the land. He found a soft plot of ground and we dug a communal grave for the dead. As I threw the last shovel full of dirt over Neil's shallow grave, four centurion knights on white steeds rode into the clearing.

CHAPTER SEVEN

I WRENCHED MY SWORD FROM ITS SCABBARD. ANGUS AND SARAH withdrew theirs as well. Beth inserted a bolt in her crossbow. Robina and Nelson still stood by the wagon preparing it for our journey north. Robina walked towards the riders. "Halt, noble lords, we have no business with you, and bear you no ill will."

I didn't understand what was happening. Angus whispered in my ear. "Be calm, don't move, slowly lower yoor sword. These are not mortal men or wizards. These are the Ancient Ones who live on the top of the highest mountain in the north. Only they know the secret o' the origins of magic. They ar' messengers o' the God on high. Even the Masters are their servants and obey at their whim. The Oldest one has spoken to ma but once. His wrath is legionary an' he is capricious as a spoiled bab. They say he is part of the Berwick events, they are the Gods' minions who invade our lives."

The stench of death rolled over the fields from the four lesser Gods towards the burial party. Robina acted oblivious to the reek of death emanating from the knights as she continued, "We honor you, but find your appearance frightening to us."

The oldest rider, the leader, still with his visor down gave a hideous laugh. "And you should, your power black witch is no match for ours. We only came to see the outsiders. We felt the shift in the balance of life."

The Roman Knights rode towards Sarah, Beth and I. "These three we sensed earlier as we did the fourth that you have buried in the forest. The other," and they turned to face Nelson, "has come we perceive to save them, yet he is the weakest of them all. He must have science, as we detect no magic in him. You are in danger. We will watch your progress. "

He laughed, "This is a new game for us. We'll be the arbitrator of the rules. If someone does not follow the rules, we will re-set the pieces to make the game fair. Remember if you don't follow the rules, your death would be just a minor result of an infraction. We wish you no luck in finding the Berwick Chronicles. Our Lord does not put any faith in the Prophecy but watches your progress with interest."

I couldn't hold my tongue, "What game, what rules?"

Another of the knights spoke, "Well, Outlander, you will have to learn them as you play the game. I know the rules, but it would not be fair to your opponents if I told you. When you succeed you will know. If you fall afoul you will know as well. The game has just started."

The third knight gave a hideous laugh, and his horse reared up on its hind legs. "Our Lord sitting in his high retreat is watching every move. He may give you helpful hints as you move about the board or he may not. You do know chess don't you? Well, this is nothing like that, but each team can move and countermove as the game progresses. It's your move right now."

Sarah yelled, "We don't want to play. We just want to return to our world. Who is your Lord to start this game?"

The leader spoke again, "Our Lord does not answer questions from mere mortals. I will say however that you started the game when you arrived. Your actions in stealing the gold and other belongings of the Red Master, including abducting Angus the Scot and Robina, Princess Witch of Black Wales, were treachery and raised the ire of the God on high. Once you killed the son of the Wizard of the White Rose, you sealed your own fate. The game is your penance for your deeds. Our Lord is the controller of this world. He knows your kind and so do we. You are a difficult race; you are insolent, full of pride and have no discipline. Your world is disgusting. Our Lord with his benevolence protects this world from colliding into others, even your miserable earth. If we find you trying to manipulate the game we'll step in and make it right."

Sarah angrily replied, "This is unfair. We're just trying to get home. We're scientists not wizards or warriors."

A phlegmy laugh emanated from the second knight, "Our point exactly, scientist, we should just kill you now, but the amusement of watching you fight magic and the Masters with their wizards and armies makes us less offended by your way of thinking. We wish you nothing but dirt." Then they rode off into a whirling cloud of smoke or dust.

Angus threw his hat on the ground. "Bloody hell."

Robina just laughed then added, "What next? I've never seen them before. I thought they were just a myth to keep the children in line. A game for death or glory is the fiercest they can do. Bah, we'll give them hell. The last game according to legend happened when Cromwell tried to unite the lands into one kingdom. It was civil war. What do you think they have in mind for us?"

Angus just shook his head and walked away. I looked around at all the confused faces and said, "We had better move. Others may find us, and we don't know the rules, but I would guess if they kill us the game's over, and we lose."

Nelson recovered his large leather bag with a shoulder strap. "I purchased a book of maps of all Great Britain." He opened the map book and found the page which showed our present position. "To the west about five miles there is an old Norman castle. Maybe it's here in this world. We could hold up there until we work out what we have to do, and how we can escape this crazy world."

"No, we have to get to the highlands as soon as possible. They could kill my son at any time. We have to go north now." Angus gestured wildly as he spoke.

Robina shook her head at Angus. "Thane of Scotland, remember the Prophecy. I don't think we want to be in such a hurry." She became silent, giving Angus time to think, and then in an amused voice said, "Both of us are right. We have to find a place of refuge and plan our next number of moves, but we have to move north quickly before they find us, or they block all roads with troops."

It confused me. I understood the merits of each strategy, and I empathized with both Angus and Nelson, but Robina's helpful statement of each put them in juxtaposition of each other. How could we decide?

Then Sarah spoke, "We'll go to the castle set up a base and plan our trip north. We'll use our science to help. Nelson, lead the way." She took his hand and gave it a squeeze.

Nelson sat proudly in the lead wagon, with map in hand the navigator of our expedition. He now had a role vital in our survival. He commanded the two wagons and almost twenty riding horses through paths, fields and forests until we arrived at the deserted castle.

Robina told us, "The land around the castle had been ordered off-limits to all by the Red Master years ago. The reason he said, was that it contained ghosts of the past and future."

The rock buildings and walls stood strong and in good repair. We stabled the horses, drew up the bridge and entered the keep. The four-story Norman castle came right out of MGM's back lot for a production of a *Robin Hood* movie. The first floor consisted of a grand hall with kitchens and servants' quarters. Twelve small two-room apartments filled the second floor. The third floor had four large apartments, more servants' quarters, a library and chapel. The fourth floor was the armory and caldrons, where the soldiers of the keep mustered awaiting for an attack on the castle.

The small castle could hold a hundred fighters in the barracks and about thirty horses in the stable. We were the only occupants and from the dust on all the simple furniture, it looked as if we were the only guests the keep had entertained in the last number of centuries. The castle had everything, from carving knives to saddles. Weapons and pottery filled their appointed places in the armory and kitchen. The keep sent shivers up my spine; it reminded me of a ghost castle lost in time, even the bedding laid in sealed wooden trunks looked fresh. In the center of the courtyard, a well stood full of sweet water and Angus pulled up the first bucket for his horse. He gave us all chores: fetch water and wood, find whatever food we could by hunting or scavenging in the fields for root crops. Angus, with bow and arrows in hand, went hunting. By suppertime, a big buck sat on the spit in the large fireplace in the Great Hall. Vegetables boiled on an old stove. Angus had located flour from the assassins' supplies for the bread baking in the open oven. I reminisced about my days camping but this experience made that pale in comparison. This was living the good life of King John. I gave a big sigh of relief. We survived the first day out of our world and in this hostile land.

The sun still sat smugly in the sky as we ate venison and talked about the adventures tomorrow would bring. Robina broke into her planning session and took command, "My new friends. We have to learn unknown skills, as well as time to plan, but my priority is to teach you magic. I'm your professor and you my students, for three hours a day I will instruct you in the art of magic. Angus the warrior king will teach you tactics and strategy of war in our world."

Sarah finally broke in. "My sister, you are wise, but we have talents too. The four of us will use our minds to bring science to your world. Swords are useful. Magic is rare, but technology will win any battle. With all three, we should be invincible."

I stood up with glass in hand. "We will study for two weeks. We'll learn, and prepare a plan to proceed to Berwick and the Chronicles." Everyone drank up the wine Robina magically conjured up. "It is the best I've ever had." I winked at her. "I think she can teach us a great deal."

Angus reminded us there was a price on our heads, both men and women. "My young lions, ye dunna' ken the customs, ye dunna' ken your enemy, and ye dunna' even ken how tae defend yourselves. Ye need this time tae learn and Robina is right. I'll teach ye' these skills. We are a team. I need ye' and ye' need me. Tomorrow I will transform ye' intae knights o' the Tartan and Thistle. Either on horse or on the ground, wit' sword or bow, ye' will master the battlefield."

Beth laughed, "You were unconscious when we defeated the White Assassins. They had skill and surprise on their side, they bloodied us," tears came to her eyes, "but we won."

"Yes my friends, you are good, but I will teach ye' to be no' just good, but the best. Then I will teach ye' how to deal with the Wizards, the Brownies, and other fairy people. You trust me, and we will all survive. You'll learn from mè, an' we'll all survive. Tonight we enjoy life, tomorrow we work."

That night we sang songs. Angus would serenade us, a ballad or a beer-drinking song, and we would sing him rock and roll or a show tune. Angus found an old barrel of grog. By midnight, the fire burned low, as did the candles, but our spirits sparkled like the stars, and we staggered to the bedrooms on the third floor. Robina and I found ourselves under bear rugs and wolf pelts. It was a wild night.

The next morning Angus and I scouted out the property. We discovered a waterwheel on the back side of the castle. When we returned to the castle I told the others of our find, and then how we could use it. "I think I can use the power from the wheel to give us electricity. I'll need you to help, but it will only take a few hours."

"What is this electricity you are talking about?" asked Robina.

Nelson laughed, "It's just the magic of our world. Without it nothing works."

We four Outlanders started talking at the same time, devising ways to use the power. Beth sat at the table drawing plans for a generator as we gathered around.

"Settle doon. Not only is Beth able tae incite ye' into rioting. She is a fabulous cook." Angus looked lovingly at her. "We hae venison for breakfast, fried with onions and carrots. On the table hot bread an' even some steaming oatmeal awaits you, all made by Beth" He smacked his lips, "I love oatmeal."

It was a breakfast I won't soon forget, not necessarily for the food itself, but for how Angus ate and how we followed his lead. Then Robina took command. "Everyone clear the table, we have lessons to work on 'till noon."

"Now class," from that moment on we returned to school, and Robina taught us magic. "See this mirror you obtained from the Red Master? It is one of his most prized possessions. One of his predecessors took it from the Black Wizard, my grandfather, who ruled my land at my birth. Cast your eyes into the mirror." Robina put it in front of Beth. She looked in it and at first she only saw her own image. Then her face morphed into a much older face, which looked out of the mirror and spoke.

"Commander, I want my mirror back, if you find it, you can keep one-fifth of the coin. The mirror, books and box I must have back at any cost. Take a thousand men and search. If a

thousand men are not enough, find ten thousand, but bring me back my possessions. Bring me the thieves alive that took them, Angus the Scot, the witch Robina, and four others. This is what they look like." He passed the Commander six large pieces of paper, each with the exact likeness of us as we exited the stable at Oxford. "Find them. If you fail, it is your life and another will be the Commander of my armies. You have ten days."

Beth put the mirror face down on the table. Robina looked at all of us and said, "That's why you're my students. You must learn and fast. That was yesterday. Pick the mirror up again Beth."

Beth followed Robina's instructions. "You lost them? How could you lose them? You rode faster than their wagons. You have trackers. How did you lose them? You found the cabin and the White Master's first son dead, but where did the six fugitives escape to? They aren't traveling up the Roman Road that is for sure. They can't have vanished. They're somewhere heading north." It was the Red Master, and he was even angrier than he had been the day before. He tore a map from the wall. "They have to be within this circle." He scratched, with a red quill pen a big circle on the map. "Seal that area off and search every square inch of it. They can't escape. We've confined them in that circle. It is imperative the thieves not escape; tighten the net until we have them. Hunt them down. If you return without them, I'll skin you alive in front of your troops. You have nine days. Now go."

Angus, sitting quietly by the fire, finally spoke, "That's your motivation to work hard. He's ruthless and right now we have most of his magic. He is at a disadvantage and must rely on his army, who are all fools. He will regain his powers soon."

Robina added, "Probably sooner than we would like."

Nelson looked frightened. "How are we to fight him? He has ten thousand men to block our way to Berwick."

Robina smiled and replied, "With magic, The Red Master's magic and with me. I'm a Witch and the daughter of the Black Wizard. I lost most of my magic being a prisoner of the Red Master. Now I can regain my strength and give you the power to defeat an army. Let's get to work, my young apprentices."

We each had a thousand questions for her, but she wouldn't listen; she just laughed and said, "I will teach you that later. First, we must learn the rules of magic." The Red Master's chest and two of his spell books lay open in front of Robina. She also had several precious stones and gold coins beside them. "Each of you forage in the kitchen and find a large pot." We went to do her bidding. On our return, she opened the box revealing many hundreds of containers. The box bore a label with strange lettering. It wasn't English or Latin or any language I had ever seen.

"Now, my students follow my instructions to the letter, and you will learn like you have never learned before. You have heard it is costly business learning. Each of you put five gold coins into the pot. Now write sword fight-ing on a piece of paper, when you have done that, put it in the pot." We did that. "Take a lock of your hair and put it in the pot. Now spit in the pot." She uncorked a bottle from the box. "Put a pinch of this in the pot." We followed her instructions. There were twenty such pinches of this and that. We then took two cups of frigid well water and poured it over the items in the pot. Once the water mixed with the other ingredients, Robina told us to drop a sparkling diamond, the reddest ruby and the purest emerald we could find from the Red Master's treasure into the mixture. Robina looked pleased with us. "Now carefully carry your pot to the stable, Angus has the smithies fire as hot as hell, keep your pot boiling over the fire until your ingredients melt into a golden simmering liquid." Like a gaggle of geese we followed her to the stable, each with our pot in hand.

After we had a simmering gold liquid in our glowing pots, she continued, "Now my brave students immerse the pot in well water for thirty minutes. No more, no less, exactly thirty minutes." We did it together. After thirty minutes, Robina looked at us with serious eyes and purred, "Drink it now, or die a stupid two-legged creature."

We drank it. It tasted cool and pleasant as it passed through our lips but once in our stomachs, it felt like a snake in our bellies.

"Good, good. You have discipline. Now you learn."

Angus took over; he had weapons for us set out on a table in the court-yard. For the next six hours, we fought. He would teach us a move and we would repeat it ten times, then another move and another. Each was more complex than the previous one. We didn't stop for food or rest. We learned and then we fought one another. Attack, parry, thrust, lunge, attack. Twist, turn, attack. Jump, roll, attack. After doing each move ten times, we retained the action and could repeat it in our sleep. It was like learning a dance, but what a dance! Each move we instantly memorized and added to it based on variations of previous moves. Each new move increased our repertoire of combat defense and attack positions exponentially.

"It's time to stop," yelled Robina. "I have another potion for you; this is the shortcut to the class in Alchemy I teach. At Oxford this would take three years to learn and another four to perfect. In the Red Master's book, the potion takes four hours to conjure up, and after an extremely ill evening, tomorrow you will know as much as I."

She put before us a large pot with green bubbling slime. I saw a severed head of a snake floating among the muck. "The Ancient Art of Magic, the written code of magic was written at the dawn of the magic age. It's considered instant learning bad form and criminal in the wizard world. If caught a student's master might give the offender a sleeping potion and put the lawbreaker to sleep for twenty years. Drink up, the rest of the day is yours, tomorrow we learn spells."

We moved into the keep at dusk, and by candlelight; we gobbled up rabbit stew with wild rice and carrots, still with the dirt clinging to them. I loved it. After dinner the science class started. First, we bandied about how to set up our electric project, and then we discussed a weapons development program to produce modern guns. Sarah and Nelson took over that project. I looked into making machines of convenience for this new world we lived in.

The next day it rained and none of us could eat. We felt like shit; head, stomach, and everything hurt. Robina laughed as she slurped up a plate of runny fried eggs and bacon. The smell of the bacon grease turned my stomach and made me run to a bucket placed strategically on the kitchen floor.

"It's time, my little lovelies, to have a lesson in potions." She pulled out the Red Master's secret potion book she had found in his chambers. "Alchemy is the ability to control your environment and animate objects in it with herbal and organic mixtures." For the next three hours, we discovered how to mix and where to find the ingredients for every potion. Of course, we knew hundreds of potions by heart since that ghastly green slop had slid down our throats the night before.

Beth and Sarah stood in the center of our makeshift class in the great hall chanting, "Toil and trouble, boil and bubble." Then in a crone's crackly laugh they stirred their brew of instant mind control.

We broke for lunch at noon, after which we fell into the hands of Angus and his collection of lethal toys. "Today ya're going tae learn how tae use the bow and arrow. Beth, I watched ye're wi' the crossbow. Noo here's an English bow, try tae pull it back." To all our surprise, she yanked it back with ease, took an arrow and shot it across the courtyard into the bale of hay set up at the far end of the yard. "My god woman, ye have strength in thae arms."

Robina smiled. "Remember Angus, yesterday they learned all about weapons. My potion works in all areas not just dexterity and learning."

For the next two weeks, we learned bewitching from Robina, six-suit magic card reading, invisibility spells and all other types of hexes. We could talk in six different magic languages. Angus taught us hand-to-hand combat, horseback riding, blacksmithing, hunting and all the highland dances he knew. Not only were the four of us becoming great soldiers, our wizardry talents ranked among the best of all the realms. The spell turned out to be the most effective of

all magic we learned. The incantations had no limits on its use, not so the potions that required time and a place to mix and brew the concoction.

In our limited spare time, we introduced the magic world to modern conveniences of heat, light, and the electric motor. Nelson invented gunpowder, "Just a pinch of this and a pinch of that, now let's see if we can get a spark." His first attempted was a small pop. The blast thrilled him. Still it was Robina with the last word. "Remember your potion class; it's much easier to make TNT than that flash in the pan explosive."

Just before we left, Nelson had constructed two crude flintlock long barreled guns with ball and powder. He had also assembled hand grenades similar to the one Robina had given to me at the gate at Oxford.

Each day we gazed into the mirror to watch the growing anger of the Red Master. He tarred and feathered his top general and a thousand soldiers, yet he still hadn't found us. I asked Angus, "Why are we so hard to find? We can't be that far from the road. They know we didn't stop anywhere further north for horses. Why haven't they marched into the castle and captured us?"

The others agreed with me, and Sarah asked, "Not only haven't they found us, but no one else has entered the area around us. There must be other people close to the castle. Why are we so isolated?"

Robina answered, "I told you, I am the Black Witch. I encased the castle in a spell when we arrived, no one can enter it, unless they know the charm. I know the charm and now you will. 'Hidden castle, water and stone, appear to me alone.' Now, repeat it ten times." We obediently repeated it and therefore, never forgot it.

During our time in the keep, Robina and I formed an even stronger relationship. We did everything together. We even thought alike, anticipating each other's word or next movement. Soon we became identical twins in thought and action. From the first night in the castle, Angus and Beth had become lovers as had Sarah and Nelson. The six of us, students and teachers, lovers and friends, learned to fight as a team and act like family. When Robina and I mooned over each other, they teased us, but we did the same to them; we played and fought and acted like combative siblings.

When the six of us fought as one, we were invincible, or so we hoped. Angus told us no army he had fought could defeat us. Robina read the magic tarot cards, and they revealed us as the best fighters in all of Britain.

"It's time for us to leave." Angus yelled as we woke on our fifteenth day in the castle. "Load the wagon and horses with all our booty and we head north."

Robina grabbed me and wouldn't let me out of bed until I properly woke her. The morning sun flew on the wings of Pegasus through the sky. As noon approached our small party finished packing the horses. Robina produced for us armor and knight's uniforms for our ride north. We rode as black knights under Robina's father's colors; Angus wore his tartan and highland fighting armor.

We had ridden a mile from the castle when a company of the Red Master's army confronted us. In the lead, we caught sight of four wizards riding in an armored coach. I felt their first spell crash against me. My eyes watered, and my mind sent confusing messages to my body. I crashed to the ground leaving my horse to whinny at me as I landed hard on the gravel path. The battle started with me and the others confused, blind and unhorsed.

CHAPTER EIGHT

ROBINA JUMPED IN FRONT OF US AS WE LAY ON THE GROUND LIKE squirming worms, the five of us unable to control our actions. Like a beautiful angel dressed in black, she spread her arms like wings and loudly enunciated a spell I should have known. I watched in horror as her angelic face changed into a mask of excruciating pain that lingered there as she repeated the spell staring at the four Red wizards in front of us. Within seconds, a cloud of mist encompassed our intrepid band of warrior sorcerers. The air surrounding us stank of ozone and the static electricity caused my hair to stand on end.

The four wizards of the Red Master had looks of murder on their faces. They waved wands, wore pointed hats, and scarlet and purple robes with stars and planets embroidered on them. An army of blue-and-red tunic clad men stood behind them on foot with pikes and swords in their hands. The green forest behind them made them stand out and magnified their numbers by tenfold. Gazing up from the ground during my imitation of a worm, it looked as if every soldier of the Red army stared right at me, and each had murder in his heart. Their arrogance, even when they stood at attention, angered me. The troopers taunted me in their neat rows like athletes expecting the start of the main event, psyching themselves for battle. I eventually had to laugh; they looked so ridiculous. My worst fears fell away, and I felt they couldn't hurt me.

The mist that surrounded us filled my nostrils. I could feel the energy-charged air into my lungs stimulate me. I breathed in and out and sensed the feeling return to my arms, and legs. I regained my feet as did the rest of the Berwick Six. That was the nickname Beth had given to our group of adventurers.

We stood proud in the uniform of the Black Master with our black tunics and gold armor shining under the afternoon sun. The four wizards no longer looked murderous but confused. Our armor flashed in their eyes, the gold chest plates, high leg guards, and our gold chain mail, enchanted by Robina to fend off enemy blows, blinded the wizards' magic. With our dark cloaks blowing like Superman's cape in the wind, the enemy stood mesmerized at our audacity to challenge them, six against an army. My gold helmet's black ostrich feather gave me just that jaunty appearance that put them on notice that I would not surrender.

With the magnificent weapons Robina had provided for us to fight the Red Master's Army, we stood ready for battle. I pulled my sword Buffoon from its scabbard and waved it at the wizards. My innards still felt like mush; I yelled insults at them even though I felt death gnawing at y heels.

Robina's voice sounded shrill and full of pain as she said, "Use your magic on the four wizards. They took us by surprise, and we must return the favor. Remember Saunders' spell eighty-four. It is a forbidden spell to these wizards. They won't expect it." Robina was fading fast. She fell to her knees trying to fight off the sorcerers' attack.

We squirmed past Robina blocking her from the wizards' view. We formed a wall holding hands and in unison chanted, "Evil spell invert your force and destroy the spell casters."

Our power was visible. It emanated from our mouths as an opaque green vapor. When it left our cocoon, it turned into a black translucent fog that choked the four wizards. They crashed to the ground in a violent thrashing motion as if attacked by great white sharks. As they undulated on the ground, they reached for their throats. I watched as their skin took on a blue tinge, as they died in front of our eyes.

In a hoarse voice, hardly recognizable, Robina said, "Thank you, you saved all our lives. They took us by surprise, and their combined strength overpowered me. Had I been able to prepare it would have been a different story." She visibly shook herself. With great distain she apprised the Red Army. "Prepare yourself the best you can."

The Red Army held their shields up like a wall, protecting them from all four sides. Then arrows came from the center of their formation. It seemed like hundreds of them at a time, flying right at us. My fear made me do something I had never done since our arrival in this land, I prayed. Death was a steel point on a wooden shaft. Like the trees from the forest, we didn't move but stood rooted to the ground in a tight circle. Our horses had galloped back towards the castle when the wizards first attacked.

The initial arrow came directly at me; I watched it with a fatal attraction. As if in slow motion, I tracked it as it came for my heart. Six feet above my head, the arrow encountered our cocoon and as if it hit a huge bowl of Jell-O, it stuck in the air. As each arrow penetrated the cocoon around us, they came closer to us. Our protective shell started to crumble.

The Red Army began to move behind their walls towards us. The armor and the shields gave off a rumbling racket almost like a slow-moving train as the soldiers moved one step at a time. The clattering train of soldiers bristled with swords and spears like a porcupine.

Robina took a deep breath. She yelled, "Run to the wagon and horses, run as if your life depended on it, as surely right now it does."

The next set of arrows hit the ground where we had stood less than two seconds before. Whatever powers we used, magic or otherwise, we found the wagons and the horses in the woods and rode as fast as our steeds would take us in the opposite direction from the Red Army. The next volley of arrows plummeted to the ground twenty feet behind our escape. We traveled along a trail that headed for the hills, not knowing where it led but knowing it went northwards.

We found ourselves at three in the afternoon riding horses along an ancient Roman road north to Scotland. The four of us 21st century city dwelling scientists bounced along on horses. Prior to this the only horses we knew were under the hoods of our cars. Yes, in my youth I had owned a Mustang, but it had a three hundred and fifty cubic inch engine, not four hooves and a tail. Sarah had ridden as a teenager and galloped like a cowboy. Naturally everything Sarah did, she qualified as an expert, as it was her personality. I had only the horse skills Robina had given us with her magic. Nelson had no talent as a horseman, and was driving a wagon of goods and gems as was Angus. I came from California; my comfort zone put me in a convertible or on a board, any board, surf, ski or skate, not a living breathing horse

We needed a break. We needed to dismount our horses and never remount them again. I knew intellectually that could not be, but my body told me another ten miles, and I would fall onto the ground in a big heap. Magic wouldn't let me fall, but my body had to have a rest.

For the last five miles, Robina did not speak or even glanced in any direction but forward. Then I watched her gaze back behind us and almost in a trance spoke, "Four hours behind us, five hundred angry soldiers of the Red Master are charging down this road. We need a plan, within minutes. I can enhance the horses, but we only have those four hours. Who knows where the roadblocks are ahead?"

Angus spoke for the first time in many miles, "I've been pondering our fate."

He looked up the long straight road, "We need one of your world's machines to carry us to Berwick and places farther north. Can you build such a conveyance? What did you call them, a motor vehicle or a train or whatever?"

I piped up, "How about a hot-air balloon? It's technologically easy to make and operate."

Nelson broke in still gritting his teeth but happy we had reined in the horses. "Why not a steam engine and mount it on a wagon? We could make good time on these roads."

Sarah rode up to Nelson and said, "My love, we don't have the time to build such a complicated contraption. I know Beth probably could put one together in a few weeks, but we don't have that much time."

"I could fabricate one much faster than that if I had the use of a blacksmith shop," groused Beth, "but as you say we don't have that much time."

I turned to Robina and then to Angus. "Either of you know where we can find a large amount of cloth and several people that can sew?"

"Stratford –Upon-Avon isn't too far and there is a cloth works near," spouted Angus.

Robina thought a moment. "Yes, there are miles of cloth there; I know the place. I believe the nunnery there takes pride in its fine seamstresses and their accuracy and speed." Her mind working through ideas visibly showed in her eyes now turning green. "I can delay the army chasing us but only for so long. I'll lay down a false trail. Ride fast, everything depends on us getting to the Stratford-Upon-Avon.

Two hours later we arrived at the nunnery. The medieval cloistered monastery had the look of a Hollywood set, everything so perfect just as one would imagine it should be. The high ivy-covered walls with the oak and iron gates surrounded a fifteenth-century French villa. On asking to enter and showing our gold, the main gate of solid oak opened gingerly, and we saw the luxurious gardens, grape vines, and fruit orchards. This was the land of plenty.

Angus introduced himself to the Mother Superior, but she refused to speak to the Scot as she said he was a heathen. Robina brokered the deal, "Most Reverend Mother Superior. I enjoyed our discussion. Can you have the material delivered here in the following hour and your charges ready to sew for the next twenty-four hours straight?"

"I do so love witches, especially the Black kind. Business is business with you. If you have the gold, all my nuns will have it done. If you extend your generosity to us in the form of more gold, we will finish that much sooner. We have nimble hands when gold passes over our palms, the Orange Master gave our order a special spell to sew as fast as the wind. We pay him to use it so your gold goes to both of us."

Before Robina answered I whispered into her ear, "We need a large basket shaped like a boat to carry us and our goods." The negotiations continued, and we entered the grounds to rest in a large glassed-in conservatory attached to the main building. The nuns cultivated orchids in the tropical atmosphere.

I marveled at the yards and yards of canvas the five ox-drawn carts delivered to the nunnery. Robina laughed at me. "Magic rules this land. The cloth merchant only channels the raw cotton and the thread together then he says his incantation, and the magic does the rest. You show him the material you need, and he transmutes it for you."

I gave her a piece of cloth. "Can he make this?"

"Of course. Where did you get that cloth anyway? I've never seen it before?"

I nodded, "Yes, when I first saw it, I thought it strange. Did you feel it? The cloth is from Beth's carryall bag. I snipped a piece of it off for the cloth merchant. I wonder what other materials we could use." I thought maybe a few hundred meters of blue denim for jeans.

I guess Robina read my mind. "If you desire some other material, we just have to ask the cloth merchant, and he would reproduce that cloth for us as he has your balloon cloth."

We strolled into the garden; I could smell the sweet aroma of the roses and a few yards away the scent of thousands of carnations wafted towards me. I marveled at the variety of flowers surrounding us. All of different colors painted a beautiful mural of the horn of cornucopia. I felt as if I entered Wonderland going to a tea party with Robina as my Alice. I could dream of no other place I would rather be. Then I felt guilty. I had to return to my world. I pushed the thought out of my mind and drank in the moment and Robina, so sensual, so alive holding me close to her.

The moment shattered as Sarah yelled to me, "We decided we'll use hydrogen in our balloon. We need the lighter gas because of the weight ratio. Bring Robina with you. We need a way to make hydrogen in large amounts right now."

Reality destroyed fantasy every time. My dream melted, and Robina's soft body against mine stiffened at the tone of Sarah's voice. We worked out a scientific-magic solution for our problem. Beth's face was aglow with excitement. "Nelson and I have an idea. We've come up with a revolutionary design for a motor that drives a propeller for our balloon. It will give us momentum if we fuel it with our leftover oxygen and hydrogen. We think we can make cylinders to carry the gas. We'll need a day to get it put together. Sarah, could you give us a hand?"

They looked at me. Nelson, a little embarrassed, asked, "Jon, could you persuade Robina to help? Actually, we need you to work with Sarah on the mathematics and Robina on acquiring the materials, you know, by magic." They looked a little sheepish asking for Robina's help.

I couldn't resist a slight laugh and asked Robina to help. She gave me a peck on the cheek, "Of course my love. I was only playing coy until you asked." I felt her snuggle up against me, and I blushed.

I looked at the others. "Don't worry, we'll do our jobs." I smiled and remembered why I became a scientist. "Once the initial balloon is ready, we can start making hydrogen. I understand the way Zeppelin must have felt putting his first airship in the air. If it works no one can catch us."

In the middle of the night we still worked on our lighter-than-air balloon. I asked Robina, "Before we arrived here you said the Red Army was right behind us. Why haven't they found us by now?"

She looked up at me with a twinkle in her eyes. "I sent off a magical image of us riding north. It will make tracks like our horses and to anyone who spies it; they will recognize the six of us riding hard straight up the Roman road north to Scotland. The army must be still following the mirage."

We worked all that night until dawn. Angus dragged us into the town for a real meal, or so he called it. "Mae friends, the tavern in this town is one I've had the opportunity ae dine at in the past. I'll buy us the best they have. Follow me."

We needed a break; our eyes burned red with fatigue, and our brains couldn't calculate two and two let alone the volume of a sphere with unusual angled bits. The Red Boar fell silent except for the barkeep's loud gasp as we entered. Our little band still wore the Black tunics of the Order of the Black Wizard. The serving wench, as Angus called her, tentatively took our order and with some fear brought us beer and bacon, eggs, roast beef, mutton and hash brown potatoes for the first course. I found the table of the publican as scrumptious as any pub I'd ever had the pleasure to dine in. Everyone agreed as we finished with griddlecakes, we would return to the Red Boar and taste the dinner menu.

I turned to Angus, "Is this a typical pub in your land?" I looked around the enormous room with two big fireplaces at each end ablaze with log fires to warm the cool morning air and sat back content with life. The red-brick building with large lead glass windows, each glass section no bigger than a pocketbook, gained most of its light from gaslights on the walls and on each table. The place didn't quite look medieval but more a mixture of times and places. It gave a cozy and welcoming feeling. On the walls were notices and paintings of Lords and Ladies and even ordinary people. I sipped my beer and resolved to while away the day in this homey atmosphere.

Four large red panted, blue tunic clad cavalrymen entered the pub. They sat down a few

tables from us. We had purposely taken a table away from the light in the back of the pub. "Wench, over here, we need beer, and plenty of it. We've been riding all night. The grub we get better be the best in the house or I'll be tanning you hide with my riding crop. Hurry I say, hurry."

"Oh shit." Sarah whispered, "The army has caught up to us. The balloons won't be ready for another six or seven hours. What are we going to do?"

The serving girl looked nervous as she carried the two pitchers of beer to the Red Army officers. She knew that six Black Army troopers and four Red Army officers didn't mix, and a brawl would be brewing. She slipped and spilled both pitchers of the ale on the soldiers. "My God girl, you're a stupid bitch aren't you?" The meanest looking of the bunch covered in beer rose from his bench and true to his word took out his riding crop, and swung at the poor girl. She rolled under the trestle table and he slashed at her feet.

Without thinking of the consequences Sarah and I jumped in front of the Red Master's officers with our swords unsheathed and at the ready. "If you lay one hand on that poor girl I'll run you through," crowed Sarah.

I echoed her challenge, "The beer gives you an almost human odor. You've been screwing your horses haven't you?" I don't know where the bravado came from, but it warmed my blood and the defender of the downtrodden felt good.

The four enraged cavalrymen forgot about the girl and charged us. With our newly gained skills, we fought them with dexterity and superior ability. I parried their first attack. On their second pass, I fell back on a table letting them thrust. As they missed me, I used the table as a springboard and with my sword waving in every direction cut four ears from my two attackers. As they fell back, I cut off their noses.

Angus and Robina could hardly contain themselves. "You two are a danger to the fighting world. Combat ae ye is like catching fish for a fisherman," Angus bellowed as he continued to laugh.

Robina just shook her head. "Remember magic. Why raise your swords in anger? Now I'll have to clean up your mess."

The two who attacked me had deserted me and were dragging the others that Sarah had sliced and diced. Robina shouted some spell into my ear, and it reached the four soldiers. They stopped as if frozen in time. "What did you do to them?" I asked.

Robina looked like my third-grade teacher. "Jonathan, I just enchanted them using spell eighty-seven, remember I taught it to you?"

I did remember. "Oh yes, you taught me the forgetting spell. They won't remember what happened to them."

"Yes my little rabbit, if they remembered the whole Red Master's Army would descend on us due to your handiwork. Ears and noses all over the floor, it's not the sword that's a Buffoon it's you my turnip." She stopped talking and thought a moment then said, "Now the bloodied soldiers don't even know who they are. They'll stumble around for the next four or five days before they start to remember."

Angus gave a sigh of agreement and said, "Otherwise I would have had to kill them, or you would."

I threw a gold coin on the table and another to the girl on the floor as we left.

On returning to the nunnery Mother Superior advised us, "If you give us two more gold pieces we can have your large bags completed within two hours. We received news of your exploits in the Red Boer and it's wise you leave as soon as possible. You are a danger to anyone who has spoken to you. As ours is an order of silence, no one here will talk. Of course, the rest of the town has eyes, ears and tongues and the Red Master's Army will eventually come by this way."

I looked deep into her ice-blue eyes. I could tell she was a beautiful woman but also calculating. I wondered in that moment if celibacy was part of her order. As quick as I thought it, I felt a hard smack on my head. A headache descended on me like I had never felt before and as fast as it came it disappeared. I could feel Robina standing behind me.

She threw four gold coins at the Mother Superior. "One hour and we leave, make it so and no more enticing my charges."

We commenced inflating the first balloon sack with hydrogen twenty minutes later. The task, which should have taken more than a day, took less than an hour. Our raw material came from a small lake. The hydrogen it made flowed from it like a river into our woebegone balloon. Once firmed up it would raise it into the sky. As the inflatable started taking shape, Sarah decided to bind the three sacks together and make one large balloon.

"No, we can't do that, our propulsion units won't work," pointed out Nelson.

Sarah started calculating in her head, "Yes we can, all we need is a little more engineering. It'll work. Jonathan, come here and fetch Robina."

With a little magic and much science, we had three propellers ready to start the voyage north. Robina shook her head now understanding the workings of the hot-air balloon, "Your basket is all wrong. We require something sturdier to travel in."

I watched as she fell into a trance. Her eyes rolled back into her skull. Her body shivered, and her hair stood up like she stuck her finger in a light socket. I held her tight to my body and could almost read her thoughts in my mind. They flew so fast through my conscious I could only grasp them in my subconscious. Then I understood what she had in mind.

I broke away from Robina's mind. I asked the nuns to bring all the basket material they had to Robina. I even ordered them to bring small trees and heavy reeds, as many as they could find. Within twenty minutes, I had a little thicket of branches and reeds.

"Robina, wake up. Wake. It's here, do your magic. Wake up."

She shook herself and her eyes opened as wide as possible, peered around not seeing anything but me. She smiled, "My love. I felt you in my mind." Then she looked around, "You understood what I saw." The glow on her face made me blush; I could sense what she felt towards me.

The team watched in awe as she commanded the pile of canes to make a real boat. It was not a boat that would hold water but one that would hold all of us and our booty in comfort under our airship. By one in the afternoon, our airship prepared to float away on the clouds. We said our good-byes and started to cut the ballast when the Red Army smashed down the Covent's gate and charged at our huge balloon.

CHAPTER NINE

I GASPED IN HORROR AS THE RED ARMY STORMED THE CONVENT. THE zeppelin rose to just over two hundred feet, and at that altitude I spotted flames leaping from the windows of the beautiful building below. The hundred or more horseman of the Red cavalry trampled the idyllic garden Robina and I loved, crushing all the delicate flowers. The aroma of the dying flowers rose in the air like the silent cries of the roses and carnations as their lives floated away. In horror I watched a wizard attack four of the nuns. Without touching them, he murdered them in the courtyard of the monastery by ripping their still beating hearts from their bodies. The Mother Superior stood defiant and proud as four officers of the Red Master ripped her robe from her displaying her naked body to their soldiers and inviting the troops to violate her on masse. The scene of the mob of soldiers crowded around her repulsed me. I felt powerless to help the beautiful but pious woman in her time of extreme need.

Sarah gasped as we floated in the air two hundred feet up in the clouds. My ears burned with ire as the screams from below drowned out the whine of the engines of our airship. The Mother Superior disappeared under the conglomeration of soldiers, but one glance at the frenzied soldiers foretold her fate.

Holding me tight, Robina observed everything I had watched; she yelled a curse and then screamed a spell I had never heard before. I could feel her in my mind trying to calm me. I didn't realize I had tears running down my face. She gently wrapped her arm around my shoulder, "It will be all right now. They will not have her."

"My god Robina! You didn't kill her did you?" I yelled with terror in my heart.

She laughed at my horror. She pointed to the ground. I looked down, I watched the mass of soldiers tossed hither and yon and out of the heap a body flew into the air, arms and legs flapping like a chicken trying to fly. I watched with eyes so wide I thought my eyeballs would jump out of their sockets, waiting for the naked Mother Superior to fall back to the ground in a crushing re-entry. I diverted my eyes from the tragedy.

"Keep your eyes on the flying nun," commanded Robina, "see her float in the air like your flying schooner."

My eyes grew even larger as I watched the tin-soldier-sized Mother Superior grow larger and larger every second. My heart raced as she approached the ship. A smile came to my face as I realized Robina had brought her from the unholy horror of rape and death to the safety of our flying ship.

"Nelson, Johnny, catch her before she smashes into the ship," ordered Robina.

The two of us snatched the terrified woman out of the air an instant before her body smashed into the side of our huge wicker basket.

"Thank god for magic," exhaled the Mother Superior as she made the sign of the cross. Then she collapsed in my arms. I hurriedly searched for one of the women to come to my aid and take this enchanting being off my hands. This was a curvaceous woman and the head of a religious order that was draped across me. The three girls watched with humor at my discomfort and giggled as I turned pink then red and finally to crimson. The three laughed at me and then so did everyone else on the airship except the Mother Superior. She had regained her composure and sat in a provocative position in my arms.

She glowered at me with eyes that could burn holes through steel. I froze. I could tell she could feel a certain part of my body turn to iron. Finally she laughed with the others. She gave me the once over with eyes of compassion. "Young man, you can let me go now. I appreciate you rescuing me and I find your hands warm on my body especially where modesty doesn't allow me to mention, but I can stand. If you could find me a garment to wear I would be in your debt even more."

Robina left the deck of our flying boat and returned with a long cotton dress in dark blue. Without shame, or even concern, the Mother Superior took the garment, slipped it over her head in front of us, and asked, "Who's in charge?"

No one spoke, we glanced at one another and finally Robina answered, "We're going to Berwick to fulfill the Prophecy. I'm a Black Witch," she pointed to me and said, "he's the outlander and these are his companions. The rough looking Scot is Angus the Thane of the Highlands."

"I knew when you asked for my help you were a weird group, but the Thane and the members of the Prophecy?" She looked at Robina. "Are you with child?"

Angus broke in, "There will be time ae discuss a' this later; right now we hae tae direct this machine north. Can any o' you scientists dae that?"

Nelson removed the map from his knapsack and examined it and finally took note of the ground a thousand feet below. "From this height I can make out the roads and the villages. Yes, if we follow the roads north, I can pilot this contraption."

Beth grasped Angus' hand but not out of love or affection, but fear, "Look below, there must be a thousand horsemen following us on the road."

We looked down. There were a great many horses, but it looked to me like only a hundred or so. Nelson laughed, "We can outrun them, and I can get this boat up to thirty–five knots." Nelson hurried off to the bridge to increase the speed and captain the ship. The rest of us retired to below decks to what Robina's magic had made as a lounge. The room gave the impression of the Orient or at least the Middle East, with beautiful fabrics, exotic cushions, lacquered furniture and lushly colored walls painted throughout. To my amazement, a large window looked out of the craft showing us a panorama of our voyage north. It had wicker woven every foot to stop anyone from falling out the window. Yet it allowed all of us to see.

We sprawled out in Robina's lounge chairs, and Angus spoke, "Mother Superior, what is your wish? We can probably set this boat down near one o' yer sister nunneries, and ye could seek refuge there."

A serious look crossed her face, "Yes that would be the prudent solution for my problem. However, I believe the Gods have something different planned for me. I know the Prophecy; my order was at Berwick when the full Council of Masters met. The order acted as the scribes for its drafting. The Masters' Seers that foresaw the future dictated it word-for-word to them. However, it changed when the Masters approved the final draft for the masses. The Masters censored the original Prophecy. It preached heresy and unorthodox ideas. My order kept a copy, and each novice since then had to memorize the first prophecy so our world would never lose or forget what the Seers glimpsed in the waters at Berwick."

The two natives to this world looked at her with surprise and then wonder on their faces. Mother Superior smiled at them and continued, "My place is with you. I can guide you and help fulfill what the council of Seers saw in the waters of the future." She took a deep breath, "It is essential I return to a secular life. The Prophecy foretells it. I've lived in the Monastery for twenty years. I will never forsake my religion. However, I must in the name of the Gods set aside my vows that I took as a novice. I shall live as the Prophecy dictates. The life the Seers envisioned for me is not one I will shirk or run away from. It is my destiny." She looked at me and winked, "As your spiritual adviser, magic and science will take their rightful place in the time of your rule."

I blushed. Robina laughed. Angus said, "Can ye tell us what the true Prophecy is and why the Council o' Berwick demanded on its secrecy from the people? Please tell us, Mother Superior."

I watched her. I observed her mind weighing her answer and rejecting one reply and then deciding what to say. Once she determined how to answer him, she paused a few more seconds, then she replied, "Mother Superior is no longer suitable; I'm neither the head of a nunnery nor bound by my vows. My name is Farica. I'm from a simple peasant family that farmed near Manchester. So I'm Farica Manchester."

Angus shook his head, "You did nae answer ma question. Tell us the true wording of the original Prophecy."

A pained look came to her face. "It's not time. When you must make an impossible decision, I will relate to you what the Seers perceived in the waters of the future. Until then, it will not help you. The knowledge is painful for all, which is why the Masters refused to divulge it. However, for the participants it is deadly, and you don't need to know the results before the time comes." On those words, she closed her mouth and sat with her arms crossed; her eyes closed and refused to answer Angus as he fell into a silent rage.

The Berwick Flyer, as Beth dubbed our flying ship, traveled north for the next several hours. The ride became bumpy over Derby as we ran into a summer storm, and lost momentum. The ship stayed airborne, but we started to drift back south.

I turned to Robina, "My love, can you brew up a south westerly wind to send us back up north? Nothing too strong, only enough weather to give us a tailwind."

She looked at me as if I just escaped from Bedlam. "No, I can't do that on a whim. Weather control is not an easy bewitching. I'd need time to prepare a spell. Can your science control the weather, stop a storm or control the seas?" She looked smug, "I didn't think so. I can if given the time."

Nelson on the bridge yelled down, "I need some help up here. The steering is sluggish, and I suggest we land soon or this wind will tear us apart."

I looked down and realized the zeppelin sped forward, not to the north, but to the west, at what I gauged to be over sixty knots.

"Where the hell are we Nelson? That does nae look like the countryside around Leeds." It was Angus peering down at the ground a thousand feet below.

"I think we're between Manchester and Liverpool, but I'm not sure. The low clouds crept in about half an hour ago and they just blew away."

Farica smiled and looked down at the ground below. "Maybe I can help, this is where I come from." She stared at the ground as it glided by, "By Holy God, right down there is Knutsford, that's where I grew up. Just north of here is Tate Hall, we could land there. I still know people in the area and since the Red and the White War of '88 no one has returned to the hall." She thought a few seconds, "I'll go up on the bridge with Nelson."

When Farica arrived on the bridge, the wind was reaching gale-force levels. The force seven winds pushed the Berwick Flyer up to another three thousand feet. The sun disappeared behind thunderclouds, and the rains poured down like Niagara Falls. Nelson yelled to Farica to tie herself down before the storm blew her overboard.

I felt Robina's hand grasping mine as a free-falling elevator ride dropped the Berwick Flyer down two thousand feet from the three thousand we had gained in the storm. Before we could gain our feet, the flyer rocketed right into the lightning and thunder.

Sarah screamed just as bolt of lightning exploded and lightning ripped through the bridge. I prayed for both Farica and Nelson. I felt the wicker under my feet start to separate. I peered down and saw a gaping hole expose the angry black clouds below the Berwick Flyer. The gap in the floor visibly widened between my feet in the few seconds I gazed at the ground. I stumbled and pitched forward and finally backwards into the breach in the airship's deck. I know now that it was my scream I heard as I tumbled in midair, but at the time, I thought someone had murdered one of my friends. The wind caught my legs as I felt my arms lash out to grab anything still attached to the ship. I could feel the storm fighting to take me. It was sucking me out of the safety of the boat. My eyes still saw the interior of the Berwick Flyer but my whole body swung under the airship.

The ship dove and then rolled on a wave of rough air. My grip slipped, and I started to plummet toward the ground. My senses were numb. All I could hear, taste, touch, see or smell was the roaring wind. Finally, a lightning flash illuminated me. I could feel the current running through my body. I tasted the bitter smell of ozone. I smelled the acidic odor of burned hair. My ears rang like Big Ben, and I was flying. Flying right back up to the Berwick Flyer, precisely up into the hole, I fell through.

"I thought I lost you. I panicked. Then the lasso spell came to me. I sent out a lightning bolt to pull you back. Oh Johnny, I thought you were gone." Robina wrapped her arms around me and smothered me with kisses.

Angus and Sarah repaired the hole with scraps of twine, small canes and hemp that Robina didn't use in making the flyer.

"Smell that," yelled Angus, "it's the ocean. The storm has pushed us far tae the west past Liverpool. If this weather continues –." A large crashing sound drowned out the rest of what he said.

Beth entered the lounge area, drenched to the skin, "I found them. I found them. They're still on board. When the wind gusted and the lightning struck it swept the bridge away, washing them into the cargo hold. Nelson is still groggy but Farica is all right." Beth took a deep breath. "The balloon has two big holes in it, the steering and the motors are gone. We're at the mercy of that fucking wind. Anyone got any ideas?"

Robina still hugging me spoke, "This isn't a natural storm. I couldn't stop it because I needed a complex spell that takes longer. I feel the rhythm of the storm, and a powerful wizard has sent this storm to stop us. The thunderstorm has just one purpose, to kill us. It can only be the Red Master." Then she stared out into the turbulence, "No. It's more powerful than him, its old magic. Nevertheless, it has his fingerprints all over it.

She turned to Beth, "Bring Nelson and Farica here. We have to use magic and with all of us in one place holding hands, we may have the power to fight the Red Master."

Two minutes later, we sat holding hands in a circle in the lounge with the design of the pentagram drawn on the uneven floor between us. Robina searched through the Red Master's book and after reading numerous pages discovered five spells, each with a different attack from the weather. She led us in group incantations with hopes our combined power could save us.

A vision blinded me to the real world. It frightened me and I squeezed my lover's hand, "Robina. I can feel the Red Master. I can smell his breath. The harder I squeeze my eyes closed the clearer the image. He is trying to read my mind. He is strong, very strong."

Robina started a new incantation. We repeated it.

Beth spoke, "I can feel all of you standing with me. I can feel the Red Master backing away. He can feel your power. Don't stop, louder and faster. Louder and faster."

Our voices screamed louder than the storm that surrounded us. My whole being became the chant. Every syllable was all that I lived for. Farica knelt beside me holding my left hand. Her chant was different, she prayed to her gods and the ancient gods of the druids, yet I could hear Christian theology in her prayers. This wasn't a conscious thought on my part. It just seeped in as I enunciated the chant.

It wasn't a noticeable change but after ten minutes or maybe an hour, time didn't have any relevance, the storm diminished and we floated north-by-north-east. I could now see the land. It slowly came closer to us.

Robina stopped chanting and we followed her lead. Farica continued her praying but at a muted level. Robina drew in a large gulp of air, closed her eyes and said, "It was the Red Master. I saw him. Our death is his only desire, he no longer cares for his gold or other objects we plucked from his strong room. I sensed he fears us, or maybe he fears what we're trying to do. That storm didn't originate from him, however he gained the power to pull it off, and it took a great deal of his physical energy and mental resources. Probably took him only about two hours of preparation. A strong force aided him, he used a forbidden spell. He'll stop at nothing. I don't trust the Ancient Ones. I have a bad feeling they have chosen sides and cast us in a game of sure death, only the last one standing will know. The Ancient Ones have never acted like this before. It's unprecedented."

"We're not out of danger yet. The ship is on its last legs. It's not going to fly much longer. The storm has damaged the balloons beyond repair. I think there's only one that's ripped but we have no way to fix it in the air and we can't fly without it," Nelson said as he dragged me up on the deck. It was obvious we had disaster chasing us.

"Can we pump more hot air into the other two sacks?"

He shook his head, "Sure, if we had heaters and motors left. We lost those in the storm. We have no way of going up or even steering this airship."

"Come on Nelson, we have the brains, think of a scientific way to get us out of this problem."

"Jesus, Jonathan, it's not that easy."

"Christ Nelson, I remember watching the movie Apollo Eleven and if those scientists could save a spaceship from two hundred thousand miles away, we can fix a balloon. Think."

Nelson sighed, "If we could climb up to the gash in the air bag we could put a patch over it. But in this weather and without proper safety equipment, it would be suicide."

"What about the steering and the motors, could we fix them and pump more air into the bags?"

"I'll have to think about that, but for the rips in the balloon we need to be on the ground to fix it."

I rolled my eyes, "Yeah Nelson, we'll be on the ground dead if we don't fix it now."

As I returned to the lounge, it hit me. I slammed the palm of my hand into my forehead and muttered to myself, "Of course we use magic to put a patch on the balloon." I fell down the last three steps and grabbed both Robina and Farica, "Can the two of you use your magic and put patches over the ripped balloon?"

Farica spoke first, "I don't have any magic. Some of my order had the ability, but I'm in touch with the gods, not the wizards. My power is in healing the sick, the wounded and the deformed, sometimes even after death. But what I do isn't magic, it is faith healing."

Robina looked amused and said, "Johnny, why ask me, you have that power. Just reach into yourself, remember your training. Just concentrate."

I took a deep breath, closed my eyes and thought of how to do it. I visualized the patch, a piece of leftover canvas. There was a large needle with canvas string attached. I watched as my mind moved them from the booty hold and then up onto the deck. In my mind's eye, they flew into the air and levitated to the rip in the balloon. I watched the patch of canvas covering the hole and staying in place with the force of my mind.

I gulped down as much air as my lungs would hold and started to push the needle into the material and from there into the skin of the balloon. Each stitch I took, I could see the hole shrink in size. In my mind I had solved the first problem. I felt exhausted and bemused. It's hard to visualize such a task but as I knew it was only a wakened dream, I chuckled at my ingenuity.

"My god, you should have seen it. It's a miracle. If I hadn't witnessed it with my own eyes I would have said it was impossible."

Sarah put her hand on Nelson's shoulder, "Calm down, what is it lover, tell us what you saw."

His eyes still a bit glazed he told us his story. "I watched a piece of fabric glue itself to the rip in the balloon and a needle and thread sew the gash closed. The airship still has enough air to fly. It's a goddamn miracle."

Robina had to hold her hand over her mouth to stop from giggling, finally she broke into Nelson's story, "You did it, didn't you Johnny? You used magic and fixed the tear in the canvas. I knew you could. All of you can do it, if you think about it and remember the training you had with me. You're fully qualified wizards. If you were back at Oxford you would have graduated with your doctorate in Magic."

"How so?" said Farica.

Robina blushed, "I used magic I found in the Red Master's book we confiscated from his chambers. It's a forbidden spell. They all learned the requirements."

Before Farica could speak, disaster struck. One of the ropes holding the Berwick Flyer under the balloons snapped; the sound exploded through the craft. We fell to the deck, the ship hung at a twenty-degree angle to the ground.

"Bloody hell, what happened?" yelled Angus, he grabbed a rope as he struggled to his feet.

Nelson scrambled up the stairs to the deck, "There are huge birds attacking the rigging," He stopped in midsentence and just a gargling sound escaped from him. Finally he continued, "They're falcons the size of a VW and they cut the ropes with their beaks and are continuing to tear away at the other ropes." The wonder and terror in his voice combined to give an almost humorous quality.

"It's that devil the Red Master again. I know the best way to fight him." Robina said falling into a trance.

I couldn't wait, I found the rifles we had made and took gun, powder and shot to the upper deck. Sarah followed with another gun.

We stood bracing ourselves against the bulkhead to the upper deck where the bridge used to be. Three falcons dove towards us. Their wings beat a tattoo as their talons reached out for us. The green eyes of the attacking bird showed no emotion, they seemed dead like a shark's. As it peered into my blue eyes it lashed out at me with its talons. I dove to my knees, and it lunged at me and missed, but its sharp nails tore away another line holding the balloon to the ship. I fired first putting a ball into the body of the bird. It reared his head and dove at me with its beak pecking wildly in the air trying to slice me in half. It snapped just above my head pulling a large chunk of my hair from my scalp. Sarah fired her shot right into one of its green eyes. The animal went berserk, flying up then down beating its wings, and eventually diving to the ground. I started to reload my gun as the second beast dove on me. I had just enough time to fall to the deck as its large claws attacked the bulkhead beside me. The claws left two-foot slashes an inch deep across the wood. It dove at me again. I had my sword at the ready. I slashed as it attacked severing the left leg that held a ten-inch slashing talons. I smelled its breath and the putrid stench of rotting meat still in its gullet. On its second attack I swung my sword madly at the beast as it attempted to fly away. It left seven feet of wing on the deck from the swipe of my sword. I watched it plummet to the ground.

I turned to Sarah. She wasn't as lucky as I. The bird mauled the left side of her body. The creature had her pinned to the bulkhead, a talon through her left shoulder. She screamed in pain as the falcon brushed its feathers against her cheek. It took pleasure in torturing her. Sarah's right hand held the dagger that Robina had given her. The creature lifted its head to decapitate her with its beak. Sarah sliced open its throat covering both of us in gallons of falcon blood.

I turned to her, "Sarah, can you speak?"

Almost in a daze she answered, "Yeah, get this damn bird off me. I think I'm going to puke."

I was about to cut off the leg or whatever you call that part of its anatomy right next to the talon when I looked down. "Oh shit." The ground was only a few hundred feet below and a big hill was flying towards us at what seemed a hundred miles an hour.

I guess I yelled real loud because the team came up to see why I was so excited.

"Nelson, do something," screamed Beth, "see that big bonfire on the top of the hill we're heading right for it."

"We're out of control. The balloon doesn't have enough hydrogen to keep us up," Nelson calmly stated, "Oh, fuck."

My mind whirled and the image of the Hindenburg, that big Zeppelin, full of hydrogen the one that crashed in New Jersey so long ago filled my mind. I could see us just like it exploding into a big ball of fire.

I heard myself say with no conviction, "Everyone tie yourselves down, we're crashing." I didn't tell them I thought death by incineration awaited us on the hill.

CHAPTER TEN

AS THE GROUND CRASHED INTO OUR YACHT, I FELT THE TREES UNDER us snap and their branches responding as shock absorbers, cradling the airship to the ground. To my surprise, the partially inflated balloon drifted down the hill towards what I later learned was the Crofton farm.

I heard Sarah shout with glee as the boat settled into the trees, "Goddamn magic. I cut the balloons loose just with my mind. Hell, we can do anything."

The boat sat ten feet from the ground in an apple orchard on top of a small hill outside Longridge. We stood upon the ground admiring our landing, when the Crofton family came to assess the damage to their orchard and the hooligans from the heavens that destroyed their apples.

Farica approached the patriarch of the family. "We are travelers from the south on our way to Edinburgh. The storm destroyed our flying boat, so we need transport to Edinburgh. We've gold to pay for your damage and for horses. Can you help us?"

That night we slept in the barn with our treasure. Farica first priority when we settled into our new accommodations was to take Sarah into one of the stables and prepare a healing potion for her. The mangled and oozing shoulder Sarah received from the falcon attack soon was completely healed.

The Crofton family, true to their word, protected us for the next ten days as they acquired horses for our trip north. The rest allowed us more time to learn about Farica's life before she joined our company of adventurers. Robina expended more gold, diamonds and rubies into her potions to conduct a quick course in magic tor Farica so she'd learn the basics to keep her alive.

I grew up in Southern California and spent most of my time living within the city or on the beach. The life of a farmer intrigued me. The ordinary people like this farmer had no magic to do their chores. Everything required manual or animal labor. Angus taught me the workings of the average farmer in the 21st century in his world. I learned to milk a cow and feed the chickens as well as other hard work the farmers had to do to survive.

"Jonathan, ma world is a tough place; war is just the cream on the cake. The people have an unyielding life either in the city or in the country. Oor world uses magic sparingly. Magic is only for better government or for the powerful tae have their way. The Crofton farm is rich in its land and so the family is prosperous. In my country, life is no' so comfortable. The highlands are rock, and the lowlands are no' much better. My people fight for every bowl of oatmeal they can eat. The gold we've taken would run my army or for that matter, my country, for twenty years or more."

I looked around me and saw the farm and its beauty and realized that this world was three or more centuries behind mine in the way ordinary people lived.

"Your world has magic, why don't they use it for the betterment of society. Why horde it and deprive the people of their right to happiness?"

A wry smile crept across Angus' face, "Ye are a man efter ma own heart. That's what I told the Red Master efter he captured me. He just laughed and said the full counsel o' wizards discussed that proposition five centuries ago and rejected it as it's against the rule of nature."

I didn't understand, "The rule of nature?"

Angus nodded, "The most vicious win and take the spoils whereas the weak obey and scramble for the crumbs. That's the law of the Ancient Ones."

The reality that one group of humans could be so cruel to the rest of society saddened me, "Angus, where do you fit in regarding this rule of law?"

"I'm neither weak nor vicious. I want what is best for me people. Most o' the other leaders believe in the rule of nature as they are wizards an' rule through terror."

The Black Witch Robina flashed through my mind and her kingdom ruled by her father. "What of the Black Wizard's land?"

"He rules more like me than the Red Master, but you must remember he's a wizard as well and the rule o' the Ancient Ones is heavy power over his head and that o' his family. It's in the Prophecy; the Black Witch wi' your knowledge will change the order o' the world. The weak will prosper and the wizards will serve them." Angus stopped and bowed his head, "That is if ye win the War of the Wizards."

"Angus, you never told me about a war. What wizards?"

"It's best left until after we reach Berwick, if we ever get there."

Angus became mute and refused to answer my questions on the Prophecy. I made inquiries of Farica but she just smiled and said how lovely the country looked and walked away. Finally, I approached Robina.

"Johnny, we live in dangerous times. The Wizards are all-powerful and power corrupts. Every one of them is a tyrant. Yes, even my father. He fights it but it is the way. I've learned much since I've been a captive. We are the saviors of this land. The Prophecy tells us war is just one of many tests for our loyalty. Each obstacle will test one or more of our strengths. We will win."

She gently grasped my hand as we walked through the fields of growing vegetables. She recounted to me the details about her life in the Black Master's castle and how she learned magic as a child. We talked for hours, and I forgot about our task for awhile. Finally as I gazed over the green fields and marveled over the gold sunset, she pulled me close to her and began kissing me. She whispered into my ear, "We must leave tomorrow. The Red Master's army is near, and he has the White Army with him."

I must have looked terrified. "How do you know?"

She took the mirror out from under her cloak. "Take a look. You can see the Red Master and his troops moving in our direction." She shook the mirror and the image changed, "That is the White Master, see his tunic? He has his army marching as well."

I could see two armies: both armies were large, and both leaders looked determined. "Where are we going?"

She laughed, "Away from them and to a place of safety or into the fires of hell, I don't know."

The sun rose over the green hills as we left the farm. We acquired twelve horses from the Crofton's endeavors on our behalf. Four Clydesdales moved away from the farm pulling the large hay wagon that carried our treasure, provisions and extra weapons. Nelson became the teamster, and the rest of us rode.

"Robina, how did they know how to find us?"

"It's magic, remember where you are. The Red Master can enchant the birds, the trees and the rocks, spies all tell him where we have traveled and are going. We just have to move faster than he can project his magic."

The hard ride to Lancaster took more out of us than we imagined. Every bone in my body ached. Every muscle screamed for relief. We used magic to aid our horses and to lighten their load. Still, when we reached the Green Parrot Inn on Market Street, we had sores where the saddles chafed our bottoms; mine was particularly raw. We obtained rooms with soft comfortable beds and sat on cushioned chairs for a hot meal. The inn had the quaint ambience of the Elizabethan age: Tudor in style, old dark wood with smoke stained beams, low ceilings and oil lamps on every table. I loved the atmosphere about the place. I could have enjoyed living in this town if I had a Norman castle. Norman Castles with all the modern technology of the world I left behind.

I said to Angus. "Do you think it's a wise idea to leave the wagon and the treasure in the stables? This place is a den for the light-fingered. Just look around at the patrons in this joint."

Sarah spoke before Angus or Robina could chime in. "You're still thinking like a scientist from our home world. Robina and I placed a spell on our loot and other property. We locked it in an invisible stall at the back of the stable. Just the best of the best wizards could find it, and only on pain of death could they unlock the charm that protects it."

Nelson looked dead on his feet. Even though he rode in the wagon all-day he received an awful beating and in a defeated voice asked, "Are we safe here? I need sleep but I fear if I close my eyes again all hell will overcome me."

Angus finally spoke, "Nae, we're no' safe anywhere in England. We are nou in the Land o' the Orange Master, Northumbria. York is where the Orange Council sits, but like the Red Master's army, the Orange army is looking for us. We hae gold and other treasures that gie us an advantage ower oor hunters, but they hae magic. No, we'll never be safe. We can never let oor guard doon, the Prophecy is on oor side. We also have the magic we appropriated frae the Red Master."

The meal arrived and I never ate so heartily. I enjoyed the joint of lamb dripping in grease which tasted to my starving stomach like the finest cut and most delicious of meats. I marveled at the potatoes, wondering how they had arrived in Britain, and then I remembered it was the 21st century.

They even had tea and chocolate. The pub style meal had the touches of an international cuisine. It mystified me.

That night we slept in peace. The seven of us needed the comfortable rest the inn offered. I fell asleep even as Robina kissed me good night. By morning, she had enticed me, or I her, and we spent a wonderful time together before breakfast. By nine we met at the pub and ate eggs, bacon and a mountain of other breakfast delicacies waiting for us.

As I took in the aroma of my meal and sloshed syrup on my French toast, I noticed, or rather felt, that someone was watching us. I whispered to Robina, "I have this feeling someone is spying on us."

To my surprise, she looked startled. "Where, who, I can't feel anything."

I turned to her with a shocked expression on my face. "Lover, you're the witch. You should feel it too. It's a prickly feeling. Can't you feel it? It's like bugs crawling up your neck. It makes my skin crawl. I just feel it's evil. I can just tell."

I watched her trying to cast a spell to find the watcher. "I'm blind. I can't see anything out there. I can't even read the cook's mind about the food." Then her eyes dilated, "Bloody hell, all I can read is my body and the food is—"

Her head smashed into the eggs on the plate in front of her. I scanned the table and to my astonishment, Angus and Farica lay collapsed in their meals. I tried to revive Robina but she was unresponsive. I attempted to cast a reviving spell, but the magic didn't work. I tried it again hoping I had mispronounced the words. It still was ineffective.

Sarah screamed, and I swung around and caught a glimpse of six large warriors in Orange uniforms with drawn swords approaching from behind. I tried to scramble from my chair, but fell onto the floor. My legs were like rubber. I used the table to gain my feet and deflect the first attacker's sword with my chair. Sarah threw her dagger at the brute charging me. It flew at an odd angle, and the pummel crashed into his teeth. He fell back in pain but still held his sword. Sarah's attack only angered him. The four of us scientists stood shakily with swords drawn.

Beth muttered a spell, blinked, and wiggled her nose like Samantha the Witch, but nothing happened other than the Orange soldiers moved closer to us. I exhaled and hoped the teaching of Angus would hold up against the Northumbrian soldiers.

I yelled in the most vicious voice I could muster, "Charge." Then I threw the lamp of burning oil at the head of the meanest looking attacker. To my surprise, the earthen lamp broke and covered the soldier in oil. The flame ignited, jumping from the neck of the lamp onto his soaked face and hair. His mates rushed to his aid, but Sarah had found another lamp and repeated my attack, throwing her lamp at a second soldier who suffered the same fate. Beth and Nelson repeated the throwing contest. Now all six attacking soldiers burned like effigies on a bonfire.

Within seconds, all the soldiers started running through the inn spreading fire and terror as they tried to escape. Sarah pushed her sword into the nearest soldier and yelled in a berserk scream, "Kill them. Kill them all."

We quickly eliminated the threat, yet I still felt uncomfortable with the sense someone had us under surveillance. The building was filling with smoke, and the fire was licking up the walls.

Nelson yelled, "Grab the unconscious and head for the stable."

Nelson threw Angus over his shoulder. I ran carrying Robina, and Sarah and Beth brought Farica between them from the inn. We were exiting as the bucket brigade started dousing the flames. We ran the fifty yards to the stables, which luckily the fire had not reached. We sat on the bales of hay breathing hard while our three unconscious friends lay at our feet.

Sarah, in a hoarse voice, spoke first, "Someone poisoned their food. They have to puke up what's in their stomachs."

Still wheezing from the effort and the smoke, Nelson disagreed. "I think it was magic, someone placed a spell on them. We have to find out what the recovery spell is."

Sarah looked confused for a few seconds, but finally she shook her head. "You said magic didn't work in the inn. Someone poisoned the food and put a damper on all magic."

Sarah started incanting. The words floated through the air. I could feel the hair at the back of my neck rise whenever the impossible was about to happen in this world. I watched as the hidden stable with our gold and precious stones materialized.

She laughed. "See, magic still works in the stable, and I bet everywhere but in the inn. A powerful wizard knew we came to that inn and cast a spell over the place and tried to capture us."

"It has to be the Orange Wizard using his soldiers to capture us," said Beth. "We have to leave this place. They'll be looking for us. Magic can fight magic, we have to remember that and never let our guard down."

"We have to find a way to revive the others, or it's going to be a difficult ride out of town." My whole body shivered as I spoke. I still had that feeling someone was spying on us. About five minutes had passed since Robina and the other two collapsed. It was vital that we leave at once and necessary to waken them. What did we have to do first, that was the problem?

Nelson said, "We have to find something that will make them vomit and flush their stomachs. That may help, and maybe some strong stimuli to wake them. Let's just hope it isn't a deadly poison. We have no way of knowing what it is or how to find an antidote."

"We need to analyze the contents of their stomachs and their blood," I said.

Sarah looked angry. "Are you a doctor or something Jon, even if we could do that what would we find? Then what would we do?"

Beth said, "If it was poison, I still want to know why only them? We're all human. Our bodies are like theirs. No, were on the wrong track. I felt wobbly when Angus fell. I think someone cast a spell over them and followed it up with another spell stopping all our magic within the inn. We can use our magic here, let's try to revive them."

"Damn, my dagger! It's still in the inn. You three try to save the others and I'll find my dagger," said Sarah as she sprinted out of the stable heading towards the inn.

I worked my mind searching for a spell or a potion that would revive our three friends. Each time I remembered one, Beth was already doing the incantation and unfortunately, each failed.

I glanced down at the three of them as their color changed from a ruddy red to a bluish tinge. I panicked and ran to the stall with our gold to find the Red Master's book. I searched everywhere, but I couldn't find it amongst our loot.

I ran back to the enchanted Robina and searched her. At that point, I remembered she carried a leather bag with her wherever she went. "Goddamn," escaped my lips, "I have to go back to the inn to find Robina's bag with the spell book in it before it perishes in the fire. Keep trying. I'll be right back." Before anyone could prevent me from leaving the stable, I had run halfway to the inn. I felt those invisible eyes still watching me but had no time to try to find them. I needed to find the book to save Robina.

The inn still burned; a bucket brigade and a pumper wagon drenched the inn with river water. Orange-clad soldiers flooded the streets, their capes visible through the clouds of smoke billowing from the inn. I run into the smoke though the front door before anyone identified my black uniform.

I heard fighting in front of me and smelled the acidic odor of burning wood. Once inside the inn, I could see less than five feet in front of me. I remembered a spell to improve vision. I uttered the spell and to my amazement, I could see throughout the inn. Someone must have lifted the hex that stopped magic.

I discovered our table doused in water by the fire brigade, only smoke and a few embers burned around the charred furniture. I searched with wild eyes, knowing the book was worth more than any object in this world and probably many other worlds. Nevertheless, for me the only value it had was to bring Robina back to me.

The leather bag lay not more than ten feet away. The covering looked charred but not destroyed. I went to my knees to pull the bag from under the broken chair that entrapped it. My focus only saw the bag. The rest of the world disappeared until three Orange soldiers charging into the room knocked over a table three feet from my position on the floor. The smoke blinded them as they ran right towards me. The first tripped over me and the two following tripped over the initial soldier.

I looked up and watched Sarah fighting three other soldiers. Her attackers pushed her back towards the part of the inn engulfed in flames. I threw the leather bag over my shoulder and charged the three unsuspecting Orange soldiers. As I pulled my magical sword from its scabbard I remembered our inability to use magic in the inn. I was about to re-sheath it when I remembered I had just used magic to enhance my vision.

I charged, slashing my sword at Sarah's attackers. My first stroke cut the left hand off the biggest of the Orange warriors. He turned to face me, blood and bone exposed where his hand had been. I stepped back into the dense smoke. He peered through watery eyes as a sailor does to see what's on the horizon. It didn't help him. I directed Buffoon to run him through and he fell at my feet. I smiled.

I heard Sarah say, "Look out Jonathan, behind you, four more of them." I turned and stumbled over the body by my feet. My sword swung wildly striking the closest of the new attackers. The Orange soldier fell next to his comrade. I pushed one of Sarah's attackers to the ground. As I rushed past him, my blade accidentally slashed his throat. "God Sarah, what's going on here? Did you find your dagger?"

She gave me a withering glance as I stood beside her, and we watched fifteen Orange tunics line up in front of us. I whispered to her, "Remember the last scene in Butch Cassidy and the Sundance Kid?"

CHAPTER ELEVEN

I WATCHED TEN ATTACKERS CHARGING TOWARDS US THROUGH THE smoke, scampering behind them another ten orange troopers. I heard Sarah say through the crackling flames behind me, "We're trapped. We'll have to fight our way through them. Hell, there're only about thirty or forty of them, we can do it. Think like Uma Thurman, do what she did in *Kill Bill,* we can do that."

I stared at Sarah and beheld the determination in her face. Her eyes dilated. Her nostrils flared, adrenaline pumped through her veins; death had no meaning for her. She just wanted to attack and kill as many as she could before she could kill no more.

I wasn't so keen to die. "Sarah, let's think about this a moment. Maybe there is another way. Do you realize we have the choice of magic? Whatever blocked it when our comrades collapsed in their soup is no more. We can just zap these guys and get out of here."

She looked over at me. "On three we charge." I could tell she didn't hear a word I said or her desire to kill blocked out all reason.

I invaded her mind and yelled, "No; we use magic, not swords. A spell or two will save our bacon in this fight."

I grabbed the *Saunders* from the bag and shouted out the spell on the top of the first page it flew open to. To my amazement, all the Orange soldiers dropped their swords, covered their ears and ran like the wind from the fire.

I stood there in utter shock as I watched through the smoke as the Orange soldiers ran out of the inn. The flames behind me flared up and the heat singed the hair at the back of my neck. I started to move forward, but a more determined company of Orange soldiers entered the building.

I could feel the Orange Master had sent his most feared troops into the chaos of the burning building to silence us. His "Storm Troopers" stomped in unison into the room. I threw out my mind and snatched the thoughts of the commander of the unit and discovered the Orange Master had protected them from the spell I had thrown at their comrades. The flames crackled in my ear and the smell of burning wood choked me. Sarah still had no reason. She itched to attack this new force. Without thinking I shouted out a spell, put on my game face and roared at the Orange elite unit in front of me. I raised my sword over my head and to my surprise uttered another spell towards them in the most vicious tone I could muster. The army in front of me disappeared in the billowing smoke.

As if she had come out of a deep sleep, Sarah blinked a few times, then said in a dreamy, almost groggy, voice, "Jonathan, let's get out of here." She grabbed my arm and pulled me into the back of the inn. I tried to resist. I knew that it was in flames, and we would both be crispy critters before we could escape, but she was insistent. I turned to face the wall of flames and looked into a frozen wonderland of icicles; snow and ice encrusted the charred wood. The back of the inn housed the kitchen, and we picked our way through the maze of stoves and storerooms to the rear door.

"Jesus, Jonathan, how did you do that? That spell you shouted was nothing we learned."

I just looked at her. I knew I had done it, but I had no idea what I said or did.

"Yeah, it was awesome wasn't it? I, at that moment, didn't think we had a chance fighting so I improvised. It's funny it came from... well I just made it up."

I still didn't understand how I had accomplished it, but it worked. We scurried back to the stable, and Beth seized the magic book from me and desperately searched for a spell that would free our team members. After about five minutes, she squealed with joy, "I've found it."

The three on the ground looked like death; their breathing came in fits and starts, and their color was nonexistent. I sat on a bale of hay with my face behind my hands and prayed for help. I slumped in a practically trance-like state trying to contact Robina by telepathy. Instead, I could nearly read the minds of the invisible ones watching us. I could also sense four other minds calculating and planning, but what and why I couldn't make out. Then I felt other minds, sinister minds, not planning but starting to take action. The new minds searched for us both by magic and with personnel. They wore Orange tunics and I could feel them close by.

"Come quick, all of you over here," said Beth. She had cast a spell over Robina, Angus and Farica. We kept a close eye on them, but they stopped breathing and the death rattles came over them. It was the most frightening experience I had ever had. They changed color like chameleons as we watched. We stepped back as they rattled and groaned like the undead on the floor of the stable. Putrid odors came from their bodies as they transformed.

"Jesus Christ, what did you do to them?" yelled Nelson, as he pulled out his sword.

I couldn't stand it any longer. I ran over to Robina and held her tightly in my arms, whispering against her ear that I loved her. She fought me and tried to escape my grasp, but I held on. Seeing what I was doing Beth ran to Angus and did the same. Poor Farica was wriggling on the ground, and both Nelson and Sarah ran to her and held her between them.

It was like holding on to an ameba. Robina's body was like Jell-O. It had no bones, or point of reference. She was no longer solid. Then I felt her starting to solidify.

It was too late; six soldiers entered the stable all in Orange uniforms of the Elite Guards of the Orange Master. The one who looked like the leader raised his sword and with a flicking motion shot a fireball across the stable which hit Nelson square in the chest.

He shouted, "Take that you horse dung infidel outlander."

Nelson fell clutching his chest where a burning hole now resided. I regained my feet while Sarah threw her dagger into the eye of the fireball thrower. Then taking her sword out she faced two of the Orangemen. Their deaths came swiftly and without mercy.

The battle began. I attacked two other of the Orange guards. I slashed then parried as they continued to attack. To my left, I saw Beth's attack, pushing her opponent back to the entrance to the stable. Sarah to my right stood on a bale of hay slashing at her two adversaries. I glimpsed her plunge her sword through one of the soldier's shoulders. A pesky fighter attempted to take my head off distracted my attention. For his adventurous move, my sword removed his sword with his arm attached.

The skirmish appeared encouraging. We pushed the soldiers against the stable wall. They couldn't retreat out of the building to the paddock. I slashed my remaining enemy across the face with my rendition of a J for Jonathan. I was getting cocky.

Finally all six of the Elite Orange Guard lay dead on the stable floor. Sarah retrieved her dagger, and we took a defensive position in the center of the barn assessing the damage. Sarah remembered Nelson, and as she ran to him the large doors to the stable burst open, and an army of Orange soldiers entered led by the Orange Wizard riding a great white stallion.

I only had time to say, "Holy shit," before I found myself frozen in a cube of solid plastic. At the same moment Sarah, Beth and even the wounded Nelson were entombed. I could see and hear, but could not speak or move.

The Orange Master spoke, "This place smells of death, not a stable." Then he appraised our three comrades still lying like corpses on the floor. He laughed. "Angus thought he was so smart. Look at him with the Black Witch, both dead." Then he glanced at Farica. "That must be the Mother Superior who deserted her cloister in flames. She can rot with the others."

I tried to form a spell and project it at the Wizard, but nothing would happen. I couldn't speak it or even project at him through the frozen cube. I moved my eyes, the only part of my body that I still could maneuver and looked at Sarah. Her eyes were on fire. I could tell she was straining to move and slice her way out of the hard plastic with her dagger.

The Orange Master just laughed at us. "You are a spunky bunch, aren't you? I can read your minds, you haven't given up hope. Well let me tell you it's over for the bunch of you. I'll feed you to my hounds, and then this cursed prophecy will be at an end, and we can rule this land without the people hoping for a miracle."

My eyes flashed hatred at the leader of Northumbria. I struggled, but only my eyes moved. I lost everything, the gold, my friend Sarah, my love Robina and now my life, all because of some Prophecy in some crazy other-world place. I thought of the already dead; my friends and lover spread out on the ground. My rage boiled over. I would not die; I would take my revenge on this animal.

I screamed within my mind, my anger more than any sane person could imagine. To my surprise, the Orange Master fell from his horse covering his ears. He stood up and looked at me with pain flashing across his face.

I noticed he was holding his right arm. I knew I had bloodied him. I had injured the Master and my anger had done it.

He drew his sword with his left hand and in obvious pain approached me. "You are powerful Outlanders. I only listened to your pitiful thoughts, yet you knocked me from my horse. I will kill you now and end it."

Before he could approach any closer another wizard ran to him, "My Lord, I've found the treasure stolen from the Red Master. It is more valuable than we thought. Come look at the gold we now have for our war chest."

The Master left me, but had written my fate on the wall. I screamed again, but the Orange Master had turned me off. To my surprise, I heard Sarah's voice inside my head. "Good work Jonathan, but you scared me with your rage as much as you scared the big Orange on the horse. It looks like we have a few minutes to plan an attack before he chops your head off. Do you any ideas?"

An epiphany came to me. If I can speak into the minds of both the Orange Master and Sarah, maybe I could speak to the mind of one of the soldiers and have him release us. I picked a soldier next to me and screamed at him as loud as my mind would let me. I watched him move and look at me. I felt success as he turned and spoke.

"Lieutenant, may I have permission to retire to the latrine? I've had a sudden urge to make water and can't hold it."

I felt silly. I thought I had the perfect plan. I heard Sarah in my mind. She was laughing, "Good try, if you do that to every guard we'll have a better chance." Large tears formed at the corners of her eyes. "Unfortunately the Orange Master will still kill us."

As Sarah spoke I felt another mind trying to talk to me. My eyes darted around the stable. Beth looked frozen and made no eye contact with me. Nelson looked dead at her feet. There was no one else that I could see. All the soldiers seemed oblivious to our communications and continued doing their military duties.

The voice was soft and barely audible but in a whisper, it said, "Wiggle your fingers. Do it slowly so no one will see."

I didn't answer the voice, but put all my effort into my right hand baby finger. I glanced down as if dejected and looking at the floor. My finger moved a millimeter then a centimeter and finally almost an inch. I cried.

"Whoever you are; my finger moved. What do I do next?"

The voice replied just a little stronger this time, "Tell Sarah to do the same. Next try your toes, then your legs and arms."

"Who are you? What's happening?" However, there was no reply to my questions.

Slowly, my body started to respond to my wishes. I saw Sarah's do the same. Nobody noticed our miniature movements; they carried the treasure from the previously hidden stall to the outer door of the stable. I noticed only the Elite Guard, and the two wizards stayed in the barn. The others were with the gold and treasure of the Red Master.

I moved my head just an inch, and then turned it all the way to the side watching the Orange Master running his hands through the coins. I pushed my head forward inch by inch until I had passed through the plastic shell. I took a breath of real air and the cube that trapped me fell away.

Now I heard the voice in my head with volume and clarity. It was Robina. "I'm all right Beth saved our lives. It's just the spell she used takes some time to rebuild our bodies. She used the most forbidden spell in the ancient book of magic; the immortal spell."

I glanced over at what still looked to be three dead bodies and could not grasp her last words, "What do you mean immortal spell?"

"In our world like all others, mothers give birth to children. They have their time upon the stage of life and then die. The ancients found a way to live forever or almost forever. For obvious reasons, the use of it became forbidden. Now Beth has used it. It heals wounds fast and no sickness can kill you and as far as old age goes, there isn't any. Only physical trauma can destroy the body." Robina was silent for a few seconds. "We can't talk now. Get back in your frozen state. Give us another few minutes and we'll help dispose of the Orange Master and his troops."

I thought, I don't have a few minutes. Once the Orange Master's wagons were filled with the gold and precious stones, we are all toast; still, I constructed a false cube around me to fool the guards and the Orange Master. I stood motionless in my fake chrysalis and spoke mentally to Sarah. "We have to take out the two wizards first, if we don't they'll turn us into turnips or something. What spell should we use?"

Sarah laughed, "Well, remember the forbidden spell's opposite."

I agreed then said, "What about the treachery spell as well. We make them members of our army."

Sarah stopped laughing. "Yes, Jonathan, but if we use both spells, there's a fifty-fifty chance the subject will not recover and either die or go insane."

My voice became hard, "And your point is? They are going to kill us any second; at least we give them an even chance to survive."

Always the bloodthirsty one, Sarah was balking at my spell choice. "Sarah, it's our best chance. You do the opposite spell, and I'll do the other. We'll wait until the guards place the last bag of gold in the wagons."

Robina's voice entered my head. "Use the voice control spell as well, Johnny, it will serve you well. Act when you have to. Nevertheless, in a few minutes, we'll be able to help."

Those few minutes never arrived.

.

CHAPTER TWELVE

THE SOLDIERS LUGGED THE GOLD BAGS TO THE WAGONS AND, THE Orange Master and his second in command strolled over to the four of us encrusted in our cubes. "You fools, you have no chance against real wizards. It's your turn to die just like your friends."

Before his next words left his lips both Sarah and I burst out of our fake tombs and incanted our spells. The shock on his face produced a smile on mine. Both, he and his lackey rose from the stable floor about six inches and spun like tops, first to the left, then to the right. They spun so fast they appeared just as a blur to my eyes. The Orange Master knocked the door to the stable wide open as he rotated.

The soldiers at the wagon watched in utter awe as their Master gyrated in the air. To my surprise, they ran, and so did the soldiers guarding the stable. The two wizards danced for another three or four minutes in the air. It felt to me like an hour as I watched in amusement. They dropped upon the ground with a resounding thud and lay motionless.

Beth and Nelson, still encrusted in the plastic, started to move. I rushed to Nelson and found the chrysalis had cauterized his wound. Unfortunately, the trauma still caused him pain. I held him in my arms and tried to comfort him as he coughed up blood from internal injuries. Sarah rushed to me and incanted a spell of healing. Nelson stiffened in my arms. He convulsed. He died, but like Lazarus, awoke. However, unlike Lazarus, nothing was the same. Nelson returned blind.

Nelson finally spoke, "I saw the white light then the four Ancient Ones riding their milky steeds, the ones we faced in the glade. They told me we broke the rules and the Most Ancient One on High had chosen me for punishment." He smiled, "I thought I'd never see you again." Then he reached out, and Sarah took him into her arms. "Thank God, I returned, and we're together."

Sarah kissed him and held him close, "You're back, don't worry. We'll find a spell to return your sight. This place is magical. We can do it."

To my surprise, Robina and the others regained consciousness. "Nelson, you're a fortunate man, when one sees the Old ones in a dream it is usually fatal. We are all lucky they didn't kill you and the rest of us."

Then she glanced at the Orange Master covered in horse manure looking like a ragged doll unconscious on the stable floor. She sneered, "A fitting place for that scum. He killed my youngest brother in a battle outside Liverpool six years ago. I should cut his throat for family honor." She pulled a gold dagger from under her robe.

Farica put a hand on her sleeve and said. "Wait, he is part of the Prophecy. We'll need him."

Robina pulled her arm away and countered, "Not the Prophecy I've heard, he's an enemy and must die."

Farica rose to her full height of over five foot nine and with her hands on her hips said to Robina, "As I told you, every member of my order knows the true Prophecy, and the Orange Master must not die. I repeat, he must not die or all is for naught."

Robina put her dagger away and then sneered, "I'll deal with him later." She stomped off to inspect the wagon with the gold.

I followed her out of the stable, but I had that feeling someone out there still watched me, "Robina, calm down," I said, "We defeated him. He's our captive. He's not going to do any more harm to you or anyone else."

She looked at me with murder in her eyes, "He's worse than the Red Master; he treats his people as slaves and shows no mercy to his captives. The average life as a captive in the mines at Newcastle is six months. In my father's mines, he employs Welsh miners. They have been happy in the mines for generations. No, the Orange Master deserves to die."

Angus yelled, "He's alive. The swine survived." As I turned I watched Angus kick the Orange Master. "See, he squeals." Angus picked the man up by his robes and placed him on a bale of hay. "My fine friend, hae a seat on your new throne."

The Orange Master looked confused, but obeyed Angus' request. I walked over to the other wizard lying on the ground and examined him. "This one didn't survive the spells." Even as I turned him over his flesh was becoming green, and he started to shrivel up. He smelled of death, it wafting through the air. Within the next few seconds I watched as his corpse transformed into a thousand-year-old mummy. I made a face and wrinkled my nose, "Yuck, what a gruesome mess." My whole body shivered, and I walked back to the circle surrounding our captive.

The one in the orange robes looked at Farica and fell to his knees, "I have sinned. Ever since I realized I had the gift of magic, I have sinned. Please God, forgive me."

We watched in amazement as the Mother Superior spoke to the Orange Master. "Yes my child, you are a sinner, do you repent?"

He looked up into her soul piercing eyes with sadness, yet with what I interpreted as hope. "Yes I repent. I am sorry for my arrogance, my pride and my brutality. To become a Master, I did terrible deeds, but to remain as a Master, I did worse. Please forgive me Mother Superior, please save me from myself."

Robina grabbed Farica by the shoulder and spun her around and beseeched her, "You can't forgive him. He's a liar." She had her dagger back in her hand ready to cut the Orange tongue from his mouth.

In a calm soothing voice, our former Mother Superior Farica said. "It is your doing; the three spells placed on the Master didn't kill him but changed him from his vile, depraved, sadistic existence to what you see before you now. He is the opposite of his former self. He will always remember his past, but his soul has changed. His reason for living has changed. He has changed from an ugly grub to a beautiful butterfly."

She embraced him and said in a commanding voice, "The Gods forgive you. Your old life will be gone forever. Your new name is—" She thought a few seconds, "Your given name is Edward, and you're from York, are you not?" He confirmed both to her. "So from this day forth you will be simply Edward of York, and you shall perform good deeds for the rest of your God-given days. You will fight evil and against the enslaving of the common man."

We looked on in wonder. We saw an aura formed around Farica encompassing the Orange Wizard. I felt a sense of well-being radiate from my heart and throughout my body. I lovingly grasped Robina's hand in mine and felt our affection for each other grow even stronger.

I said, "What are we to do with this born again wizard?"

Our Mother Superior answered, "He's to come with us. He's part of the solution."

Farica didn't convince Robina, who did not feel the love and snarled, "If he steps out of line just once I'll kill him. Listen up well, Edward of Orange, one sign of your old self and you're going to be like your friend on the floor."

The Orange Master, now just Edward, replied, "Robina, I've known you since you were a baby, and Angus, I've known even longer. I've betrayed you both and done worse to both your families. I've manipulated and lied to get my way. Today I do neither. I tell you from my heart, whatever happened to me, I have changed. Please call me just Edward, even Ted, which is what my friends use. Since I became a Master no one has called me that in thirty years. Please call me Ted or Edward, if you must Edward of York. I'm no longer the Orange Master. I know the Prophecy, and now I understand my place."

So our group added a new member, and the eight of us prepared to leave. With Nelson and Edward on one wagon and Beth and Angus on the other, the rest of us rode as outriders. We reached the gate leading out of town along the road to York where we met hundreds of the town's people. They surrounded our wagons and horses.

A man riding a white stallion cantered in front of the gate and spoke directly to me. "I'm the mayor of Lancaster, and I have watched you since you arrived. I have felt you probing for me. Like my Master, I'm a wizard and hide myself from you. You are the Jonathan of the Prophecy. I bow to you. We know you are the ones to fulfill the Prophecy. The whole city is here to protect you. The Red Master's army is going to arrive at the city in the next hour, and if you leave now you will ride right into them. Our friends to the east and the south have seen them coming."

Angus spoke for us, "Thank ye for your warning." He pointed to Edward, "Your Master is noo a member of our quest. Your land will be in civil war. I fear the Red Master will try tae take possession o' all o' Northumbria. We must leave, or he will sack your city looking for us."

The crowd now noticed the Orange Master in simple Orange robes. Since his transformation, he reminded me of a Buddhist monk, not a powerful warlord.

"Hang him, draw and quarter him. Kill him," came the cries from the masses, spreading from a grumbling to a roar of anger.

Robina stood up and said, "I know what you feel, he killed my brother. I guard him, and you will do him no harm. However, if he steps out of line, as my brother's dead spirit is my witness, I will feed his liver to the rooks of Cardigan that guard my brother's grave. I'm the Black Witch, and this is Jonathan beside me."

A hush crept over the crowd, and finally Farica spoke, "Your Orange Master is the Emperor's Steward of Britain from the Prophecy. You cannot kill him, or all our hopes will die. Look on him now, see the change in him, see how he will bring back the truth to the world we know as Great Britain. I am the Mother Superior in the Prophecy, and I know his heart is now pure. Listen to your hearts and pray for us."

The mass of people looked confused and started to grumble among themselves in small groups. Finally, someone stepped forward and said, "I'm Miles Silversmith. Take the old fart with you; he'll do better in Berwick than he'll do in Lancaster or York. Follow us; we'll lead you to the North Gate. Then ride like the wind, the Red Army is flying on winged horses to find you. Let's go."

We paraded out of the town with the Orange Master's two wagons, one a fine coach fit for a duke. The other wagon was a working wagon carrying all our gear and the gold. We rode as Orange Guards with silver breast plates, on white stallions with orange plumes waving from their heads.

The pageantry of our exit brightened my mood. The fact the Red Army rode a few hours behind our parade didn't diminish my mood. The cheers from the city's inhabitants gave me some peace of mind. The people supported our quest. We strutted the first five miles out of town and eventually fell into an easy canter with no one talking. Everyone was mulling over the last few hours.

I finally rode up to the beautiful carriage and started talking to our new comrade in arms. "How do you feel after Sarah and I zapped you?"

The Orange Master looked at me quizzically, "Zapped. You mean bewitched?"

I nodded.

He continued, "I feel like myself, except I have a different set of priorities. I have changed. It's beyond belief."

Then he became introspective for a few minutes. Eventually, he continued, "You used two forbidden spells on me, didn't you?"

I corrected him, "I believe it was three."

He looked cross and said, "That will not do young man. That will not do at all. That is not cricket." Then a diabolical look crossed his face. "You are a rogue aren't you? The Prophecy said you would be; you and your Black Witch wife. If I still called myself Master, I would try to kill you this instant for your treachery. However, now I commend you. I still possess my magic and all the ways of a Master. I'm your servant, and we'll change this land as it is foretold. I just wonder if it will be for the better, or will we destroy the fabric of England and the other territories of Britain."

"You commanded the Orange Army as a leader of Northumbria. How can you be so philosophic about your new life and your fall from power? With the hubris of a Master of a great house, you should be threatening us and trying either to kill us or bribe us. Why are you so complacent? I know we enchanted you with the forbidden spells, but that cannot explain your mood and your joy in being on the quest with us."

He chuckled and replied, "The Mother Superior hasn't told you much about the Prophecy has she? The quest has many difficulties to overcome and some will not see the end. If the Prophecy is true, you and I have the greatest to gain. What I left behind is nothing; both our futures will show that. However, if the Mother Superior is mute on what the true Prophecy foretells, I cannot enlighten you." A smirk came over his face. "From this moment onward we are one in the betterment of mankind. In this world, our fate is in each other's hands."

I implored him to tell me more, but he sat soberly in his carriage. Angus sat serenely on the largest of the white stallions leading the orange carriage along the road. The Scot just smiled at me. I rode up to him and asked about the Orange Master.

Angus' smile broadened, "Wae Jonathan, in times past he was ma biggest ally in the wars. Oor armies fought as one, but that was during the Alliance. I married his sister, an' we had two girls. However, as her passion towards me cooled and her politics burned, she showed her true colors by enticing ma two lieutenants, and they killed each other in a duel for the right to seduce her. The fools dinnae realize she bewitched them and seduced them by her magic. She laughed in ma face and ran back tae her brother wi' half my treasury an' ma two darling girls." I could see the anger in his face and attempted to change the subject. Then he laughed and a twinkle came to his eyes,

"That's when I married ma bonnie boy's mother an' he arrived nine months later. I told everyone that I would have gladly given the Orange Witch ma entire treasury for the like o' my son."

I looked back at the carriage and then to Angus, "Does he know who you are?"

"Aye my lad, he knows me weell enough, but even in his new altered state he will nae speak directly to ma or look ma in the eye until I speak to him. Otherwise, I would have to kill him for his dishonor."

I rode with Angus for a few more miles. He spoke to me in loving terms about his land. The further north we traveled the more he talked of home and kin.

Finally, Robina rode up behind me and gently poked me with her sword. "Johnny, you rogue, you've been ignoring me since we left Lancaster. Now it's my time with you." Her eyes and her smile were downright flirtatious, and I couldn't resist her. "Come back and we'll ride in the baggage wagon and talk." When she said talk, I took it to mean some other form of intercourse and acknowledged her comment with a smile that not even a fool could misunderstand.

I said so all could hear me, "Sure my love, my backside is starting to chafe. I do want to chat with you about the strange day we've had." All could tell I had other more personal duties on my mind. "Let's climb into the wagon."

When we sat in the wagon I said, "I was talking to the Orange Master, and he told me that he would gain more power with us than he had as the leader of Northumbria. What did he mean?"

Before she could answer, or we could fulfill our desires, Sarah yelled from the front of our parade. "Look to the west, coming over the mountains. See it? A cloud of dust."

Angus yelled to the rear, "Its cavalry and they're moving fast." He looked back at Edward, "Are they your men?"

Our new comrade said no, but added, "It's probably the Red Master's troops. They invaded Northumbria a week ago to find you. He probably tracked us by magic and sent them to deal with you just like I did, but it looks like he sent a few more men than I did." He scanned the dust cloud. "I'd say there are about two hundred of them; they're about two miles away and traveling about three times our speed."

I turned to Robina, "We can use the spells from back at the clearing to defeat them, can't we?"

Before she could speak the ex-Master shook his head, "No my boy, we Masters are smarter than that. Once surprised we defend against that attack. You can be sure there are several first class wizards traveling with the army. It wouldn't surprise me if the Red Master is traveling with his troops by proxy. I've done that many times, it allows me to be in three or four places at the same time."

I looked at the Edward not understanding his meaning. "By proxy, what's that?" I asked.

Robina piped up, "My father used to do that. You bewitch one of your wizards and send him off to spy for you. You can see and hear everything he does, and if need be you can communicate with others through his mouth. It's a powerful spell. I have it; it's in the Red Master's book."

Edward looked stunned, "You have the Red Master's copy of Saunders on Wizardry and other Craft?"

Her eyes twinkled as she replied, "Yes, my new friend. I have it right here." She took the book out of her backpack.

Edward of York cried, "I've wanted to see that book all my life. I knew it existed. My great, great-grandfather had a copy, but his castle burned to the ground in an Irish raid with the book inside, or so says the legend; even so, to see one. Can I touch it?"

Robina held it tight but let Edward touch the book. He visibly jolted as if an electric current surged through his body. "Oh, I feel the magic."

Robina smiled. "We have a few minutes Edward; let's sit down and find a spell that will

get us past this red cloud of horsemen."

CHAPTER THIRTEEN

THE RIVER FLOWED TO OUR WEST; ITS LUSH UNDERGROWTH HID THE wild rabbits and other fauna of the untamed English countryside. The different shades of green reflected off the water. Our orange uniforms caused us the most concern as the Red Army marched around a bend in the river to fight us. We had our backs to the river which in turn protected our rear. We hid the horses and wagons on the other side of the watercourse on a small path winding through the woods. Our army of eight stood motionless as the first fifty rode by us as if we were invisible.

"I told you it would work," whispered Edward, "all the soldiers see are green and we look just like the bushes around us. I used this spell when my Northumbrian army fought in Ireland. How is your illusion working Robina?" Edward, still thinking like a Master professional soldier, and master of deception, had used his magic to turn orange to green.

Angus scrutinized the enemy as they rode past. "We won't attack until the wizards ride by, and we use oor powers tae vanquish them afore we assault the others. The General will be right wi' them. We attack and cut off their heads and the army will crumble." We agreed that his plan had merit and prepared to execute it. We lay in wait as the Red Army rode by in tens and twenties. Not one soldier observed anything except what Edward of York wished him to see.

I watched in awe as the troops passed by. They rode tall in the saddle with lances and gold breast plates over their red tunics. All carried swords and shields. The shields sported the embossed coat of arms of the Red Master. It showed a griffin with a dead eagle in one paw and a mauled lion at his feet. On the top of each rider's helmet stood a red plume dancing as he rode past.

Sarah whispered, "I see the wizards." Then she corrected herself, "I feel the wizards, they are on the other side of the rise."

Edward whispered in our minds. "You are a blade of grass. Remember, just a blade of grass."

We stood as a blade of grass, we moved only as the wind would move that simple little piece of vegetation. We neither spoke nor breathed. The army blissfully rode by. Then the wagons moved past the waving grass that consumed me. Each wagon held twenty infantry troopers crammed into the eight-horse-team. Ten such wagons rolled by, then we saw the artillery section. A dozen huge catapults followed, each pulled by twenty Clydesdale horses. Next in the procession, I watched six large wooden contraptions, each able to fire twenty arrows in one shot; not ordinary arrows, but a bolt that was six feet long and as thick as two inch doweling. Just one such arrow would kill an elephant. If I still possessed my right mind I would've run as far away and as fast as I could, instead I stood in my Orange tunic and thought I was a blade of grass.

Next in the procession rode the flag bearers and trumpeters followed by the General riding his ivory white stallion. Behind him five officers of his high command bounced along on their high-spirited steeds. The leader's entourage all pranced; not one of them looked left or right but held their heads high and haughtily as they supervised their troops.

The wizards' wagons and specially trained Red guards followed the military parade. Whereas the army was Spartan in its accouterments, the wizards traveled in luxury evidenced from their carriages to their wardrobes. Their wagons looked like mobile homes pulled by a twenty mule team. Once the wizards were in the radius of Robina's spell, I heard her in my mind speaking the words that she had taught us regarding the ancient hex. I watched it crash against the green shield of the wagons and roll harmlessly over them like a wave.

She muttered, "On my father's grave." And she threw a fireball at the lead wagon. A green glow filled the sky as the fireball ate its way towards the wagon but burned out before reaching the target. To my surprise, Sarah threw her own fireball at the same wagon and at the same spot as Robina's ball of fire. Sarah's fireball crashed through the green shield and ignited the wagon in a huge explosion sending blue flames hundreds of feet into the air.

We dove to the ground as various spells crashed against our position. Our protective shield glowed as it repulsed spell after spell. We crawled back towards the river. Angus threw the imaginary army spell. He created fifty soldiers that rose from the greenery and charged the wagons. Each soldier had the ability to fight to the death. The seven foot, kilt- wearing Highland berserkers charged the enemy soldiers with their claymores, screaming a bloodcurdling Gaelic curse.

The guards protecting the wizards thought the phantom soldiers real and stepped to the road's edge in a defensive position to shield the wagons and the wizards. The distraction allowed us to fall back even farther into the shallows of the river. I cast a spell to turn the road into a quagmire to stop the wagons from moving forward and to consume anyone walking to or from them.

The wizards tried to freeze us like the Orange Master had but Nelson sensed the spell and blocked it in mid-flight. The spell only reached the Red Master's guards defending the wagons, killing over half of them.

I cast a spell to take away the magic of one of the wizards. Robina told me the spell worked for up to ten days. I just hoped it worked for a few minutes. The spell smashed against the lead wizard in the bright purple robe. He held a fireball in his hand and as our eyes met I read in his mind the fireball was for me. When my spell hit him, the fireball exploded consuming him in flames. Like a Roman candle his whole body shot up in the sky, He exploded showering his army with body parts.

Beth stood next to me shooting arrows from her magical bow; a bolt struck a red-clad wizard between the eyes. The wizard crumbled to the floor of his carriage. I cheered, that was two down and six to go.

Robina and Sarah had become a team of death. Two further wizards fell to the combined spells of their magic. Death blows learned from the Red Master's book disintegrated not only the wizards but their carriages.

The battle was in our favor. We marched from our position at the river's edge back up the bank and next to Angus's berserkers who had now defeated the Red Guard. The eight of us charged up the hill to meet the four remaining wizards.

Farica pulled on my sleeve and said, "We must retreat; this is in the Prophecy, no good will come of this."

The Red Army stood motionless unable to protect the wizards. They could not enter the battlefield as Edward had created a protective wall around our force and the wizards'.

I smiled, "We're winning, what do you mean?"

"Jonathan, you don't understand. We must leave now."

I heard Edward of York's voice in my head. "She's right, there's nothing we can do. The Prophecy controls everything we do, we can't change it. We're slaves to it."

The four remaining wizards met us; all four were hovering over the quagmire six-inches above the ground. They stood wands in hand and garish robes blowing in the wind. It reminded me of a gun fight in the Old West. The eight of us stared into the eyes of the four. They returned the steely stare as they stood motionless.

Waiting for battle with my adversaries, my mind became clouded with a multitude of voices incanting different spells. My vision failed me. I saw chaos surrounding me. I tried to speak. I had to tell the others but my mouth wouldn't move.

I tried to remember a spell to ward off the one that had attacked me. I couldn't think. The smell of death infiltrated my very being. With every ounce of strength and self-control I had left, I yelled in my mind the only spell I could remember.

I found myself on the ground back down by the river under a tree. I could see no one else. I cast a spell to project my eyes to a raven I saw in the air above me. The horror the bird's eyes sent to my brain almost made me lose control of the creature.

Beth lay across a large rock on the side of the road. Her body grotesquely twisted in a way a body cannot contort. I grieved for my friend. I wondered how she ended in such a manner. I had no time to dwell on her as I saw other devastation.

Two of the Red Master's wizards lay in the quagmire with their bodies inverted, that is their innards were on the outside. The hideous vision turned my stomach. Yet I cheered for their deaths. What parts I could recognize oozed blood and other bodily fluids. I momentarily wondered what spell had caused such devastation and how could I learn it.

I looked for Edward the Orange Master, thinking he had cast the deadly spell. I couldn't see him on the battlefield. But I did see Sarah. Like me she was some distance from the action. Like me she was lying under a pile of natural debris. I couldn't tell if she still lived or not. I prayed the Prophecy was right and she survived to be part of the rebirth of this world.

I thought of freeing myself from the tree. But instead I diverted my energies to the raven so it could see more of the battle. The force field stopping the Red Army from entering the battle had collapsed. Red troopers started flooding into the firefight. I watched Robina cast a spell turning the first line of attackers into flames. On the other flank Angus had sent his berserkers to the attack. The conjured troops charged swinging their claymores at the Red Army, who fell at the Highlanders' feet.

The two remaining wizards exchanged spells with Farica and Nelson. Farica stood like a majestic oak, serene and tranquil in the middle of the battle, throwing orange fireballs at the Red wizards with no fear on her face. Nelson was casting an ice spell at the other wizard. The ice spears flew through the air, some hitting the wagons, others were crashing to the ground. In horror the wizard cringed using his powers to melt the bolts before they pierced his heart.

Then a fireball exploded on Nelson. I cried when I saw him on the ground with both his legs severed from his body. Both his eyes glowed red. I know they saw nothing. It was his mind that screamed in pain.

My raven still gave me a view of the battlefield. The Red Army, even with its losses, had progressed towards my friends. The bog of a road had slowed some of them down. The war-machines of the Red Army started throwing arrows and rocks from the catapults. The projectiles started to rain down on us.

The raven flew higher; it gave me a view of the army and the artillery section. The Red Army troops grunted as they pushed the large arrow launchers into position to fire on our band of wizards. I cast two spells, one to stop the catapults and the other to attack the arrows from the other machine. My first spell set the grease on the catapult on fire. The spell cast an explosive chemical fire. Within seconds the flames lit up the sky. The second spell sent the arrows back towards the Red Army's troops.

I felt pleased with my endeavors. My raven found the General of the Army; I put all my energy into a spell I cast through the eyes of the raven aimed at the General. The bird showed me the horse and rider turn to stone just like a monument to a Civil War general. My glee in eliminating the head of the army paled when I saw my raven fall from the sky with an arrow through its black body. My eyes in the sky plummeted to the ground in a feathery death.

Seconds later, I heard Sarah's voice in my mind, "We have to save the others. I can see them struggling. The Red Army has slaughtered all of Angus's warriors, and they're flooding in from the south and the north. Four of them are within ten feet of Robina."

I crawled up the bank to see our little force falling back to the river. The wizard who had been fighting Nelson joined the others in the attack. The wizard never noticed my mind reaching out for him. He concentrated his attention on destroying Farica so he never felt my spell coming. I plucked his heart from his body and exploded it in front of his terror-stricken eyes.

The sight rejuvenated me. I knew we had a chance. I started aiming the spell at the soldiers running towards us. One after another their hearts exploded in front of their eyes. Even so, for each I killed five more took his place. It slowed the attack, but we still had to retreat.

"Back to the waterline, Johnny," I heard Robina.

I turned to see Sarah carrying Nelson and Angus pulling Farica and Beth towards the water. I could see blood flowing from a wound on Farica's head. I muttered an oath or a spell, in any event the brush between me and the charging Red Army bursts into flames, and the rocks turned a pulsating red with eight hundred degree heat.

"Hurry, we'll cross the river and ride out of here with Edward's carriage." I watched as Robina searched the area. "God damn it, where is that big Orange bastard?"

Farica coughed then gave a small laugh. "We need that big Orange. We can't let them kill him. He's to be mine."

Her statement shocked me, but before I could voice my questions, ten horsemen rode through the fire and down on us. I turned with my magic sword drawn for combat and Sarah with hers stood beside me. Angus had joined us and we now stood three strong. Sarah yelled as the horses bore down on us. "All for one and one for all was our call to arms. Kill the buggers."

The first rider rode right toward me with his sword swinging at my head. To the right of me, I glanced up to see Sarah throw her dagger at the fighter closest to her. I heard her battle cry, the battle cry of the Amazon Women, "You dickless asshole, fight me now."

I had no time to linger. My sword slashed, and I rolled out of the way of the charging horse. I cut the horse's legs off as it rode over me. The Red soldier fell from his mount at my feet. Buffoon did its worst beheading the rider.

Angus dismounted his opponent. They engaged in a sword fight, a fight the soldier could not win. Every advance the soldier took, Angus parried. Every lunge Angus took, he scored a blood wound.

The five became two. Then Sarah was on the back of the horse of one of them. She plunged her sword through the Red cavalryman. The sword continued on into the head of the horse. Both fell dead on the ground. She dismounted without a scratch. The remaining soldier fell to a combined attack by Angus and me. He panicked. Pulled so hard on the reins to avoid us the horse fell on the incline crushing the rider.

Sarah recovered her dagger and we moved back to the river as the next cavalry attack came on us. This time fifteen horses charged down the hill towards us.

Robina yelled, "These are not mortal men riding these steeds. I can feel the vibrations of sorcery in them. They are like Angus's soldiers. They are a magic army. Our weapons will do us no good. We must destroy them with our own magic."

I enchanted the rocks to roll from the top of the hill to the river below. The horsemen slid down the hill gaining speed as their horses stumbled. From the rocks, I erected a sturdy wall in front of them with rose vines forming a bramble. Each rose thorn possessed a deadly poison. In less than five seconds, I watched two die pinned between the wall and the bramble, with hundreds of thorns piercing their bodies.

The others concocted other magic to kill most of the magical army. The remaining soldiers attacked Angus. He fought heroically disabling the four that surrounded him. A dying Red Officer slashed out at Angus severing his Achilles tendons. Our Scott fell upon his knees sword still in hand. He slashed back cutting the soldier's arm from his body. Even so, the last magical soldier wouldn't die and cut Angus's left hand off at the wrist. Angus uttered a curse so strong the Red soldier exploded. Body parts flew with the wind. Angus fell in a Punic victory. We rushed to his aid.

Farica stuck his hand back in place and started to bind it. She mixed a small packet of natural herbs and a dash of magic powder. She mixed the concoction with a handful of water she scooped from the river. She did the same for his Achilles tendons. Robina uttered a healing spell from the Red Master's book.

With all the strain, Farica collapsed in my arms. Sarah, Robina and I fought as the only functioning warriors left. We formed a fighting triangle and waited for the next attack. Just like at Oxford, the three of us stood back to back to defeat the Red Army.

With our powers combined we levitated our wounded and carried them across the river. Using all our remaining strength, we placed them in the Orange Master's carriage and sealed it in a hidden place that only we knew how to find.

"Damn Jonathan, no one could defeat you. You're the savior of this place; the one the Chronicles of Berwick prophesied would rule this world," Sarah uttered in a sarcastic tone.

Robina rolled her eyes and said, "It's not over yet. This is part of the Prophecy. I know it looks like the end, but we have many more trials to go before we gain the prize at Berwick."

Sarah gave a cruel laugh, "I don't think so. Here they come."

"Sarah, dig us a trench." Our Amazon warrior bent down using her hands to dig, "No stupid, use magic," chided Robina. She turned to me and added, "Make a fog, thick fog now and quickly. It must cover us and all the soldiers. I'll plant hawthorns throughout the riverbank and make them grow to five feet high with many thorns."

Five seconds later, a forest of thorns protected us in our hole in the ground with London's pea soup fog everywhere, giving us safety in the middle of the Red Army. Shouts of pain and frustration surrounded us. We never set eyes on a red tunic, but at times they cried out so close we could smell their breath of stale beer and garlic sausage.

Robina whispered, "Now with magic make images of us appear at the outer edges of the fog. You must project yourself, not just your body. It must be your whole being otherwise the wizard will know it isn't real."

Seconds later, we heard the soldiers yelling, they caught a glimpse of us trying to escape at the north end of the fog.

The area around us turned into chaos with soldiers trying to run to the north, stumbling over the ground, tearing their clothes and bodies on the sharp thorns, and seeing nothing by their efforts in the fog. We slowly emerged from our hole and crawled through the fog down to the river. Each step we took opened a path through the hawthorn to the river.

The fog still surrounded us as we stepped into the river. Like a tsunami, the river receded, the fog cleared. Then it engulfed us in a huge wave. We didn't move, and the water pinned us in place as it surrounded us burying us under its force. Of course, it was magic. We couldn't move in the liquid, but we could breathe.

As the clear water held us, a wizard walked within five feet of us. He looked amused. "You are a formidable force. You have cost me greatly, but now you are mine. I will keep you like my butterfly collection pinned in my album, but of course I have to drive the pin through your hearts."

I heard Robina speak in my head, "It's the Red Master speaking through his wizard. We have to escape and fast before he kills us."

The Red Master continued to speak, but I didn't hear him; I was thinking of ways to escape when I saw Edward the Orange Master at the top of the hill laughing at us.

CHAPTER FOURTEEN

IT DIDN'T TAKE THE RED WIZARD LONG TO FIND OUR WAGONS AND the other members of our quest. He had defanged us with a forbidden spell from the Saunders Book of Magic and paraded us before him. I observed the Red Master using the wizard as his surrogate; the Red Lord's personality and voice permeated every movement and every word of the wizard.

"You scum. You steal from me and kill my soldiers. You sealed your fate once you stepped inside my treasure room."

I followed his piercing eyes as they scanned our bedraggled group of which the others had appointed me the nominal leader.

"Jonathan," he pointed at me, "yes you. You're the impersonator of the Prophecy of the Berwick Chronicles. You're just a crazed wizard from the land of the Gaul's. You will die first."

Two soldiers pulled me away from the others. Before I could resist, a brutally strong soldier pulled my head down towards the ground and placed it on a three-foot tall round of wood. Out of my left eye, I glimpsed a flash of hard cold steel, the type executioners fancy.

I now smelled fear sweating out of my body. I saw in the shadow the executioner swinging the large axe practicing his death chop. I had no hope. However, I knew that this couldn't happen, the Prophecy wouldn't allow it. That's when I realized I had bought into this world's mythology. I didn't even believe in my own world's religion.

"Do them all. Death is too good for them, but I don't have the time to waste on such garbage," The Red Master spouted through his puppet.

I could hear the soldiers seize each one of my friends. I reached out with my mind to connect with Robina. I knew I had no magic, but love surely must have a way. I felt her in my mind just for a fleeting second, and it was bliss.

The grunt of the executioner told me he was lifting his axe. I knew at the count of five I would be in two parts. A headless body doesn't walk away from the executioner's axe. I just didn't want to think anymore. Two soldiers held me firm to the block. My face tasted the raw wood. My eyes stared straight ahead but saw nothing; bile crept up to my throat. I had no tears just regrets that my life had no meaning. I ran out of time to give it some.

As the blade swished down towards my neck, I felt static electricity surround me and every hair of my body stood on end. I felt the slap against my neck and heard the Red Army cry out in horror. A voice I knew echoed from behind me and across the river,

"No, not now, and not here; I forbid it. This is my domain, and he will die in York. The Council of Masters will be present as will the people of York, all watching as the axe comes down. They will all die and so will the Prophecy, and we can continue our rule over this land."

I wasn't dead or injured; a lifeless chicken lay across my neck. I turned to see the Orange Master standing beside the mouthpiece of the Red Lord.

The Red Lord answered, "This is my victory; I saved you from this wretched band of misfits. Your own army couldn't save you. You have no influence here. He must die now before he can escape from my hands."

The Orange Master shook his head and said, "No, you didn't save me. I defeated this lot. It was my curse that deprived them of their magic. I uttered the words that now make them as harmless as newborn kittens."

"It's time. The longer they live the more chance they have to escape. Don't forget these are the strongest wizards in the Realm, one slip, and they could kill us all. No, we must kill them now. Listen to me, no talking, no examining who and what they are, just off with their heads."

A great sigh escaped the Orange Master. "If you execute him and the others hear rumors they will spread that he made his escape with his warriors, and another pretender will surface. If we have a public execution with all the Masters present the people will realize the foolishness of believing in the Prophecy. We will have crushed all their hope. They will know there is no rescue from our power, and the people will never trust in the Prophecy again. We will no longer have this resistance to our rule."

The Red Master's anger flashed across the wizard's face. "I see your point, but he must die now. No more of your magic, I have other means to take his head. Let's get on with the executions."

Out of the forest thousands of Orange tunics filled with warriors appeared from both directions along the road. "No, my friend, the Council is with me, and they have commanded me to take the prisoners to York. If you resist they have ordered me to drag your Doppelganger to York in chains."

The red in the surrogate Red Master's face matched his blood-red robe. "I have stronger magic than you my friend. I could crush you where you stand," he said.

A smirk came over the face of the Orange leader.as he said, "No, my dear friend, I have the magic now. I have the book you so dearly wished to have returned to your library in Oxford. I have the spells that will make you comply. We will dispose of the villains as you planned but in the right time, the right order and in the right place. One week henceforth in the York square, we will put an end to the Prophesy. With all the Masters present, we will show the people we control everything.

The Doppelganger screamed at his sergeant at arms, "Find a jailer's cart and transport them to York. Bring all of them, even the woman who no longer responds."

The Orange Master smiled and said, "Now you're seeing reason, guard them well. Send the treasure with them to show their crimes to the people and the Masters. Display them as common criminals and murderers, the Masters can be their judge and jury, and we can wash our hands of their deaths. With the Prophecy destroyed, and the Thane of Scotland dead, we can take over all the northern territory, even some of the Black Master's lands. His daughter is one of the condemned."

The trip to York was a harsh journey in the prison wagon as The Red and Orange Armies escorted us across England. The seven of us lay or knelt in the confined cage. It was a four-foot cube, set on top of a buck board wagon. We ate, slept and complained for three days in our moving prison. Our mobile cell stopped at every village and hamlet where the army encouraged the locals to throw spoiled vegetables at us. Beth was unresponsive to all stimuli except light. Nelson didn't complain, but his stumps of legs oozed blood and the pain of his ordeal silently cried out with every movement he made.

"See it moves. I can wiggle my fingers." It was the third day, and Angus' reattached hand now moved and his fingers, which had wilted to a corpse's gray bloomed pink from their roots to their tips. The rest of us licked our wounds, nevertheless we faired well in our captivity. We planned and schemed, but the result was always the same. We could do nothing until the soldiers incarcerated us in the Orange Master's castle. The Orange Master we determined had used one of the spells from Saunders Book of Magic on us. No matter where the wagon traveled, the spell placed on us stopped us from performing any magic. However, we watched the Red Wizard do whatever he wished.

Robina was confident her father, the Black Master, would be there. "He won't let them execute me," she said. "He only tolerated me as a captive, because his spies watched over me. The Red Master knew my death would mean war."

Angus shook his head. "No, my Black Witch, he has no choice but to watch the axe fall over your head. The Red Master has branded you a common thief and, in the eyes of the Masters, a murderer. Remember the White Master's son; he died at our hands. I know yoo and I were under a spell, but the Masters aren't going to observe the niceties of the law. They want oor blood."

The prison cell in the castle's dungeon projected a mood of foreboding. Its dank and dark atmosphere with its old, rat- infested, smelly straw caused me to vomit when I initially entered. However, after the first ten minutes of horror, I saw it as heaven; the cell didn't move, jarring me every second or even crashing me against the roof and then back down to the floor. I would never have to ride over the rough road of the English countryside ever again. I stopped and thought hard about that statement.

We awoke on the day of the York Execution; the Masters called it the purification of the Age of Magic. They gave the citizenry a holiday throughout each Master's domain. We had a fantasy plan of escape. A battalion of Marines storming the castle in a helicopter rescue would drop out of the sky and snatch us up and fly us back to the good old U. S. of A.

The night before we all voiced our hopes, fears and regrets. Farica, the eternal optimist, gave the pep talk. "My fellow travelers, it is not the end. The Prophecy is just working itself through."

Robina turned to Farica and said. "Mother Superior, no version of the Prophecy I've ever heard tells of our execution or even our capture by the Red Master. I fear we are not the right adventurers to discover the meaning of the Berwick Chronicles."

Farica looked sad and replied, "Robina, you just think with your heart, and not with your head. We are magical people. Nothing is impossible. Nothing is as it appears. I tell you this is the Prophecy in action. I know. Trust in what you know; magic. Never surrender, never give up. The Prophecy is true. This is but another step toward our goal. We are now at York. Berwick is close in distance, but in our journey, we have many trials to meet before we succeed. We will overcome all obstacles." The rest of us clapped, and murmured our positive feelings about our escape and success. Nevertheless, it was obvious to me the others felt like I did, the next day would be our last.

That night I slept with Robina in my arms. I held her close knowing she carried my child and unless something drastic happened, the child would die in the womb. I wept thinking of the children Robina and I should have, but never would. I held her closer to me and felt her heart beat as fast as mine. I awoke with a start as the cell door clanged open and an escort of soldiers waited to take us to meet our fate. They interrupted a disturbing dream. All I remembered came to me in a searing phrase, "What is black and white and orange all over; beware of the checkerboard."

A sergeant in his bright-red tunic prodded me with his sword, "Get up, a man is waiting with an axe to put your head back to sleep for you." He laughed. I groaned. What drivel.

Angus sloughed behind me and whispered into my ear, "Be strong lad, there is no shame in death. We are warriors. The wizards fear us. We are the real masters of this world."

Angus and I carried Nelson and Robina, and Sarah dragged Beth as the soldiers marched us through the dungeons. I looked at the walls surrounding us, the huge blocks of granite which at one time had a plastered finish, but now looked worn and in places green with mold. The broad circular staircase led to the main floor of the castle. We entered the great room which the Orange Master had decorated as a medieval court. Banners hung from the ceiling thirty feet above. Over a thousand people filed the great room. My eyes blinked from the glare of the light streaking through the narrow windows and the thousands of lit candles.

I remarked to Angus. "Jesus, what the hell are we in the middle of here?"

He gave me a knowing smile. "This is the gathering of the Masters. They will conduct the mock trial here an' after hearing evidence will sentence us to death in the courtyard outside. There is twenty thousand or more waitin' for the trial tae end out there. They won't have to wait long. The trial usually lasts around an hour, most of it taken up with pomp and pageantry."

Everyone watched us as the guards paraded us into the hall like zoo animals. I thought of growling but held back remembering Angus' words; we are warriors. The dignity of a warrior had to be upheld. The seven of us ended up in a stall-like enclosure the sergeant-at-arms called the accused docket. No chairs occupied our pen. We stood. The raised platform we occupied was about two feet higher than the surrounding floor.

Moments later, the hubbub in the large room subsided. The sound of shuffling feet and the hushed conversation of the Masters echoed from the stone walls as they entered the great room from a staircase leading down from the upper floors of the castle.

The Orange Master, our erstwhile friend, led the procession; followed by the Red then the White, Black, Green and Tartan Lords, for Lords, of their lands they were, even though they called themselves Masters. They were impressive in their richly colored robes with the gold ornamentation of office. The Guards who followed them carried the Master's banners displaying their coats-of-arms. These soldiers arrogantly strutted down the stairs. No magic display needed, the pageantry accompanying the trooping of the Masters would have made the present monarchy of England proud.

Soldiers dressed in Red, White, Green, Orange, Black and Tartan stood ten deep and fifty across to give a rainbow of color and push the crowd back.

I inhaled deeply, gently grasping Robina's hand. Her hand shook as did her whole body. I pulled her closer to me to let some of the warmth of my body calm her and give her strength. I gazed into her eyes, marveling at her beauty. I felt her body calm. She smiled while she stared at the Masters. We watch with intensity as they sat upon the thrones prepared to sentence us to death. Then she beamed at me and whispered into my ear. "That's my father in the black with the gold adornments. He will free us. The council never met at the time of my capture, but now he has his chance to save me." She squeezed my hand. "He is strong, and he's defied the Masters before, he will be our savior."

He had his head lowered as he sat, then he raised his head and faced us. I saw a broken man, not one of power or defiance, but one who already surrendered. It reminded me of the victim of a bully, who knew if he complained or stepped out of line, he would receive another beating. It was the eyes; the life drained from them. His cheeks were sunken and his skin a pasty white. I felt Robina's anguish, not by magic, but as a soul mate. Before the first tear dropped, I held her close to me giving her as much support as a man in the docket can give anyone before he receives his death sentence.

A man dressed in black and gold robes sent a fire ball from the Masters' high bench to the wall at the far end of the Great Hall. Then he opened the trial. The head of Security for Oxford presented the first evidence. He related our exploits during our time there. I had to credit him; he did not falsify his testimony. It was accurate down to destruction of the gate and the number of bodies we left behind. In a dramatic move he stood up and said, "For all to behold, the treasure they stole from the Red Master." On these words, forty pairs of Red soldiers carried on poles over their shoulders boxes containing the loot of the Red Master's treasury that we possessed at our capture. The Grand Hall exploded in surprise at the volume and our audacity to take such valuable items.

The next witness told the court of the finding of the White Master's son and his troops and how they discovered evidence of our treachery. I disagreed with the emotional words of the witness, as he didn't see the true attack of the White Prince. However, I had to agree we did kill the bastards. I couldn't help myself and smirked thinking of the aftermath with Robina.

A few more witnesses took the oath and told of our criminality then we heard from the Orange Master's wizard, he, being the most senior of the witnesses to give an oath against us. Again, the wizard's facts were correct as he told of our killings of his soldiers, the Orange wizard and abducting the Orange Master himself.

The Masters closed their case. In such trials we had the opportunity to answer, Angus advised us not to say a word but stand tall. To open your mouth was to ask for the rack. That's how they determined if an accused had a tongue that told the truth or lied. The verdict was a given, unless someone on the Masters' bench threw their lot in with us. No one spoke, not us or them.

I looked over at Angus. Then at Robina whose tears dropped from her eyes like golden pearls. Angus's teeth held his mouth tightly closed, but I heard him mumble. "That's a lowlander Englishman in ma Tartan. They hae annexed ma country." His body was as tight as a wound up watch. I could see him ready to charge the Masters. He didn't stand a chance. We stood in the middle of the Orange soldiers. I closed my eyes and willed him to stay calm, to stand still, and to stay speechless. Every fiber in my body, every thought in my mind concentrated on Angus and those three thoughts.

The Red Master gave us a wolfish grin. "Well, you impostors, you thieves, you murderers. The Council has made its decision. You are all guilty of every crime. Your silence is an indictment against you. The council has decided your sentence." I didn't see any of them converse with each other or write down notes and pass them around. They all just stared at us.

The Red Master continued, "Out of mercy for the Thane of Scotland, and the Princess of Wales, we are taking you outside and beheading you before the crowd. There will be no torturing or drawing and quartering. Once I have your severed heads in my hands, I will personally remove your entrails and burn them. Your miserable bodies will hang in front of the main city gate of Oxford to rot for one year. That is our sentence. Take them away."

It was a warm July day, and the sun blinded me as they dragged us outside. The scaffold we climbed stood only twenty feet away from the castle. The rainbow army marched all around us clearing a path to our execution.

I heard Farica's voice behind me yell, "This is only the beginning. Immortal life waits."

I'm not a religious man, but her words calmed me, instilled hope and faith in me. I turned to her and yelled back. "Thank you, Mother Superior. How can I ask for forgiveness from your God to reach this life after death?"

I saw the quizzical look upon her face, then the smile of understanding. "Stupid, I wasn't talking about religion but about the Prophecy. Have faith Jonathan. We aren't going to die."

Before I could reply, a soldier grabbed me and pushed me up to the stairs to the axe man. The soldiers bound us together hands and feet in a line with four long strands of rope. When I fell up the stairs, the rest fell with me. The crowd roared with excitement the violence had begun.

Robina helped me to my feet. I noticed the two soldiers who were carrying Nelson helped the zombie-like Beth to her feet too. Our procession hobbled up the stairs, and we faced the crowd that now yelled in frenzy for our deaths.

The sea of people looked on with an expectation in their eyes and various foods in their mouths. It reminded me of a football game, the crowd wild, waiting for the last five minutes, consuming food and beer in quantities only a herd of elephants could match. Everyone was waiting with anticipation for the next play. However, in this game, it would be a head not a football flying through the air. To my surprise, the six Masters joined us on the scaffolding carrying gold daggers. I realized the purpose, and my stomach turned. I felt the bile rising and forced myself not to embarrass my comrades. I squeezed Robina's hand and whispered, "I love you."

She whispered back. "No matter what, I'll love you forever. I always have and always will. You were my first lover, and I will have no other."

I had to laugh, where would she find another lover after the scaffold? The ridiculousness of the statement brought me out of the melancholy of death. I decided I would die with a smile upon my face, and love within my heart for the magical Robina.

The drums started to beat, and the thousands calmed to complete silence. The Red Master said more words. I didn't listen, and then I stepped forward to place my head on the block. To my surprise, two soldiers in red tunics carried Nelson toward the front, and placed his head on the block. Three soldiers held him in place.

I heard the swish of the axe which was about ten feet from my head. I could not help myself, my eyes would not move, all they saw was Nelson's head on the block and the silver axe gleaming from the sun's rays. It reminded me of the last minutes of a football game, the quarterback stepping back to take the ball, everyone in the crowd silent waiting to cheer for the home team victory on the expected touchdown. The crowd with beer in their hands and food in their mouths all stopped, waiting for the axe to fall. I looked up and watched the executioner swings his axe in a big circle to gain momentum for the touchdown.

CHAPTER FIFTEEN

MY BODY CONVULSED, AND MY EYES BUGGED OUT IN HORROR AS Nelson's head dropped into the basket. I promptly threw up. I killed many recently but witnessing an execution knowing that your head would soon sit in the wicker was sensory overload. The thought was too much for my stomach, it turned. The reaction from the assembled crowd was in contrast to mine, they cheered and hooted for more blood and more severed heads. The Masters wanted to please. It wasn't me next, but Beth's, in her zombie state. She was like the proverbial lamb going to slaughter.

The guards flung her down on the deck of the platform putting her flopping head on the block. I hollered out in pain for her. She stared off, oblivious to her fate. The executioner swung his axe in a wide circle showing off for the crowd. The Red Master gave him a slight wave with his hand as a signal to dispatch Beth to the next frontier.

The executioner acknowledged the Red Master with a cavalier wave and swung the axe back with a loud swish. Beth's eyes popped open as if from an alarm clock's scream. She shook her arms, and the two guards holding her down flew over the roaring crowd. The axe, still in midair, crumbled to dust in the executioner's hands. I felt a new sense of power. My magic returned. My bonds had turned to water and left a puddle on the scaffold by my feet, next to the puddles of my friends. We were free.

I heard voices in my head, I identified them all but one. Robina shouted at me. "Attack the Masters. They'll destroy us if we don't act quickly."

Angus threw fireballs at the Masters standing behind us. They hit the Masters causing fireworks like on the Fourth of July. Roman candles exploded over the crowd. Panic filled the square. Everyone ran to escape from what they sensed as a battle between good and evil. The crowd turned.

I looked at my friends and then at the soldiers, "Jump into the crowd. They'll give us some protection from the enemy." I screamed.

We bounced from the platform into the masses. The six of us formed a phalanx and pushed forward, still throwing spells at the Masters. The retaliation was swift, with wave after wave of hexes hitting us. We fought off each as we ran for safety. Once an Immobilization curse stopped us for a few seconds, but we forced the Red Master to stop it by casting a spell to turn him into a tree. I felt another presence there fighting with us, a sixth mind. It was close by, stopping many of the Masters' spells.

The soldiers of the six Masters mixed in with the panicking crowd surrounded us as we ran. The soldiers from the Black army formed a shield for us as we battled against the Red, Green and White army. The Tartan and the Orange armies disappeared from the square. In the chaos, Red soldiers started to slash the crowd with their weapons to cut us down. Many fell and many resisted. The six of us still had no weapons to fight with and continued to run. I saw the stables only a hundred feet away.

I yelled for the others, "Horses, run fast, they are our way to get out of here. I crashed against an invisible barrier that felt like a stone wall. I fell onto the ground, with my nose bleeding and my ass sore as hell. All of us lay tangled in each other's arms and legs like a giant bowl of octopus and squid trying to escape from becoming soup.

I struggled to my feet and turned to face the enemy. Four of the Masters strutted towards us with swords in their right hands and evil in their hearts. I felt my comrades behind me ready for battle. I tossed a spell to turn the cobblestone plaza in front of the Masters into quicksand. They stopped, and I felt a searing breeze singe my hair. Angus swore and added, "Where's a sword when ya need one, I'll cut the head off that impostor."

Robina tried to conjure weapons for our little band but the Red Master blocked her efforts, "By gods," She uttered, "you bastards."

As fast as the quicksand appeared, it disappeared and the four Masters continued their advance. A swarm of huge wasps attacked us. In retaliation, Robina pulled strands of her hair and threw them into the air, in an instant; they became an enormous net that trapped the buzzing killers. She laughed, "At least I can still stop them. The Masters can't anticipate everything."

We weren't as gullible as before, when we had sent out protective spells against the previous magic with which the wizards had attacked us. Now the war escalated to new and exotic spells. We learned well from Robina and the ancient book of spells. However, the book in our hand would have given us more confidence and assurance in our defense.

Beth turned towards the invisible barrier; and cast a spell on herself. In a second, she metamorphosed into a wispy cloud of water vapor and slid through the barrier. Her voice echoed through my mind reciting a spell to me. I repeated it and turned into nothing but vapor and escaped the trap as she had. Three seconds later, our team stood on the other side of the invisible wall and ran like hell towards the stables.

I could hardly breathe, with my hands against my thighs and my head down by my knees. I croaked, "Jesus. I thought they had us back there. Let's get out of here."

Robina grabbed my hand and pulled me back up. "Not so quick, look at the wagon."

We looked where Robina was staring. "Oh my god," whispered Sarah. "It's impossible."

All the treasure we had appropriated from the Red Master and twice as much again sat in four large wagons with four horses hitched to each cart. Our weapons stood stacked beside them. I turned to my friends, "Which one of you had the forethought to do this? It's brilliant."

Each one of them denied it. "No, we didn't do it. It must be a trick or possibly the Red Master's preparations for his own hasty departure," pondered Robina.

Sarah dashed to the weapons. "One-way or another we now have weapons to fight and my Reaper is as sharp as ever." She picked it up and swished it through the stale air of the stable.

Then she spotted her other belongings. "Ah, here is my dagger, my black tunic and armor. Let's meet those bastards, they're all old men. We can take them in a fair fight."

Angus shook his head. "Ma brave heroic Sarah, they dinna believe in anything fair. They will hae archers on the parapets, or even two or three companies o' swordsmen hidden waiting for us to show oor heads. Let's find a way oot o' here an' leave."

We quickly donned our tunics and armor. "There's no other way out. We're trapped." Yelled Farica and she picked up a sword. "We have to leave the way we came in."

I gave a great sigh. "It's show time my friends, Robina, bewitch the horses to follow us; we'll have to fight our way out. Let's give them hell, warriors."

Having entered the stable as fleeing prisoners, we exited as seasoned warriors. It became the classic shoot out scene in the movies. We proudly marched out like the Earps, and the Masters as the gangster gang the Clantons waiting for us. The four Masters stood in front of the troops waiting for us in the bright sun.

In my mind, I could hear that haunting music from a Fistful of Dollars. The soldiers stood at attention on three sides to the square as the crowd looked on in disbelief. The Red, Green, and White armies cordoned the civilians from the center of the plaza. The Masters' faces had cunning grins when we came out of the stables but their expressions quickly changed to, if not horror, at least to dismay as they realized we now had weapons and armor.

My force of warriors took up combat positions. Weapons drawn, we slow marched forward to meet the Masters. Robina whispered into our ears, "They all have combat magic as good as yours, and some even better. Angus knows. He's faced the Red Master before, and even though he's the best fighter in Scotland, the Red Master bested him. That's why you found him a slave at Oxford. If you have a chance, discretion is the better part of valor; retreat, if you survive you've won."

Here we were six desperate heroic figures facing an army ready to fight the best of the best in single combat. At stake were not only our lives, but all the lives of this world depending on us to win. It reminded me of an old western or Japanese Samurai movie. I spent my youth watching cowboy movies. High Noon crossed my mind. I now imagined myself as the sheriff outnumbered and outgunned facing evil.

As we stepped out into the open, the four Masters blew a foul wind at us. We blew it back in their faces. Spell after spell they attacked with and each time we returned it to them. Cold steel was the only way they could defeat us or so I thought.

A hail of arrows rained down on us from the parapets, hundreds of bolts flying through the air. I winced expecting the arrows to pierce my heart. My eyes grew large as the arrows redirected themselves in flight either by magic or divine intervention. We stepped five paces closer to the Masters.

Farica sneered and yelled at the Red Master, "You know the Prophecy as well as I. Remember what happens next. On the other hand, have you set this up to aid yourself in the outcome? You can't change it no matter what you do. It is foretold."

No further magic assaulted us. Brute force entered the stage, eight warriors appeared in front of the Masters. They stood over seven feet tall, all muscle, decked out in shining silver armor with scarlet cloaks and long blond hair flowing under their helmets. They reminded me of gladiators. We stood like prey soon to be dinner for these carrions.

"Goddamn you," I yelled at the Red Master. Robina whispered into my ear, "His name is Jasper, but he likes Henry in private."

I taunted him, "Jasper's a chicken; he goes cluck, cluck, cluck and sends his roosters to do his fighting for him. He's just a pantywaist chicken."

He pushed his way through the giants in armor. "You'll eat those words when I spill your guts and feed them to my dogs. You'll beg me for mercy, you worm."

He scared me and I felt my bladder trying to empty, but I kept up the bravado, "Sticks and stones, my friend, but your words won't hurt me. Bring it on, old man, show me your stuff."

The Red Master charged me leaving magic behind as his rage brought back the warrior of twenty years before. I parried his attack and fell back. My still enchanted sword waved like a flag on the Fourth of July stopping his every blow. I danced like Travolta in *Saturday Night Fever*. I could see the frustration on the Master's face. "Come on Jasper. You know that name suits you much better than the feared Red Master." His swordplay was outstanding. Mine was pitiful, but he never touched me.

Three of his giants swarmed me. Like a good basketball player on the midget side, I darted between their legs. Instead of dribbling the ball, I slashed with my sword. They aimed their swords at my head. I weaved and bobbed. My luck held. Not a hair upon my head suffered. However, one of my attackers lost his kneecaps. Another would need a doctor to complete the sex change that my sword had started. I stared down the third and darted to the rear.

I had a breather as Jasper collected his giants. He ordered them to attack me in his new plan of attack. I watched Angus in a fight till the death with the impostor Thane of Scotland. The impostor didn't have the skill of Angus. It cost him dearly. Angus pushed him backward with one blow after another. The fake Thane fell backward tripping over his own feet. Angus stepped back and bowed to him. The true Thane of Scotland allowed the imposter to regain his footing. Angus then charged him, leaving the impostor's right cheek flapping with blood pouring out onto his face and the ground. Nevertheless, there was no respite for the pretender. On Angus's next thrust, he pierced the sham Thane in the belly. The blade of the claymore entered only about three inches but enough to rupture the stomach.

I saw no more of Angus and his battle. The Red Master and his toadies charged me. One to the right and the other at the left, they had murder in their eyes. The giant on the right was on me in seconds. I did a pratfall and rolled as if I were on fire. Surprised the giant stood gaping where I had been. Exasperated the Red Master swung his sword where I had stood a second before. Unfortunately for the giant, he stood in that exact spot. The Red Master's sword found him. A large slash wound just above his navel dispatched the Red Master's giant.

I jumped up from the ground, like Johnny Depp in some pirate movie. However, I foiled my own illusion of the fleet-footed, dashing pirate, when I tripped over the White Master. Both of us fell hard to the ground. I watched as he regained his feet. He didn't come for me but charged Sarah. She parried, and like a matador gracefully led the White Master running off in opposite direction, moving his head in almost in a circle trying to find her.

The White Master screamed at her once he saw her standing behind him, "Bitch, I can feel it. You killed my son. You surprised him when he slept. You cut his heart out. You used the Black Witch's magic to kill my son." He puffed himself up, his face now beet red with veins bulging as he yelled, "Women are good for only two base functions; making babies and killing. I'm going to rip your womb from your body with my long sharp sword, and watch you wriggle as you die."

The White Master never spoke another disgusting word. Sarah yanked her dagger from her belt and chucked the bewitched blade with all the strength her powerful body possessed. The hilt was all that protruded from the White Master's forehead. The steel helmet showed no damage other than the hilt firmly stuck to it.

The Green Master retreated to his force of Irish soldiers. He had not returned unscathed. His left arm was useless, and he had lost an eye from Beth's sword. He collapsed as he regained his force. Only the Red Master stayed on the battlefield. His whole force of soldiers now charged towards us. It was no longer mano a mano. It was his army against us. I threw a freezing spell out to stop the army. However, as before, the dampening force had returned to the battlefield. The inability to cast spells made our fight desperate if not hopeless.

We stood in the middle of the square with the roaring crowd now on our side watching the Masters fall to our swords. Suddenly, the Red Army lined up in a formation of twenty across and thirty deep. The drums started to beat a rata-tat-tat, a rata-tat-tat. After each combination, the troops marched forward five steps to meet us. The basketball team that had faced us earlier was dead at our feet, but the ones marching forward looked even meaner.

The Green Army, also marching in formation of twenty across, joined the Red Army holding the left flank. The red and the green tunics gave a Christmas flavor to our impending demise.

I almost cried when the White army formed up on the right flank. In all, I counted fifteen hundred soldiers in a line of sixty strong and at least twenty rows deep.

"Damn." Was all I could utter. I appraised my sword and hoped it could slay at least two or three hundred of the colorful enemy. Even so, I realized I might kill ten or even twenty before their sheer numbers would do me in.

Robina put her hand on my shoulder. "I had cast a spell earlier to put a dead zone on the battlefield when the battle was one-on-one. As the odds changed I attempted to remove it. This is the Red Master's magic I tried to stop it. I cast ten spells that would save us, but nothing works. Whatever the Red Master did this is a dead zone. There are a number of dead zones throughout the realms, but York was never one of them until today. Stand firm my lover. If the Prophecy holds true we'll survive this ordeal."

I looked at the troops massed against us, then at the barn behind us and finally at the castle wall. There was no escape. If magic didn't work, death was a certainty. I prayed. To what god I can't remember, but I prayed.

Farica whistled a happy tune and in a cheery, voice said to us. "In the darkest hour is when you forge your courage. Think of this as a character-building moment. This is all an illusion. Like you, the men marching towards us are uneasy. They saw their Masters fall to our strength. Their hearts aren't in the fight. Stand tall. The Prophecy tells us they will die like the oak leaves in fall. My friends gaze on all the beautiful colors from the green to the right on the red in the middle to the bleached out white at the end. All will fall like leaves from a tree, dead. So say the Seers. We have the Halloween colors to protect us. The spooks and the goblins are ours." I liked Farica from first, I saw her, if not when I held her naked body. Now I feared she had gone over the deep end. She made no sense, and the rata-tat-tat echoed in my ears. I now could see the whites of the soldiers' eyes.

Angus yelled his Highland battle cry and shouted, "Charge the bloody bastards."

Without thinking the six of us rushed with swords raised high and voices screaming charged the enemy line. The drumbeat of the enemy increased to double time. The line was now at most twenty yards away on a crash course to our six berserkers. I yelled so loud my fear evaporated, and just red-hot adrenaline rushed through my veins pushing me onward.

I saw the first line falter, and the second line run into them pushing them forward. Our band of berserkers slashed and ran. We attacked up and down-the-line we staying in no place more than a second our blades' cutting and our legs running. The front line of the enemy stopped. It then started to curl around us. We left bodies wherever we attacked and retreated to the entrance to the barn. We had destroyed the front row of the enemy attack but sixty more marched over the dead.

It was a fabulous gesture. The last scene of Bonnie and Clyde came to mind as Robina put her hand on my shoulder. "I love you my Emperor and this is not the end, I trust the Prophecy. Like, Farica, I know we will win, have faith in our strength."

CHAPTER SIXTEEN

I LEANED BACK AGAINST THE STABLE DOOR FACING A THOUSAND OR more warriors. My sword poised to kill as many as it could reach. I knew my friends stood beside me with similar thoughts. I picked out one Red Army soldier, if nothing else I would die with his blood on my sword. I only wished I could have killed the Red Master when I had my chance. I exhaled with a great sigh. It had been fun, and like nothing I would have ever experienced in my own world.

My time on earth had expired, only a sword blade through my heart still awaited me. The enemy rushed forward with no more than ten feet between us. The six of us charged again at the enemy. Without a nod, I thought they all knew we would die in battle but as the aggressors. As my sword swung on its own volition, I felt it bite into chain mail and then flesh. Above me, I heard a loud swish through the air. I glanced up as my sword cut through another of the Red soldiers sending him to the gods in the sky. I watched the descent of hundreds of colorful arrows falling on our enemy. Whoever shot those arrows gave my little band the inspiration to slaughter the force in front of us. My sword never stopped. Buffoon moved of its own accord. It killed one after another of enemy soldiers. The enemy was in a frenzy to escape the arrows rain down. The army in front of us retreated into the castle leaving many of their numbers dead or dying on the cobblestones of the square.

I turned to Farica and asked, "What happened?"

She smiled. "The fates have more in store for us than a death in the square of York Castle. Look up on the parapets." I turned squinting behind me. The Orange and the Black armies stood with bows in their hands peering down at us.

Robina grabbed my hand. "Look up, there's my father and the Orange Master. They saved our lives. My gods, my prayers were answered."

Angus yelled to us. "It's time to leave. We'll take the wagons and two riding horses each. Robina and Farica, stand guard in case they attack again. Jon and Beth help me. The Red Master isn't going to surrender so easy."

The three of us saddled six horses and had the wagons out of the stables in less time than it took to lead us to the chopping block. As we exited the stables, Robina was hugging a huge soldier in gold armor and a black tunic and cape. The Orange Master was giving Farica a hug as well. Both Orange and Black soldiers surrounded the stables.

"Jonathan. Johnny, this is my father. He saved us." She dragged him over to the wagon that I sat on. "Dad, this is Jonathan. He's the Emperor foretold to us in the Prophecy, and I carry his child."

The Black Master had an amused look upon his face. "Well, my son, you have your hands full with Robina. I gladly give her to you. I've been trying to marry her off for years. The Red Master even offered, but you know Robina. She threatened to place a pox on me if I even forced my hand and gave her to him. She said she would rather be his prisoner for the rest of her life than be in his bed." He chuckled. "Well finally, I'll be a grandfather. You know. She is my only child now, and her heir will be the ruler of my domain."

The Black Master frowned. "Oh yes the Prophecy. If my daughter's right, our world is about to change even more than it did today."

Angus jumped down from his wagon and ran to the Black Master, "Arthur. It's been a long time; I was sorry tae hear about Julna."

A black cloud crossed Robina's father's face as he looked with sad eyes at Robina and then back at Angus. "Yes, she was older than me and when Elliot died in battle and the capture of Robina, she pined. She used every spell she knew to revive our son even years after his death. She did everything in her power to release Robina. She burned her magic day and night to have her children back. It aged her so and with no success, she had no strength to fight that old age sickness."

He frowned and stopped talking. Finally, his eyes sparkled and he looked lovingly at Robina. "Julna would have marveled at the events of the last few months, and her happiness would fill the realm knowing that Jonathan of the Prophecy saved and is your true love."

The Black Master slapped Angus on the back. "My old friend, it's been a long time indeed. We'll ride together, and I'll tell you the news. First tell me about this Jonathan fellow. The Prophecy is happening as we speak, if my daughter's correct. I know the Red Master believes it." A wry smile came to his maturely handsome face. "But first tell me about the man who my daughter chose to be the father to her children."

Angus nodded, and I heard him say, "Weell Arthur, he's a good man, brave, loving, loyal, and I think honorable. He fits the Prophecy weell and so de your daughter and the others wi' us." Then he paused. "You know the Prophecy ma friend. It doesnne bode well for oor future. But then again the change tae oor island an' tee Irish will be worth the sacrifice, don't ye think?"

The Black Master nodded. The Orange Master joined his two friends. "You didn't think I turned on you did you Angus?" Angus had his claymore ready to attack Edward of York.

Finally, Angus spoke, "Ma dear ex-father-in-law. I should cut ye in two right here, ye cunning bastard." To all our surprise, Angus grabbed Edward of York and gave him a bear hug, "Ye are a sight, ma friend, wonderful sight indeed. A' past deeds, even your daughter, will no' come between us. I have forgotten the past." He released Edward and they shook hands. "Aye, Edward o' York, we hae a bigger reason tae be friends, Jonathan and the Prophecy. As I said I have forgiven and forgotten, and I hope you do the same."

Edward beamed, "Thank-you Angus. The outlanders are powerful sorcerers no matter what I thought or tried to do. They changed me, and all I could think of was saving all of you." He gazed at Sarah and me. You didn't think I had turned against you did you?"

I walked over with the rest of my band. "Jesus, I did." I had my hand upon the hilt of my sword. "It was hell for the last week; why did you wait so long?"

He turned to Farica. "She told me the Prophecy dictated my actions, and if I acted too soon misfortune would strike us all. I had to wait until the Council of Masters met, and the first of the heretics died on the block. I'm sorry about that, I liked Nelson, but I had no control over it."

A flash of anger came to me, and I raised my hand to strike out at the ex-Orange Master, when Farica grabbed my arm, "He had no choice."

I gritted my teeth and scrunched up my eyes as I watched Sarah come to grips with Nelson's death within the context of what we had just learned. She started to cry, and looked so forlorn. Robina spoke to her, "I feel your loss. I know it rips your heart to pieces. I promise your true love will find you, and this will be just a bad dream."

Sarah who never liked to show emotion in front of others wiped her tears on her sleeve and looked daggers at Edward. He gave her a sad eye, "I'm sorry my dear. I haven't forgotten my oath to you my friends. I have forsaken my title and my lands. If you search the wagons, you'll see the treasure of Northumbria with that of the Red Master. I'm now Edward of York or just simply Edward York. Let's be off, before the Red Lord and his army regroup. Most of the Orange army will stay to protect our rear, and Arthur and his band will travel with us. Angus' Tartan army is waiting for him outside the gate." Angus sprinted into the stable and rode out a moment later mounted on a magnificent white stallion. "Off tae Berwick," he shouted with his highland brogue almost unintelligible.

The march was on; we are high-tailed it from the castle with a force no sane general would attack. We had a few hundred soldiers, three Masters of the realm, three trained sorcerers from the real world, my lover, the Black Witch and the Mother Superior of a religion I didn't understand. I knew we still had the Red Master to deal with, but I felt confident we could overcome all obstacles in our path. My spirits couldn't have been higher.

Robina, her father Arthur and I rode together for the first day.

We took turns telling about our lives and amusing stories that put us in fits of laughter. I noticed that Edward of York and Farica rode together speaking quietly to each other. Angus rode with the Highlanders, and the conversation took on a jovial mood, with much back slapping and loud laughter. Angus had several years to catch up on with his friends and relatives who had soldiered with the lowland impostor.

We spent our first night at the village of Norton twenty miles from York. Our March took us north and east towards the coast road. The ride was leisurely with the marching troops beside us, and our entrance into the village was exciting. The whole town's folk turned out to meet the procession to Berwick, and their Lord and Master Edward of York. We received a hero's welcome. A feast awaited us, and afterwards a festival of entertainment, songs, dance, readings and even a one-act play, a farce with the Red Master as the foil of all the jokes.

Later that night Robina lay beside me. "Johnny, this is one of the best days of my life; the rescue, the fighting, the near-death experience, my father, the entertainment and now being with you. Pinch me so I know it's real."

Taking her at her word, I pinched her, "Johnny, I didn't mean it." Then a smile came over her face, and I felt her pinches all over my body, yet she didn't move a finger.

"Damn," I said, "you're using magic against me." I retaliated by kissing her all over her body, but it wasn't magic. We both slept well that night.

The next morning Robina woke me with a peck on the cheek, "Up and at em, Emperor, come and meet your subjects."

I squinted with blurry eyes at her, grabbed her and pulled her down to the bed, "We have a few minutes before the Emperor rises," Then I thought a second. "What do you mean Emperor?"

"It's the Prophecy."

I felt confused. "Damn, that Prophecy. I'm no Emperor. I'm just a guy trying to go home."

She gave me that oh sure you are smile and planted a sloppy kiss upon my lips. "All right, Mr. Average John, let's go downstairs to breakfast. You'll see what I mean." My black tunic was gone, and a dark-blue uniform was in its place with gold epaulets, gold buttons, gold sash and sword.

"Robina, my sword is missing. This gold one is no good. I need Buffoon, my magical sword." I was in hysterics.

"Johnny calm down. That is your sword. I coated it in gold to match your uniform. Its Buffoon, he'll still serve you well. We have to hurry; everyone is waiting."

Whoever organized the breakfast had set up five or more trestle tables and a head table with eight place settings. Robina led me to the head table and sat me down in the center. The rest of the team sat to either side of me; including Arthur of Wales and Edward of York.

When I sat down the standing citizenry of the town screamed my name and chanted, "Emperor, Emperor."

Edward stood up and addressed the people, "Everyone sit." Then he stretched out his arms. "You know me as the Orange Master, your Lord. Today I am no longer your lord or master. From this moment forward I follow Jonathan, Emperor Jonathan. I am like you, an ordinary person, who will follow the Emperor wherever he orders me to go." He pointed to Angus.

"You know Angus the Scot, he also believes in the Emperor, and so does Arthur of Wales, the Black Master. We follow the Emperor. All of us put our armies behind him. We are going to Berwick to fulfill the Prophecy."

The crowd went wild with excitement. Robina grabbed my hand and forced me to my feet. She spoke, "This is the Emperor. He is the bravest of us all and won many battles with his heroic comrades. I call upon you no, I demand that you spread the word the Emperor has arrived, and you have sat with him. You have seen the Masters that support him, and you have broken bread with him."

She poked me in the ribs and whispered into my ear. "Darling speak to them. Tell them how you will bring justice, liberty and freedom to them. You will listen to their voices and help them." I felt like a politician who had forgotten his speech. I pulled up every politician I recalled listening to and used every platitude and hackneyed line ever spoken. They loved it. No one ever said anything like that to them, especially someone in authority. I became their ultimate authority figure with the help of my sword and my friends. I could think of nothing to do after the words, so I cast a spell, and provided every person seated at the tables with eggs, bacon, hotcakes, orange juice and tea. I also scattered butter, jam and English muffins on every table.

My esteem raised a hundred fold with the meal. I accepted their praise with humility and grace. Farica sat on the other side of me and whispered into my ear. "The Prophecy tells of what you said today but your exact words sounded more elegant, and it came across as a brilliant delivery and the meal, a stroke of genius. The Prophecy just states a miracle caused the people to believe." Then her voice became serious and sadder. "Keep close to Robina today. She'll need you more than she ever has or will in the future. Remember she carries your child. I'll stay close as well. Everyone has need of you today, and all in different places."

I tried to ask her why. However, the three Masters pushed me to my feet and pulled me up onto the table so all could see. They raised their swords, and I followed suit as Angus yelled, "Tell the Red Lord that he has reached the last days of his rule. Tell him you have seen the Emperor, and he has come to cleanse the land of tyrants."

The villagers, who had heard the speeches and had eaten the meal, swarmed us. In groups of twos or threes, they came forward, bowed before me and offered their allegiance. I kissed babies and full-grown women. I shook every man's hand and gave them a blue and gold tunic with my new coat of arms on it; a shield with a diagonal gold bar crossing from left to right. On the left side of the bar, a crown above a Norman castle stood out in gold and silver. I saw on the right side of the gold bar a lion holding a sword in one hand and a book in the other, glared at the observer. When I asked what it meant the only answer I received was, "It's in the Prophecy."

By noon, we left the people of Norton and headed north to Pickering. The festive mood of the morning still filled the soldiers and the band of adventurers. I could see no reason to fear, for the day was sunny, and no army's dust followed us. We traveled north towards Angus' country and away from the Red Master. The Orange and Black armies we left at the battle of York had joined us on our march to Berwick the previous night.

The Black army was at the front of the column with the Black Lord in the lead. Robina and I rode alongside him; she related to him stories about our adventures. He turned to me, "Jonathan, tell me about your world."

I smiled. "No one has asked me that. My world is different, yet the same. People are alike. There are the average people who work, have children and scrape out an existence for themselves. Then there are the rich and powerful who control the others. In my world, it's done with technology and commerce. We have machines to do what your magic does. We transport objects from place to place in wagons like carts, just much bigger and faster. In your world exclusively the most powerful use magic, in my world most people use technology."

We spoke about the similarities and the differences for some time then he gazed toward the sky. "Do you see that up there close to the hills in the north? It looks like two, no three, giant birds."

I peered up into the sky, and I could see only little spots moving towards us. He saw me straining and said, "Use your extended vision spell. You'll see them better." The Black Master appeared grim, intense concentration etched across his face. "My stars, it's something this land hasn't seen in a millennium." He stopped for emphasis. "It has to be a dragon; no it's three of them."

I stared at the dragons with my magic eyes, and sure enough they looked like the spitting image of what dragons appeared like in children's picture books. "Do they breathe fire?" I whispered loud enough for all to hear, but to no one in general.

Robina answered, "The ones that used to live in Britain did, but who knows about these." as we gawked at them. They approached us at incredible speeds as if they had jet engines. I rode closer to Robina remembering Farica's words. The three dragons came at us like fighter planes strafing a column of infantry. I yelled as they came out of the sky, "Scatter." I edged Robina's horse to the left side across the road and saw Arthur go right. The original dragon spewed fire straight down the column. Looking back I stared in horror at twenty of my infantry burst into flames and those that survived ran in every direction.

The second dragon dove from the sun to do his damage upon the Orange Army. I dismounted and stood near the center on the road and cast a spell to tear the creature apart. It came closer and closer to me, yet the spell hadn't taken effect yet. I continued to repeat the magic but still nothing occurred. The creature glared at me, and his fire descended from the sky right at me. I dove to the ground, and the fire singed my hair, and my clothes ignited. I rolled across the road and tried to smother the fire. I felt a ton of water hit me and heard Robina's yell.

"Johnny, are you all right? Johnny, talk to me."

"Thank god you splashed me with that water. Was that magic water? I felt myself burning up and then ice water all over me."

She peered down at me and smiled. "Thank the gods."

The first dragon attacked again. It didn't even bother with the front of the column, but attacked the wagons incinerating the horses pulling them. The Tartan Army took the brunt of his flames.

Once I regained my feet, I appraised our force and the disposition of the column. It was shambles. Burning bodies lay scattered on the road. I called for Arthur of Wales. "Why didn't my magic stop the dragons?"

He sighed. "Dragons are from a time before we discovered magic. They are ancient creatures; magic has no effect on them. We have to kill them the old-fashioned way with swords and arrows. We'll need cunning and luck. They never attack in threes. They're a solitary animal. Even when they mate they only stay together for less than five minutes or that's what the legends say."

I scanned the lands around our force. "We need a defensive position to make our stand.

The road is a killing zone. See those rocks off to the west?" I pointed to a rocky outcropping. "If we can make it there we may stand a chance."

Edward of York over heard me and agreed, "Yes that's our only chance, let's go." We mounted and rode as fast as our enchanted horses could gallop onto the rocks. The army followed at magic double time, but it wasn't quick enough.

Beth shot her bow from the saddle as the dragons made their second pass. Her arrow hit the lead creature in the thigh of the back leg. To our horror, the dragon pulled the arrow out of its flesh with its beak. Then it burned the arrow in midair. In a fit of anger, it flamed another column of the Black infantry.

The other two dragons caused more havoc as soldiers by the dozen burned trying to reach cover. The dragons flew back up in the sky regrouping for their next strafing of our position. I searched my mind to remember how the army dealt with fighter attacks on the infantry. I decided we needed anti-air-missiles. Even so, our bows and arrows didn't have the power to knock them out of the sky. In the rocks, we had a better chance.

The first dragon made its next attack. As it came in it had to fly low. The leader of the Black army and I waited on a rock outcropping at the front of the rocky ground. We stood on the highest point and the roughest area on the hill. The dragon came in low, and I attacked it with my sword as it flew over. My attack targeted its underbelly. I thrust my sword up and flew the twenty feet to puncture its belly. The animal went wild, and swooped low to scrape me and my sword off him. I twisted the sword, and the dragon turned and spat fire at me.

Arthur of Wales swung his sword at the head of the dragon as I still held on to my sword embedded in the creature's belly. His blow pierced the dragon's eye and tore half the scales off the dragon's face. The scream that escaped the wounded dragon was ear shattering. The pain the animal suffered had to be unbearable. It breathed fire that ignited the air right into the space occupied by the Black Master.

CHAPTER SEVENTEEN

I WATCHED IN HORROR AS THE FLAMES LICKED UP THE LEFT SIDE OF
the Black Master's body. I could smell the burning flesh and the screams
of Arthur as he made one final slash at the dragon. I couldn't keep my eyes
away from the burning Black Lord, or his last attack on the dragon. I gasped
in horror as everything slowed down, and I watched in slow motion as he
gouged out the dragon's remaining eye. The mythical creature was blind
and wild with pain. It crashed into a rock outcropping and fell heavily to the
ground. I jumped at the last moment as the dragon broke its neck in the fall.

I ran to Arthur of Wales and rolled him in my cloak to extinguish the
flames. He still cried in agony, but once he realized it was me, he said, "Did
we get that demon? Is it dead?"

I softly grasped his burned right hand in mine. "Yes, my lord, you killed
him." As I spoke to him, I also tried to cast a spell to save him. The first hex
was to relieve his pain. The second started to lay new skin and flesh on his
charred body. I gave a sigh of relief. He was coming back.

He gazed up at me with a look of futility. "No, my son, I can feel your
workings, but I'm not injured by mortal man or beast. This wound is fatal;
you can't heal the damage."

"No, my magic is good. I learned from your daughter and from the
ancient book. My spells are strong and powerful."

He squeezed my hand. "Yes, I feel how strong you are. My physical
wounds are healing. The flesh is back and the pain is gone, but my soul is still
burning and there is no magic that can save me."

"Tell me what to do! Tell me what spell I should use. Hurry, I can save you!"

"My daughter was right. You are the best among the best. You will fulfill
the Prophecy. You don't know defeat, yet you are compassionate. You are a

warrior. I saw you attack that dragon with no fear. No one can save me. All you can do is protect my daughter. Love her, and care for her as I would."

Then he stopped talking, and his eyes rolled up into his head. I still held his hand and felt for a pulse. His heart was beating slowly and faintly. I heard him take a deep breath, and then his eyes came back and focused on me. "Even though my heart beats I'm dead, I have little time. I will give you a wedding present to carry all your life. Your magic is not only what you have learned, but it is innately part of your soul. I sense you are a true wizard. I'm going to transfer to you my knowledge and wisdom of the Order of the Black Masters. On the death of each master, he transfers to his successor the experience and learning of all masters to the new master. I give you that responsibility."

I breathed in heavily, and my eyes glazed over. I remembered a spell, one I saw in the Red Master's book. As I sensed the Black Master's last breath, I pulled every thought every brain cell of knowledge he ever had into me. Not just magic, but everything he thought, his whole conscious and unconscious mind I snatched from him as he died. The dead Black Master's lips moved. "My Emperor, death has no bounds for you. I live."

Before I could reply, Robina was standing beside me, her smooth features twisted in horror as she stared down at her father and me. "Father, what has happened?" I knew I had repaired his wounds; my magic powers fixed his physical damage. However, I knew; the body would no longer rise from the ground. The beast consumed his soul and stole his life.

The Black Master's voice echoed in my ears, but didn't come from the corpse's slack mouth. "Daughter, I love you but I no longer have the spirit of life."

She yelled in pain. "Father, I sense—No, no father." She threw herself on him. "I just got you back. You can't die. I won't let you." She closed her eyes, and her face took on a scrunched up appearance. She was concentrating so hard she almost passed out. I could tell she was using magic to bring him back from the pit of death.

She turned to me. "What happened?"

"The dragon burned his left side, but I healed him. He told me his soul was dying."

I shivered throughout my body. I knew he finally passed. My whole head felt like it expanded. The pain came and overtook me for a few seconds and floated away. Finally, I heard the Black Master's voice within my mind. "It's done. Whatever spell you used worked. I am a permanent resident in your brain. I have no soul. I have no place to reside but in you. Our spirits are one. You have saved me from oblivion. You now have me for better or worse. We are one in body and soul."

I blinked trying to recover, but the voice continued. "I can't direct your mind or your body in any way. I can only advise you. If you can do magic or other skills you couldn't before that's because you have tapped into my experience and knowledge. I'll always be with you." Then he paused, and I sensed an uncomfortable feeling in my mind. "I have to confess I have heard of this spell before, but no wizard had the power to succeed. No one has ever survived this transference in the last nine hundred years. Two entities and one soul, I hope it doesn't destroy both of us."

Robina was crying and pounding on my chest. "He's gone, and I couldn't tell him how I feel. Oh, Johnny, it's so unfair. It's so unfair."

Before I could tell her what her father did, the second dragon attacked. He flew over us but flamed the army. I cursed as the dragon incinerated one after another of the soldiers. That's when my mind found the answer to our problem. "Beth, Sarah, come here fast."

Seconds later, the three of us planned our strategy in the dirt and Beth conjured up the material we would need, while Sarah and I worked out the science for the construction. Robina held her father's body, while the Black Master talked to me incessantly about the plan and how science mystified him.

Sarah asked, "How hot are the dragon's flames?"

Beth asked, "How far can he shoot them?"

Sarah shook her head. "We need to know what gasses he is expelling to cause the flames. Does he have other ways to kill other than his breath?"

I piped up, "He has claws, sharp teeth and a vicious looking tail. He's big enough to pick up a man and fling him back to the ground from fifty feet. I think that would be a good way to kill us."

Beth sighed. "Conjure up the equipment we have some testing to do before we kill that son of a bitch."

When the next dragon attacked we had our experiment ready, unfortunately his blitz killed two more of the soldiers. However, we had the data we needed. The three of us stood on the highest peak waving our hands to attract the attention of the other dragon. He swooped in order to incinerate us. The fire came in fireballs that almost knocked us down. Nevertheless, we stood our ground.

Beth's muffled voice reached my ears. "Shit, that's scary."

Sarah replied. "Beth, you're a genius. These suits took that thousand degrees and didn't melt, but I feel the heat now."

Beth yelled back, "We have thirty-five seconds before we have to remove them, or we'll fry inside. Here he comes again. He's plunging right at us like a dive bomber. Is everyone ready?"

We set up our huge bow and placed our aluminum arrow with the poison tip. The magical bow had guided targeting. We waited until the animal reached its flaming range. That's when it opened its mouth to spray us with hell-fire. It gave us a perfect shot into its vulnerable insides; his scaly skin did not protect his innards. The poison would enter his bloodstream so much faster from piercing into his palate. Sarah released the arrow.

"Oh, my God," yelled Beth. We ran down from the rocks into any crevasse we could find. The dragon crashed into the ground in the middle of our position, landing on top of me. I lay in a small natural crevice in the rock. The dragon wheezed. I felt the heat from the suit building up and the weight of the struggling dragon on top of me. It rose and fell towards the left of me. The screams from the dying animal were terrifying. As I scrambled to my feet and tore off the suit. The dragon looked right at me, the arrow still embedded in his mouth. I could tell it had thought that I had shot the arrow. It had enough life to swat at me with his front legs. I tried to move away from it. Nevertheless, the beast's claws now fully extended cut across my chest just barely reaching my skin.

I heard Arthur in my ear. "His claws are sharp, but not poisoned. Just don't let him breathe on you."

I looked into the dragon's eyes. I saw the hate. It turned his head to flame me or just breathe the gas on me. I could tell it had me. I struggled to find my sword and in desperation swung it towards the beast. I swung at the dragon with my first my swing cutting off its arm that slashed my chest. It turned just to my left. I slashed again and this time my sword bit through its scaly hide. Buffoon ripped open its throat spewing dragon blood all over me. His blood mixed with mine from the claw wound.

Arthur yelled in my mind, "I feel the dragon blood. It's mingling with yours. Legend tells us that once dragon blood combines with a warrior's the man's strength increases a hundred fold. We are invincible." His words reverberated in my mind. "We are invincible."

I climbed back to the top of the outcropping to find the others. Sarah took one look at me. "Christ, Jon, what happened to you, you're covered in blood." She wiped the blood off my chest. "That damn dragon sliced you up good."

I looked down and blood bubbling out of my wound. She grabbed my right hand in hers then taking the middle finger of her other hand ran it across my chest. "Jesus, this will take time to heal."

I watched the wound come together, and the blood stopped flowing. In a few seconds, she sealed the wound. I looked down and there was no blood, no scar, and no pain. I winked at her and exclaimed, "You're a miracle worker you healed me."

Sarah's eyes bulged from her head. "Holy crap, that's not supposed to happened. Robina told us the spell would stop the bleeding and leave a messy scar for some time before it would disappear. It's like it healed a hundred times faster than it should. What have you been up to, Jonathan?"

I told her about the dragon blood, and that led to the Black Master residing in my head.

Beth looked at me with amazement. "That's just too weird to believe. It's like Bones and Spock in Star Trek."

I knew what she meant. "Yeah, but he talks to me. I can access his memory, and all the past masters before him. It's scary, but interesting at the same time. He talks to me and gives me knowledge I need to know. It's like having a telephone in my head."

Sarah laughed. "We have that already." Then she spoke to my mind, "See. We are telepathic with our magic. How's that different from talking to Arthur in your head?"

I didn't reply. He did, "Sarah; you can hear me, can't you? Once you're in Jonathan's mind you're in my mind as well. That's how I can talk to you. I can even see you through Jonathan's eyes. Thanks for fixing him up. It's true about the dragon's blood and how he is now much stronger"

Sarah jumped away from me. Her eyes dilated to the max. "Holy shit; he is in your head. Jesus, that's impossible. I saw his body even after you repaired him. He was dead. Robina has taken him back to the trees. She is preparing him for cremation. Is that really you Arthur?" He did not reply, but she knew it was him.

Both the Black Master and I reacted in the same way, "Damn; we have to get to Robina. She must be in hell right now."

Sarah and Beth re-armed the bow and donned their firefighting suits to await the return of the last dragon. I left them to locate Robina. I found her in a grove of oak trees preparing to cremate her father's remains. My memory told me this was the tradition of her people. No, not my memory, it's the memory of the Black Master who now resided in my brain. He laughed at me.

"Yes, Jonathan, you know all I know, and you can't get rid of me. I've been poking around in your head too. Not only are you a scientific genius, you're a randy individual aren't you; especially with my daughter."

I blushed and felt crimson with embarrassment. "Stop it. Some knowledge is better unknown."

Then I realized I could block him out of some of my thoughts, if I drifted into a dream state.

He laughed. "No, my Emperor, your being naughty you have blocked me out of your personal thought and memories. We must share everything if we are to rule the universe."

I laughed, "no, we don't my feeling for your daughter is well-known, but my bedroom antics with her are off limits." Then I realized what he said, "The universe, no one told me that. What do you mean?"

"Well search my mind and find out." Then he added. "No, on second thought that's not a good idea." I felt a blinding headache then it vanished. "I blocked off the Prophecy from you. If you need some information, I can retrieve it later."

I looked amused, "So you have secrets from me as well. I guess that's alright, therefore keep out of my private life." Before I could continue my inner conversation, Robina wrapped her arms around me and said, "Hold me, I feel so lost."

Angus, Edward of York and Farica gathered around us. I held Robina close to me, and the others listened as I told her. "You have your father's body in front of you. I repaired his body the best I could, but the dragon had taken his soul."

Farica gave a sigh and said a little prayer. Then she looked at me with a knowing glance, and I continued. "Your father transferred his memory into me like the Masters do when they pass on the mantle to the next Master."

Edward nodded. "Yes, I have all the memories of the dead masters."

"But I did something more. I transferred his conscious mind into me." I let that sink in for a few moments.

Edward broke the silence. "That's impossible; no one has done that in nearly a millennium. The last time... Oh mother of god, if I ever had doubts, they are gone. It was at Berwick when it previously happened during the time the Wizard Council gave the Prophecy."

Robina's expression changed from mourning, to disbelief, and finally to hope. "Is it true Johnny, is my father within you?"

I nodded and told her, "Speak to me telepathically."

She entered my mind. "How can it be? It's impossible, Johnny. It's just inconceivable I'm preparing his body for the final journey."

I didn't respond. The Black Master's voice echoed in my skull, "Robina, nothing's impossible now that the Emperor has arrived. He makes anything possible, and I stayed to see how it will all work out."

They talked about ten minutes, and I just listened holding her hand and caressing her. I felt like an intruder, even though he was me, and I him. I just enjoyed being with her and making her happy, even if her father lurked inside my mind.

That night we camped beside the rock outcropping. We collected the dead and cremated them with the Black Lord's body. The last dragon never returned. The wagons needed new horses, so in the late-afternoon Angus took ten riders to buy what we needed. We slept beneath the stars in the glow from the burial fires. We gave thanks that we had survived another of the Red Master's attack on our lives. Hundreds of our soldiers had died, as the Black Master had done in the attack. We mourned the dead and celebrated our survival.

The morning brought a warm sunny day. I sent the Black Army to sweep our rear and to head back to Wales to tell of the happenings. Before they left, I had a heart to heart with the general, while actually the Black Master spoke to him through me. The general was to take orders back to the council.

"General Jones, you're to understand the Emperor is now the leader of our clan. If he calls on you, or any of our people, you are to obey him as if the order came from me. As you see I'm now him, and he me. If he calls on you and yours, remember it's me, your Master." The general nodded and the Black army left.

Six hundred and fifty Tartan and Orange soldiers and the seven of us moved up the road towards Pickering on our way to the coast.

The sky darkened. The ground moved slightly at first, just a light rocking sensation. Then it heaved. I yelled to Sarah, "Feels like a good old California quake."

Beth yelled back, "We're in England, there's no San Andreas Fault here. It's the Red Master."

The shaking continued then the earth started to split open in front of us. I watched as the land to push up and molten rock spewed out of the earth.

"Fire and damnation," muttered Farica, "it's going to test us."

Angus stamped his foot on the shaking ground. "That loony Red Master is playing with the earth. He can't control it. He'll kill everyone."

Robina agreed. "He's playing with fire. Magic can change weather, control man and beast but the earth is too great a force for him or any of us to fool with."

Behind us the ground erupted in molten lava, isolating us. We stood on a small island of native rock with smoke, hot steam, ash and lava in front of us and behind. The air was now super sizzling. The odor of brimstone filled our nostrils. It was hell.

I saw no natural way of escape, but we had magic so there must be a way to overcome Vulcan the god of volcanoes. I asked Edward, "This is your land, is there not a place close by for us to hide?"

"There are the caves toward the west. They are large, but I fear the lava is flowing from them like it is to our north and south."

"What about to the east? What is there?"

He thought, "There's the old deserted Norman castle. It's built of solid stone, and it's on a high rock. The owners deserted it a few hundred years ago."

"On a hill you say, how high is it, and how far away?"

"Not far, maybe a couple of miles. It stands about two hundred feet above the surrounding land."

Angus spoke, "I knew that place. The castle's bewitched. No one can stay there overnight. The goblins and the ghosts will kill ya. It's no' a place for mortal men tae stay."

I started to laugh, Angus the most fearless man I knew, afraid of ghosts and goblins. What insanity. Then I remembered that this land is not like home. Maybe, no certainly, there were ghosts and goblins, and they did inhabit this place. To my surprise, Arthur spoke to me. "Yes, my lad, you're learning. The story about the dead is true. They will try to drive us from their homes. Remember you are the Emperor, everyone, even the ghosts know of our coming. They will be wary of you. Do we have a choice?"

I breathed the air and realized we didn't have an alternative. The super-heated atmosphere, now saturated with deadly gases would soon make it impossible for us to breathe the air, or walk the ground. The shaking continued, and with each violent upheaval, more lava covered the ground. Ash floated across the sky turning the blue sky into gray.

The column headed east to a safe haven from the red molten rock, or so we hoped. Each step we took we fought to breathe. The air was foul, and the ash started to land all around us like snow, but it was black, and it was hot. The animals bayed like sheep and tried to run, but we led them on. I noticed soldiers carrying their friends, and then one fell to the falling ash and after that another. I ordered the army to pick up their fallen comrades. One of the seven of us could magically repair their lungs. We would abandon no one.

The hell we faced an hour before had seemed like paradise compared with the hell in which we now lived. I found the castle through the blizzard of ash. The hill surrounding it looked un-climbable. I didn't see a road, and bramble and hawthorn trees covered the hill. I bowed my head in defeat, but Edward spoke to me.

CHAPTER EIGHTEEN

"THE WAY UP TO THE TOP IS FROM THE INSIDE. THERE'S A TUNNEL through the base of the hill that winds its way up to the castle. It's slow, but with the ash and the toxic gas, it would be advisable that we find it as soon as possible. I'm having trouble breathing." Then Edward of York coughed violently.

"Where's the entrance? I can't see at all with this scalding snow." I said squinting as if I were snow blind.

He blinked, trying to wash away the burning ash. "I don't know. I think it's on the north side on the hill. I've never been up there. I've had no reason none of my people go up to the place. It's just an old piece of history."

Sarah rode next to me. "I know where it is. I've been concentrating on it, and my sixth sense felt it. The tunnel is not far from here. It's hidden behind a hawthorn tree."

Even with magic, we searched for ten minutes before we discovered the opening. For our reward, we each received hundreds of puncture wounds from hawthorn thorns, but we cleared a path into the tunnel. Once inside, we realized it wasn't a tunnel, it was a natural cave. The ancient warriors who built the castle had widened the cave to make a road to the top of the hill. The ground rocked under us as we pulled the wagons and the troops into the cavern. All of us breathed a sigh of relief inside the mountain's protection.

Beth was huffing and puffing as we started to climb toward the top of the hill the rest of us were even worse. It was long ago since Beth was our couch potato. She now dedicated herself to be an Amazon, the best physical specimen of our team. She looked back to me and in a hoarse, voice said, "What a bitch, this mountain cave has a ten percent, if not fifteen percent incline. I'll be dead before we reach the top."

Sarah laughed. "It's not that bad, look at the horses; they're prancing up the hill."

Beth rolled her eyes. "Yeah, they have a spell on them. They don't feel any of the weight of the wagons full of gold."

Sarah giggled and said a few words under her breath.

"Jesus Sarah, what did you do to me? I feel like I'm floating."

Robina broke into the conversation. "She reduced your body weight so you only weigh thirty pounds. You now have more than enough energy to climb to the castle."

We climbed about a third of the way, following flaming torches on every wagon as guides up the tunnel. The air inside was fresh and had none of the foul smells of the outside. That's how I noticed we had a problem. Robina and I fell toward the back of the column wanting to be alone for a few minutes.

I smelled it first, then looked back and saw the red-hot flowing fire behind us. "Run!" Is all I said to Robina. She didn't even look back. She knew what was happening,

I heard Arthur talking to me. "Think, Jonathan, use your powers. All you need is a little time. Once you reach the castle everyone can help. Fire and ice, think of a twenty footwall of ice and then another."

I whispered, "I hear you."

Robina looked confused, "What did you say?"

"Oh, I was talking with your father. He said to make an ice wall behind us from where we stand to the liquid fire." We both cast a frozen water spell. It's hard to do on the run, but it became cold extremely cold. We raced up the hill until we crashed into the rest of the team. Out of breath but trying to explain what was behind us, I croaked, "Lava is coming up the tunnel. The cave must be a prehistoric lava chute or something." I took a deep breath and continued, "I blocked it with ice, but it will break through. It's only a matter of time before it reaches us. We have to hurry."

Our pace quickened, and half my mind watched the fiery rock burn through the ice. I gauged the castle was only a few hundred feet ahead of us. I felt a shaking on the ground then the world rocked back and forth, and finally I fell onto the ground. I had been through many earthquakes in California, but this shook like no other. The quake lasted five minutes. Holes opened on the floor, rocks fell from the ceiling, and finally the walls collapsed around us. We felt helpless; the dust-covered everyone and made visibility impossible. We communicated through telepathy and crawled forward. I reached a large rock pile blocking the tunnel. I heard cries and agonizing screams from behind me. I threw my mind out to read the consciousness of the injured.

I cried in pain as I felt their distress. Many of my army died, others survived with crushed limbs. I felt the last thoughts of many of the soldiers as they succumbed to the tons of rocks. The worst pain came from the few at the end of the column who couldn't move because of the debris. The lava was closing in on them. The heat and gas were a slow brutal death.

For each of the injured my mind touched, I cast a spell to save them, with many I succeeded, some I lost and a few died before I could find the solution to their agony.

Robina's mind spoke to me and her father. "We must find a way out of the tunnel. I've tried to move the rock slide, but a magical force is holding the rocks in place."

I was learning a lot about myself. My pessimism overtook me. When I found myself trapped inside the cave I was terrified even more than with the molten lava. Blind, gasping for air and about to die by a creeping boiling rock, without even being able to run, froze my mind. I felt Arthur scolding me, "You are the Emperor, and you never give up, think how we can find a way out. Remember, my life depends on your survival, so does my daughter's and your unborn heir. Fight, never give up."

I felt Robina's hand in mine and her comforting voice, "We can make it. We've come this far; nothing can stop us." I took strength from her. I knew of the sacrifice many had made to get us this far. We needed to escape from the tunnel.

Robina joined hands with me, and added her strength to the spell I cast. I winked at her with confidence I did not feel. "I can get us out of here." I could feel her power, Arthur's power, and mine unite. The cave shuddered and then rocks started to fall around us. The ground to our right crumbled and finally opened into a path. Rocks smashed down and turned to gravel. Eventually I saw a speck of daylight shining through the cave wall. It became bigger and finally a hole opened at the side of the mountain. The dust settled as I ran toward the opening. I looked out and watched lava surrounding our hill, but the slope going up to the castle didn't look steep. I laid eyes on the castle walls as I craned my neck out of the hole near the top of the mountain. The fortress stood only about twenty yards away.

I yelled, "This way, everyone up here, hurry."

I climbed out first and started up the slope below the castle. The gentle slope I saw from the opening was much steeper. I had trouble climbing over the castle wall. I clung to the stones and started to circle the castle looking for a way in. The full team now followed me around the castle.

Halfway around the fortress Angus became impatient. "Let's just punch a hole in the wall and enter the damn place."

Edward of York shook his head. "No, we may need these stone walls. We'll find a gate. Every castle has a gate."

Angus glared at him. "Ma dear friend, this castle has nae road doon tae the plane below. It's entered frae inside. Why would they have a gate?"

Farica laughed. "No squabbling you two. I'll tell you why there's a gate somewhere on this wall. Feel under your feet. There's a cobblestone road. There must at one time have been a road up to the top, and we're now walking on it. If we follow it up, we'll find the gate."

I said, "Duh, how dumb are we? Nevertheless, let's hurry. That ash is getting thicker, and it's raining molten rock."

The entrance into the castle was like others that you see at the movies, a drawbridge over a moat. Over time, the moat had filled in and the only remnant of it was the foundation where the bridge ends sat.

"My God," exclaimed Sarah, "it's what I imagined the Sheriff of Nottingham's castle to look like. It's straight out of an Errol Flynn movie."

Farica said, "What's an Errol Flynn movie?" Sarah and I laughed; Farica looked nonplussed, but then added in a vexed voice, "Anyway. It doesn't look like the Sheriff of Nottingham's castle at all. His is considerably bigger and not in such a dilapidated condition. The Sheriff's style is a lot more modern."

Sarah agreed. "Yes you're right Farica, but one day if we ever return to our world, I'll show you what a movie is."

As we chatted Edward and Angus had lowered the drawbridge and opened the gate into the castle. They performed the simple magic involved even as they listened to Sarah's and my conversation with Farica. Edward asked, "What is a movie?"

I thought for a minute and then from my memory flashed a scene of *Robin Hood* with Errol Flynn on the castle wall. The darkness against the sky made the light I projected on the wall sparkle with color.

"Oh my," was Edward's only reply.

Robina's was much more intriguing. "My lord, your movie is like my magic, it is wonderful, what a tool of magic your movie is. I've written on walls with a hand as big as a horse, but this, it's like real life. Show us more."

My memory failed me, and the wall turned back to its dull gray self. "When we get inside and out of danger I'll show you more movies that I remember, and maybe Sarah and Beth can help. It would be an excellent diversion from the death we face out here."

The good condition of the interior of the castle surprised me. It took us almost ten minutes to bring all the survivors from the tunnel. We had twenty horses left, and they brought the wagons into the castle with the gold. Magic was the motivation for the horses.

I stared at the hole I had punched through to the surface. Minutes after the last soldier climbed out of the hole the hot magma started to pour outflow down the mountain side. The lava was like a river of burning rock flowing down the mountain, setting everything on fire as it poured like water towards the plain below which was covered in the same red hot lava. The smoke gushing out of the hole choked me. It surprised me that any of us had escaped the hell the Red Master unleashed on us.

The walled fortress which housed our depleted army stood as one of the most defensible havens in Britain. The sole problem was that the castle now sat at the top of a volcano. I could see from the battlements, even though the ash filled air, six vents of lava had sprung leaks on the hillside and one at most twenty feet from the walls.

Edward of York gazed over the land. "What power he has. I could never conceive of a wizard doing this. The energy and the mental stamina involved are incredible. Just one thousandths of this would take the whole wizardry of my Orange force."

I heard Arthur respond by speaking through me. "I know of this power. Its dark and it comes with a cost. No Master has dared to do what he has done in six hundred years. The Yellow Master used the power in uniting the kingdom, but we know the consequence. I fear my enemy will suffer the same fate."

I had no knowledge about the fate of the Yellow Master, or even that a Yellow Master ever existed. "Who is the Yellow Master, and what happened to him?"

I heard Sarah echo my questions. "I thought there were only Six Masters and two—, oh sorry Arthur, three of them are here. One is dead, and the Green and Red are chasing us."

Angus cleared his throat. "Sorry ma oot world friends, but at one time twelve Masters ruled different areas o' our land. The Yellow Master turned evil after ma clansmen butchered his whole family. He dabbled in the devil's magic, learned frae a far place called Greece. There's a rumor the Ancient Ones helped him. He traveled there an' then to Egypt. When he returned he devoted his life and soul to Isis."

"Isis, Egypt and Greece, we have them in our world too. Egypt is an extremely ancient place, and the religion of Isis is as old and mysterious. This is getting interesting." I said in awe.

Angus continued. "Well, no' for the Yellow Master. Isis an' the Ancient Ones had their revenge. For ten years he controlled all the land. Isis took his soul an' aged him, for each year ten clicked by. The Ancient Ones crumbled his castle, destroyed his cities an' lay waste tae a' his land. Since then yellow connotes evil an' bad omen. If you notice, nobody wears yellow clothing."

I couldn't help myself. "What magic did the Yellow Master leave that the Red Master found to do this havoc." I pointed to the lava and the ash. As I spoke the earth shook again throwing us down to the stone platform on the parapets. I watched as part of the castle started to twist and shift in front of me. Finally large blocks of stone started to fall from the castle.

As suddenly as it started the earthquake stopped. "Christ, are we ever going to get out of this hell?" I shouted to no one in particular.

To my surprise, Edward of York replied, "He can't sustain this spell for much longer. He has probably aged five years since we last saw him. We have to take cover. He'll have one more attempt to destroy us."

I looked at him with skepticism in my eyes. "I didn't know you could read the future."

Angus and Edward laughed, "No. I just know the power of Isis's magic from the writings of Harold the Scribe of Berwick. The Isis power lasts only as long as the sun is in the sky. Look on the horizon. We have only an hour before the sun sets."

We found our way back to the great hall of the old castle. The surviving soldiers set up a defensive position with the great hall as the hub of our defense. Farica used her magic and prepared soup, bread and wine for everyone

A bitter cold raced through the castle. Everyone felt it. The smell of death followed the eerie cold wind. Edward shook his head, "I told you ghosts haunt this place. We can't stay here. The evil ones will kill us."

I felt loneliness and danger and them. I observed images floating in the air like wisps of smoke. Incorporeal creatures carried axes, swords and other weapons of war.

Robina stood by my side uttering a spell and for her effort a spirit came to her and bit her finger leaving the flesh flayed back to the bone.

Farica rushed to her and administered one of her medical potions to repair the damage. Robina, still in pain, said through gritted teeth. "We have to leave, they are beyond

magic. They are evil."

I let my mind drift with the wisps of fog that floated in the great hall. I found an active mind. It was like nothing I had ever encountered, but a mind nonetheless. "I am Jonathan from the Prophecy. Who are you?"

To my surprise the wisp spoke to me, "I'm George, the third Master of the Blue realm. The last Blue Master. I know the Seers foretold of your coming. I bow to you. Is this your army?" The wisp of fog spread thought out the room encompassing all my force.

"Yes, Blue Master. I request that you allow me to take possession of your home and use it as my fortification. May I enlist your help in my ordeals? With that he disappeared; and I never saw or heard from him again. Yet I knew he guarded this outpost of freedom for me. With that problem faced, I had a hundred more to take care of before nightfall.

It was during the meal the sentries yelled the warning. The magma started to flow from all sides of the castle encircling it. The castle began to sink. I felt the first jolt. The mountain's interior had turned to molten rock. Slowly the castle began to sink into a crater of magma.

The wall in the center courtyard started spewing out lava. I watched as ten soldiers turned to stone in front of me. Edward yelled, "Everyone up to the turrets, up to the high ground. The sun is starting to set."

Another earthquake hit us. The ground surrounding the hill started to explode shooting huge plumes of liquid rock into the air and more ash than the sky could hold. It was a scene from Dante's Inferno. My eyes recorded it, but my brain couldn't understand it. A wave of liquid rock hit the wall of the castle splashing death on a platoon of soldiers on the parapet at the east side of the wall.

The ash rained down and I caught sight of four more soldiers still standing but turned into statutes like those found at Pompeii. The seven of us had climbed to the highest turret under a rock roof with arrow slits for windows. Even there the burning hot ash floated through and piled itself on the floor with inches accumulating every few seconds.

"Oh, Jesus," I heard myself yell as the whole castle dropped ten feet in one second, then without warning it dropped another ten feet. I looked down and the bottom floor was now under molten lava.

The air was thick, my lungs burned with the super-heated air. The ash started to clog my breathing. I fell to my knees into the hot ash. I could feel the life starting to seep out of me.

"Jonathan, get back on your feet. Think: you can get us out of this. In your brain you know how. Get up."

I looked around and the rest of the team was in worse shape than I was. I wondered who was talking to me.

Then I heard it again. "You're the Emperor, remember you have the power to save everyone, get up and fight." The voice was reverberating in my head. "Jesus," I whispered, "It's you Arthur." In my panic I had forgotten he was still with me. "What can I do?"

The voice just said, "Look at the sun, it is dropping behind the horizon. Think fast and you can save everyone, but you must act now. Just think."

I struggled to my feet. A large explosion almost burst my eardrums and the molten rock crashed against the turret encrusting the lower parts with at least three feet of new rock. I smelled the sulfur and the burning wood of the interior of the castle. I choked again on the ash and fell to my knees trying to regain my breath.

CHAPTER NINETEEN

MY MIND DUG DEEP INTO ITS MEMORY AND LOGIC. IF I HAD SCIENCE working for me what machine could I use to save my team and soldiers? My head was spinning, I could think of nothing. It flashed through my mind. How was I going to save my trapped company of soldiers? It came to me in a lightning bolt. A helicopter rescue mission would save all them. I looked outside and moaned, not even a fleet of helicopters could fly in this ash. If science had no answers, then magic had to solve my problem. Arthur was shouting at me, but all his ideas lacked any chance of success.

Every second I knew death came closer. Then like all great ideas, it came from the subconscious and just popped into my mind. The audacity of the plan made my head ache and my stomach turn. I took a deep breath and searched my memory for the spell. I heard Arthur begging me not to put my plan into effect. "It won't work. You'll kill us all, Jonathan, look at reason. It's impossible."

Death is death, if it didn't work, we would all die anyway. I cast the spell and then another. I concentrated with every fiber of my being. I felt a tingling in my body. My ears rang and eventually nothing was audible. The strong smell of brimstone faded until not even my sweat was perceivable. Next a blinding light came from my mind and like bricks, built a wall blotting out my vision. Finally, inch by inch my body went numb, and I stood with no senses telling me how the outside world had reacted to my spells.

I don't know how long I stood oblivious to everything, but scalding droplets falling from the sky awoke me. Robina was holding me tight, and the others looked on in awe. Angus spoke first. "Jonathan, how did yae doo it? Ma God, it's a miracle."

I heard Robina reply for me. "No, it's magic, the best magic, pure and powerful."

My vision had returned, and I looked around me. The hot droplets that brought me back to life turned out to be rain, a deluge drowning all the fires in the castle. I looked at the ground below and took in a gasp of air. It worked. The castle was no longer on the top of the hill. It was floating through the air over the melting landscape below. The sun into the west was setting behind the horizon, with half of its body sunk under the earth as if it caused the rock around it to boil.

"Holy Shit," escaped from Sarah's lips. "Look at Jonathan's hair." Everyone stared at me, and I didn't understand the amazed looks on their faces. Finally, Sarah told me. "Jon, your hair has turned white. Not just colorless, but a brilliant white and your eyes, the blue is dramatic." She just gawked at me. "You are the same, yet you're so different."

Robina squeezed my hand, and seemingly from nowhere she offered me a mirror. "Look my love; you are now the image of the Emperor whom the Prophecy described to us. Every child will recognize you as the Emperor."

Arthur prodded my mind and from his memory showed me a picture that of the image of the Emperor, the Monks at Berwick had drawn nine hundred years before. I compared the mental image to the image upon the mirror; they looked identical. "What happened to me? Can anyone tell me what's going on?"

Edward took his time and then said. "It's your power. None of us could've done what you just did. The use of the power has changed you. With no preparation or special spells or black magic, or even a secret ancient scroll to help you; you levitated the castle and moved it away from the erupting volcano. Not only did you do that, but you removed all the molten rock from the castle. You even put the castle back to its previous glory of ten centuries ago." He looked at the others. "Could any of you have done that?"

They all shook their heads. Farica smiled. "This is the Prophecy, no one could do what you have done. Nothing can stop you."

I frowned. "That's not true. The Red Master's powers are greater. Look around you, look what he can do. He almost destroyed us today. What is going to happen tomorrow? I don't see us reaching Berwick."

Farica wouldn't let me say another word. "Today has weakened the Red Master. He is not long for this world; just as you have proven your power his is on the wane. Yours is a righteous power. He has shown his evil dark side. Look at all the land around us. Five miles in every direction he has scorched the earth. Twenty-five square miles of volcanic rock, he has destroyed the fabric of the land. He will pay. The Berwick Chronicles tell us so." She gazed out the window of the turret, "Look. The sun has set. Isis has departed the battlefield, and the Red Master's attack has ended with the last ray the sunlight. Find a good piece of land and set this castle down. That will be the location from which you'll rule your Empire."

The next morning Robina and I awoke in our new home's master bedroom. Sarah named the castle Camelot. Beth conjured up a large round table where we sat eating breakfast. All the others relished the idea of such a unique idea of equality. Beth and Sarah just winked at me and laughed.

The only one to understand the humor was Arthur, who sang in my ear songs from the Broadway Play which he'd found in my mind. He then fell silent as he dug deeper finding all he could on King Arthur and the Round Table.

"If the Chronicles are right, I'm King Arthur of this magical kingdom of Camelot."

I blinked a couple of times. "Hey, I'm the Emperor, and you're just renting a bit of space in my brain. What do you mean you are King Arthur?"

He sighed, "Just a little joke. It's Edward that will be king. I'll be with you wherever that may be."

I tried to have him clarify his words, but breakfast turned into a festival. All the people of the nearby villages came to see me and the new castle that had landed out of nowhere. Minstrels, clowns and even an acting troupe arrived. Breakfast stretched into the afternoon. I finally took Robina for a walk along the battlements to appraise our new lands. To my wonder, the abandoned fields surrounding the castle now sported a village. Pubs, blacksmith shops, stores, cottages and buildings of every nature and kind spread out below me.

Edward strutted up the stairs with a cocky smile on his face, and said, "While you ate and listened to the minstrels, Angus and I built a village for our castle. Many of my old subjects came to see the Emperor of Prophecy and stayed to serve the castle and make a better life for themselves. The farmers are happy as well; they now have a place to set up their market. With the treasure, we have we can provide well for our subjects."

I looked at the joy on his face. "My friend, I'm no administrator. I'm a scientist with a little ability in magic. You've shown me that in the time it takes me to eat a meal, you can organize and make a kingdom. I appoint you my administrator with the rank of King of the South. Now all you have to do is conquer everything south of this place. Defeat the Red Master and bring peace and prosperity to your new kingdom."

We stayed in the castle a week. Every day more and more people arrived, many displaced from the lava fields. Others heard we could provide a safe place in Camelot to live. The town now had over five thousand inhabitants, and a large city wall surrounded the houses. To my surprise soldiers of all areas of Britain came to serve in my army. Our numbers swelled, and all received a fair monetary bonus for joining my force. Nevertheless, many refused it and joined only to defeat their old master.

On the night of the seventh day, we had a Thanksgiving dinner. The castle now had seven of us and three hundred of the townspeople all at the banquet. I had strewn the hall with the banners of our exploits, the battle flags of our victories, the flag of the defeated White Master, and the Red Master's flag. In the place of honor flew the Orange, Black and Tartan flags. Trumpeters announced my arrival at the hall with Robina by my side. I found the pageantry exciting. We drank and entertained our three hundred guests with a magical evening. I showed movies on the wall with Beth and Sarah helping. The crowd understood the fantasy movies. However, they were disturbed by the science fiction and war dramas. The works of Shakespeare enthralled the crowd. By midnight, my mind ran out of clips to present yet the audience wanted more; that's when I start showing cartoons, which brought down the house.

I thought of the first time I held Farica, and I turned red for the hundredth time. She and Edward had formed a liaison which the night before I had legitimized by marrying them. My authority came from me. As the Emperor, I made the laws, appointed the justices and ruled the church. I still didn't understand the religion, yet as its head, I dictated dogma and policy.

At the wedding, I watched Sarah. She lost me and then Nelson. She looked so lonely I felt sorry for her. I had Robina and Beth had Angus. Sarah the warrior princess had no one. As I pondered this sad subject, the bride came over to me. "Don't despair, your friend Sarah will find happiness; not here, but somewhere and soon." Then she giggled as only bride can. "When are you going to make an honest woman out of Robina? She is showing, soon you'll be a father."

That thought scared me. I shuddered, but said, "If I won't spoil your special day I would do it right now in front of the assembled folks here."

Without batting an eye, she raised her voice, and in her Mother Superior, demeanor called us together. "The Emperor is going to marry his betrothed tonight. In honor of my wedding, I will preside, and the ceremony will take place in half an hour."

True to her word half an hour later, she magically transformed the great hall into an Emperor's wedding cathedral, fitting for the greatest magnificent wedding ever in this magic land. I was decked out in my finest military dress uniform and Robina in the most beautiful gown of white and gold with every precious stone imaginable adorning her. I looked at her in awe. Robina took my breath away as the most beautiful woman in the world. The goddess Venus could not look as gorgeous and sexy as Robina did that night. Sarah had dressed her and added all the special twenty-first century tricks. That night will always stay in my mind as the best memory I will ever have.

Arthur encouraged me throughout the ceremony. I needed him with me. I needed him to accept me. I needed him to give his daughter to me. I needed him as a friend to tell me I was good enough for her. I needed him to approve.

Our column left Camelot at ten the next morning. In the great hall, we said our good byes. Farica held on to Edward of York. I thought it would take a crowbar to separate them. She whispered into his ear, but the acoustics of the hall allowed everyone to overhear her muttering. "Darling be careful, we haven't tamed the Red Master yet. He still has big teeth. I know the Chronicles by heart, but I don't want to lose you. After my time cloistered away, you have ignited the fire in me."

What horrors awaited us at Berwick flashed through my mind as I smiled at Farica as she said her good-byes to Edward. I took Farica's hand and said, "We've got to go. Edward will be fine. He has fifty of his soldiers and more are coming every day. You must lead us to Berwick and tell us when we reach a milestone in our journey."

Our force left the castle much lighter and more mobile than when we came. Our baggage train consisted of only one wagon with our equipment and stores. We traveled with two hundred mounted soldiers whom I had dubbed knights. All wore magical armor with new black tunics with my coat of arms emblazoned on them. Our infantry consisted of one thousand trained soldiers.

We raced towards Scarborough and then north along the coast road. The sight of the North Sea gave me goose bumps. It felt so good with Robina at my side, the sun shining, and with the cool fresh sea breeze pushing against my chest. Sarah, Beth and I sang, I'm Henry the Eighth I Am. Angus and the rest had never heard it before, but they caught on fast to the words. We crossed paths with a battalion of the Red Master's guards just north of Whitby at a crossing of a small river. There were about fifteen hundred of them. We could make them out at two hundred yards, and they also had spotted us. Both groups urged their horses to a gallop, and then we drew swords and charged. It was our first battle as knights. The horsemen charged, and the infantry ran behind in tight formation. We started to yell, and everyone broke into the chorus of Henry the Eighth bringing the adrenaline pumping faster through our veins. At this point, of the attack, even if we wanted to stop it, we couldn't. I had bewitched the infantry who ran like gazelles, and the mounts that carried the knights flew as if they had the wings of Pegasus, faster and faster into battle. It takes my breath away even now thinking about the power of being on an enchanted charging stallion.

I led my knights into battle with my golden sword, Buffoon. I thought of calling it Rambo, because it killed without effort, but decided against that. However, Buffoon described, me not the sword, and I couldn't be a Rambo if I tried. The rest of my knights charged in one long line across the road. At fifty yards, we could see the scared faces of the Red Master's soldiers. Our swords shone upon their faces from the sun's reflection. I stopped my infantry a hundred feet behind to kill any of the Red Army that passed through my knights. My horsemen faced odds of seven to one. In any battle that isn't good. However, when they were charging us a hundred abreast, twelve deep; it wasn't a fair fight. Well, not for them, we had the advantage.

My sword clashed first with the leader of the Red force. He was six feet and on a horse as tall as mine. A crashing blow from Buffon severed the man's arm in one swing. That's all I saw. I was in combat. I feigned a head swing at the next horseman, then thrust under my opponent's raised arm. I felt the crash of my sword against his chain mail. I remember only swinging at the next attacker. The third cavalryman hit my breastplate a glancing blow. I saw his sword break in half. I drove my sword through his armor into his shoulder. The attackers retreated. My horse wanted to continue charging forward, but I pulled back on the reins. It reared up in the air and clawed the air with its front hooves. I looked down seeing fallen enemy soldiers dead at its feet.

Our first charge disrupted them. Two hundred Red soldiers and their horses strewed the battlefield with blood and gore blanketing the ground. Farica dismounted to tend to our five casualties. Just five of my soldiers suffered injuries and only one fatal.

I glanced over at Sarah, who had a look of rapture on her face and the blood from her enemies glistened on her sword. The battlefield gave her life meaning and definition.

I threw my mind out to listen to the new commander's plans. I received a shock. The Red Master's voice sounding much older projected from one of his wizards, "Use the enchanted arrows in the Da Vinci rapid firing arrow machine.

Da Vinci, how did he know about Da Vinci, and what was a rapid firing arrow machine? It didn't take me long to find out.

As we formed our line, ten wagons set up facing us with the Red Army's cavalry behind them. As we charged forward, the machines started spitting out arrows like bullets from a machine gun. Twenty of my men died before I yelled the order to fall back. The six of us used magic and cast a spell to revive our dead and injured and to regain their fighting status.

Angus shook his head. "The Red Master is violating every code of the Wizard community. " The disgust in his voice showed the contempt he held against the Red Master.

I glared at the wagons. "We have to eliminate his cavalry. If we attack, he'll just shoot us with the arrow machines as we approach."

Robina shrugged her shoulder. "Then we just won't approach. We set up a defensive position and let them attack."

I frowned. "They'll simply move the wagons up and shoot us down."

Angus looked over at the wagons, and said, "So then we merely destroy the wagons." A few seconds later, the wagons burst into flames, "Is that what you wanted?"

Arthur laughed and purred, "With generals like Angus. I need only relax and watch him destroy the Red Army. If ye need me simply ask." I could feel my belly jiggling as he laughed again.

Farica shook her head. "That's too easy. He has something else planned. That was just a feint to give us a false sense of security." She closed her eyes, and her brow wrinkled. "He must have a screen protecting his force. I can't penetrate it. It's strong. I can't read anyone's mind."

"Right," I said then thought. "We know it's a trap, but we have to play out the hand. He dealt us. As soon as we see his intention, we must adapt and use it to our advantage."

Beth hadn't said a word for the last few minutes, and finally spoke, "If he's not playing by the rules we have no way of knowing what he's going to do. We saw his power with the earthquakes and volcanoes. Out here with a large army, he could do almost anything. If we trade three of his soldiers for each of ours, we lose, even if it's five to one. I say we retreat and find another way to Berwick."

Sarah with eyes blazing put her hand up to stop all conversations. "This is war. If we don't defeat them now they will follow us until they have us trapped. We have to attack and wipe them out. Christ, they're a bunch of weasels. I've read their minds as I killed them."

I agreed with Sarah, but put my arm around Beth. "Sarah's right, we have to attack. We can't give up the initiative."

Then I turned back to the others. "This is the plan. We charge. When his army advances to meet us, we cut a trench line six feet deep and ten feet across in front of the galloping horses. The whole front will fall into the trench, and then we retreat to see what his next trick is. If we do that we never get within a hundred yards of his force. We must use magic and technology. Beth, can you conjure up a simple water cannon? It needs to have enough force to peel the flesh off the bone."

Beth's eyes fogged over for a few seconds, and then she replied, "Give me about ten minutes. I can work it out."

Ten minutes later, the attack began. Our force charged forward. The Red cavalry charged towards us. On my order, my wizards activated the spell. The first line of a hundred horses and riders fell into the trench. The next line stopped dead in front of the barrier. Beth drove her wagon forward and started hosing the enemy with her hydraulic weapon. The pressure was deadly. I watched as soldiers turned to mush under Beth's direction. Her water cannon killed more than three hundred of the Red Army's horsemen before they struck back.

Then a sound echoed through the air. I knew immediately what it was, but my soldiers and companions from this world had no idea. Many died still trying to understand the sound of sixteenth-century cannon fire.

CHAPTER TWENTY

"THE RED MASTER MUST BE DESPERATE IF HE IS RESORTING TO TECH-nology to fight us." The Black Master echoed in my head.

I had to do something before the Red Master destroyed my army. "Pull back our troops," I order to my commanders. Then I gave the same order to every soldier by telepathy. As they fell back, my stomach turned a somer-sault. I watched in terror as a unit of musketeers entered the battlefield. Two hundred Red soldiers discharged their muskets on masse just as another volley of cannon fire hit us. Beth and her water cannon took aim at the mus-keteers. The cannon fire missed our retreating cavalry. Instead it obliterated the wagon that Beth was standing on. I turned my horse in a violent jerk and rode as fast as I could to my retreating soldiers.

Sarah was covered in blood, and in horror screamed to me. "That bastard has cannons and muskets, where the hell did he steal them? This land is too low tech for that equipment. Anyway, I thought they despised technology."

As she spoke, the artillery shot another volley of explosives into our lines. Death lay all around me, even Sarah suffered from a musket ball wound. I roared inside. I channeled all my anger and blew out hot air from my lungs. Six hundred yards away my breath hit the line of cannons setting everyone on fire standing near to them and melting every barrel, so they drooped impotently to the ground.

Arthur coughed. "Holy father, I felt the power of your anger. I've never seen that done before. You used no spell, no potion. You just thought, destroy and kill and it happened. My God, you're all powerful."

I shook my head. "No, the Red Master has delved into my time to bring weapons to fight us with. He is going to stop us."

"No, Jonathan, he has done something that is against everything decent. He has searched the mind of one of your otherlanders and created weapons they have seen or studied. These are not of our world, but of yours." As I talked with Arthur, the Red Master pressed his attack. The cavalry dismounted and formed a skirmish line and marched double time firing their muskets every twenty paces. My troops dove for cover and lay motionless hugging the ground.

Once the bullets started to fly, I commanded my team of wizards to turn the bullets into snowflakes. The fluffy flakes drifted harmlessly to the ground. My wrath subsided, and I turned all the muskets into poisonous vipers to attack and kill the Red Master's troops. The musketeers tumbled to the ground writhing in pain.

I looked over the battlefield, and cried as hundreds of soldiers lay dead or dying. The waste of such brave men on both sides sickened me. Nevertheless, in my anguish, I stretched my mind to find the wizards of the Red Master who directed this attack. My pacifist feelings changed to aggression when I saw him dissecting Beth. Her mangled body lay on a wagon, and the wizard held a curved bladed knife and started to cut into Beth. I felt a shield around the wizard, a strong protection against magic, one I'd felt before outside Lancaster. I wouldn't let it stop me.

I picked up a small rock from the ground and visualized it as a slab from Stonehenge, but four times as big. Once I had that image in my mind, I transported it to three hundred feet above the wizard then dropped it on him. The shield didn't go above the wizard or Beth. His master only thought in two dimensions, not three. He died, crushed to death with his toadies, their bodies mingled with Beth's.

We wheeled our horses around and trotted back to the mayhem. Nine hundred soldiers lay dead or dying on the battlefield. Sarah and I knew there was no help for Beth; we had both tried to bring her back. Sarah's wound was easily healed but there would be a scar just below her right shoulder. "Hell, if I can still swing my sword all is well," she told me as I applied my magic to seal the wound.

Robina soothingly said, "I loved Beth too. She gave our team balance, and we'll all miss her zest for life. However, the ones on the field of battle need us now. We can save many of them if we work quickly."

Angus cried openly. He lost his love. "Not only hae most of ma kin died in this battle, but I hae lost the woman of ma dreams. The gentle Elizabeth died in this land o' death." He rode off to where her mangled body lay under the huge stone. He left us to deal with the horror of the battlefield.

We immediately jumped from our horses to give aid. Farica directed us to remove the living to the one side of the road and the dead to the other. We even sorted the horses similarly. The ones still breathing black or Red tunics, we carried them to the left shoulder of the road. The dead were dragged to the right shoulder. The wounded soldiers and horses fell to Robina to cure with her magic.

I still had the heat of battle burning in my gut. "Robina, how can you work like a surgeon on the Red Army soldiers after hacking them to pieces? They killed Beth. They don't deserve to live."

"I am a Master's daughter. I know soldiers only take orders. They are men; and like all men deserve to live. Wouldn't you want the same for your soldiers? I will save them all, ours and even the enemy. None of them deserves to die for obeying their general. Their horses were just doing what horses do."

Robina and Sarah treated the injured. Farica instructed me to make a potion for the dead. I stared at her, "They're dead. What do they need a potion for?" She just winked at me and told me to make it.

I started a large fire and mixed the ingredients that Farica carried in her saddlebag. She directed me to stoke the fires as hot as the oak would burn. Her next order surprised me. "Jonathan, melt fifty gold pieces in your brew." I look shocked, "The fire isn't hot enough"

She winked, don't worry Jonathan, I'll make it melt."

Following Farica's instructions I dragged the lifeless soldiers one at a time to the caldron of bubbling liquid and poured one large wooden spoonful of liquid in each of the dead soldiers' mouths. I then repeated a chant Farica told me to say over each body three times.

The cauldron ran dry, and I repeated the process throwing more gold into the pot. I asked her, "Have the Wizards found the philosopher's stone?"

"What's that, Jonathan?"

"It changes base metals into gold."

Farica laughed. "You got it all wrong. Wizards here knew the power of gold. It's gold that you've been using; it changes all tangible and intangible objects to whatever you need. Gold is the most powerful ingredient to any potion. You'll find in life if you don't have gold, you have nothing."

I smiled at her. "Isn't that the truth?"

Once the next batch of potion was ready, I started pouring it down the throats of the rest of the dead soldiers. I shook my head and wrinkled my nose. "Are you serious with this?"

She gave me an amusing glance. "Yes, I'm deadly serious. We have little time, please do it now."

I followed her instructions. Then we returned to the injured warriors. They all looked better; some completely recovered and others were on the mend. Some still in pain, others unconscious, but all showed much better vital signs than just a few minutes before. I turned to Robina. "You're the best nurse in all of Christendom."

She laughed. "What's Christendom?"

I just smiled.

I had a chilling thought, "Farica, why didn't we use this potion on our dead friends? We could have saved them."

She looked at me with sadness in her eyes, "It is a battlefield potion from the most sacred book of my order. Only when hundreds have died does it work. It's so the land can be repopulated. We need big strong man to make robust children"

Farica sat Robina and me down beside the horses. "We have to go soon. The Red Army will return. They're not defeated yet. The injured will return to their barracks, and will tell their comrades of our hospitality as well as our taking on seven times their number and winning. It will put fear in their hearts, and we'll have made our reputation. We don't take prisoners or slaves. We release the living. We take the dead."

I looked at her as if she had grown a second head right in front of me. "I'm not carrying any dead guys around with me." I shook my head, "No way, there are too many of them. I just moved ours and theirs, and there are over five hundred of them."

"You don't have to, they will come of their own accord."

I glanced at the dead not really seeing them. "Last time I looked, they were not going anywhere. For Christ's sake, you severed one of their heads."

"Yes, but I'm still a Mother Superior in my soul with charity in my heart, look at your dead now." Robina, Sarah and I stared at the dead. I gasped.

They were moving. Just not wiggling in the grass, they were standing and talking to each other. I almost fainted, and Sarah looked amazed.

"Come on you bunch of old women." Farica put her arm around me, and passed me a bottle of Bickster wine. "Have a drink and meet our new recruits." She herded us over to the resurrected soldiers. They stood talking to one another, Black and Red tunics comparing wounds that were still bloody, but now healing with big angry red marks.

Farica commanded them, "Stand at attention."

The dead complied. "This is the Emperor of the Prophecy." She pointed to me. "You can serve him or return to the dead. If you serve the Emperor, you shall live out your life as normal soldiers. However, if you are disloyal, you will immediately revert to your previous state." She pointed to the soldier who had just recovered from a severed head. "For you, your head will fall off and all your blood will spurt out of your body. For the rest, it will just be as you died. All of you remember how you died, the pain, the emptiness. That fate waits any who are disloyal. Those who choose the Emperor, step forward, those that don't, die now."

There was some hesitation, but all stepped forward. I turned to Farica, "Are they zombies now? You know the un-dead without a mind, without emotions?"

She laughed. "No, why would I want soldiers like that? They are just ordinary men again. They will love, hate, kill and even die if it is their fate. I have just given them another chance. Their death was violent and unnatural. Don't you think they deserve another chance? We gave their compatriots another chance; don't the dead deserve a second one?"

I frowned. "Yes, but do you have that power?"

I heard Arthur grumble. "Yes she does. That's what the nuns have the power to do. As a Mother Superior, she can raise the dead. No wonder she is part of our band."

Farica nodded. "I suspect the Black Master told you my one main purpose as Mother Superior. I will in time teach you the magic, you'll just have to read page 258 in the chapter, Raising of the Dead. The book of course is rare, and I have one of the only ten copies given to Mother Superiors of my order, The Holy Scriptures of Mary."

She then turned to the resurrected Red soldiers. "Take your uniforms off and wash them in the river." The soldiers did as she commanded. "Now put them back on." As they did so, their uniforms turned black with my coat of arms embossed on them. "On your horses, we've business to complete."

My army increased in size after the vicious battle, a wish every commander hopes for, but never receives. I led as Emperor; my four captains riding behind me. Following us was our army, as proud and happy as any army that ever marched in England. Many of our soldiers were undead and ecstatic to be now alive. We rode all that day, and by nightfall with the help of a little magic, we dined in Middlesbrough. The soldiers constructed our camp in an open field just outside the town. I used a little magic and set it up to resemble a medieval festival with colorful tents, games and other entertainment so the town folk would come to see the victorious army.

The five of us dined at the King's Venison Tavern with four of the Red Army's recently deceased generals. They were a friendly lot, all from around London, all professional soldiers who had served in many campaigns. Actually, once you forgot they were dead, they were an amusing bunch of blokes. We ordered four suckling pigs, a large roast of beef, whatever fish the kitchen had, and all the beer we could drink. It was a feast. We ate until we couldn't anymore, then they brought the apple pies and other pastries. It was almost midnight when we started back to the camp. We had just exited the pub when they attacked.

I must say I never try to eat or drink in a public house anymore. Every time I entered one I ended up in a battle with smoke filling my nostrils and fire trying to roast me alive. A pub draws the worst of the worst. Take my advice and eat, drink and be merry at your own castle.

The first arrows struck the door as we closed it. We ran back into the pub as their arrows whizzed by us. The door burst open before we could bolt it. There were shouts and six warriors with swords flashing attacked. The resurrected Red Army generals attacked the intruders and showed their ability to fight. As I said, I hate this close quarters' bar room brawl fighting. I quickly found a back door and found ourselves in a wood yard. We scrambled into the midst of hundreds of cords of wood. We formed a hastily prepared defense in the center of the wood yard with piles of lumber surrounding us, this wooden breastwork giving us protective walls to hide behind. The nine of us stood vigilant with swords drawn and eyes scanning in every direction for the enemy. We didn't have to look far; there must have been a hundred soldiers. The full moon gave a dim light, but I could tell these weren't the Red

Master's men. They wore black silk robes with red piping, and they looked to be slim and athletic, not like the overfed gorillas of the Red Army. The general standing beside me confirmed they were not members of his former army. I sent a telepathic message about our situation to our army camped about a mile away.

They attacked in waves of twenty-five soldiers as there was little room to maneuver in the stacks of wood. As the soldiers crept up on us, a volley of arrows crashed down on our fortification. Angus didn't wait for the next flight of arrows. He attacked the nearest group of the crouching enemy. The rest of us charged behind him.

It was all close in fighting, swords and daggers, fists and heads. Within the initial two minutes, the ground was slippery with blood, and the screams of the wounded were disturbing. We fought through the first wave and then back across the lot. Only about twenty of their soldiers could attack in the confined area and twenty at a time fell to the ground.

I decided this fighting so close to bedtime had to stop. I cast a spell, but nothing happened. I felt confused. I looked closer at my attackers; they appeared oriental, and on a closer glance at their uniforms, I identified them as ninjas. What caused me more concerns, many of the fallen had crawled off the battleground and returned to attack us again. I surmised, they had the same recuperation magic as we used only hours before.

A determined attack pushed us back into our defensive position, as the ninja warriors were persistent. The Japanese blades our opponents wielded cut through the raw wood of our fortifications as if it were paper. I slashed back with my still bewitched Buffoon and hacked at my enemy. The fiercest ninja's attacked me Buffoon parried and attacked as usual, but it bounced off his silk robe of my opponent as if it had ten inches of steel reinforcing the fabric. The swordsmanship of this warrior surprised me, every thrust I took he parried, every feint I made he anticipated. Back and forth, we fought. I twisted to my left and struck with my full force. His sword crashed with mine, and we both stepped back feeling the vibrating steel in our hands. He charged me. I tripped, and he took the advantage. His excellent sword dug into the ground inches from my ear. In a rage, I swung my sword from my prone position catching his blade. The ensuing crash broke his delicate sword in half and drove my sword into his neck severing his carotid artery.

The oriental force withdrew from the wood lot, but could not recover the dead ninja.

"Jesus, who are they?" I asked Angus.

He looked puzzled as well. "I have no idea; they're not the Master's soldiers. I've never seen their kind before. Have you?"

I grimaced. "Yes, I've seen them, but not in action. They're called ninjas, and they're from a place called Japan. They are good soldiers; surprise and stealth are some of their abilities, but as you saw they are good with the blade."

Robina ran over to me. "Do you smell it?"

I sniffed the air. "Shit," escaped from my mouth. "It's smoke and you know what they say."

Sarah answered, "Fire."

I peeked over our defensive wall, and five arrows crashed against it. "The bastards have us trapped in here." They had surrounded the wood lot and fired flaming arrows into the dry wood, flames ignited everywhere.

Angus thought a second. "Maybe if we crawl we can escape through their lines. It's still dark tae the north."

"Works good in the cowboy movies, but with the fires burning, it'll be like daytime around here in a few seconds. Every bit of wood is dry and will burn with bright flames. It would be suicide."

Robina cursed, "If only we could use magic." She uttered a few words under her breath, but nothing happened. "I can't even move this stack of wood. They have put a dead zone around this place."

The fire started to lick against the outside walls of our defenses, and the wind blew embers from one wood pile to the next. "Quick Farica, brew up some of your elixir of life, and we'll bring the dead ninja back to life. Maybe he can help us. We don't have much time, hurry."

We started dismantling our wooden defensive wall and tried to clear a no burn area. It seemed hopeless. The fire was spreading quickly, and the choking smoke billowed from every direction. The enemy dashed my hopes by firing more flaming arrows and throwing Molotov cocktails at some of the non-burning wood piles. The whole area burst into flames. We dragged our dead captive over to Farica, and she pushed a large dose of her medicine down his throat.

He lay as stiff as a board, not even his eyes moving. The heat was starting to crackle like the skin of a roasted pig. Still the dead man didn't move. Farica took another spoonful of her potion and forced it down the ninja's throat.

Sarah had perspiration dripping from her head. "It doesn't look good guys. We've been through a lot and to think another firestorm will do us in. Shit, I'd rather die with an arrow in my heart than by the smoke or the flames. I'm ready to leave this inferno."

"Arthur, do you have any ideas? There's fire everywhere. Do you have any trick to stop the fire or get us out of here?"

Arthur spoke softly to me. "The spells I know I already heard my daughter chant them. With magic dampened in this wood lot, it is up to you to find another way out of. I'm sorry, but I can't help you."

I fought too long and won every time to give up now. There had to be a way out of this situation. I picked up the dead ninja and slapped his face hard. There was no response. I felt the smoke start to irritate my eyes and lungs. I knew time conspired with the ninjas to kill us.

Angus rubbed his eyes. "Wit'oot Beth an'" in this intolerable situation, "I vote tae charge the bastards. All o' us have chain mail on; we can survive, or at least take a couple o' them wi' us when we die. Let's dae it."

Farica grabbed his sleeve. "You old warrior, this is not the place to make a desperate last stand. We'll survive this. Think. There is a way out of this. It is staring us in the face. We just have to be smart enough to find it. Think."

I was coughing and looking up at the moon wondering when it would disappear into the clouds of smoke when I heard the ninja stir.

I grabbed him and yanked him to his feet. I slapped his face, "Speak to me asshole, or I'll send you back to hell. Talk."

CHAPTER TWENTY-ONE

HIS EYE FLITTERED, AND A DRIBBLE OF SPIT SLID FROM HIS MOUTH AS it twitched. I felt his fingernail brush against my arm. The ninja was alive. "Wake up you bastard. Your life depends on your ability to speak. Wake up asshole."

His eyes opened lazily, exposing themselves to the horror surrounding him. I still held him, and he shivered in my grasp. "We have about a minute before the smoke suffocates us, and we turn into crispy critters. Do you understand me?"

He nodded his head. "Don't shout. I'm not deaf." He croaked. "What's happening?"

In as few words as possible, I explained to him his predicament and ours. "You either help us or you die; not tomorrow, not the next day but now and forever. Remember what it felt like when death took you away? Right, well that's how you'll feel for an eternity." I looked him straight in the eye, "How do we escape this fire and your men? If you trick us, you die. Not from us, but from the potion, it's poison for anyone other than our allies."

He shook his head. "If I choose to live I must desert my master. I have served the masters of my house all my life. My family for a thousand years has been loyal to my master's house. I know of no other life but to serve my ancestors."

The flames flashed up around us, and a rolling fire ball flashed ten feet over our heads. "Decide fast or it's a moot point."

He frowned. "What does that mean?"

"Just tell me if you want to live as a free man and have your children and their children free from your master. You must decide now, or we die."

I watched as the dilemma he felt flashed across his face, and then I yelled, "Decide!" I pulled my sword from its scabbard and pointed it at his chest.

I didn't need the gesture. Our defensive wall flared up spraying us with sparks and telling all imminent death waited in the wings.

He blinked, scavenged in his inside pocket and pulled out a gadget from under his black robe and pushed a button, "Use your magic and get us out of here."

I stopped time for two minutes. I didn't know how I did it. I had read the spell in the book we took from the Red Master. Robina told me no one had ever tried to use the spell as it altered the universe and shifted dimensions. Hell, I thought that was what I wanted. My adventure to Berwick had one purpose, to alter dimensions and return to mine.

Stopping time didn't affect any of us in the defensive position in the wood yard but everything else stopped; the fires, the smoke and even the ninjas outside stood as statutes. We had two minutes to run as fast and as far away from the inn as possible. I led everyone towards our soldiers' camp. The world had no noise, even our footsteps made no sound. The air didn't move and we couldn't speak. People stood like stone, as did everything around us. I liked the silent non-moving environment. However, I realized it would be a sad world if time stopped forever and just the nine of us survived. No, now we were ten counting our ninja.

I ran across a patch of gravel and heard it crunch under my feet, then the wind in my ears and finally Robina yelling to me. "You did it, but are we still in the same dimension?" Her question received an immediate answer; we saw ten Red tunic clad guards riding towards us obviously ordered to investigate the fire we just escaped. They didn't even notice us as they rode hard towards the smoke and flames.

Back at our camp protected by my army, we started interrogating our captive.

Angus started the questioning. "Which master do you serve?"

The ninja captain just laughed.

Angus was not in the mood for humor and had his claymore ready to take off the captive's head. I stepped between them. "Angus, I didn't save him so you could kill him five minutes later. I'll ask the questions but you can keep that sword ready, just in case he tries to escape."

VICTOR SIMPSON

Angus ground his teeth, but when I said he could use his sword if the ninja tried to escape, he flashed me a brilliant smile.

I conjured up sake, sushi and rice for our captive and me. I picked up my chopsticks and dug in. "Do you want to eat with me. It's good."

He tentatively picked up his chopsticks and tasted the rice. He picked off a piece of the raw fish and slipped it down his throat. A smile came to his face. "Have you been to my world?"

I smiled back. "And what world do you come from? I'm not from here either."

He closed his eyes and breathed out. Finally, he sipped his sake. "My world is geographically similar to this world. The people have the same motivations and desires, but in my world honor and conquests are what our leaders desire more than life itself. My Shogun rules a quarter of the world, and he has felt a tremor in the force."

I immediately thought of Star Wars, "What's the force?"

He looked at me as if I had no brains. "The force is what controls matter throughout the universe. It keeps dimensions from colliding and destroying each other. He sent out four teams of ninjas to find the place and people disrupting the force and to fix the problem. We found you, and your deaths would solve the anomaly in the force."

"How did you stop our magic from working?"

A broad smile spread across his face and he rubbed his left eye with his fist, "That's the rub. In our world, magic dominated for a millennium. Our science finally discovered how to defend against it; we developed a way to make a dead zone. It stopped the creation of all magic in the area covered by our electronic signal. Existing magic prevailed, but the device stopped all other magic created by spells, potions, appeals to gods or even natural magic. My Shogun is a tech leader who never uses magic just force and technology. He is also a traditionalist and loves the old ways." He pointed to himself. "That's why he uses the ancient arts of the ninja."

"Do you have the gadget that stops magic?"

With a deadpan expression, he answered with the simple, "Yes, of course."

I closed my eyes and thanked whatever god was looking down on me with favor. "How does it work?"

The ninja smiled at me, "I have the small portable model. It has a hundred yards range in every direction." He took it out from under his robe and was about to push a button when Angus brought his sword within an inch of the ninja's ear. "Now my fine friend, you hand that to Jonathan, our Emperor, or I'll take your head off in one swift swing."

The ninja slowly handed the device to me. "The red button turns the dead zone operational and the green button turns it off. It's quite simple."

I looked at the instrument that looked much like a TV remote control. "What do the other buttons do?"

A pained look came across his face. "This is also an instrument to communicate between dimensions, and its other purpose is as a transporter to bring my force back to our own dimension. I'm not a techie; I'm a samurai trained as a ninja. As you're aware, I'm a soldier and my family has been soldiers for the last two thousand years. My Shogun has only ruled us for ten years since he defeated my father's army in battle. He is my uncle, but he has no honor. He just believes in destroy and conquer."

"I'll hold on to this device for now. What's your name ninja?"

"Oshiro, I'm just Oshiro. I lost my personal name when I became a slave to my uncle. I would have followed my father and obtained the title of Shogun, so he removed my name. He made me write it on a piece of paper and then burned the paper in a holy shrine telling me the Gods don't know who I am anymore. I'm just Oshiro, the name of the village of my people."

Robina stood next to me. Sarah and Farica stood on my other side. I could feel their compassion. I thought for a few seconds, and then said, "Now that you are a free man and can choose your destiny. I give you a fresh personal name. Your new name is, Leonardo, the man in our world that envisioned a future in technology."

Sarah poked me in the ribs. "You bastard, Leonardo is one of the ninja turtles."

I whispered back to her. "Yeah I know, but I liked him the best. I think this ninja could be my best friend someday. I just have a feeling, call it clairvoyant or what."

I felt Arthur smirk. "Remember, the Red Master acted like my best friend before he tried to kill me and kidnapped Robina. I'll cover your back for you."

Farica just clucked and finally said, "Remember the Prophecy."

I scrunched up my brow and looked quizzically at her. Eventually I asked, "Tell me what I should remember."

She just shook her head and looked away.

I turned back to Oshiro, "Is Leonardo agreeable to you as your new name?"

You would have thought I gave him a million gold pieces. "Thank you, Emperor Jonathan. I will serve you to my death."

I inwardly winced. I could almost hear him say those exact words to his Shogun. Didn't every tyrant require absolute loyalty from their armies, and subjects? I smiled and said, "Thank-you, you are so kind."

He bowed to me. Sarah spoke directly to him. "Can your machine transport us to other dimensions?"

He shook his head, "No. The technicians didn't want to make it complicated. They thought we would confuse ourselves and go to the wrong dimension. It is preset, once we set it to return we go right back to the Shogun's throne room as if we had never left. He will then await our answer and check to see that we have indeed corrected the anomaly."

Sarah and I looked at each other and at the same time just said, "Shit!"

Robina broke the tension we had caused. "Let's see if this gadget works."

We walked about a quarter of a mile from the camp into a large field and following Leonardo's instructions turned the magic damper on. "Robina, let's see some magic."

She said the fireball spell, and nothing happened, then she tried the make a wall of ice spell again. Nothing happened. Finally, she tried the invisibility spell with the same result.

I nodded to Oshiro, "It works."

He replied, "Did you think I would lie to you?"

"You never know in this strange land. There are several bizarre people here."

Angus heard me. "Come on, ma friend, we're al' normal wizards and noblemen ye have surrounded yourself wit'. We arenae't bizarre or even weird; we're just your friends."

I rolled my eyes at Angus. "Yes, you, Robina and Farica are just people. You're not weird. However, your society is cruel. There are the haves, and the have not; the wizards and the people. I go through villages, and the people are just people. However, they live an existence of drudgery and serfdom. It sounds like in Leonardo's world, there are slaves as well. Leo, tell me how the common people in your world live? Does your Shogun keep them in hovels like this world? Conversely, do your Shoguns treat them more humanely, allowing technology to help them in their daily lives?"

The ninja frowned. "I have nothing to compare to, other than this place. In my world, we have—" he thought for a few seconds, "wagons without horses, wagons that fly, even houses as tall as mountains. Most people live in large cities. The farms use technology to raise food. With technology, war is brutal. As a result of so many people reside together, diseases spread rapidly, yet our people have a long life, some over two hundred years."

Angus and Robina nodded their heads. "Jonathan has told us about such times. They sound interesting. Disease is something new to us. We have little sickness here and the average farmer lives about two hundred years as well. The wizards and nobles do not fair so well because of war and the drain of mental ability casting spells. Seventy to eighty years is the average for what the Emperor calls the haves."

They both looked at me and the ninja asked, "Tell us about your world. Why do you scorn ours, is yours such a utopia?"

Sarah answered before I could. For half an hour, she talked about our world, telling them about politics, our history and most of all about the people, and their diversity, wishes and desires.

Robina nodded her head, "I see where you two get your drive for freedom and your fighting spirit. Your world must be full of warriors. Your society has great diversity in all areas of thought and humanity. Our world is lucky you are the ones the Prophecy predicted." Then she looked at the ninja. "He is a warrior, but honor doesn't give a soldier his ability to win. Honor dictates death, not survival at any cost. Our teachings tell us our Ancient Ones believed in survival of the fittest. If one stands on honor, one does it for the stupidest principles. A wizard knows that, but you and your world, Sarah, have taken that slogan to heart."

I shook my head. "We believe in honor too."

Robina smiled. "Sure you do, who stole the gold from the Red Master?"

I could see the discussion going on forever so I ended it with a simple. "We can't stay here. We have to move on; the Red Army will find us. We'll move up the road another ten miles or so and set up camp."

For two days we marched up the coast road without incident. Our new companion told stories of his battles and life in his world. We told him about our journey from Oxford. I could tell from his facial expressions, he didn't believe half of what we said to him, but soon, he would believe.

In the sea to our east was a large island. Looking at it, Angus became quiet and seemed concerned. Arthur gave me a warning. "This is a Holy place, the dead of many Ancient Ones rest in eternal bliss on the island in sacred tombs. The rumors are the tombs are full of riches; the Brownies guard them."

I smiled. "Yes, I've heard of Brownies. They're little nymphs like fairies. They live in the woods."

Arthur tweaked my nose by snapping a synapse in by brain. "No, Brownies are fairies yes, but huge mean beasts. They're very nasty creatures to mix with. I've seen one eat a man in two bites. We don't fool with them. Even a strong wizard is no match for them. They are by nature immune to bewitching. The Ancient Ones created them to guard the Holy Places and the Holy Island."

I looked out to sea, "They won't bother us. We aren't going near that island." I gazed out and saw mud flats and five ships, all the size of small frigates of the 15th century, their sails full of wind and heading straight for us. I stood rooted to the road watching in fascination then I saw the red sails and the coat of arms of the Red Master on them. At first, I thought the ships would fire on us, but as they came closer I noticed huge man like creatures chasing the ships.

Angus grabbed my arm. "Run. We have to run. The Red fleet is going to crash on the shore any moment. They'll be less than a hundred yards from us. The Brownies chasing them won't be particular. They'll kill and eat anyone in the area."

"What is the fleet doing near Holy Island when they know the Brownies guard it?"

Sarah slapped me hard on the side of the head. "Stupid, the Red Master is using his fleet to bring the Brownies to us. He must think they will kill us as well as his own men."

"But his fleet?" I mumbled this time Robina slapped me on the other side of my head. "Don't you get it? He's sacrificing his navy to kill us. We have to move. Let's get this army moving."

I rode to the front of the column cast a spell on my force to march at fifteen miles an hour for the next hour. We would be in Berwick soon. Just as I started to hike north, the first boat crashed into the land disgorging a hundred or more soldiers. The soldiers charged my army with wild battle cries and swinging swords. I had no choice but to engage them.

I heard Arthur telling me. "Remember, this attack is only to slow you down so the Brownies will catch you."

I understood the Red Master's tactics, but I had to fight. I had read Arthur's mind, and we had to defeat the Brownies, or we couldn't fulfill the Prophecy. How to defeat the Brownies didn't appear in the Prophecy or in Arthur's mind, and I had no idea how to do it without casting a spell.

"Cut doon the Red soldiers then run as fast as ye can for Scotland, do it quick." We all heard Angus' voice echoed across the battlefield. Each of the Red Master's ships puked ugly vicious looking soldiers in front of us. Still in front of my men, I gave them another spell, one to increase speed, "Everything is at double time." Each sword stroke, each parry, each thrust, and every movement were twice as fast as the Red soldiers they faced.

The battle still took time. I noticed a group of ten wizards on the ship also casting spells. I used my long-distance hearing spell to eavesdrop, thus casting a reciprocal spell as they throw theirs. The army formed a semi-circle around me and fought off the Red army. I watched as the Brownies left the sea. Each was over twenty feet tall and, as their names implied, they dressed in brown. As I cast a spell to turn the ground under the Red army's feet to mud, a vision hit me, brownies with chocolate, almost mud colored icing, and whipped cream. It used to be my favorite as a teenager. Those brownies I ate by the pan full, now I faced the Brownies' revenge, Twenty-foot tall man eating Brownies were racing as fast as their long legs could carry them to eat me.

CHAPTER TWENTY-TWO

THE RED ARMY FOUGHT LIKE A BEAR CAUGHT IN A TRAP. IN FRONT OF them my army slashed and retreated, but behind the Red Army the Brownies attacked like savages picking them up and eating them. They took a bite and threw the half eaten soldiers to the ground. The Red Master's soldiers died in their ranks one man at a time. Moving forward became a slow deadly process, moving north or south brought our force into immediate contact with the Brownies. The protectors of Holy Island impeded movement in every direction but west.

The fast moving giants ate every straggler and then started on our rearguard. They nibbled through our lines like children eating chocolate squares at a birthday party.

I invaded the minds of the Red Army soldiers, imploring them to throw down their weapons and join my retreating army. I flashed a vivid picture of the Brownies eating one of their officers. To my surprise within seconds the Red army joined mine in a full run towards the trees to the west.

As we sprinted to the tree line, I dared to look behind me and watched in horror as the slower fleeing soldiers fell into the grasp of the giants stamping behind us. The lead Brownie would pick up a soldier and pop the poor man's head into his mouth, seconds later the body minus the head landed on the ground. To my astonishment, the Brownie behind would stop and chomp on the remains of the headless soldier. They didn't stop chasing us; they just slowed down to enjoy the meal laid out in front of them.

My army now hid in the woods, climbing trees behind them and even hiding under the fallen branches. I stretched out my ears and could hear the wizards screaming as the Brownies ate them. Most of the Red wizards had big pot bellies, wore ornate shoes, and were not accustomed to physical endurance. The Brownies surrounded them. It struck me the Brownies enjoyed their work. They laughed as they tormented the wizards with a nibble on a finger or a foot, devouring a leg and then a nose, an ear or even a face. For the moment, they had lost interest in us. It was Brownies at play. I watched.

We could run and hide or stand and fight. I looked around me and decided if we ran they would have us. If we fought like the Red Army, they would have us. No magic would work against them. I didn't have a machine gun, or even a stick of dynamite to use to defeat them.

"We have about five minutes, and then they will be back and we can't stop them," yelled Angus.

In my head Arthur echoed the same thought. I looked at Sarah and Robina. "I've an idea." I told them what we needed to do. My force and the captured Red Master's force would have run in all directions, if I had not a spell on all of them that glued them in place. I could feel their fear, a seeping damp feeling in the pit of each of their stomachs. In fact I could smell it on my generals who stood next to me. In a calm soothing voice I spoke to each of my soldiers. "This is not the end. It is only a new part of the road to travel. We'll be victorious as we have in the past. Settle yourselves; we have a battle to win."

It took Robina only seconds and she had trees falling. Sarah found material to make rope by the league. I levitated rocks and boulders to the clearing we had made. With Farica's help Sarah and Robina used their psychic powers to change saplings and old oaks into logs and then into machines.

Angus watched with utter amazement as catapults and other war machines built themselves. I scoured the soil for trace elements of the raw material for explosives. I needed iron, coal and the right temperature. I needed steel for my cannon.

It took the Brownies ten minutes to play with the wizards and the unfortunate Red Army soldiers that didn't make it back into the forest. The weather had changed; a storm blew in off the North Sea. Visibility in the forest was yards and in some parts mere feet. In some places a man five feet away disappeared in the foliage. I felt the dampness and the wisps of fog coming off the sea. I just hoped the Brownies didn't have infrared vision.

In my youth I watched every fantasy and science fiction movie I could find. The Star Wars series stimulated me to become a scientist. Yet the mysticism of the Force always intrigued me. The Ewoks gave me inspiration. As a child I was small and resembled the little creatures, more than I cared to admit. The antithesis of a warrior, and the proverbial underdog, I admired their tenacity.

The first Brownie attacked through the dense forest. He pushed his way through the bushes and knocked down small trees. His bulk caused him to have to fight his way through the tangle of trees and bushes. I placed myself with Robina in the top of a large tree with ax in hand. I waited. On my signal, six of my soldiers rose from the underbrush as if the Brownie had flushed them out like wild birds. They flew as fast as they could towards my tree and away from the lumbering giant. I saw the glint in the giant's eyes as he increased his stride to scoop them up in his hand and devour them.

I yelled to Angus in a tree across from me, "On three; one, two, three." We both used our axes to cut lines holding back two large logs suspended on ropes from the tree to swing inward. It was a Ewok trick and luckily for me the Brownies had never seen the movie. The two logs crashed together crushing the Brownie's head between them. He never knew what hit him. Throughout the forest, many other Brownies met the same fate.

The next Brownie who passed my tree met a different fate. I turned to Robina and winked. My next move took my breath away. I jumped on the head of the Brownie and with my two, daggers reached over his brow and dug them into his eyes. The creature went wild. He tried to reach me with his huge hands, but Robina pulled me back into the tree by a pulley, and a rope tied around me like a parachute harness.

Throughout the forest, Brownies fell to the ground dead or in agony. Hidden in the undergrowth, Sarah sprang from the ground. Using an axe she cut off the foot of a marauding Brownie and then when a fellow Brownie came to his aid, she used her dagger, springing up to castrate the beast. He crumbled to the ground next to his incapacitated friend.

I retreated from my treetop position and climbed a hill that overlooked the tiny valley that we had chosen to defend. Another four Brownies charged up the valley from the sea following a tiny stream. The Brownies entered the clearing we had prepared. Five of my soldiers, led by Leo, released ten logs, which rolled down the side of the hill, each gaining speed as they rolled closer to the unsuspecting giants. The logs acted as steamrollers rolling over the four and crushing them like delicate China figurines.

The lucky Brownies who reached the end of the valley in the large clearing met the cannon I had built. The gunpowder was not the best, but it exploded throwing large and small rocks at the approaching Brown giants. The Brownies stood tall and had huge muscles, but they had the same organs as a man. They died when shot, like any other creature in the 21ˢᵗ Century. The ones that survived the initial volley of cannon fire had their bodies incinerated by my flamethrowers; fifteen soldiers carried napalm on their backs and pointed the nozzle of their guns at the few approaching Brownies. The smell of napalm and burning flesh brought the sound of Wagner to my ears. Even Brownies burn if they get too close to the flames.

The two Brownies that had survived retreated to the sea. We regrouped our force and watched. I threw my mind out to read their thoughts, but death came back to me in waves. I didn't understand it. I felt death in their spirit. It frightened me. I slowly had my force move north through the forest. We didn't regain the road until we had passed the village of Hagerstown.

We set up camp at the Black Rocks of Cheswick. I wanted to march the remaining few miles to Berwick, but my army had to rest. I turned to Angus. "My friend, why don't we take ten soldiers and our loyal band and ride off to Berwick tonight. By morning, we could be out of this place and back in my world, and you could be closer to your people."

A weary smile came to his face. "It's no' time yet, Ma Lord. Wait, everything comes tae those wi' patience. The Prophecy tells o' more adventures afore we reach oor goal."

I took a deep breath and said, "Why won't anyone tell me the whole Prophecy but only give me hints and veiled warnings? Jesus, I'm the Emperor I should know what's going to happen."

Angus laughed. "Why don't ye dig aroun' in Arthur's mind, he knows as much as I dae, and more."

Before I could speak, Arthur's voice resonated in my brain. "I've hidden it; you know too much as it is. I tell you the more you know, the less spontaneous you'll be. Your unorthodox thinking is what has gotten us this far. No, I'm keeping silent and you'll never find the information." Then he laughed at me.

Sarah nodded, "I agree with Jonathan. It will only take a few hours, and then we'll finish it. Let's do it."

Farica shook her head. "The Prophecy supplies us with the knowledge that the Red Master has more tricks up his sleeve. I can explain this much to you before we reach Berwick, we have one more confrontation with him. It's best we rest tonight and be ready for tomorrow."

"Thanks, Farica." I said, "Why am I the last to know what's going to happen?" I just walked away with Robina following me trying to smooth my ruffled feathers.

It was dark; we sat around a large fire. The siege towers and catapults we had erected to fight the Brownies faced north ready for a surprise attack by the Red Army. The mood took on a jovial nature. Angus sang about the clans and the warriors of old to the bagpipes of one of the Tartan soldiers. By the end of the evening, we all spoke with a Scottish brogue.

In the morning, Angus had prepared a feast for us. Oatmeal and venison topped the list of breakfast delicacies. The mood of my companions turned jolly. We only had a few miles to travel. Everyone just wanted it all to finish. The army felt the same sense of joy. Their spirits had never been higher. Even the recruits from the Red Army who now took the oath of allegiance to me. They all knew if they broke it terrible, consequences would befall them. When I administered the oath, I told them in grave detail what I had in store for traitors.

Leo looked confused. "You took into your army your enemy's soldiers. Isn't that dangerous?"

I put my arm around his shoulder and in a grave, voice said, "My friend, didn't I do the same to you. Should I fear you? Are you going to sneak up on me one night and slit my throat? Should I fear them in the same way?"

"No, honor forbids me. Yes, I understand," he said with just a trace of ten-tativeness in his voice. "I'm a warrior who has no allegiance to his master. I am his slave and only serve because I have no other way to use my talents. When you freed me, I saw your way as the way of my heart."

I smiled. "My point exactly, these troopers of the Red Master are like you, virtual slaves. They think of me as their savior. Loyalty to me is loyalty to the Prophecy. Who knows, the Prophecy might even be true."

The army started its march to Berwick at seven. I had magically pro-pelled them at twice their normal speed. I did the same to the horses pulling the towers, and catapults. I wanted to get back to my own world as quickly as possible.

The army marched steadily along, but with foreboding as they neared Berwick. All knew the Red Master waited for our arrival. In contrast, I rode with a song in my heart; Goin' Up Country by Canned Heat.

Two miles from the Tweed River, I stopped the army and declared, "Everyone inspect your armor and prepare for anything and everything. We'll be under fire in the next mile, or at most, a mile and a half."

Robina stood in front of the troops and commanded, "Everyone repeat after me, I serve the Emperor and will protect him with my life." After the roar of voices she proclaimed, "I have bewitched each of you who repeated my words and took them to heart with a spell that will protect you from arrows, rocks, sharp objects and hand to hand combat. If necessary, I will bewitch you with protection from any other treachery you may encounter."

A roar came from the troops. We marched forward into battle. We faced all sorts of discomfort from the Red Master. I didn't know what he had in store for us, but I prepared myself for every kind of offensive encounter. Since our first encounter with the enemy, we imbued our soldiers with protective spells to make all previous spells against us ineffective. It was an easy safeguard yet it was impossible to protect against newly created dangers. Angus and Arthur told me it was the way of the Masters always to attack with a different plan and never use the same spell twice in a campaign.

The Red Army stood on an open field in front of the old low arched bridge that crossed the river Tweed. On the hill on the Berwick side of the bridge was Berwick Castle, Norman in design. Surrounding the castle and the city stood a wall that came right down to the river's edge. The bridge led to a large gate in the wall. The Tweed at this point was a wide river with a serpentine quality. I looked at my force and the Red Army facing us, both on the plain in front of us and on the walls of the city. Finally, I looked at the castle, and my heart sank. To my eyes, there must have been ten thousand soldiers, if not more.

We marched forward slowly in a long line three ranks deep with my siege engines in the rear. I rode about ten yards ahead of my army with my companions beside me. We assessed the enemy's formations. As we drew closer, I noticed the crimson robes of the Red Master in front of his troops. I waved to him. I saw a smile come to his face. However, his face had changed. He appeared different, no longer the man I had seen just weeks before in York. He had aged, not years, but what looked like generations. The wrinkles, the age spots, the shrunken body, he no longer looked forty-five as he did before, but a hundred and five. I watched as he waved his sword. He still had the power of a warrior, but did he have the endurance?

We marched closer to the Red Army. I anticipated arrows flying towards us. In medieval battles, they usually started the festivities with the archers, yet nothing came as we continued our advance. I looked over his army, and I saw soldiers standing like statues with only the occasional blinking of an eye. No panic on the enemy's soldiers' faces; no reaching for their swords, just an almost bored nonchalant appearance.

I ordered my archers to send their first volley. The arrows filled the sky and arced down on the soldiers standing between the bridge and my army. We held our breath as the arrows rocketed to the ground. I watched as the arrows plummeted into the ranks of the enemy soldiers. I could hear the cheer of my men behind me. What I saw turned my heart into ice. The arrows pierced the soldiers, but the arrows passed right through their bodies and landed on the ground behind them. The soldiers never flinched; they looked as bored as they did before the attack.

"Archers fire another volley." I watched as the bowmen strung their arrows and pulled back hard on the bows. The arrows raised high in the air and fell as before right into the midst of the enemy. Again, I saw the arrows find their targets, but again the arrows landed on the ground behind the soldiers.

The Red Master laughed and raised the staff he held in his right hand. He crashed the staff on the ground three times in a show of arrogant force. On the third thumping, thunder rumbled all around my army and the enemy soldiers behind the Red Master vanished. He stood alone in the field. My whole force stopped. My horse stood no more than fifty yards from the Red Master.

I acknowledged his magic with a nod and then pulled my sword out and pranced forward. I had Angus on one side of me and Robina on the other when I grabbed the halter of my steed. "No my lover, wait, he is baiting us. He has planned this. We must retreat and plan this attack. We must take his trick and turn it to our advantage."

I took a deep breath. Our goal stood in the castle on the hill on the other side of the river not far from us. We had magic. We had technology we had Leo's gadget to stop all magic. God damn it. We could stop the Red Master in his tracks.

"Leo," I yelled to my ninja still in his black robes who looked to all the world like one of the Black Master's wizards. He rode towards me. "Will your dead zone gadget work at this range?"

He gauged the distance, "We need to move just a little closer to be sure."

"The rest of you go back to the army and Leo and I will ride closer to engage the dead zone. Then we can fight a real battle with this wizened up old wizard."

My faithful friends all circled my horse and Farica spoke, "The Prophecy tells us we must face the Red Master." Then she surprised me. "All for one and one for all is what the prophet wrote for the crossing of the Tweed."

I looked at her. "Jesus, tell me more, I need to know what to expect. I'm the Emperor, I command you. I make plans, and yet you leave me in the dark. Hell, I feel like a mushroom not an Emperor."

I looked at Leo, "Press the buttons on your dead zone gadget and we'll deal with the Red Lord."

I turned to look at the Red Master. He winked at me. I gave him the finger. He looked quizzically at me, and then threw what looked like a boomerang at us. It floated in the air moving like a ripple on a pond. As it passed through the air it made a waving motion and blurred everything behind it. The team looked up in surprise. The Red Master turned to vapor and then I heard Arthur yelling in my head.

"May all the gods damn that foolish bastard. He's activated a temporal wave. He's going to take us back in time. I would think probably to yesterday when he had a dead zone around this area and a thousand soldiers just waiting for us to appear. This is his worst infraction of the Wizard's code, he has done many ignoble deeds but this is the most hideous."

Leo pushed the buttons. The dead zone should have stopped the wave; but to our horror, the wave was coming like a tsunami crashing over us. I felt it crushing me and then knocking me off my horse. My vision faded.

As I gained my feet I yelled, "How is everyone?"

I expected to see us in the arms of the enemy, but instead I stood in a primordial forest, a jungle that no human living or dead had ever seen before. The undergrowth came up to my neck. I searched for Robina. Then I heard her voice.

"Help me; I'm caught in a slimy pond. Yuck, it's not a pond it's a large pile of dung."

I found her by the sound of her voice and pulled her to her feet. That's when we first saw it. It stood forty feet tall and must have weighed twenty tons. I'd loved dinosaurs as a kid, but I had never seen a picture of one that looked like this creature. It had armor covering its body with fangs for teeth and a hammerhead tail. Its long neck allowed it to turn its head in a three hundred and sixty degree arc, without the body moving, Robina looked around, "Obviously the Red Master made a mistake, this wasn't where he wanted us." Then she thought for a second. "It must have been Leo's dead zone, it modified the temporal wave. My God how? Are we going to return to our time and fulfill the Prophecy?"

Farica smiled. "The Prophecy tells of this, but no one thought this part was true. The scholars interpreted it as a dream. We now know it isn't a dream." Then she yelled. "Run, that creature is sizing us up for dinner."

As I looked back, I glimpsed the long necked creature clamping its teeth around my horse. We ran like the wind.

CHAPTER TWENTY-THREE

THE AIR WAS FETID, THE TEMPERATURE IN THE NINETIES, AND THE humidity close to the same. After running a few hundred feet, I felt that my lungs would explode. Then I had to laugh. Just those few months ago at the lab in Oxford, all I wanted to do was move a drop of water from the future back to the past. Now I looked on the world sixty or seventy million years in the past.

The color green in all its shades surrounded me, but mixed among the green plants and trees grew fauna and flora of every color; this was a world of variety, unlike the world I knew with oak forests with deer and squirrels. This was a land of every possible variation. As I held my sides and gulped in air, I saw at my feet a small mammal, not a mouse, but of that size. Its bright eyes looked up at me, and I imagined it winked at me as if it knew that in 60 million years it would be like me, human.

Angus half bent over next to me wheezing, and said, "Where the blazes are we? I've never imagined such a place like this. Is it hell?"

Sarah, covered in guck, shook her head. "No, we're in your world's distant past, before man ruled. We're in big trouble." She threw her hand out as if to cast a spell, but nothing happened. "Jesus, what happened?" Then she hit her forehead with the palm of her hand, "Leo's spell has deadened this area." She looked all around and said, "Oh hell, where is Leo?"

We looked, but Leo our Ninja had disappeared. Robina spoke, "He was right next to me when the wave hit. I saw him push the button on the magic damper. When we landed here I didn't see him or his horse."

Sarah said with concern, "I don't think he came with us. When we materialized here I was facing where he should have been, but he wasn't there."

She looked upset. "He must still be confronting the Red Master. I hope he survives. Damn, if I'm right—"

I tried to object, "We have to find Leo. We need him and that gadget. He's one of us, and we don't leave our team behind."

Robina shook her head. "He's not here. He stayed behind, the wave hit us because his machine didn't have time to deaden the magic around us, only distort it, but for him it stopped the Red Master's magic. He's still in our present standing alone in front of the Red Master with a dead space around him. We must go. I've a bad feeling about this place." She looked around her and wriggled her nose, "Please."

I still searched for him. "Look, we need to find him, with his magic deadener we can get back to where we were. He just has to press a few buttons—" I stopped in mid-sentence, knowing I was babbling about my hopes, not reality.

"He's not here, Jonathan. He's still back in the present," Sarah said in a firm no nonsense voice. "He's not here with us. He's not dead. We have to find a way back to the present ourselves. We need a time machine." A stupid expression crossed her face. "Shit, that's what brought us to this crazy world. Jonathan, how do we get back to face the Red Master?"

Before I could answer Angus yelled, "Run."

I looked up and saw a huge Tyrannosaurus Rex twenty feet away. He stood on his hind legs with his two short front legs pawing in the air at us. His large mouth was open, and huge sharp teeth filled my whole field of vision. I ran.

It blended in with the color of the forest but its roar made its presence known to the primordial jungle. As we ran, Angus' hoarse voice reached me between gasping breaths, "He licked his lips, that's how I saw him. His tongue is gigantic. It came out of his mouth at least four feet. We'll never outrun him. This is his home. We are having trouble traveling through the underbrush. We have to fight."

As we talked, I heard the beast running behind us, knocking down small trees, crushing the plants underfoot and roaring in that impossible high nasal pitched screech. A large group of trees blocked our way. "Behind the trees we'll make our stand." The five of us ran as fast as the terrain would allow, but Robina didn't make it. She fell just a few feet from the tree line.

The creature stooped down with his front paws slashing her across her body. I couldn't let her die in the wilds of the Cretaceous period. As the Tyrannosaurus Rex lifted its arm to stuff Robina in its saliva dripping mouth, I took my sword and hacked away at its foot. My adrenalin must have been flooding my system, for I cut through skin that looked like armor, cutting the tendons and smashed into raw bone.

The creature cried out and dropped Robina to swat at me. Angus didn't want to give all the glory to me and attacked the dinosaur's other foot. The creature wobbled then fell backwards into the undergrowth. He roared and fought to regain his upright position. His feet hadn't the strength to support him. We ran and hid behind the trees to regain our composure. I tried to stop the bleeding from Robina's chest where the T-Rex slashed her with is sharp claws.

Farica had the forethought or the knowledge from the Prophecy to carry a well-stocked first aid kit. After swabbing Robina down with a medical potion, she strenuously rubbed a second bag of herbs over the bloody wound. It helped that Robina wore her fitted steel and titanium breastplate. The six-inch claws had a hard time piercing it and only about a quarter of an inch sliced through. Two of the claws had caught on the breastplate itself, never breaching the armor, but staying embedded in the steel.

Farica looked pleased. "It will sting for a few hours my dear, but all being equal, tomorrow you won't even have a scar."

Robina patted me on the arm and said, "See my love, my breasts will be as good as new. You can kiss them better for me later."

I blushed at her battlefield humor. She lay on the ground topless, with all of us trying to repair her wound, and all she thought about was making me turn red.

I could see the pain in her eyes, but her voice sounded strong and deter-mined. She laughed and continued, "Let's move before his brother comes looking for him. We need to find a safe place to plan our escape."

I looked back at the T-Rex. The king lay dead in the undergrowth with twenty or more raptors tearing his flesh away. It was the throat I noticed first, slashed open with blood still pumping out. Surrounding its body many more raptors lay dead or dying. The T-Rex had put up a valiant fight, but with no mobility, it didn't have a chance. The idyllic jungle of picture books in fact nurtured death, which just waited to spring on the unsuspecting.

We escaped to a clearing some half mile away. We followed an animal trail, knowing that we put ourselves in danger, but anywhere we stood, we faced death.

Robina felt better, Farica had given her natural herbs that acted as pain relievers. "Baby, how are you feeling? Where does it hurt? Is there anything I can do?"

She looked up at me with glistening eyes. "Yeah, get me back to Berwick." Then she gave me a lopsided smile.

Arthur gave a little moan. "My poor daughter, this place is a death trap. The Red Master might have sent us here after all." And a little tear dripped from my eye as he asked me to give his daughter a kiss for him.

Farica patted me on the shoulder and reassured me, "She'll be all right. Her wound is healing at an accelerated rate and it appears almost healed. I put healing powder in it to stop fever and poison from killing her. She's just groggy from the painkiller powder I gave her."

I felt frantic. How could I return my team to Berwick to solve the riddle and fulfill the Prophecy, whatever the end could be? I looked at my warriors. They all looked to me to solve the problems of our survival and return. I had no answers. I came from the twenty-first century, not this land of terror.

I had to say something, but what? "We have to find high ground to make our camp, something defensible. I suggest we head south." Then I looked at Robina and asked, "Are you strong enough to trek through the jungle with us?"

"Johnny, I told you, wherever you go I go. If you can walk so can I. Let's start moving. I don't want to meet up with another of those beasts."

We headed south, or as best we could with the primitive compass I had carried since I became a tenderfoot in scouts. It was the geek in me. We had moved about three hundred yards when we came across a field of beautiful colored plants. I scratched my head. In my world flowers didn't evolve until after this era. What were they doing here, and were they real flowers? I didn't have time to think, we had to move.

The flowers stood almost seven feet from the ground and each flower head had a radius of four feet. They looked like giant daisies with a large round center and petals stretching out like the sun. The aroma of the flower was bold and pleasant and the variety of colors could fill a Crayola box of sixty-four and still not capture them all.

The blooms swayed back and forth as we pushed our way through them. Sarah spied a rock outcropping some half-mile ahead and we picked up our pace. I held Robina's hand and hurried her along. Farica ran ahead of us to catch up to Sarah. The fragrant smell of the flowers was over-powering, it acted as a stimulant. I felt my strength improve and even my mood brightened.

Farica stopped by one of the larger red and blue flowers. It moved closer to her as she smelled the blossom. I could see her move closer to the plant and in almost a trance; she touched the bright red petal. Before I realized it the flower grabbed her and encased her in the petals that rolled up into a pod with Farica trapped inside.

As Angus and I ran to the plant, all the other flowers expelled a noxious powder which gave the air a fog like appearance. I covered my mouth, but Angus stumbled and fell to the ground. I noticed a vine from one of the plants move along the ground and wrap itself around Angus' body. I didn't know which way to go, help Angus or try to release Farica from her encasement?

"Jonathan, you go to Farica. I'll free Angus." Out of the corner of my eye, I saw Sarah using her dagger to slash the vine to free Angus. I observed that plants around us expelled poison powder.

"Jesus, Jonathan, this stuff is pure heroin. Keep at a distance from it or you'll be like Angus. The plants are trying to kill us."

I drew my sword from my belt and slashed franticly at the pod. Each gash caused the plant to cry out in a loud hissing sound. I attacked the plant for almost a minute to cut Farica free of the pod. The plant fought back, smashing the pod into me, trying to knock me to the ground. A large vine lashed out at me, trying to curl itself around my body. Robina, who had not regained her full strength, cut the vine, hacking furiously at it until it spilled green blood and slithered into the primordial jungle.

My sword did the work. My last swing severed the stem, dropping the pod to the ground. Farica rolled out of the encasement. The petals that held her tight now lay on the ground in shreds from my hacking.

Farica's breathing was shallow and her heartbeat slow and weak. I sur-mised that pure heroin was in the center of the flower and when it encased her, the plant smothered her in the drug.

As I pulled our injured to safety, I slashed every stem of the hideous plants I could reach. With two of the five of my team unable to travel, Sarah and

I manhandled them towards the top of the rock outcropping, which over-looked the jungle, and sat exhausted waiting for the next disaster to strike.

Sarah looked at me with fatigue in her eyes and perspiration pouring down her body. "I need water. This heat is killing me."

"We need water, but I bet one of the faunas or flora will kill us first. Keep a watch out for danger." Then I said, "I'll wander down into that hell below to find something."

She smiled at me as I left. "When you're down there can you find me a Big Mac," she asked, I'm dying for one. I haven't had one in months. Maybe some Dino legs from KFC would be good too."

Robina shook her head. "Big Mac, Dino's legs, KFC, what language are you two talking? There are such things in the jungle?"

Sarah laughed and answered, "No, Robina, it's a joke. Those are foods back in our time not in this weird jungle."

"I'll see what I can find," I promised. I held Buffoon firmly in my hand. I proceeded back into the jungle.

I made no noise as I returned to the primordial rain forest and the home of the dinosaurs. I moved with a fluid motion, always watching in every direction before I took a step. To my surprise, I saw an exotic looking bird like creature trotted in front of me. I crept up to him on his downwind side so he wouldn't see me. He had green feather-like scales and was the size of a large dog. He moved faster than I could run, but I had my dead friend Beth's bow and arrow. I stopped and took aim, but the beast disappeared in the undergrowth. I could see no further use for the bow and arrow. I started to sling it on my back when a second creature similar to the first, but a little smaller walked about five feet in front of me.

I shot the poor beast through the back of its head. It died on the spot. I shook my head and wondered aloud, "How could such a stupid animal survive in this world of survival of the fittest?"

I tied the animal's legs with a vine I found hanging from the nearest tree. I threw the carcass over my shoulder and started on the hunt for water. I had continued about another ten feet when the heavens opened and more water than I had ever seen came rushing from the sky. In seconds, I stood ankle-deep in a stream. The water crept up my leg and every second I was in the water, I feared that some creature would attack me. My premonition came true; it wasn't from the water but from behind me. I heard a sound so foreign, but blood curdling. I ran as fast as I could with the forty-pound chicken like creature on my back.

The climb back up to Sarah and Robina further exhausted me. My heart raced and I wished only to collapse. I was dead on my feet. Sarah had made a dam out of pocket-sized rocks, mud and leaves, which formed a tiny reservoir for us. It was almost a foot deep in water and ten feet long. I scooped up a large handful and drank. It took another six such gulps to quench my thirst.

Robina rushed to me and hugged me. "God, I thought you would never return," She cried, "I don't like this place." She looked down at Angus and Farica. "We need them back. Farica would know what to do. By all that is holy, there must be a way home."

I put my arm around her and kissed her forehead. "My love, no matter what it takes I'll get us home." Then I thought what home, mine or hers, or did it matter?

As Robina and I held each other tight, Sarah had gutted the creature and hung it to cure.

"Holy shit, where did you learn that?" I asked with amazement dripping from my voice.

"I told you, I spent my summers on my grandparents' farm, don't you remember? My granddad showed me how. He raised pigs, turkeys and chickens for his own use." She poked the hanging beast, whatever it was with her dagger. "It'll make a good dinner, now all we need is fire and dry wood."

I tried to remember how we started a fire by rubbing two sticks together in Boy Scouts. I know I needed to have wood shavings and a bow to spin a stick and a block with a hole or dimple in it to hold the stick. That's how I made the friction to ignite my shavings. However, that's all I remembered. As I was working out the design in my head, the rain stopped. The clouds disappeared, and the intense sun dried everything out. The rocks became unbearably hot.

Robina put her hand on my shoulder. "If we still could do magic I'd just say a few words, and a fire would be burning," she said, "however, we've lost it in this wild and dangerous land."

I had no answer for her, so I looked out into the jungle and in distance to the south. I caught a glimpse of wisps of smoke or steam rising from a distant escarpment. My mind raced. It had to be geo-thermal venting, a source of heat and fire.

"Sarah, I found a place for us to set up a permanent camp. Look to the south where the smoke is coming from, it will have everything we need. How are our patients doing?'

She sighed. "Farica is in pain and still not responding, but I think that's not unusual since a plant almost ate her. Besides that she has no broken bones and is not bleeding. Angus is not responding. He's in a coma. He has a puncture wound on his leg. That vine must have had barbs on it covered in some poison."

"Is there anything we can do for him?" Without waiting for an answer I gazed at the sun and the distance to the escarpment. "We need to move, or we won't be at the top of the escarpment before sunset. I don't want to be in the jungle at night."

Robina walked over to me rubbing her chest. "I'm better," she said. "It still hurts, but I can walk faster or even run if we have to. Show me this smoky place you want to go to."

I pointed off into the distance, "Johnny that seems a long way to go. Are you sure it's worth the effort?"

Behind us, I heard movement and swung around with Buffoon ready to kill. To my surprise, Farica stood behind me. Her eyes still glazed and looking the worse for wear. She rubbed her head with both hands as she spoke, "I thought I was dead. The dreams—they seemed so real. I fought off the poison by mentally cleaning my body in my dreams." She sighed. "I almost died."

Then she saw Angus." Oh my god! Hand me my packsack." She forced a packet of green guck down his throat.

"We'll have to carry Angus. He's still not good." She looked beat. "That plant took a lot out of me when I struggled inside it. I could feel its mind, or whatever primitive thoughts' plants have. Food was the thought I received. Food! That's all I was to it." She shivered, "To think I came millions of years into the past as food for a plant. I must say a beautiful plant, but a plant nonetheless."

It stunned me that in her dreams, she could heal herself. Only a few minutes ago Farica was in a coma, and now she was back with the living. "Farica, are you sure you are O.K?"

"No. I'm not all right. A plant tried to eat me and I dreamed of death, death for us all. However, I'm not dead and neither are you. I can walk and talk and carry on."

I gave a sigh. She was back to her old self. I quizzed her, "How's Angus, will he live?"

She shook her head and replied, "It's time that's most important. If I can work on someone soon after their injury or death, then my potions and faith healing will bring them back whole. If time goes by, the body passes beyond my ability to repair. I can only help within the first few hours of the injury or death."

I shook my head in frustration. If only she had gained consciousness sooner, maybe she could have done more for Angus. We had to leave. The sun dropped low on the horizon even as we talked.

It took us less than five minutes to start our trek across the jungle to the escarpment. Sarah and I carried the litter with Angus, and Robina carried the gutted chicken-like critter. Farica led the way. We found an animal trail that led almost directly to the escarpment. The light started to fade as we approached the base of the hill. The team stayed silent as we gingerly continued, watching for any movement in front and behind us. We spotted huge animals everywhere, but avoided any contact with them. To my surprise, most of the dinosaurs that came close to us ate plants.

Once at the escarpment, we realized we had a problem. The cliff was steep, and it would take all our efforts to climb it without carrying the litter. Farica's face showed her exhaustion. Her body swam in her sweat. I felt the same. Sarah was the freshest, but she looked as if she had just run two marathons. Robina and I sat with our backs together to support ourselves.

I spoke with little enthusiasm in my voice, gasping every few seconds. "We have to reach the top before the light goes. We can't stay here. The night feeders will devour us. How are we going to get him to the top?"

A smile came to Sarah's eyes as she replied, "We use magic. I only wave my hand, and he floats to the top."

I almost did it, but remembered Leo's dead zone gadget. "No, we need a practical way to transport him up there."

Farica took a slow deep breath and said, "Back when I initially joined the order at my original convent, we had our cloisters at a summit of a tall rock with only a winding path to the top. One side was almost vertical. We used a rope and pulley to bring up a basket with our supplies. We could find some twine and three of us could climb up to the top and pull him up. The other can guide the litter over jagged rocks and free the rope from snagging. I'll stay with Angus and guide him up to the three of you as you pull him up."

After rooting around in the jungle, we found enough vines to make a rope of about three hundred feet. I took Robina's hand and said, "Let's do it. The three of us can do it! If the nuns can, we can!"

Sarah scouted the side of the escarpment and found what looked like a path, not wide, but big enough for us to travel to the top of the escalade.

After climbing a hundred feet I could hardly breathe, "Jesus, I hope we can make it to the top."

"Oh fearless leader, Emperor of this world, you can do anything if you put your mind to it," Sarah said with a smile.

Robina barked at her, "Don't make fun of him, he's the chosen one, and he'll find a way to take us back to our time and Berwick. He will fulfill the Prophecy."

We reached a natural terraced area. The ground was flat giving us a small but safe area to rest. I collapsed. Sarah gave a huge groan, "Oh God!" Then she looked down. The litter was directly below us. She shouted towards Farica, "How's everyone doing down there?"

In a faint voice which wavered in the storm that blew in as we started the climb she replied, "I'm all right, but he's still not with us yet. Why don't you pull him up from there, and I can climb up with him?"

I looked at the ground, it appeared rough and un-climbable.

"It doesn't look good, Farica. Are you sure?"

I heard the edge in her voice, "I see the jungle moving behind me and the sounds are not pleasant. I think being on the hill will give me more confidence in surviving the night."

I looked around. The sun looked low on the western horizon. Maybe a half-hour to forty minutes of light left. "Okay, we'll start to pull him up."

My muscles cried out on the first pull. Angus weighed more than I thought. On the litter, it seemed as if he floated along. Now I prayed to whatever god could hear me, to give me strength to pull Angus up to where I stood. After pulling him halfway up to the top, I called a stop. A big rock stood beside me. With the others' help, I tied the rope around the rock then the three of us collapsed in a heap.

As we lay on the ground trying to regain our strength, Farica screamed from below. It was a scream of terror, and my blood froze. I scrambled to my feet and looked down. Three Pterodactyls with their leather wings circled the defenseless Angus. Farica with her sword drawn fended them off, but they kept coming.

The birds of prey attacked vigorously. Farica swung her sword with more power than I could imagine. The sword appeared as ten blurring arcs swinging around her. The birds attacked from all sides, yet they stayed just outside her arc. To my dismay three more of the birds appeared. With a wingspan of twenty feet, the six covered my view of the litter and Farica. In a blur of sword, talons and beaks, one of the birds fell from the sky.

Even with this victory, I could tell by the prehistoric bird diving on my friends and they were closing ranks and they were looking for blood. This battle was not over and had only one conclusion. I cursed the sky and my stupidity.

Without warning and from the very top of the mountain, a huge arrow slammed into one of the Pterodactyls, driving the bird-like creature to the ground. The animal tried to fly. The arrow was embedded in the ground and impaled the creature

CHAPTER TWENTY-FOUR

ANOTHER PTERODACTYL FELL FROM THE SKY, SUFFERING THE SAME fate as its fellow attacker. I watched in amazement as the others flew away. I looked up to the top of the escarpment, but I could only see the shadows cast by the disappearing sun.

"Pull them up fast, we only have a few minutes until we lose the light," yelled Sarah. Then she started pulling on the rope.

The five of us lay on the outcropping of rock, which formed the platform halfway up the escarpment. I turned to Sarah and Robina and asked, "Did you see where those arrows came from?"

Both shook their heads. Sarah asked, "Who's here? It's too early for humans to develop, but only a human mind could develop complex tools like a bow and arrow. Who can it be?"

I pursed my lips. "Maybe in this world humans developed sooner and it's a primitive tribe."

"God, Jonathan, you're a scientist, you know that's impossible. No, like us, there must be time travelers here from some other time, but from when? Who are they?"

Robina had listened in silence but now she spoke, "There's only one way to know, we'll have to climb to the top and see who saved Farica from those birds. What do you say, Farica, are you prepared to climb up the next part of the mountain?"

She looked up to the top and replied, "It's extremely steep the rest of the way, you better tie a rope around me. You'll probably have to pull me up some of the way."

The sun had dropped below the horizon almost an hour before all of us reached the top of the escarpment. The jungle at the top thinned out, but in the dark with no moon, it looked like a wall of black. I felt a cool breeze coming from the west and debated whether to spend the night in the open or find a place in the fringes of the jungle.

"No, Jonathan," replied Sarah, "it's better for us to camp here tonight. The cliff at our back and open ground around us will protect us better than in the jungle. We'll take shifts so one of us is always awake."

At dawn, I almost nodded off, but a movement in the trees about fifty yards away brought me back to life in a hurry. "Everyone up, I see something."

Angus had regained consciousness in the night. He still had a serious headache, but otherwise he had returned to his old self. He picked up his claymore and yelled, "Come on ye little beasties, let's see how ya like the taste o' ma blade."

I could see the Thane of Scotland slay any beastie, little or not, that came into our makeshift camp. The look of killing in his icy blue eyes frightened even me. Once he postured in his killing stance the rest of us stood back and awaited the attack.

Farica saw them first. She pointed, and then said in almost a whisper, "Oh my God and all the dead wizards."

I thought my eyes deceived me, six men exited the jungle, each dressed in the colors of the Masters; red, white, green, orange, black and tartan. Farica ran to them. I could tell she was crying and laughing all at the same time. They reminded me of the knight guarding the chalice in Indiana Jones, tall, gaunt looking, and of an indeterminate age.

As she ran, she yelled to the men in a strange form of English. However, I could understand it with no difficulty, "Ye be the Soothsayers of Berwick, the ones who foretold of the coming of the Emperor Jonathan, be ye not?"

Hearing the words my mind clouded with confusion. By then the rest of us had run after Farica. I shook my head to clear the cobwebs and looked sternly at her, "What nonsense is this?" I said. "You told me the Prophecy of Berwick was almost a thousand years old, how could these be the soothsayers who predicted my coming?"

The six Seers embraced Farica as we approached. The Black robed soothsayer spoke, "It's a miracle beyond hope. Jonathan, you are as I saw you in my mind, and this must be Sarah the warrior." He looked at Robina. "Ah yes, the Black Witch. You look like your ancestor, the wife of the Black Lord I served." He then looked back at Farica, "Mother Superior, it is you. Oh what an amazing turn of events." He gave her an extra big hug.

Sarah looked astonished, "You know us?"

The Red Soothsayer answered, "Of course we do, and we foretold your coming. We know everything about you. However, we never imagined we would meet you."

I was skeptical. "If you know so much, why didn't you know we would meet you?" Then I paused, "How did you get here, and why are we here?"

The Tartan Seer laughed and replied, "Too many questions, my young Emperor, wait an' a' will be clear." He looked at Angus. "Ah, it's ma kin, Angus the Highlander." He waved us into the jungle. "Follow us we have a safe hide-away not far from here."

Tall trees formed the ramparts of the hideaway; the inside was a stout stone keep with wooden out buildings. The keep stood thirty feet high and was thirty feet on all four sides.

The Red Seer saw the creature Robina was carrying. "I see you killed yourself a dinochick. They're wonderful when cooked with wild rice and chives." He took it from her shoulder, "Let me cook it up for lunch."

I scanned the inside of the keep. It had all the conveniences of home, strong walls, a cook stove and a plethora of weapons attached to the exterior walls. Everything looked new, not ages old or even worn. The wood seemed freshly cut, not dark with age or rotting.

"It is time," I said, "to tell us what's happening."

"Come upstairs and sit with us in our meditation room. We have nothing to hide. Come."

We followed the Black Soothsayer up a rough set of wooden stairs to the top of the tower. It had large windows on all sides and a large round table in the center of the room. Twelve chairs circled the table. "We started this adventure with twelve. The Blue, Yellow, Tan, Violet, Gray and Brown soothsayers all died after we arrived, many in the first few days until we understood the ecology of this time."

He stopped talking, and stared off into the jungle. "Those kingdoms don't exist anymore do they? I understood the meaning of their deaths."

It was the first time in hours that Arthur spoke to me, "I heard the Legends of the past Masters and their domains. I thought them mostly fiction, stories told on dark nights in the winter to amuse the children."

In a soft voice, Robina asked the Black Seer to continue. He sighed, "We've been here about four years, as we count time. It must be longer in the world you just came from. The scientists of the Gray and the Blue Masters built the machine. They knew technology. They had many different machines to perform magic for them. They pushed a switch and light came from a lantern, but it was not oil or candlelight, it was as bright as the sun. They didn't travel on horses but in wagons that propelled themselves.

"I digress, they built a machine which would travel in time, but it didn't work. It took people to different dimensions. Or that's what the returning travelers told us. Our physical world holds many alternate realities. One came back distorted and brought another human from the dimension he left. Another traveler came back with a duplicate of himself attached to his back facing outward, it was hideous. The fabric of our world started to change. First magic became much more powerful and then the scientists started to fade away. I watched one just vanish. The last of them told us they disappeared into the other dimension.

"With the powerful magic came the Prophecy, we aren't magicians, we can only see into the future. First we saw only a week or so in the future: who would die, or if it would rain. Then the twelve of us started seeing events in the distant future as well.

"The magicians feared us, as they feared the scientists. They imprisoned us at Berwick, but wanted us to foretell their futures. When we told them about the terrible catastrophes that would befall them, they feared us even more. When we told them about the coming of an Emperor to destroy their magical world, they wanted to kill us, but they still needed us to tell them whether to go to war or not."

He took a deep breath and looked at us. We sat spellbound around the table. This was not history that any of our friends had heard before. It frightened them. I could see it on their faces. Arthur, inside my mind, gasped. The Black Seer continued, "The Red Master read the Prophecy out loud then tore it up and threw it on the floor. We had given each of the Masters a copy, as well as the few scientists who had not faded away. The Red Master's rage consumed him. When he turned twenty-five, he wrote Saunders on Wizardry and other Crafts. The magic spells and potions in the book destroyed the need for science and brought magic to the forefront of society. The book that he published and gave to the Masters contained only half of his work. The full volume told of spells that could destroy the world, violent storms, earthquakes, volcanoes, instant armies, and all the misfortunes you successfully conquered." He stopped talking for a minute, then added, "The Red Master rediscovered the earliest religion of our world, that of the Ancient Ones. The first time they came to our world they brought fire, with his rediscovery of them they brought magic. It is from them that he derived his knowledge. He brought them back to our land so he and his minions could worship them. He used this new magic gained from them against the people."

The Soothsayer looked pathetically sad. "But for us, he chose to send us back to the time of the giant beasts. He chose this time because of the violence, and he told us because in a short time, everything would die. He called it the great extinction; a rock will fall from the sky and kill us all."

The Green robed soothsayer broke in, "We have seen it. It's not pleasant. Everything will change. We have three years, give or take six months, to wait."

He bowed his head but then looked up with bright eyes. "Your coming has told us we'll all survive. You have a date with destiny. You will fulfill the Prophecy."

I didn't have the light in my eye. I felt defeated. "How?" I bowed my head as he did, "How are we to return to complete the task?

His eyes now twinkled as he replied, "You are the Emperor. You'll find a way."

I looked around the table at my team and the soothsayers. "How do you know?"

A brilliant smile spread across his face. "Because that's what we do, we predict the future. We don't know how you'll do it, but you'll find a way."

I scanned the table again then gazed deep into his eyes. "We can't even do magic!" I exclaimed. "We had a gadget to put a dead zone around us, and we activated it when the Red Master zapped us here. We tried to use our magic, but it won't work."

He laughed and said, "We predicted the oriental would join your quest, and he would have that device. It only works in a small area, does it not?"

He shook his head at me. "Once you moved away from where you entered this time your magic returned. Try it now," he urged.

My whole team did a small spell. I filled the table with food and drink. The Seers all laughed and the Green robed soothsayer exclaimed, "See, you still have your magic! You can find a way to return to defeat the Red Master."

Robina spoke, "I have a copy of the Saunders on Wizardry and other Crafts. Maybe it has the time-travel spell."

The Orange Seer spoke, "If you have a copy of Saunders it will be a condensed version not the full version. Only the Red Master has a whole copy, and it's always kept at Berwick with the machine."

Robina tried to continue her conversation, but I drowned her out, "The machine, the one that takes people from dimension to dimension. It actually exists?"

All the Soothsayers laughed. "Yes, Emperor, it exists, and no Master dares to destroy it, or it would destroy our world. It awaits you."

The eleven of us sat around the table brainstorming the rest of that day on strategies to return to the world we left behind. Robina's solution to the problem of time travel had only one answer, magic. She determined that with the minds we had in the room, we should be able to come up with a spell to propel us forward in time to when we had left the field next to the Tweed River.

Arthur yelled in my brain, "That damn daughter of mine doesn't realize the best wizards for the past thousand years have tried to make a spell to time travel. The ancient Red Master had help. The wizards tell he traveled in the Berwick machine and returned with spells and potions never before known to us. No, we cannot repeat his findings without help from another dimension." I repeated his words to the group around the round table.

We argued for another hour about magic and how spells came into being. The old Seers shook their heads. The Orange robed soothsayer spoke, "We see no magic in our return."

Robina turned to Angus for support, but he too shook his head. "No, Robina, oor magic is not able to travel through time." He looked away from her, and I could see a small tear drop from his eye, "We're trapped here until the rock from the sky destroys everything."

I took a deep breath, "No. We have another way out of this problem. Sarah and I in our world are two of the brightest scientists in the field of time travel. We have a few years to solve the problem of how to build a machine that will take us back to the future. It's our only way to return."

Sarah had a stunned look on her face. "Jonathan," she said, "science has tried for hundreds of years to understand the concept of time travel, and no one has ever done it." Then she looked around at the primitive setting of our present existence. "We don't even have the most rudimentary tools of science to start our inquiries."

I smiled at her and said several words under my breath. A hefty square rock in the corner of the keep turned into a large mainframe computer. The table in front of Sarah became the monitor and input system for the computer. "It's the one we saw in New York that Professor Stafford tried to buy for our lab. It's just magic. I thought of what I wanted, did the acquisition spell, and presto, we have it. With magic and science, we'll be out of here in no time."

"Yes," Sarah said," but where is the power coming from?'

I laughed, "Silly girl, did you see that fast moving river at the bottom of the cliff. I also used magic to build a dam and strung power lines to the compound. Yes, we have good old electricity."

Sarah and I made the room into a top-notch science lab in minutes. We even called up all the research papers we had read in our construction of the machine in Oxford that brought us to this world.

I explained to the others the scientific method and how it resembled magic. Potions in science took the name chemistry, and spells worked like physics. This interested every one of the trapped Wizards and Seers. They enthusiastically wanted to help.

I devised a learning spell like Robina had made for us. I used pure gold from a lava flow instead of gold coins and raw diamonds and rubies instead of polished stones. I trained my team of scientists in all aspects of chemistry, biology, physics and even engineering. The Seers found physics their specialty, but astrophysics enchanted them. Robina couldn't get enough of chemistry, and Angus took a liking to biology. Farica amazed me. She had a natural aptitude for engineering. Her innate ability surpassed even Beth's understanding and ability to take a concept and make it functional.

With a team of ten beside me, we started to work ten days after our arrival. My plan had a simple structure. Time resembled a string and like a string, it was either tight or loose. When it was loose, it could touch another piece of itself. All we had to do was slacken the string, so we could move from one point along it to another. In its normal state, time did not bend or slacken, but once the underpinning which held it tight loosened, we could travel to any point along the string. Time was no longer linear, but three dimensional. We could jump from one time to another when the string of time formed a loop and two parts of the string intersected. In the model I constructed, time was finite. It had a beginning and an end. Once we found them, either we pulled them together or untied one end of the long string of time.

As we began working on the idea, a personal problem arose. Robina came to me crying hysterically. She said she was no longer pregnant but had not miscarried.

"Has the Red Master put a spell on me?"

The Green Soothsayer overheard her deep pain. In a soft sympatric voice he said, "No child, you are not with a child in this time. When you return to your time the pregnancy will continue as if you never left." He smiled with a twinkle in his eye in the kind manner he had, "We have foreseen this. The Emperor's child exists in your time. I promise."

Robina patted her stomach, "Thank you. I miss it."

Her efforts were tenfold more inspired to return us to our own time and her impending motherhood.

We worked on the problem for over a year. Each step took months. New principles took shape. One day Sarah said to me, "My god, Jonathan, I think the accelerators are ready to test. If it works, time will slow down, and we'll have just a moment of slack in the continuum. We'll feel it, and I believe we'll see it."

I gave her a mock frown. "Sarah, I know, remember this is my theory."

She laughed. "Sorry, but it's so exciting, I keep telling myself it'll work. To think we had the wrong idea of time when we worked in Oxford. No wonder we jumped dimensions. Your theory is so pure and simple, one could imagine that any dullard physicist would have come up with the idea."

I rolled my eyes at her. "You think I'm just a moron that came up with the most obvious solution? I don't get any credit for original thought?"

It was her turn for the mock frown. "No, no, that's not what I meant. I expressed myself badly. You are brilliant. It's just that once seen from this perspective it's so simple."

Our measurement of the time slipping and joining still hadn't a calibration. Therefore, when we did our first test, we had no idea if we went forwards in time or backwards in time. The jump would only last a few seconds then the string of time would snap us back to our primordial existence. Or so we hoped.

All of us stood in the courtyard of the compound. Our time machine resembled a bus without wheels. The body housed twelve seats and all the miniaturized compartments that now held more computer chips than ten thousand desktops, and more uranium than five one hundred megaton bombs.

"Is everyone ready?" I yelled over the hum of the machine. None of us knew what to expect. Would it be a flash and searing pain in the brain, or a sharp cold experience? It was just like our expectations when Sarah and I departed our own world to come to this one.

We had constructed the frame of our machine of steel and aluminum, and the upper half we encased in a clear Kevlar bubble. As I pushed the lever forward less than an inch, I waited for the change in time, and the change in the world.

CHAPTER TWENTY-FIVE

NOTHING HAPPENED. ONLY A LITTLE SHIVER AND MY VISION BLURRED. The compound changed just a little. More weeds and debris crept into my sight. Nothing changed in me, nor did I feel any of the symptoms I expected. I checked the others, and they all smiled back.

Robina looked quizzically at me and asked, "What happened? It doesn't seem like we traveled anywhere. Everything is the same. Are you sure this contraption of yours worked?"

The excitement in Sarah's voice caught us all off guard, "We've moved forward in time. The astral reader tells us it's almost four years since we first arrived or two years one month and two days we've traveled ahead."

The Black Seer cried out, "We must return and now."

All the other Soothsayers gave the same command and started chanting. The Seers stayed in the machine, but the five of us exited and examined the courtyard. I looked up in the sky and noticed a spot against the sun. It was tiny but growing bigger, just noticeable to the naked eye.

"Sarah, what do you make of that?" I pointed up into the sky.

"My God, it's an asteroid. It must be the one that kills off the dinosaurs and devastates the earth's plants and animal, making the planet a wasteland for millions of years." We watched as the spot grew. She spoke again, "Theory has it that it crashes into the world to form the Gulf of Mexico. However, the world's continents don't have the same configuration as when we lived. God, I can't remember how far away from England the asteroid hits the earth. I should know that, yes I do know that."

Before she continued, I grabbed her. "We have to return to the past. Once we work out the calibrations, we can return to Berwick. We can't stay or we'll be like the dinosaurs."

She pulled away from me. "We're scientists. We have to stay and record what happens. There is no record of this. There are only theories and they are unclear."

Before I could answer, the rock in the sky blotted out the sun and seconds later the whole earth shook and vibrated. I grabbed her by the collar and dragged her back to the machine. The eleven of us sat in our seats watching the outside world change. The way the heavens moved was awe inspiring. In a blink of an eye, the sun changed places in the sky. I had my hands on the instruments to return us to the past, but waited as Sarah said this was a chance to see the world change dramatically.

The first ripple from the collision hit us like an atomic blast with winds of three times the force of a hurricane. Trees everywhere flew from the ground and now became projectiles to destroy any plants or animals in their way. I didn't wait for the next ripple of destruction. I moved the lever to put us in time travel, but instead of backward. I went forward only a few days.

Chaos filled our vision. The keep was in rubble, and the jungle lay as ash around us. A fire of epic proportions swept through the land. Now ash fell from the sky, which was a murky gray. The wind tore through the land in whirlpools bringing all the fine ash into the clouds.

Sarah and I exited the time machine. Sarah shivered, "My god it's cold. Feel that wind, it's going to snow, and it should be summer. And where is the sun?"

I scooped up a bag of ash and walked to the edge of the plateau. The land-scape reminded me of photos of the moon, greyish and barren. No animals, no plants, the ground looked radiated and unable to sustain life. Just gray moonscape reflected in my eyes.

I thought aloud to Sarah, "I wish our time machine could fly. Then we could watch the world in this state of flux and why life died and started over. We could return afterwards to our world in the 21st century with all the data showing how devastating an asteroid's collision is."

"Return us to the compound", she said." Before we start this trip we have some modifications to make."

The Soothsayers exited the time machine discombobulated. When we entered the fort I overheard the Green Seer telling the Red one, "I couldn't read the future when we saw the rock heading to the earth. I didn't feel anything. I thought I would die."

Sarah put her hand up for silence. "Our trip succeeded. We have a functioning time machine, but it needs further changes. We leave in ten days but, first I need everyone to help."

With magic and engineering, we redesigned the time machine so it now sat twelve passengers and two pilots. Its design incorporated retractable wings with the capacity to take off and land vertically. It had caterpillar tracks to travel through the roughest of terrain. Sarah also designed it with remote-controlled cameras and digital recording machines.

After breakfast on the tenth day, we prepared to leave. The craft sat in the same spot we left it from eleven days before. This time it would take us back to Berwick to defeat the Red Master and then return us to our world. As I started the machine, I asked Farica. "When and where should we return?"

She looked confused. "After the discussions we've had, I'm not sure if we should return while we are on the battlefield or some time before. What do you think will happen? You know if there are two of us facing the Red Master, will that tear this time-space continuum, or will it snap the string of time? What are we to do?"

I had to smile, the magic world's wizards and sorceresses on my team debated the concept of the space-time continuum paradox in the same way as my world's physicists and science fiction buffs have debated it for years.

I turned to my Soothsayers and asked, "Can we exist as duplicates of ourselves in the same time and place that we left, or will we die? Will the world end? Tell me when we should arrive back at the battlefield."

They eyeballed each other. "Aye," said the Scottish Seer, "I see ye arriving in a cloud o' smoke behind the Red Master some seconds after ye disappeared frae the battlefield." He stared off into space and finally continued, "I didnae see ye disintegrate intae powder or the world start tae disappear in areas that ya and the others hae been. The world just continued. Therefore, the events we predicted will happen."

Before I pushed the lever of the time machine forward to engage the mechanism, I turned to face the Soothsayers and Farica. "What is it with this Prophecy that no one ever tells me what's going to happen? Why do you keep me in the dark? Just a few helpful phrases would be useful, so I know what to expect."

No one said a word. They stared back at me with the look of the cat that swallowed the canary. Then I heard Arthur laugh in my ear and say, "Farica is trying to protect you. The other sons of bitches like me are not willing to tempt fate by outlining your future for you in case you try to avoid it, and in the process wreak havoc with the Prophecy." Then he laughed again. He spoke to me all the time about life in general, and specifically about Robina and my relationship with her. He loved her and dug in my mind to make sure that I was the best man for her. He became my best friend and worst critic.

To no one, specifically, but to them all, I shouted, "Let's do it, you mother fuckers. What will be will be. You're right; no one should know their future." I pushed the lever forward and watched the digital read out show the seconds, minutes, hours, days and years flash ahead in green. The years flashed by, so at most the first digit was readable. The others numbers I could only see as a blur. At one million years before the modern era, I slowed the machine down and every hundred thousand years I slowed it even more. I didn't want to overshoot the time of our arrival or undershoot it. Both could be disastrous to my team and to my army on the ground.

My technology of time travel made it impossible for me to pop into a time without notice. My flying machine had too great a mass to hide in your back pocket. Half an hour before the confrontation on the banks of the Tweed, I landed the time machine behind the lines of the Red Master's army.

We marched forward into the rear ranks of the Red Army. We continued down the High Street when trouble found us. He stood in the center of the road at a checkpoint. I wore the red tunic and blue pants of a colonel in the Red Army. The sergeant who stood at the checkpoint, as fate would have it, turned out to be the sergeant who had commanded the guard those many months ago in the dungeons at Oxford.

His eyes widened in a stare and then recognition. He stood in front of me with his sword out, and in his parade square sergeant major voice yelled, "Stop, and defend yourself."

The company of soldiers loitering on the street all turned to see what the sergeant was about. In my mind I squeezed his throat so he couldn't speak then with a fast thrust disarmed him. I glimpsed another non-com rush forward.

"Sergeant, put this man in irons, he tried to assault me. I commanded him in Oxford when he was the sergeant of the guards. He's a good man. He has just had too much to drink in anticipation of our victory. Hold him in solitary for forty-eight hours."

As I stopped him from talking, I had filled his bloodstream with high proof alcohol. In moments, I had him as drunk as a one of the Black Master's poets and twice as giggly.

We marched past the roadblock deeper into the city. The Red Soothsayer looked in awe at the town and whispered to me as we passed a group of stone buildings surrounding a square with a statue in the center, "See over there?" He pointed to a pub called the Fortune Teller, "That's where I started my foretelling. I did it for pennies then my reputation grew and one day the Red Master kidnapped me. He put me in a tower suite in the Tower of London. He kept me there with the other Masters' Seers. He gathered us there to foretell the future of his lands. He brought us all to Berwick to foretell of the Realm to all the Masters at the Council of Berwick. He was arrogant and craved the adulation of the others. He kept us in the tower where we wrote the scrolls and he told us he would not let the scrolls out of that room. It was our new prison. It's where we first laid eyes on you almost a thousand years ago. I would guess the original scroll is still there."

The five other Soothsayers looked at me and said in unison, "We know what happens next."

One Soothsayer continued, "You don't need us. We're going into the pub and relax with a good meal. You and your friends take care." With that, they turned and walked into the Fortune Teller Pub.

The rest of us reached the old bridge across the Tweed. Five thousand troopers blocked the road in front of us, all waiting to charge across the bridge and slay my army. I gave orders to destroy the will of the soldiers to fight. Our spells incited some to rebel and either leave their ranks or fight their officers. Others we turned into drooling idiots. Each soldier we messed with, we used his predisposition to our advantage. So we changed each mind in a predisposed way. If he hated his officers, he rebelled. Cowards we made run, drunks we made intoxicated. Many we just gave a sleeping spell, so they would sleep for the next twenty-four hours. Those slow of thought, we stopped their ability to think. The soldiers who wished to fight we took away their skills and allowed them to cut themselves on their own weapons.

We had almost reached the bridge when we came upon the main strength of the Red Army and our minds came up against the wizards. Not one or two, but over a hundred of them, all focusing on my army. I sought out the weakest of the bunch and attacked his mind. It became a struggle, for although the weakest, he had strength of mind and character and fought like a tiger. Unfortunately, for him, I now tamed dinosaurs so a tiger, saber tooth or otherwise, didn't faze me.

Our battle to cross the river started. We defended ourselves against spell after spell thrown by the wizards. I had repelled a viper spell before, unfortunately this hex threw me into a pit of ten thousand snakes. Like Indiana Jones, I hate snakes with a passion. I remember as a toddler seeing one and telling my mother I didn't like it and ran and hid. The wizard must have read my mind. I almost froze, but the Black Master acted fast and commanded me from inside my mind to turn them into protozoa. In response to the wizard, I turned him into a Roman candle and his head shot up in the sky and exploded into an array of beautiful colors.

The Battle of the Hundred as it became known continued unabated for what seemed like hours, but lasted only for a few minutes. Every spell that hit us we parried, and then we hit the wizard with a deadly counter-hex. Yet with a hundred of them, we parried many more than we attacked.

I glanced out over the river and saw our other-selves race out to meet the Red Master with Leo by my side. We looked so arrogant on our horses facing the only man in the realm who could defeat us. He for his part looked as his troops wished to see him, proud, haughty and the commanding Master of their world, strong and mighty, facing the renegades and the outlanders. From this side of the river he didn't look old and wasted, but virile and strong.

I yelled at my team, "Draw swords, we're in for it now." Then the scene from the movie Kill Bill flashed into my mind with Uma Thurman fighting the Crazy Eighty-Eights.

I raised Buffoon, kissed Robina and bragged, "If we can kill dinosaurs this will be easy. There are only about forty wizards. Oh yeah, and two thousand troops in front of us and maybe another ten thousand behind us. The Red Master is our target, don't waste your skill."

All of us felt it in the pit of our stomachs and in a searing pain behind our eyes when our doppelgangers disappeared. As my mind cleared I realized all our magic had disappeared with them into the past.

Leo stood alone on the battlefield with the Red Master and we six stood alone close to the bridge with the Red Army. The confrontation between Leo and the Red Master kept the attention of the Red Army and its generals so they didn't realize the danger we were to them.

The army behind us still hadn't organized itself so we marched forward as a unit of the Red Army slaying every wizard. Some tried to defend themselves, but even the Soothsayer trained by Robina during our stay in the keep had the abilities of a mean fighting machine. We marched forward like a threshing machine, swords cutting down the stalks in front of us; one, two, three, every step killed six, then the next another six.

The panicking wizards had nowhere to go. With the dead zone and the lack of magic, they had no defense. The army beyond them stood firm guarding the bridge. They watched their leader and the renegade army, too excited to worry about their rear.

I fought five Red Army soldiers who noticed my handiwork as I killed three frightened wizards in one, two, three strokes of my Buffoon. Almost nonchalantly I thrust my way through the lot. After I dispatched the last of the five, I waved my sword in the air and behind my back in a flourish that would have put a champion baton twirler to shame. As the sword twisted behind me it crashed against a sharp object deflecting it from hitting me. I spun around to find the Red Seer pulling his sword from the belly of the Red Master's personal body guard, from whom I had confiscated Buffoon back in Oxford. He must have recognized his old sword and tried to attack me. The Red Seer saved my life from the brute, or was it fate or the magic that seem to surround me, using the Red Seer as its instrument? I'll never know.

As my mind wavered on that thought, Sarah yelled, "Cut them down. Don't let them escape. Without them the Red Master stands alone." I watched her brutality beheading two of the unarmed wizards with one swish of her sword. The blood of my killing soaked me and the smell made me sick. However, I continued to swing my sword and destroy the enemy.

I paused for a second to catch my breath and saw Leo. I waved at him, and to my surprise, he waved back. I also saw the Red Master trying to cast a spell on Leo, but the dead zone that covered us still covered the battlefield and he could do nothing but charge Leo.

The Battle of the Hundred ultimately became the Massacre of the Hundred. As my small band of warriors came closer to the bridge, the wizards threw themselves into a frenzy, they tried to pry cobblestones from the street to throw at us. Some even used lengths of wood as clubs. Yet whatever weapon they found, it had no effect. They died where they stood.

The Red Master had his attention taken up with our ninja and had no inkling of the fate of his army or his wizards. He charged Leo, meeting him in the center of the field, both slashing out with their swords. The collision stopped both armies, everyone waited to see who still stood. To the surprise of both armies, the riders wobbled on their horses, but both returned to their lines to charge again.

On the bridge behind the Red Army, we pushed our way forward through the ranks as the officers and some of the men allowed us to pass, while others ignored us. The latter group found themselves dead floating in the river. When Leo's second charge took place we had crossed the river and stood next to the commanding general and his staff.

I positioned myself next to the Field Marshal of the Red Army as the clamor reached the front of the army. The general had two duties, one to charge his army across the open fields once the Red Master had killed the ninja, and second, to protect the city and ultimately the castle. He didn't realize his second duty was badly in need of his attention.

Both sides watched in anticipation as the second collision of the horses took place. This time the outcome had both sides yelling. The general had to make a decision or face the consequences, unfortunately for him; he didn't know which to choose.

CHAPTER TWENTY-SIX

THE ORDER WAS GIVEN TO ADVANCE. THE RED ARMY CROSSED THE bridge and formed a line next to the river. After the first line measured five hundred yards, the second formed in front of it and so on and so on. My team of counterfeit officers stood to the right of the forming army and watched.

The contest between Leo and the Red Master had the whole field enthralled. After four passes, both riders looked fatigued, but rode to meet the other with swords high. In the background, I heard the bagpipes of my Scottish Army encouraging our ninja to victory.

I was now in direct sight of Leo. He made eye contact with me after his fourth charge. With a slight nod of his head, he acknowledged my request. As he charged on this last round, he pushed the button on his magic dampener and the six of us acted in unison.

I whispered to Farica, "Horse." I heard her spell, and the Red Master's horse stumbled and fell during its charge.

"General." I signaled to Angus. Seconds later the field marshal and his staff all fell to the ground foaming at the mouth. They had all succumbed to brain aneurysms.

Robina acted on her own. She collapsed the bank of the river Tweed with four rows of the Red army disappearing in the cold waters. I spoke quietly to both the Red Seer and Farica, and they sent a wave of sleeping gas towards the front ranks of the Red Army.

The Red Master must have felt the return of magic from his prone position on the ground, since he pulled Leo from his horse. Leo tried to return to his feet, but the ground below him opened like the mouth of a shark and consumed him. I watched as he struggled to throw himself back onto solid ground. I cast a spell to pull him out of the abyss, but the Red Master blocked my attempt. In retaliation for my actions, he caused the rent in the earth to spew out crude oil, which pulled the ninja down. Leo sank beneath the surface of the ground to drown in oil that came from a reservoir deep in the earth.

My rage overtook me. I attacked the Red Master even as he arrogantly brushed the dirt from his gold braided jacket and jumped back to his feet. My spell caught him off guard. I blinded him by plucking his eyes out. I watched as he realized I was his attacker. He cast hex after hex to find me. I should have killed him then. I felt so stupid when he came at me with a pack of charging elephants. He turned the blood filled flies preying on the gore of the battlefield into pachyderms three times the normal size. They charged my army and scattered my forces to the four winds.

I turned back to the Red Master to do what I should have done before, but the blind despot had abandoned the field of battle.

"Christ, I'm so stupid. I should have killed the bastard." My team stood around me trying to make sense of the last few minutes.

"Jonathan, what happened? Where did the Red Master go?"

I shook my head and groused to Sarah, "I screwed up. I had him in my grasp and only wounded him. What's that saying about an injured animal with no way to escape?" I felt the regret and now the sorrow. I knew my arrogance had caused my army hundreds of casualties that wouldn't have happened just a few seconds before. I muttered, "If only I could turn back time." The irony of my statement did not register. The Red Seer smiled. "You can, any time you want. However, the die you cast today I saw a millennium ago, and when you read the dice, you'll see your winning roll."

I didn't think so, but I kept my own council. I watched as Robina metamorphosed the charging elephants into little brown mice. I breathed a sigh of relief, but I realized the war with the Red Master had not ended, and our final victory had not arrived.

The remnants of the Red Army on the south side of the Tweed retreated across the bridge. I groaned. "Oh hell, we're on this side of the river, and our time machine is on the other side. I'm so stupid. Why didn't I go to the castle where the machine is and take it? Then we could have left the Red Master to regret his loss."

The Red Seer just smiled and shook his head. "That's not your fate."

My heart still raced and beat the same rat-a-tat tat which I remembered from the castle in York, but my mind, was in a faraway place. I thought of the friend I never had a chance to know. Leo died because of my hubris. I should have stopped the combat between him and the Red Master. I knew the ninja had no hope, yet I let it go on so I could wipe out the Red wizards. I mourned him, for he had a taste of freedom, and my arrogance snatched it from him.

A roar of wild rage coming from the other side of the river brought me out of my reverie. I knew it had to be the Red Master. I stretched out my mind and finally we crossed minds. His rage didn't stem from the loss of his vision, but the annihilations of his wizards. He lost all reason. His insanity seared my mind. I felt his power trying to encase me. He tried to squash my mind like one of his large elephants stomping on a grape. I felt the enormous mental power that made magic happen. However, he didn't have focus, just rage. I sidestepped him like a judo move using his strength against him. I entered the Red Master's mind as his mental grip slipped off me, his power was terrifying. I reached deep in and found he had endowed his troops with weapons of magic to fight my men. I also learned that he would fight the war from a distance using magic weather to attack my army with a falling rain of fire and brimstone and arrows of molten lead. I gleaned from his warped brain trickery and deceit, but the where, the why or even the who I could not see because of his insanity.

"We have to force the bridge," yelled Angus. We set up a command tent. The five of us including the Red Seer, sat around a table in the tent looking at a three-dimensional map of the city. Angus continued, "We hae tae break through an' reach the other side o' the river to destroy the Red Master an' his army."

Robina looked disgusted and asked, "How are we to charge through his army? You tell us he's insane and will use every magic spell he knows to defeat us." She shook her head. "It's Horatio on the bridge again."

I looked amazed and asked her how she knew about Horatio.

She gave me a quizzical glance. "Everyone takes the classics in school, both Greek and Roman. I know my Homer and my Virgil. Ah, Caesar, what an Emperor. Even so, you have already surpassed him. Soon, you'll eclipse even Alexander the Great, my Johnny."

As she spoke the fiery rain started to fall. Our tents burst into flames and the fire spread to our encampment. I couldn't let this spell destroy my army.

I had to do something to protect my force. The cries of the injured spread across the field, I watched in horror as soldiers fell to the ground covered in flames.

I puckered up my eyes and using all my force as well as Arthur's, causing the sunny early September day to turn dark with snow clouds. Within seconds, huge flakes of snow started to fall. The temperature dropped thirty degrees, and the snow amassed by inches every minute. The fire and molten lead from the sky died.

My band of friends stood watching the snow form drifts across the open ground. Sarah ran to the river as fast as she could stumble through the drifts. "Christ, Jonathan, you're a genius. You froze the river over, and it's now solid ice." She had to take a breath then continued, "We can charge our army anywhere over the river. The bridge is their choke point, not ours."

Our army formed up in a phalanx, this time my four comrades and I took the point. We cast a spell to deflect all projectiles and spells from us. Then our march started to the city. The snow continued and the temperature was now below zero. I gave each of my soldiers' special clothing that made them impervious to the cold. How much I loved magic and science when combined, they gave me whatever I needed.

I heard cheers from my army as we advanced. Farica pulled at my arm, "Jonathan. We have the Black and Orange Armies joining us."

I didn't understand who had sent them and why they had come. As far as I recalled, the Black Army had returned to Wales and the Orange Army had retreated to York. Why had the Black Army come to Berwick? Robina had assumed her father's place as the Black Master, and controlled the Black Army. I heard rumblings in my head from Arthur. "Robina," I asked, "why is your army here? I thought you told the general to withdraw to Wales."

Before Robina could reply, my head buzzed with Arthur's thoughts on the subject. "Fornicate with the devil, it's my nephew. It has to be him. He's the vilest of creatures. I banished him to London when Robina fell into the hands of the Red Master. It was my nephew's doing. Simon the Snake is his name in our land. Simon the Wise is what the Red Master called him. Whatever it used to be I now call him Simon the Traitor. It's him leading the army, and he will bring all my wizards to fight us. He's a coward and would only come with a large army and powerful magic."

As I related what Arthur had told me, Farica broke in, "Edward is in battle with the New Orange Master. It's Edward's bastard son Richard. Richard commanded the Master's Loyal Guards. During the combat I watched from the keep's battlements."

I looked at her with skepticism. "How do you know this? How could you see Richard from Camelot's battlements?"

She gave me a smile without humor and answered, "The Prophesy, and of course I've been talking to Edward."

"You've been talking to Edward?"

She nodded. "Remember the mirror you took from the Red Master's room? Well, my husband Edward of Camelot has one too, so we use them to communicate. I watched Richard's army try to destroy our Camelot. The spirits of the Blue lord scared his army away. Richard must be leading the Orange Army that is here." She thought a few seconds. "The Orange Army is about four thousand strong, and made up of mainly disgruntled ex-soldiers. They call themselves the Master's Loyal Guards. In fact, they are only here to reap the spoils of war."

I cursed every foul word I knew then ordered the rear half of my army to turn around. I spoke loud and clear with a spell to bring snow falling at twenty feet an hour to blanket the back half of the battlefield. The Orange and the Black Armies behind my army would freeze to death buried in cold white snow.

The flakes came down like wheat out of a grain elevator. Then everything stopped. The clouds evaporated and the September sun burst through. In North America, you'd call the day an Indian summer. I called it hell. The Red Master, as deranged as the mad hatter still had the cunning to put a blanket over magic again.

The six of us stood on the river, as around us the ice cracked and evaporated. I ran for the shore, but I saw the Red Seer fall into the river and the current whisked him faster than I could swim out to the ocean. He looked up at me not with fear in his eyes but joy. I heard his shrill voice yelling to me, "I predicted this. Everything is coming true. Don't worry. I don't die here. The Red Wizard in the Prophecy has more adventures for you. Return to your battle with the Red Master." The last words floated to me on the wind as he disappeared down the river.

I shouted at the rest of my team,. "Robina, Farica, lead five hundred of our troops to the bridge. Don't let any of the buggers get on this side of the river. The rest of us will lead most of the army to fight the Blacks and Oranges. What a surprising trick or treat these two impostors have brought us."

We now had a pitched battle on our hands. The Orange Army led the vanguard of the enemy. I had to kill the fake Orange Master and rout his army. If my plan took more than twenty minutes, the enemy would encircle my army, and the Orange archers would pin us to the ground, like bugs in a display case.

Sarah, Angus and I pushed our way to the front facing the Orange enemy. To my surprise, I glimpsed the Orange Master standing on the back of a wagon, not an ordinary farm buckboard, but a fancy gold ornate carriage with an awning over it, and a table with maps and miniature soldiers placed strategically on it. It was the Orange Master's command center, horse drawn; of course. Similar to what a modern commander would use to direct his troops close to the battlefield. I noticed five soldiers standing beside him on the platform.

My sword in one hand and my shield in the other, I attacked. To my surprise, my sword, nonetheless, possessed the ability to kill on its own initiative, even though the dead zone covered that part of the battlefield. I swung at the first attacker, missing him but severing the head of his friend who had tried to attack me from my right side. Sarah, Angus and I pushed, swung and thrust our swords, and even our shields, into every enemy who came within a ten-foot radius of our position.

The enemy didn't fall back as we attacked, they enveloped us. The three of us formed a triangle facing out and swinging at anything orange. I could see the podium and the impostor. He sat watching the battle in front of him. He looked over the battlefield with a smirk on his face watching his troops fight their way around my army. His elite guards consisted of gigantic grizzled warriors. They looked more like a biker gang than soldiers.

I handed Angus one of the explosive contraptions I made during our holiday in the Cretaceous period. I built them to resemble a baseball. It was the perfect shape to throw. Over our time in that primordial era, I had taught the Seers and my team the venerable thinking man's game. Angus as it turned out, was a born pitcher. Sarah and I stood on both sides of Angus as he tossed my hand grenade into the masses of the false Orange Master's soldiers. Seconds later, a large hole lay before us. Where there once fought soldiers, now lay corpses. Angus threw three more strikes, and we soon stood in a field of corpses in all directions. I know it's morbid, but I laughed out loud. The bombs or balls had not a rawhide cover, but a dinosaur casing, and the shrapnel inside didn't have steel projectiles, but razor-sharp raptor teeth.

"Charge!" I screamed, as we stepped over the pulp of the squished Orange soldiers. I could see the Master in Orange robes try to mutter a spell, but nothing happened. We stood thirty feet away facing his Imperial guard a hundred strong. The Master's face showed concern. I saw him squirm on his podium. I had science, not magic on my side. He had to fight or run. Brute force and the spirit of the warrior would win this battle. I knew my compatriots and the fact the Orange Master had only mercenaries and freebooters on his side. A hundred of them had no chance against three real soldiers.

The Orange Master had to decide whether to stay or to run. He didn't know if his army had won or lost the battle. Those questions flickered across his face. I thought I could smell his fear. I knew I could smell his soldiers' panic as the three of us cut them to pieces. Our combat experience shone off our swords. We had the skill and the right weapons to survive an attack of ten or twenty of his guards and kill every one of them. Once we showed our mettle, the grizzled biker types shied away from us and stepped back. All they saw behind us was their dead and dying comrades.

The Orange Master's remaining guards tasted my sword as they retreated to the wagon with the Master. That's when my archers fired a volley over the open field the grenades had created. The three of us fell to the earth as the arrows whizzed over our heads and pierced the remaining guards. The first twenty fell without moving. The next twenty couldn't retreat any further so they charged like crazed rhinos looking for fresh mud.

The gap behind us was now filled in with an orange mob of retreating grunts. They came from the surrounding force leaving the circle only half completed. My next trick came out of my knapsack, a small ivory gun, the barrel made from the hollow bone of a flying dinosaur. The handle of the pistol was crafted from a tusk of another beast I couldn't even classify. The firing mechanism was a stretchy material from a tree that had to be the predecessor of the rubber plant.

My zip gun used bullets I magically made and machined. The raw material came from nature. It fired a single shot that would rock any of the sons of bitches in an orange uniform. Sarah, Angus and I shot one gun each and then reloaded. After four rounds of fire, the guards no longer existed. The cry of a banshee didn't compare to our war cry as we charged the Orange Master's podium. He stood transfixed as we charged through his retreating mercenaries. We swung our swords with gusto as the enemy started to leave the battlefield. The rear guard retreated with dignity stepping backwards. The next set of ranks hurried their steps trying to avoid the middle ranks retreating in front of them. The central ranks pushed each other and tripped over the ranks behind them trying to escape. The lead ranks of strikers fell over themselves to get away from Angus' claymore, Sarah's sword the Reaper and my swinging sword Buffoon. In all the commotion, the army disintegrated and deserted their commander, the phony Master.

We ran to the podium passing retreating soldiers. Every few steps we would swing our weapons cutting down one or two of the enemy. No one stopped to fight us. No one even noticed us until it was too late. The only orange clad person on the battlefield who saw us was the Master. He just stood on his platform and watched in horror as we came forward. It was the classic case of the deer caught in the headlights. He had time to run. He even had part of an army between him and us. However, he just stood there, not a muscle moving, except the terror causing his face to convulse and his eyes to twitch.

I reached the podium first and yelled such an inhuman cry all eyes on the battlefield looked at the platform. The make-believe Orange Master reacted by giving me a bewildering look. I saw his mouth open, and words start to form. "Don't sir, I—"

My blood was hot and before he could utter another sound, I held his severed head aloft and his warm sticky blood baptized me in front of my troops as the supreme warrior. My army went wild; they attacked every orange rag that still lay on the back of a breathing warrior. The slaughter continued until blood and the dead covered the battlefield, we were winning.

In the midst of our victory Angus whispered in my ear, "We usually don't kill Masters on the battlefield. We might assassinate them, but it is bad form to kill a leader in front of the rabble. They might get the wrong idea and kill their own Master. Your action showed the whole battlefield the old order is gone. You are the true Emperor."

I still held the Orange impostor's head, "But we killed the White Master in York."

"Yes that was in single-handed combat. Here the Orange Master did not draw his sword. And you summarily beheaded him on the platform in front of both our armies. You are the hero of every common soldier in every army."

I shrugged and looked back to the bridge. Robina and Farica's army held its ground. The Red Army had not moved from the bridge and was content to watch. The Black Army of five thousand soldiers marched in good order through the retreating ranks of the fleeing Orange mass, which had once been an army.

I had worn the black uniform of the approaching army and seeing the well-groomed efficient units marching towards me, I felt dread in my heart. They reminded me of the Nazi storm troopers; the SS. Arthur yelled in my mind in rage, "That ungrateful son of a bitch has usurped his authority. Emperor Jon, I grant you the right to kill my nephew. I choose you as my champion to defeat him in battle."

I looked at his men stretched across the field with the sun reflecting off the officers' gold breastplates. I almost ordered my men to attack, when the Black Master within me spoke again. "He's so predictable. He's feigning an attack with his veteran infantry. Watch, he'll parade his light infantry to the front and parade them for twenty yards then shuffle them back into his lines with the old-guard infantry to confuse you. He has hidden the archers in the third section of his advance; once he starts his attack, they will advance and rain arrows on your attacking force. He'll pull back his light infantry, move forward fifty yards with his veterans, and then have the rest join them. He'll repeat this until he meets your remaining force in battle. He'll lose no one, yet half your army will lay on the battlefield because of his archers."

I swore again. "I didn't see it coming. I'd have ... well, thanks, Arthur, I guess that's why you're the Emperor's adviser or should I say part of his brain trust."

I passed the word to my troops to march forward and meet the Black Death. After marching fifty yards in tight formation, the archers of the Black force discharged their initial volley. With well-trained precision, my force formed a turtle with shields placed on all sides of my alignment. The troops inside the ranks held their six-foot shields over their heads forming a roof over the army. The Romans devised this technique and I fashioned my troops' shields a month earlier for this defense. My archers returned fire at the enemy aiming for the archers who had shot on us.

"If I hadn't been here I'd never believe it", Sarah remarked, "who would have guessed that a nerd like you having the talent to be a general beyond compare?"

Under my shield, I smiled at her. "Remember us nerds read books, even history books sometimes. However, who are you to talk, you're my fiercest warrior. Who would have guessed it?"

The volleys continued for another fifteen flights, but then they stopped. In a battle such as this, each archer has a limited number of arrows and relies on the enemy to re-supply him with ammunition. I read about the English in the Hundred Year's War using the longbow and fine string in their bows. Their enemy, the French, couldn't use the British arrows to return fire as the slit for the string was too small. However, the English had a full quiver of French arrows to sling back. The Black Army had to develop a new plan, but unfortunately for them the battle was at this moment in full force. The armies stood fifty yards apart and no one could stop the battle now, not even to revise the attack plan.

I looked at the three thousand soldiers of the Black Master still standing, then at my small army. I prayed.

CHAPTER TWENTY-SEVEN

SOMETHING MADE ME LOOK BEHIND ME AND MY HEART FELT LIKE ICE. The Red Army attacked Robina's force and pushed her troops back from the bridge and into my soldiers. My army stood between the Red and Black Armies. The tyrants' armies squeezed Robina's troops like the jam in the middle of a sandwich. The armies, Black and Red, would soon devour us. My mind was whirling. What could I do? What bit of history, science or magic could I use to save my soldiers and my friends?

Angus looked at me with fire in his eyes. "Jonathan, I knew it would come down to this. It's been a pleasure serving with you. Don't worry my ladies, you'll find a way. We are but mortal men, but you, you are a true angel."

I didn't understand, nor did Sarah, who stood beside me. "What's gotten into him? He sounds like this is the end."

I shrugged, "It does look bleak, but we have come through before."

He heard us and turned with a flicker of amusement on his face. "Aye ma friends, we hae faced many desperate struggles, but alas, the Prophecy tells o' this battle wi' certainty." Then he grabbed both Sarah's hand and mine and clasped them together. "Swear tae ma that ye will never give up. Swear tae ma that wherever ye go, ye'll fight the evil o' the despot. Swear. Swear on yoor blood." Still holding our hands with his left he plucked his dagger from his belt and sliced each of our forearms with a slim line, blood oozing out of the wounds. He took his knife, licked the blade clean of the blood, and then rubbed it on each of our wounds again. "Jonathan, lick your knife also." I did it, and then so did Sarah.

"On the blood o' each other ye will swear." It was barbaric, but it felt good, the warm salty blood from each of us infused me with confidence that the

Prophecy would bring us through. However, Angus' confidence made it a certainty.

The Black Master whispered in my head," Tell Angus for me, I always thought him the worthiest of enemies, the most trusted of allies and the best of friends. I wish him well."

I told Angus this as we stepped forward to meet the enemy. He chuckled and said, "Listen ye old bastard, if the fates had smiled at me at the battle in Dunbar, I might have been your son in law."

Arthur laughed and it vibrated in my head. "She would have killed you my Scottish friend even at the age of twelve. No, the only man who could have tamed her, and who has, is Jonathan the Emperor of the lands, seas and skies."

I didn't have time to tell Angus his reply. The battle started. The Black Army was a much better trained army than the ruffian Orange. We marched in formation to meet them. The Red Army marched steadily towards Farica and Robina's forces in the rear. My optimism of a few minutes before started to evaporate in the hot September afternoon.

I led my army into battle hacking and thrusting my way into the core of the enemy. I felt that tingle that spoke of power. I felt the awakening of magic in me. I cast a simple spell, which caused the four attackers in front of me to drop their swords and run. Just the fact that my magic affected four soldiers, and the Red Master hadn't retaliated, gave me strength. If not my knowledge of history or understanding of science, then my magic would win the battle for me, and the Red Master couldn't stop me. I fought my way past the radius of the dead zone. With confidence and power, we could now defeat the Black Master. I stretched out my mind and found the nephew of Arthur and cousin of my wife. His mind was devious and cunning, yet he still didn't realize my magical strength and power. He had set his army so when we reached this point he would use his magic to crush us. He misjudged my power and my ability to read his mind.

I felt him start his spell and I used a reverse spell so it acted on his soldiers and not mine. The spell he incanted I had never heard or read about, yet I memorized it. The results at first were not obvious, but after another five minutes of battle, the Black Army en masse fell to the ground. I rushed to the nearest soldier and found he still breathed. However, he inhaled only every thirty seconds.

The Black Master was now alone on the battlefield, his army lay all around him. He tried to cast another spell to revive them, but I blocked his incantation.

Nevertheless, from somewhere a powerful presence entered the fray. The power of this being, for I didn't feel a human mind, made the hair on my body stand on end, as if directed by static electricity. I felt that someone or something invaded my mind. I blocked attack after attack, and I could feel Arthur wriggling in pain. I could sense that he couldn't withstand this attack forever.

Angus exclaimed, "We have to eliminate the impostor. We must put him to the sword. Follow me!"

He started to run through the rows of incapacitated soldiers towards the Black Lord, who sat on his stallion. My mind was cluttered with ideas, too much happening so that I couldn't think clearly to stop Angus, so I just followed him. I absentmindedly sliced the throat of every soldier who lay at my feet as we ran towards our enemy.

The Impostor watched us come closer to him, and as we approached, he charged us sitting on his black beast. I threw a lasso of liquid fire at him and he parried with a flaming spear. My lasso grabbed the spear and impaled his horse. The rider fell under the dead beast.

I could see him screaming and crying out in pain. Angus took his claymore and ran the imposter through.

Angus and I turned our attention to the Red Army charging us from behind as our whole force now marched towards the bridge. I knew that this battle would end the war. My troops stopped and stood in a solid single line across the battlefield. The crème de la crème of the Red Master's force stood in front of us in six rows. The Red Master sat on a pure white stallion in the center of the front line of his ranks.

Both armies stood appraising the other. My army earned the distinction of veterans, many stood with me with injuries that would have killed lesser men. With Farica's healing powders and Robina's magic, they mended more than seventy-five percent casualties on the battlefield. Even as my army formed a single line of attack, Farica had used her potion on many of the dead Red and Orange soldiers to swell our ranks for this upcoming battle.

I looked at the enemy and instead of feeling the rage of glory and the desire to kill I saw the same-old battle that we had faced many times before.

There in front of me remained hundreds and thousands of the enemy. With only my sword and my wit standing between me and a sword waiting to slice my heart into little pieces, I didn't want to do it again. I wanted to go home and sleep in my bed, in my own apartment in Oxford. I needed to read the New York Times and see if the Yankees would make the playoffs. Robina's father tried to perk me up, but like a spent bullet, I had no energy left to fight. I had no desire left to win another battle. The alien mind still attacked me, and most of my energy fought him, leaving me with the feelings of despair.

I stood waiting. A scraping noise made me turn and look behind me. Robina's cousin dressed in the Black Master's garb had dragged himself from under his dead horse. Even with an obvious broken leg and a deadly wound, he stood directly behind Angus, who hadn't heard him. As I turned, he thrust his sword into the Thane of Scotland's back and twisted it through my friend's heart. He practiced this cowardly attack. The smooth swift stroke slaughtered my friend. Then he uttered a magic spell that my wracked mind didn't understand which tore Angus into shreds.

My rage overtook me. I swung madly with my sword severing the head of the Black Impostor with a single backhand stroke of Buffoon. His body didn't fall to the ground but stood for all to see, and then he turned and tried to walk away. I charged the headless impostor and severed his arms and next his legs from his body and finally sliced his trunk into a myriad of pieces.

I regained the leadership of the Black forces for my wife. I heard Arthur cheer even in his pain. "I hated that sniveling nephew of mine," he said. "He always slunk around my throne. I caught him once trying to steal my scepter. Good riddance to him."

I grabbed large pieces of Angus and yelled for both Robina and Farica. Farica came first and held the shattered Angus in her arms. She rocked him back and forth with tears dripping onto his shocked face. She cradled his bloody remains as she would her own baby.

"Make him right. Bring him back to life," I screamed at Farica.

"It's impossible, Jonathan. The fake master cursed him and took his most important organs. It's a mortal spell. There isn't enough of him to resurrect. The spell sent his soul directly to the gods. The evil killer destroyed his heart and mind sending them to the four winds, so we could not resurrect him. He had no time to transfer his knowledge from his long line of Thanes to you or anyone. It's a devilish curse, but to its benefit, he is now in a far better place than us. He has entered Valhalla and is with the warriors of old."

I yelled in rage. I was no longer disinterested in the battle but sought the blood of my enemies and the death of the Red Master. I looked at the battle-field of the fallen Black Army. I recalled the words of the dead Black Master as he tried to revive the army. I uttered the spell the impostor had tried to speak to his frozen army. Using Arthur's voice and cadence, I spoke ancient Welsh in the Celtic tongue. After giving the spell, I added my own, which made the Black army loyal to me and their New Black Leader, their rightful master and Robina my wife. The army jumped to their feet from where they had fallen. Now with their weapons they joined my army. They filled in the ranks and at present the Red Lord faced a seasoned force almost as large as theirs in striking range.

I wondered when the Red Master would send a deadly spell to incapaci-tate my soldiers. I knew he had to. It would enable him to have a surprise attack on my army. I marched slowly forward sensing every change in the force. Nevertheless, I still struggled with the inhuman power that racked my brain and had Arthur in a death grip. I compartmentalized it, and let my subconscious fight the disruption it caused in my mind. I knew it drew power from me, but I had no way to stop it.

As I walked forward with my army, Farica stood on my left with her sword brandished and her helmet firmly on her head. "Jonathan, don't despair, Angus knew, like I did, that he would never reach his homeland. It's the Prophecy. We realized if you knew his fate, you would not fulfill the Prophecy. We didn't tell you for your own good. The Prophecy sealed his fate before you left Oxford, in fact, a thousand years before you, or he existed. We will celebrate his life when we defeat the Red Master. The Prophecy tells us his son will take his position on your ruling council."

I pushed back the tears and gave a hard-fought smile to Farica. "He was my friend and he was my mentor. Why did he have to die?"

She just shook her head. We continued to rush forward. Robina stood on my right and whispered to me, "Lover, I know how you feel. Remember you have my father with you. This will all end soon, and the rest of our lives will be happy and fulfilling. No matter what, I love you and our son will bring us joy and happiness."

Farica on my other side just gave a clucking sound.

However, I glanced at my wife with a quizzical look on my face. She smiled. "Yes my husband, the baby I'm carrying is our son Emperor Jonathan the Second. Remember I'm a witch and know the future."

I gave her a jaundiced look knowing she couldn't read what would happen in the future. She wasn't a seer. She just knew what others had told her about the Prophecy. However, before I could answer, I heard a swishing sound and my flying time machine blinked out of nowhere ten feet in front of me. The Red Seer jumped out and ran to me.

The Seer had a big grin on his face. "You looked like you needed help." Then he pointed behind me.

Set up just behind the army stood four huge catapults and twelve of the biggest brownies I'd ever seen.

He continued, "I appropriated the catapults and the Brownies volunteered." He pointed to the brown giants. "I visited my old friends before returning to the battlefield. Those ten centuries ago when I lived in Berwick, I was an honored guest of the Brownie Kingdom. I told the fortunes of the Holy Island rulers. Five Brownie Kings called me their Seer before the Red Master stole me away. King Ethelbert rewarded me with the title of Brownie Prince of the Future. If I ever needed help, I was to strike the holy gong of the Dead three times, and the Brownie Kingdom would come to my aid. That's what I did."

I gazed at the Brownies and shook my head. "We are in need of their help. That's for sure."

The Red Seer showed his tooth in what I realized was a smile. "I know. I really do know." A cloud crossed his face. "I'm sorry about Angus. I knew a thousand years ago that his death would affect you greatly."

He changed the subject to relieve my pain. "It took us no time using the time machine to bring them here and now we're ready to go." As he spoke, the initial volley of fiery burning oil crashed into the Red Master's lines. The Brownies only took about ten strides, and they led the attack.

I yelled, "Charge!" and as if by magic, the Red Army started to panic. First, they moved back a few steps, then I watched the line of red like a wave recede across the river. I braced myself. I knew the Red Master would use his sorcery to regain the advantage.

I felt him as soon as he started his spell. I stretched out my mind and invaded his thoughts. His madness overwhelmed me and for an instant I tried to escape, but I knew I had to finish him off. In any event, he wouldn't let me go. My mind split in two with my subconscious currently entering my realm of understanding. The inhuman attacker still undertook to meld my mind, and with the Red Master's insanity trying to overwhelm me, I dueled them both.

In my mind, it became the classic sword fight. I was Douglas Fairbanks, Errol Flynn, Viggo Mortensen and Johnny Depp all rolled into one. Thrusting and parrying, jumping from table to table, swinging from the chandelier, rolling on the floor, doing all the classic movie fencing moves. My two opponents matched my every move, yet I felt that the Red Master could not continue for long. He faltered ever so slightly. My other adversary had strength and endurance. He fought with reason and cunning. I defended against him and attacked the Red Master.

Out of nowhere, I felt an ally at my back. I glanced and saw the Black garb of Arthur the Black Master as he had stood before his death. "Yes, my young Emperor. When the beast attacked you, I came, nothing is impossible in the mind."

Damn, it was like I was in the Matrix; I can dodge bullets and even walk up walls. I tried it. I charged the Red Master, and as he retreated, I did a back flip putting myself behind him and slashed with my sword as I flew over him cutting his left ear off. He spun around to face me, but he now looked awkward, and I slashed his right arm putting an eight-inch gash from his wrist to his forearm. I heard him yell, and the other charged towards me leaving Arthur. I had seen the other before, I could not place where, but his image in my mind depicted a tall gaunt figure, old but wiry. His armor shone like gold and his sword had weird runes writing on it.

He yelled at me as he dashed past the Red Master. "You shall linger in the land of the un-dead for the rest of eternity. Hephaestus, or as you know him by his vulgar Roman named Vulcan, forged my sword in the depths of Hades. Not even Zeus would dare to fight me."

I sneered at him. "You sound like an evil villain from a bad fantasy movie. Who the hell are you any ways?"

It was if the sky turned black. "I'm Ares or as you prefer, Mars the God of War."

I finally looked into the creature's eyes. They had an inner glow and they flashed like a strobe. "What the hell are you doing here?"

I received no answer. He charged me with sword swinging. I lay flat suspended six inches off the ground. When he had exhausted his attack, I jumped into the air. We met six feet off the ground with our swords crashing together making the sound of thunder with the flashing of lightning from our blades.

I pushed him away and we both floated in the air. I yelled, "How can you be Ares or Mars? They're just myths of the Romans and Greeks."

He didn't answer, but threw a fireball at me. I sped up time and flipped over him as the fireball floated past me. As I levitated head first above him, I poured hot lava on his skull.

For an instant, he was a bronze looking statue. Then he disappeared from my mind. I searched for my friend, the Black Master and the evil Red one. They fought on a stairway that looked like it led to heaven. I ran the five hundred steps to meet them in less than five seconds. Neither had injured the other, but the Red Master's skin had a slick shining coat of sweat and specks of blood. I could tell he had a fatal wound for his body was excreting blood from his pores. I attacked him with full vigor. He fell back on the stairs, and I hacked away, my sword biting into him with every blow. I heard his screams, but only thought of my friends who had died on this journey. I could not stop.

From behind me, I heard Arthur scream. I turned and saw Mars and four others of his sort all dressed as Roman Warriors trudging up the stairs. "Jonathan, look out," Arthur yelled before the enemy swarmed him. I charged down the stairs in a blink of an eye and stood between my friend and the enemy.

I grabbed Arthur and jumped from the stairs. They seemed to be half a mile above the ground. I soared down like an eagle. I could, however, feel the Red Master's pain. It told me he still lived. The five Roman clad warriors led by Mars stood on the stairs. I needed time to assess what and who these warriors were, and why they sided with the Red Master. Using every ounce of my psychic power, or magic, whatever you called it, I broke away from the mental war and rejoined my friends on the battlefield.

The bodies of red uniformed soldiers lay strewn across the battlefield. I no longer stood in the middle of the plain in front of Berwick, but at the buttress of the main bridge into the town. My body directed my sword to slash at the retreating Red Army. Sarah stood to my left and Robina to my right.

Both, like me, had blood stained uniforms created by the splatters of our enemy's blood. Our catapults still threw fire at the city, and flames roared across the bridge from where I stood.

The Brownies had advanced before the main force. I could see their mayhem as I hacked my way to the other side of the bridge. As I came back from the fight with Mars and his friends, a dead zone engulfed the battlefield. I searched the area for the physical form of the Greek Gods, but could find them nowhere. I did see the Red Master. He directed his troops from his gold encrusted carriage; it reminded me of the Coronation carriage of Queen Elizabeth. I charged the coach with Robina, Sarah and Farica following me. The best troops of the Red Army surrounded the carriage, but the four of us were no match for any army, even without magic. However, as I didn't think suicide was for me, I had the Red Seer take the flying time machine in the air and with its weaponry open a path to the Red Master for us.

The coachman watched us hack through the defenses, and as we approached, he whipped his horses mercilessly and drove into his own men, running them down to escape us. I watched in horror as the wheels of the carriage stopped in the mass of the dead bodies.

The four of us reached the coach when I felt the dead zone disappear and the full force of magic returned.

CHAPTER TWENTY-EIGHT

THE AIR TURNED FRIGID, I FELT MY LIMBS LOSE THE ABILITY TO MOVE. Everyone around me froze in place like game statues. My army looked like the Chinese army in Xi'an of the Chin Dynasty, frozen in time in terra cotta. This spell was a mind freeze, unlike the Orange Master's immobilization hex. The spell that held me was powerful and controlled everyone on the battle-field, including the horses. I fought with every magic power I had to unlock myself from the force which held my body.

Even though my body would not move using all my power, I could unlock my mind. I stretched my psychic powers to their limits and found the source of the spell that froze the world around me. I reached out, touching his thoughts gently, not letting him know I had found him. I could sense his arrogance, his megalomania and his feelings of superiority over me and all humankind. I crept through his mind, sampling bits and pieces of his per-sonality and thoughts.

This mind didn't belong to the Red Master or even Mars. This mind saw itself as the high-and-mighty force in the universe. I analyzed the mind and determined it was my real foe as everything that had happened to me had the hallmark of this villain. This world jumped to his manipulation. That is, everyone except me, and the ones who followed me.

I poked harder and the pure hate it had for me burned deep within the beating heart. His passion had only one outlet, my defeat. I searched for his weakness. I trolled through his mind and the sole flaw I found related to me. He had simply one obsession, my death.

I retreated into my frozen body. My mind started running through ideas and ways to defeat him, each rejected in the millisecond it took to develop the thought. However, I knew that I had the knowledge to win this life-and-death struggle.

I searched the battlefield for another active mind. Every mind I found had limited functions. Only their autonomic nervous system continued its natural process. In almost everyone, their brain slowed to a suspended animation condition.

To my horror, I noticed some of my frozen soldiers dying of fright. I invaded as many minds as I could, speaking to their subconscious, trying to soothe and reassure them. Several soldiers didn't survive and one didn't die, but lost himself. The body lived, but the mind no longer had personality or a template of being. This body had all the prerequisites for Arthur. Without thinking, I deposited Arthur's mind into the brain of this soldier. Regardless, the connection between us continued. We knew we had to be the only two active minds on the battlefield.

"My Emperor, what have you done? This body is excellent. It is young and vigorous. If only I could move it. Holy shit— damned be the wizards." His words reverberated in my mind.

"What, what's happening?" I shouted in my telepathic voice.

"I—I can move. The body freeze must be a mind spell because it doesn't freeze the body, it incapacitates the brain."

Out of the corner of my eye, I could see Arthur's new body move. He continued to talk to me. "I hid in your mind and he didn't know I lived there, so he didn't freeze my mind, only yours. What do you want me to do?"

I had to think. I needed a plan. I needed to be free. I needed to use my magic. If this creature only attacked my mind maybe I could get loose, I began to analyze my mind. It felt like a diagnostic check I used to run on my computer. Brain cell by brain cell, I looked for the bug that had crept into my brain and froze my body.

I placed myself in a state of suspended animation, arresting my heart and my breathing to such a low rate, that they wouldn't register on any monitoring machines. I couldn't gauge time or even space. I stayed inside my brain not daring to look outward. Finally, I found it. The spell had placed a rogue red blood cell in my brain. It blocked a thin capillary that brought blood to ten synapses. The synapses controlled all movement of every muscle in my body, except my autonomic systems.

I allowed my heart to start beating again and then I let my mind drift and waited for my subconscious to come up with an answer. I felt it before I realized what happened. My subconscious contracted all my blood vessels and raised my blood pressure to Everest heights and rushed as much blood as my brain would take through my mind. The offending red blood cell, like a small cork in a violently shaken champagne bottle, blew through my body drowned in the flood of perfectly fine blood cells.

A second later my blood pressure returned to normal as did my ability to function.

The revived Black Master and I moved through the monuments of war that had been my army and the Red Master's Army. Slowly we proceeded towards the source of the magic that transformed life into a slow terrifying frozen death. The creature with such power now resided in the castle, the home of the Berwick holy of holies, that housed the machine or whatever it was that could transport me back to my world.

As we entered the city Red troopers cluttered the roads frozen like statutes. It surprised me that even the town's folk stood like the soldiers. Everyone looked like a frozen Woolly Mammoth pulled from a glacier. An eerie feeling came over me, the town had no sound, nothing reached my ears. I could smell raw animal waste and even the sweet smells from the town's bakeries. I could taste the bile in my throat. This new menace's power frightened me. It felt almost omnipotent. I needed to defeat it, but didn't know how.

The castle at the top of the hill stretched for almost a quarter of a mile. It had high walls of large hewed stones. The gray facade looked ominous and appeared impregnable.

Arthur spoke in a low voice, "Do you still have your magic?"

My mind had been numb since my body had regained its ability to move. "Yes, yes, I can feel it. Why?"

He rolled his eyes and in a mocking voice said, "My Emperor, the two of us are attacking this castle, we either need a large army or some powerful magic. Do you have it in you?"

I laughed when I said, "My Black Lord, you have powerful magic as well, you should have us in there in no time with our enemy bowing to our superiority."

Arthur, in both mind and body, stood beside me egging me on to bolster my spirit. "We can do it, let's show them who they are up against."

In his new body, Arthur stood tall, young, blond and as handsome as a Viking. We climbed the hill to the base of the castle wall. I used a simple spell changing the stone to water. The castle looked as if it was crying as the rocks in a six foot square at the base turned to tears and flowed down the side of the hill. We entered without anyone noticing.

The castle like the town stood still, not a soldier, not a servant, not even a stable boy moved as we stealthily crept deeper into the fortification. As we entered the keep, Arthur cast one of his black spells that would make us invisible. He purred, "This spell is undetectable, not even your super wizards know we're there." In an instant we faded away.

I strained my eyes to find anything that would help defeat the inhuman wizard that cast the statue spell. The castle contained more rooms than a Cambodian bordello and each had as many ante-rooms as Windsor Castle. We had searched the first three levels before we found the cabal of wizards.

The flamboyant throne room of the great Khan spread before us, huge columns, rich fabric and everything else that decorated the room was gold. On the throne sat an enormous figure at least seven feet tall dressed in ancient Greek garb. Standing before the august ruler, stood six of his minions, Mars being one of them, standing proud with full Roman armor as a legion commander.

They spoke in a foreign language, but to my surprise, I understood every word because of the magic schooling Robina had given me.

Mars gave a slight laugh then continued his conversation with the man on the throne. "Yes Zeus, my celestial King, we have defeated Jonathan and his feeble attempt to fulfill that damned Prophecy. Once we find him among his stone army, we can destroy him and all of Berwick: town, beasts and men. Once we do this our rule will be absolute."

One of the other retainers spoke, "My Lord, why did you order us not to destroy him when he first appeared? When we had them trapped at the forest meadow after they killed the White Master's son? Why didn't you let us kill them then? Why did we wait until now?"

Zeus jumped up from his throne. "Achilles, you are human and godlike, that's why you don't understand. The vibration between the worlds would have splintered. We could never again travel between dimensions, and we would lose our magical powers. He had to kill the Red Master before we could destroy him and all the others. No, now it's time to destroy him and take away the peoples' will to resist our rule."

Mars snickered, "It's too bad we have to kill them all, that human Sarah would have borne me a fine line of warriors." He laughed even louder, "Achilles, you could have had Robina, the Black Witch. She would have kept you out of trouble with the wenches."

The whole room burst into laughter, even Zeus chortled. "That's enough, go find him, and bring him to me. I'll kill him here and that'll end this cursed Prophecy."

A large evil smile crossed Mars' face as he said, "I love destroying cities and their people. Carthage was such a sweet success, then Hiroshima, such misery. Thank you my lord." The six minions left the throne room in quick military double time.

I swayed back and forth as my mind raced. Who and what were these monsters? Could they be the gods from Earth or just imitations? How could I stop them? They would soon learn I was not with the army. A simple magic spell would show that. Would that save my people, or would this Zeus go into a rage and kill everyone?

Before I could think, the Black Master pulled me from the room and whispered, "Emperor, he is sitting in your throne room and your destiny is to recapture it."

I looked back into the room and saw the King rest his elbow on the arm of the throne and place his head in his cupped hand. He stared out the window at the frozen city and the plain covered with frozen soldiers. I had seen this image before, but could not remember where. I wondered what he thought. Then I heard his inner feelings.

My spirits rose as he said to himself, "If only I could make the Prophecy fail, but I feel he has tricked me. I cannot find him on the battlefield. That damn Prophecy foretells everything, even my death."

Arthur and I sat in the private library of Zeus. He couldn't find us even under his own nose. I perused his books; they spanned Earth's history and that of many other worlds, all neatly organized. I searched for his magic books. I needed a spell to re-animate my army and another to destroy his band of evil. I searched with feverous intensity, yet I found nothing.

I ravished his papers and tore through his neatly placed files, still nothing. I had to find an answer, a way to defeat him before he found me in his castle. I decided I could face death, but I must save my friends and pregnant wife. My search took on more intensity as I tore books and pictures off the wall, turned over chairs and the large desk. Panic had consumed me. I needed the tools to defeat him and could not find them.

"Slow down, Jonathan, you have the knowledge in your mind, just search and find it."

I knew the Black Master was half-right. However, I also knew there was something I was missing. A book, a spell, a talisman, an object in this room that would bestow on me the power to defeat the King of this world, the King of every world he chose to invade.

I fell to my knees in utter fatigue. My manic search had taken all my energy. I knew I had to continue but couldn't get up from the floor. The deep pile Persian rug felt like a soft cloud. I lay my head down and something rubbed against my ear. I moved to see what had scratched me, causing me such pain. A five-pointed gold star the size of a silver dollar lay on the carpet. It must have fallen from the desk when I searched through the pile of papers. I picked it up and held it in my hand. It radiated heat and power. I held it up before my eyes and read the inscription on it, 'Power requires Responsibility only the Responsible can command me.' The Greek letters came from an early time, not the Greek of Homer, not the Greek of Agamemnon and Troy but from the first writings of the Greek language.

I held the star tightly in my hand and rocked back and forth on the floor. I had my edge. This star had power, but Zeus couldn't use it for he couldn't act responsibly. The question that crossed my lips was, could I?

"We have to leave," I heard Arthur whisper. "Someone's coming and if it's that big fellow we're in trouble."

I had trashed the room and no matter who came in we would be in the middle of a bad situation. Without thinking I cast a spell and everything but the star returned to its place as if we had never entered. To my amazement four women in traditional Homeric Greek dress entered the room. Statuesque and beautiful, three looked to be in their late teens and the other in her thirties. The eldest was obviously their teacher. She pulled a book down from the shelves and in the way of Socrates started to lead the others in discussion.

Arthur and I crept out of the room and found our way out of the castle. "We have to free our soldiers and our team before that Greek has his way with them," said Arthur.

I still had the star in my hand as we rushed across the bridge to where Robina and the rest still stood frozen in time. I flipped the star over in my hands as one does a coin. I did it absentmindedly, but on one revolution, I glanced down and saw the back of the star. It showed the seven-foot giant sitting on his throne just as I had seen him in his royal room with his captains. The Greek inscription said, 'Zeus, the living God.'

I stopped in my tracks and brought the star close to my face to see the tiny writing over Zeus's depiction. It read, 'Cronus' gift to his son with the power of all the gods.' I almost dropped the ancient star on the bridge, but I regained my poise and headed towards Robina and the others.

I held the star to the sky. The clouds had covered the sun except for a small opening. A ray of sun splashing down on me, and flashed off the star as I repeated an awakening spell to my soldiers, my small band of companions and especially to my wife.

"My god, my husband, where was I? I feel like I have been in a block of ice. I feel so numb with cold all over my body, even my mind felt frozen." Robina's whole body was shaking as she spoke.

We had no time to talk. The captains of Zeus, or Jupiter, his Roman name, or whatever he called himself in this world, raced towards us. Mars led five warriors after our small band of fighters. I turned to my wife as they approached, "My dear, may I introduce you to your father, Arthur the VII, the Dark Master and Lord of Wales." I pointed to the six foot blond haired, blue eyed young warrior.

She gave me a skeptical stare. Her voice had no amusement in its usual teasing manner, "This is not the time to play the fool. Who is this warrior?"

"Don't let this new body fool you, daughter. It's I, your devoted father, who sent you to bed without pudding because you turned your mother into a toad, and made me kiss her to bring her back to her human form."

Her eyes welled with tears. She ran to him and threw her arms around him kissing both his cheeks. "How can this be?" she cried.

He pointed to me, "Ask your husband."

Before I could reply, the battle started and I saw Achilles eyes on me from three hundred yards away. A flash from the star I held hit Achilles right in his heel. I could see the flash as it melted everything below his ankle. His eyes blazed at me in anger and pain. He and I knew it wasn't the first time the Gods hadn't been kind to him. I pitied the great warrior who would never win in battle.

Mars saw what happened to Achilles and came after me with the fury of his name. He slashed, prodded, pushed and thrust his sword at me yet his attacks did nothing to me. I paid little attention to him, letting my reactions fight for me as my mind attacked the problem of defeating Zeus.

I could still feel the Red Master's powers trying to control my force and me. He attacked my mind as he had in the past, but now it was a pleasant buzz like a babbling brook giving me peace and a feeling of contentment. I could tell he realized his powers over me and mine had waned, but he still had teeth and so did his soldiers. But I didn't have time to think of the Red Master now, all my focus was in defeating Zeus.

Streaming from the castle I saw what I took to be ancient Spartans come down to the bridge to stop our advance. The battle would soon be vicious as the Spartans joined the Red Army. To my amazement, the Red Army seemed to be commanded now by Zeus, which actually made sense since the Red Master's powers were waning.

With one hand, I warded off Mars, with the other I pointed the star to the sky and muttered a spell. The clouds crashed together, the sky turned dark and rain fell from the heavens. Not as drops, but by the bucketful. The battlefield turned into a lake. The ground turned to river bottom mud. No one could stand let alone fight. I saw the Spartans slide down the hill to the bridge, landing in three feet of water. Many in heavy armor had trouble regaining their feet and some even drowned in the muddy water.

"Charge," I yelled and pointed to the high ground around the castle. My army moved with speed through the rain, the water and the mud. I had cast a spell on all my troops so the weather had no effect on their movement.

As I darted through the city I came across the Red Master's coach floating down the street. No one sat perched on the driver's seat, nor did I see any guards protecting the Red Master seated inside. I reached the door to the carriage and swung it open. My eyes fell on the Red Lord. He sat erect in the carriage seat staring straight ahead. His eyes now just empty sockets. His body was bleeding from a hundred slashes. His robe had stains of red rust covering the bright red of the material. He heard me, and moved his head in my direction.

"Ah, so we meet again, Jonathan. I hope you're proud of your accomplishments. You have destroyed this world and its way of life. The Masters are gone and the Ancient Ones are angry. You are worse than the plague that struck before magic, millions died in that pestilence, but all will die because of you."

I looked at the pathetic creature that had controlled most of the inhabitants of the Isle, and spat on him. "You vile beast, you enslaved this island and your kind kept them slaves for over a thousand years."

He stared at me through his empty eye sockets, "You bleeding heart, you'll never rule a nation let alone a world. You don't have the stomach for the hard choices. I give my people food, happiness, and they want for nothing. You give them the freedom of chaos. You will understand your folly sooner rather than later."

I could stand no more of his blather. I took my sword and lashed out with such force, I removed his head with one swing. A flash of lightning zinged past my head and I looked up to the castle holding the Red Master's head by his hair. Zeus stood high on the battlements throwing another thunderbolt at me.

CHAPTER TWENTY-NINE

HE STOOD ON THE BATTLEMENTS LIKE A WEATHERVANE AND LIKE A weathervane; I had the sky shooting lightning bolts at him, not one, or two, but a hundred or more. I watched the most powerful King in the universe run for shelter. I threw down the Red Master's severed head and charged forward with my army. This time I vowed to end the bloodshed by defeating my enemies and having their heads.

Farica ran beside me as my army charged up the hill to the castle. "You're about to fulfill your destiny my Emperor. You have come this far, now it's time."

I smiled at her and asked, "Yes Mother Superior, but what should I expect?"

She shrugged her shoulders. "I don't know, the Seers never wrote what happened after you defeated the Red Master. They only stated you won the war against the rulers."

I had forgotten about the Red Seer, and wondered what had happened to him. I asked Farica where he had gone.

"He returned to the time machine and disappeared just before everything stopped, and the cold dead feeling overtook me."

On the castle battlements, a legion of Roman soldiers readied themselves to withstand my army's attack. The walls of the castle gave off a greenish light. I could feel the evil magic surrounding the fortress.

I stopped my force thirty feet from the walls and encompassed us in an umbrella of protection. I imagined the force field all science fiction stories give their spaceships. I did the same for my army.

I felt it first, it came from high in the sky, and it felt like rain hitting the force field. The sky became black as a rock bigger than a city block blotted out the sun. It smashed down on my umbrella. I felt the ribs of my force field start to crack. The roof of my umbrella started to push inward. I gave a big grunt and mentally pushed it up as hard as I could. My mind had to stop the rock from crashing through my force field and crushing my army, or the Prophecy would never come true.

Time stopped as I felt my whole-body strain, then felt as if the moisture within me rushed out of every pore. I rubbed the star and in my last gasp turned the large rock into helium gas. I awoke moments later in the arms of Robina down in the village.

"My God, Johnny, I thought we had lost you. You stopped breathing and then— well." She continued to caress me, "Nothing's happened since we came down from the castle. Your army is awaiting your command. Only my father and I knew about your collapse. I animated you so no one else would realize what was happening. What do we do now?"

I threw my mind out to find the enemy and determined what his plan entailed. He stood again pompously on the parapets looking over the city. His mind flowed with victory and a sweeping plan to invade the city with his army all imbued with powers of their own to kill with death rays from their eyes.

The rain had stopped when I lost consciousness. I now cleared the sky of all clouds and intensified the sun's rays by adjusting the atmosphere over Berwick.

I had to laugh. Zeus's overconfidence had him making mistakes. I looked around at my surroundings. My companions stood beside me in this tavern Robina had found for our headquarters. "Barkeep," I yelled, "your best meal for us and your finest ale. This is a day you'll talk about for the rest of your life. Join us and we'll all eat hearty before we see if the Prophecy is true." I scanned the bar. "Barkeep set us a table, outside so I can see the sun. I've been in many pubs lately, and they all bring me trouble."

The meal we ate brought my band of warriors together. We had fought our way across England, and now we awaited the final battle. Farica smiled benignly at me. She laughed saying to us, "Everyone enjoy your food, but save a little room for more. Tonight, my friends, the kitchens of Berwick Castle will supply us with the banquet of a lifetime to feast upon."

However, that afternoon I enjoyed the joint of beef. It made my taste buds run riot with joy. The sweet smell of the bread fulfilled all my expectations as

I smothered it in creamy butter. Equally as good, the lightly steamed vegetables in their cheese sauce boiled over my tongue tasting red, green, orange and also violet. I ate that meal as if it were my last, for if I were a betting man it was even money I wouldn't survive the rest of the day. I thought as I stuffed another piece of bread into my mouth, I was lucky but I didn't believe in luck.

As I predicted, the Roman Legion started marching down the hill to annihilate my army. They marched in individual cohorts of a hundred men, ten men in ten ranks; all ranks straight, all men organized, all under the command of Zeus. I could feel their power and their magical changed eyes just waiting to kill. I led my army to an open field on the other side of a hill east of the castle. The Romans would not be able to see my troops until they charged down the hill. The afternoon sun shone into the eyes of my soldiers, and they all waited in fear and wonder for the enemy to appear.

As we waited, I issued new shields to each of my warriors and the same to my companions. The steady drumbeat and the rumbling of the ground from the rhythmic crash of sandals told us the legion would be on us in less than a minute. I stood in front of my army. "Raise your shields as I directed, swords at the ready. We have come too far to end in this field, remember you are my Immortals."

I heard the enemy cross the top of the hill. I looked back at my troops standing behind their six-foot shields, their body hidden behind the brightly-colored Kevlar and fiberglass defenses. I uttered a spell and then turned, hiding behind my shield.

I could see in my mind's eye Zeus peering over the walls of the castle trying to see the battle. He had little imagination about his powers. I changed my focus to the army bearing down on my soldiers and smiled. In the lead, riding a black stallion and standing in the stirrups, was Mars.

"How brave and how stupid," I said directly into Mars's mind, letting it reverberate throughout his brain. "How brave, but how stupid, you can't win. It is foretold." It was the first time I believed it. I gripped the star in my hand so tight that the points dug into my skin and five small streams of blood trickled from the sharp edges. I licked my hand and tasted my blood; a copper metallic taste met my tongue. The bloody taste re-instilled in me hope that this was the last battle to win, and I would never spill blood again. This world of magic would gain its right course and control its own destiny.

I heard Zeus give the order subconsciously to each of his soldiers to use their death ray weapon and destroy my army.

The mild reflection from the shields I directed at Mars caused him momentary to go blind. Mars' horse swerved to the left and he blindly rode from the battlefield. I then directed every shield in my army to face the legion. I transformed the shields into powerful reflective mirrors and with the sun's late-afternoon intense glare, as the enemy shot their death rays, the rays bounced back from the mirrors and burned out their eyes, thus killing every soldier who used a ray gun. From every cohort, the first five rows died. The rear five rows had orders to wait until the initial rows had done their damage before letting loose. Their obedience to their commander saved them for the moment.

Blinded by the light from the mirrors, the remaining enemy infantry broke and ran. Many leaving their weapons behind, all had serious eye problems, many with retinas burned beyond repair, others just momentarily blind, shrieking in pain. My army marched forward.

Should I use my powers and have a magic blackout in this area? This would let me, and my soldiers fight it out with the remnants of the enemy force. I had to decide should I use my magic or blackout all magic in the fight. I had no idea. What did the Prophecy say? I asked Farica, and she answered in a hushed voice, "All it says is you will win, how I don't know, but it foretells of other deaths. Whatever you do it must be fast. The Prophecy says it ends before the sun sets behind the castle."

I was a fool. As I talked to Farica, I had not kept my mind alert. As my first wave of troops chased after the retreating Romans, Zeus sent a wave of fire across the top of the hill burning a hundred of my men. I watched them run down the hill in flames. My rage overcame me and I pulled the beating hearts out of a hundred of the Roman soldiers as they raced back to the castle. Many kept running for more than a hundred paces without their beating hearts, which through my powers I sent to the feet of Zeus.

My rage knew no bounds. I turned the walls of the castle into wax and then intensified the sun to melt them. My mind collided with Zeus's. We wrestled and we stood as at the games in ancient Greece, naked in the ring. Zeus, the seven-foot giant grabbed me and threw me to the ground as all of Greece stood watching us. In an instant, I transformed myself into a ten-foot wrestler to match his power. Within seconds, he lay upon the ground.

I dodged a flash of lightning from his eyes and responded with a sledge hammer for a fist to his torso, knocking him back to the ground.

Anger grew in his eyes. He didn't know how to take personal pain, let alone defeat. The earth shook as he roared from my blow. The air turned super-heated and I could no longer breathe without burning my lungs. A ball of fire appeared on his hand and he threw it directly at my face. I breathed out frigid air, which chilled the surrounding earth and turned the ball of fire into a sloppy snowball that fell harmlessly at my feet.

The fight continued with javelins, shot puts and rocks. We both had the added danger of magic. Neither of us had the advantage. I needed a psychological advantage. I thought back to my time in his castle, in the library. Who were the young women? I still had an accurate vision of them. As we took up the sword, I threw my mind out to find them. I caught their minds. Each was a witch of sorts. Each was a daughter of Zeus. Each was a goddess, yet I now controlled them.

With sword in hand, I changed the place of the battle. From the Olympics in old Greece, I took us to the sadistic dungeons of Tomas de Torquemada during the Spanish Inquisition. Three of the four goddesses hung from iron shackles suspended from the walls of the dungeon, and the fourth lay stretched out on the rack. I covered her beautiful body with sores and festering wounds. She looked up from the rack pleading with Zeus to come to her aid.

I looked into his eyes. "You choose my friend, your daughters or me." I tightened the wheel on the rack and the young woman screamed in pain. "Who will it be? Or do you favor one of the girls in chains? Cast your eyes over there." A dozen rats the size of the cats scurried by the hanging women, one stopped to lap up drops of blood from the bleeding wrists of the goddesses suspended by their hands.

"By the bones of my child, I'll eat your heart if you harm any one of my young daughters."

I gave him a wintry smile and said, "Your heart is black my friend, much blacker than mine. I remember your deeds. Look at your daughters, should I scar them and make them ugly?" I opened a six inch cut down the most beautiful goddesses' cheek and let the blood flow.

"Stop, stop!" screamed Zeus.

"Make me," I said with no compassion in my voice.

"You're the devil. Leave my children alone."

I could feel him reaching out to ensnare one of my company. I grabbed him, slapped his face, and then introduced a cauldron of fire under one of the hanging goddesses. The heat started to blister her feet.

"Stop, Stop!"

I removed the heat, but left the caldron. "We can make peace. From what I know there are many dimensions, we can divide them up. You take half, and I'll take half."

He looked at me with hate in his eyes and spat out, "How can I trust you? How do I know you won't attack me and take my half?"

I healed the slashed face of his daughter. I lowered her to the floor. She still wore her shackles, but now she could stand without the body weight pulling on her arms. "We'll have to trust each other. We can make a pact like the city-states in your ancient Greece. If you're attacked, I'll come to your aid, and if I'm attacked, you come to mine."

He frowned and replied, "Those pacts never worked. I had to push them to help each other, they said the feast to the gods or celebrations to the gods took precedence. I used the Oracle to prod them to support each other, nothing worked. Only when their self-interest was at stake did they cooperate but never for long."

"Well, we know the oracles here tell the truth, and we know if harm comes to one of us, it will soon visit the other."

I lowered another of his daughters. He looked over at her and smiled reassuringly.

"I don't trust you."

I snickered. "I don't trust you either. That's what binds us closer. Why don't we have emissaries in each other's inner circle?"

He looked over at his beautiful daughters. "No, you are a barbarian. You cannot have one of my daughters as a concubine."

This time my smile was genuine as I said, "No, I don't think my wife would allow me to take a consort. She is a powerful witch and would turn your daughter into a flea or worse. I think maybe Mars would make a good emissary, and I would send you my wife's father the Black Master."

Zeus laughed, "I've ruled this land a long time, and I know your wife and her father. I know their bloodline and have followed it for a thousand years. You have made a good choice."

I released his daughters and they ran to him. We stood over ten feet apart in the dungeons. It took only a second, but I read his mind. His captains surrounded me with swords drawn and murder in their eyes. In the blink of an eye, my trusted companions stood next to me. We now fight in the sixteenth-century castle like the knights of old.

"Zeus, I thought your word had honor."

He sneered at me. "A God doesn't need honor. He rules by intimidation. If you don't obey me you go to the underworld, only humans have the need of honor."

Sarah attacked Mars. Her sword slashed and parried. The two fought as if they danced the tango together. Robina took on Vulcan and I had the seven-foot Zeus to fight. Zeus backed me into a corner. His sword slashed at me. I defied gravity climbing walls. I flipped landing behind him. In the world of the mind, anything is possible.

I knew from the injuries I had observed on the Red Master that any damage done in this mental battle, one received in the real world. "Surrender your weapons, Zeus, we don't have to fight. We can live with the agreement we arranged."

"This is my world and you are not going to take it from me. All the worlds are mine. I'm Zeus the God of Gods. I'll rule this land and all lands forever."

I saw Sarah take her dagger from her boot and throw it at Mars. The blade pierced his heart, and he fell upon the ground without a whimper. Arthur in his new body had downed his adversary and so had Farica. Robina's talents came from her spells and her ability to teach. She didn't fight as well as she taught. Vulcan had her on the defensive forcing her back and eventually pushed her into a wall. She matched each stroke of his blade with hers. Nevertheless, I could tell in time she would miss, and he would cut her in two.

I needed to stop this battle before more of my warriors died. I needed to save my pregnant wife. I grappled with Zeus letting my sword fall to the floor and kicking him in the groin. He just laughed. "Remember, I'm not human."

I used a judo move on him. I flipped him to the ground, and dove for my sword. His blade reached out to cut off my arm. He missed only because I willed Buffoon to come to me. Our swords clashed against the raw stone of the dungeon floor. They flashed like the birth of a new star. I looked over at Robina. Vulcan's attacks had broken her sword, and she dripped with perspiration. Robina's exhaustion from the fight showed in every moment she made. The fatigue and pain of the fight showed on her beautiful face.

I rolled across the floor and did a cartwheel landing next to one of Zeus' daughters. "Stop everyone, stop or I'll slit her throat." I had my blade across the teenager's throat. The blade had barely bit in, and a thin line of blood escaped her neck.

Zeus had his sword about a foot from my heart. "By all the ancient gods, damn you to hell if you touch her again with your blade. I have beaten you Jonathan." He pronounced each vowel with a doubling of the sound.

I watched him nod his head giving Vulcan a secret sign. I yelled in pain. "Noooo," as I saw Vulcan swing back for the killing blow to Robina. My blade cut the throat of the beautiful goddess, in reaction to seeing Vulcan's attack.

Zeus's blade plunged right through my body; I heard the sword break against the wall behind me. I still stood tall and erect, and my blade struck home with one swift and un-aimed attack. It sliced through his armor and into his gut, deep into his stomach and intestines. The magic sword knew how to kill. The war ended, however, at what cost to me and mine. Sarah rushed to me, and the Black Master rushed to his daughter. Farica was to minister to all of us.

CHAPTER THIRTY

I HAD MY REVENGE. IT WASN'T SWEET OR EVEN BITTERSWEET. IT WAS just bitter. I acted swiftly and without thought or remorse. I uttered a spell which didn't exist. I turned Vulcan into a puddle of piss. Disgusting as it might be, he drained away among the cracks in the stone floor. Zeus fared no better. I corrupted his body; it bubbled, and rotted away until only bones lay across the floor beside me. My body still had the hole in it, where I had deformed myself to allow Zeus' blade to go through the hole in my middle, missing body parts.

As I readjusted my bodily form, Farica gave a cursory glance at my body, and saw no blood or wound. All of this action was still cerebral and took part in my mind. However, I knew the ramifications that bodies of the people killed and wounded in the inner space would be real in the outside world. The battle had its consequences and Farica, as was her lot, tried to repair all the damage. She sealed the wound on the young goddess's throat and then felt for the girl's heart, which started it beating in the fragile body. I rushed to Robina. I sealed my hand on her wound and with all my powers took her pain into my body. The pain dug into every nerve of my live carcass; it exploded like an atomic bomb. I felt the cloud erupt from my head, and it covered me in death.

I fought it, as if death was a dark Knight with a sword and shield. I knocked him down, slashed him with my sword and bit his face. With my bare hands, I tore at him pulling his heart from his corrupted body. As he disappeared in front of me, I could only see Robina. She could hardly breathe, but every second it sounded stronger. She looked up at me with smiling eyes. I collapsed in her lap. I knew death did not exit alone. With him, he took our unborn child.

I awoke seconds later, in a heap upon the ground. Surrounding me stood my comrades. I couldn't tell by their faces whether they were alive or died after the battle of the Inquisition castle. Robina spoke first, "Thank you my husband. Thank you for saving me. I died, but you brought me back." Then she cried.

I grabbed her hand and pulled her down to me, hugging her tight, letting our tears of sorrow come together on our cheeks. "Yes, my love, I know. I know. We'll have another son, many other sons and daughters. Your body is better than it ever was before. Never fear, my love, we will have a lengthy and fruitful life. Remember, I chased death away, and he'll not come back, not for a long, long time.

She smiled, but I could still feel her pain and absorbed it into my body. "We have defeated the Old Rulers, the Usurpers of your world for the last thousand years. They lived in my world for a thousand or more years too, but they will never interfere with humans again."

I made the statement with conviction, but I knew I hadn't defeated all of them. I saw four of them crawl away, with the daughters of Zeus leading the way. How many more lived in this strange world, I had no idea.

The room had brightly-colored garlands strewn around to make a festive atmosphere. The next morning I sat on the large golden throne in the castle with Robina by my side. On our right stood Sarah and Arthur, the Black Master, both dressed as warrior generals which titles I had just bestowed on them. Standing on my left was my darling wife as well as Farica and her husband, Edward of Camelot. Edward had ridden hard with his army once he heard of our troubles with the Brownies. The Seers stood in front of me explaining the Prophecy, and what I had performed. Each trial had shown to them and to the Britons, that I deserved the title of Emperor.

"Yes, Jonathan, you are the one, but there is one more test you have to complete," the White Seer sneered at me. "Now you have to enter the cave of lost dreams and bring us the machine of distant places. That's what you wish, is it not, Jonathan, the Outlander?"

I looked at him. The friendliness in his voice of a few minutes ago had vanished. He challenged me, no. He threatened me. His eyes glared flashing contempt at me. He continued with his lips cured and pointed at me, "You are a spineless academic with no tradition of the warrior class. You come and take my land. That's not the vision I saw. You're an interloper. The member of my blood line you killed in the glade was to be the one."

The Red Soothsayer pushed him back, as the speaker tried to force his way to the throne. "Mandrake, it's not your place. Your vision had no merit. The rest of us saw the outlander. Your eyes deceived you. Your emotion blurred your inner eye."

The White Seer would have none of it. "You are just a lily-livered paper-consuming egghead. Go find your destiny in the cave, if you dare."

I stood glaring down at him, the older than dirt naysayer. "Lead the way asshole. Bring it on. I can take your shit."

The Red Seer chuckled, under his breath. I heard him say, "Mandrake is an ass, but he's sure lit a fire under our Emperor. Nothing will hold Jonathan back now."

The Red Seer told no lies. I would have gone to hell and back to prove to that old fool he was wrong. Robina grabbed me as I started down the stairs of the throne. "Johnny, don't. This isn't part of the Prophecy I've ever heard."

Farica also spoke. I didn't hear her words but for the first time I heard the concern in her voice and on her face, it told me she didn't know how this new adventure would end.

The Red Seer led the way down into the lower regions of the castle. The spiral staircase went deeper and deeper into the raw rock, which formed the base for the castle. The air smelled stale, and I could taste the calcium deposits that showed on the walls. The dull light from the torches, which hung from the wall in iron sconces, threw ghastly shadows on the rock.

All the way down the White Seer threw insults at me just loud enough for me to hear, but not the others. I ignored him. He was a gnat in the events of the day. I won or lost this challenge on my own merit. The Red Seer told us as we walked out of the throne room only I could face the cave of lost dreams, I must go in and no magic would help me. Whatever dwelled in the cave would die protecting the machine. I had to find a way to recover the machine and defeat its protector.

I felt naked. My band of heroes conquered these lands. Now I must go alone without magic or my friends. I wouldn't give the White Seer the plea-sure of seeing my concern so with all the confidence I could muster, I said, "It is time this is over, let's do it." With no further ado, we marched into the dankest place I had ever been.

A huge door made of wooden beams, each a foot wide, barred our entry to the cave. The White Seer gave a cruel laugh. "It bars the guardian from escaping and running amok in this world. Whatever god you pray to, it's time to speak to him now. Your soul is in mortal danger, you coward."

I looked on him with contempt. "When I return, your life is mine to do with as I please. Prepare yourself accordingly."

It took ten of my soldiers, pulling on the rusty chain, to open the door. The iron hinges creaked like the hounds of hell as it opened. If I thought the air smelled like death in the tunnels, the air that escaped from the cave sprang from the death trenches of Auschwitz.

I looked into the cave and after the first two feet, everything looked black. Not outlined in black, but just black, no reflection, no light at all. The air of death did not move; nothing moved. All sound died at the entrance into the cave.

Sarah handed me a torch and her dagger. She whispered in a hoarse voice that I barely heard, "It never misses. Whatever you meet in there," she pointed into the blackness, "you'll need it." She gave me a hug and kissed me on the lips, "For old times, remember those days so long ago in the lab?"

I did, and I wanted to return to that time and never have to use magic or fight again. I wanted to return to my old life. As the poet said, you can never go home. I had that thought in my mind, as I stepped into the darkness.

Robina grabbed me and spoke so softly no one else heard her sweet voice except me, "I love you more than life itself. This is a secret spell." She slipped me a piece of parchment. "Even in a dead zone it will transport you from the cavern to me, and I'll take your place in the cave. If you are in mortal danger, just say the spell, and I'll take your place. You cannot die. I won't let it happen." Tears ran down her face. "Johnny, I love everything about you, from your cute little smile, to your bravery, your commanding nature and yes, your playfulness when we're alone."

A tear came into my eye. I would never sacrifice her. I loved her in the same way she loved me. I broke away from her and stepped deeper into the darkness. The cave I found myself in continued down far under the ground. After some time, I started to see. The walls of the cave came into view, then the roof, and sparkles like gold and even diamonds reflected from the raw rock. Gradually as I advanced deeper into the cave, my vision allowed me to see more clearly. Nevertheless, as I crept farther, in what felt like a crypt, the air became more sickeningly sweet with the cloying and fetid odor of death. It gagged me. After five minutes in the cave, I came to another enormous door. A large iron ring acted as the doorknob. I pulled the ring, and the door opened with the sound like a woman screaming her last breath. A small piece of my mind tried to panic, but I grabbed it, and tucked it into my childhood. I feared nothing that this world could throw at me. If I died, I died. If I lived, it would be inasmuch as I conquered my fears.

I entered a cavern with thirty-foot ceilings and an expanse as big as a football field. To my surprise, I heard the flapping wings of a large bird. I felt rather than saw it swoop down on me. It attacked me, digging its claws and then its vicious beak into my side. I beat it off with my sword. As it flew away, I saw it was an eagle, but none like I had ever seen before. This bird was huge with a wing span of over fifteen feet. I looked down. Blood dripped from wounds the bird had inflicted in my side. The flesh covering my liver was flapping as I moved. The raw flesh sickened me. I felt light headed, but pushed the pain and fear from my mind.

I continue into the cavern. I saw a huge rock in the middle of the expanse. Alongside the rock stood a large wood box, not a house or even a weapon, but a machine. The closer I came the more complicated it looked. I noticed bright pieces of metal attached to it. Then I saw glass gauges and levers. I finally found the object of my quest. I had found the machine that Berwick had hidden for a millennium. This machine would take me home to the world I knew. The closer I came the faster my heart beat. Everything I had done, since I left Oxford, had a meaning and a conclusion.

My eyes had no other purpose except to examine the machine and to understand how it worked. The bird had vanished from my mind's eye and I gave it no further thought. I touched the ancient wood, and then the solid gold that held it together. I could not contain myself. I yelled in utter joy.

A figure emerged from behind the rock. He stood twice as tall as I, and he was wearing only a torn rag across his middle. Like me, his side oozed blood, but on his face, I could see pure rage. I realized in a second the object of his wrath. I tried to run.

Within one stride, he had me. I rolled upon the ground as he tried to grab me in his hands. I scrabbled on my hands and knees. I knew I couldn't escape him. His huge arms reached for me. He attached himself to my ankle as I kicked him away. I pulled myself forward two more feet. He tried to take hold of me again. However, to my astonishment he couldn't move any closer to me. I stood up, and realized he was on a tether. The chain had links of solid platinum, each as big as my hand. The giant couldn't go more than twenty feet from the machine in any direction.

He stood at the end of his chain in frenzy. I stood just outside his reach wondering how I would kill the beast. It looked like a standoff when the huge eagle circled us. I reached to my side and so did the giant. It was unclear who the bird would strike. Then the bird like a dive-bomber attacked his target. The ache in my side increased as the bird covered my field of view. Its talons again dug deep into my side. I wrestled with the bird and finally broke free from him. The blood no longer oozed from my side but flowed freely. I tore my shirt and used it as a bandage to stop the bleeding.

Both the giant and I watched the sky and waited. Now I saw dread in his face. He had been through this many times before. The bird swooped down and attacked my opponent. I knew I couldn't watch this creature attack him. We both faced the same agonizing death if this raptor continued attacking us. As the bird's beak pulled flesh from the side of the giant, I attacked using my sword.

The winged beast still tearing flesh away with its beak struck me with three razor-sharp talons each as cutting as a Japanese samurai sword. The foul creature knocked my sword from my hand and slashed my arm from the wrist to my shoulder. The giant looked at me and acknowledged my wound with sadness. He showed compassion to my plight.

I took Sarah's dagger, dove into the back of the eagle, and plunged the blade into the bird's neck. I repeated the stabbing motion a dozen or more times. Once I felt the bird turning its neck to attack me, I slashed the blade across its throat, digging it in as hard as my hand would allow. To my surprise blood spurted from the animal's neck, splashing over the giant and me.

I looked at the giant, and he smiled at me. No longer did I see rage or even anger in his eyes. To my amazement, he started to shrink and in seconds he stood in front of me the size of a man and he easily stepped out of his fetters.

"You have saved me," he said in what I recognized as simple Greek. Then he added, "That eagle you have slain was eternal, it could not die yet you killed it. Its blood touched both of our bleeding wounds. Legend says if the bird blood mixes with yours, you will be immortal like the eagle." He laughed again. "Legends may be just old wives' tales, but you killed the bird, didn't you?" He then added, "They say the same about dragons as well. Have you ever killed a dragon?"

I could feel my body change. Only time would tell, but just maybe I would live forever. I answered his question. "Yes my friend, I have. I guess I did save your life. Do we have to kill each other now?"

He laughed. "It seems like a foolish task since we both are immortal. No friend, we are at peace."

I shook my head not understanding what had happened. "What are you doing here, and why did you attack me?"

He blinked a couple of times. "Zeus sent me here and has tortured me for the last millennium. That bird attacks me and kills me every day. If I guard the machine, I am reborn each night at midnight. If I fail, the bird eats all of me. I've prayed to die for those thousand years, but only Zeus has come for the machine. I am your servant, master." He lay down on the floor before me.

"Stand up my friend. What is your name?"

"Prometheus is what they call me."

I smiled. My knowledge of Greek mythology placed my new friend as an ally, he was an enemy of Zeus. "Well, Prometheus, help me move the machine to the surface and you can see the sun and moon again."

That night we celebrated with our new friend and ally. He and Edward became fast friends and he joined the ranks of Edward's newly formed United British Isles Defense Force. As my Regent, Edward would act on my behalf in the country until I returned. Prometheus would sit by his side as a symbol to man's humanity to man.

Two days later, we combined both the time machine and the Berwick machine into one new contraption that traveled through both dimensions and time. With all preparations completed, Sarah, Arthur, Robina and I stepped into the machine. Farica and Edward of Camelot stood near the door. I would miss all the friends I had made in this land, but I dearly wanted to return to my world. "Farica, take care of my Empire for me, and make sure Edward doesn't bring back the rule of the Masters."

Edward the retired Orange Master, laughed, "Emperor, there is no need. You have given my new wife all the power in this land. I'm but her slave and do her bidding. I'm happy basking in her power. The four of you take care. Remember, this land is yours, and anytime you want it back just return." The five Seers stood back all chattering among themselves. I waved to them and the Red Seer came forward.

"Emperor, last night the five of us had the same dream. It is a window to your future what we next see for you..."

I quickly slammed the door of the flying machine; I didn't want to hear more.

Robina took my hand, and we sat down in front of the controls. She whispered into my ear, "Did you actually take the White Seer back to the time of the dinosaurs?"

I nodded and gave her a little smile, "Yes, my dear. Prometheus thought it would be a good punishment. We tethered him to a rock."

"You didn't?"

"Oh, yes, Robina, we did, but with a spell. He will have nourishment forever," I chuckled remembering the fear in his eyes then said a little more, "and he will never die even when eaten by a dinosaur every day."

I pushed the levers forward to the day we left the lab. The machine flew with the speed of light back to Oxford. The contraption landed behind our lab in a small grove of trees. We exited the flying bus and I scurried everyone over to one of the tall windows that looked into the lab. It was May again, the smell of the trees and the old university made my heart jump. We made it back.

Sarah whispered to me, "It's been a long journey. I'm a warrior, and you're an Emperor. Who would have ever thought it when we left here?"

I remembered the time when I was the pacifistic clumsy nerd of a scientist. How many had I killed since then, how many had I enjoyed sending on to the next world? What wealth did I now hold through thievery and conquest? How could I cut a beautiful woman's throat for my own purposes? I changed, but the world I saw hadn't. It looked the same. The students going to class, the buildings, it was all so familiar. None of the other trappings of the university had changed from the day we had left.

I peeked in the window and watched as my old self and the others prepared the experiment which sent us off on the deadly adventure. Everything looked the same, then I noticed the calendar on the wall; it read April not May. I knew it had to be a mistake. Maybe the Professor didn't change the month on the calendar. Nevertheless, I didn't remember it being like that when we left. I looked closer at the professor. He appeared different. He still dressed and groomed to look like Einstein, but a younger version of the same. As the experiment came to its climax, I watched Sarah and that other Jonathan. That's when I noticed she carried a child, she was pregnant. This couldn't be; that didn't happen.

Sarah poked me. "Jonathan, this can't be us. It's the same but different. We are in the wrong dimension. We're not home. We're lost."

"No, wait and see. Everything is all right, only wait and see." I didn't believe what I said, but maybe it would turn out all right.

The accident happened as we remembered it, but nothing changed. Everyone stayed inside the room. I heard my voice in the room say, "Doctor, are you okay? That was a bummer."

I just stared in the window watching the mundane work I used to do, as the scientific team prepared to redo the experiment.

Robina took my hand. "Johnny, let's explore this world, and see if by magic, we can conquer it and add it to our Empire. That's why you're called Emperor. The Prophecy says you will rule many worlds."

"Damn, no one told me that."

Sarah laughed. "Even I knew that." And she took the Black Master's hand as they walked toward the entrance to the classroom block, the same one we entered those many months before. The University boldly displayed its name in gold letters over the main door, King James the X's Oxford Military Academy for War Studies. Then the adventure began.

CPSIA information can be obtained at www.ICGtesting.com
Printed in the USA
LVOW10s0533311215

468236LV00011B/33/P